I dedicate this saga
to the maligned heroes
and the forgotten victims of
several fratricidal wars in our century -
men and women, brave beyond belief,
who hurled themselves against the forces
of the New World Order

First publication in March of 1998

Samisdat Publishers, Inc.
206 Carlton Street, Toronto,
Ontario, Canada
M5A 2L1

Cover illustration by Ernst Zündel

Text set in AGaramond Semibold 12

Written and published in the United States. Printed and bound by KNI Incorporated, Anaheim, California, USA

ISBN 1-896006-01-9

This is Book I of a trilogy. Book II and III are available by writing to:

6965 El Camino Real, # 105-588
La Costa, CA 92009

Fax: 760-929-2268

Lebensraum!

A Passion for Land and Peace

A Novel
by
Ingrid Rimland

Book I

*Lebensraum! spans seven generations and 200 years.
It is a story told to me a thousand times in many
different voices: that there was once a place called
"Apanlee" that fell to the Red Terror.*

*A novel is, by definition, fiction against the backdrop
of genuine emotions. This novel has been my attempt
to grasp and to extract the interplay between opposing
ideologies, to find the core of human tragedies that
make up cold statistics.*

*The novel's voice belongs to "Erika" who, in this
saga, is older than I was when I experienced World
War II. She is, however, of the transition generation,
as I am. Hers is the ethnic voice in this novel, trying
to find the right words to own up to the pride and
courage that were the hallmarks of her people.*

*She learns to say: "Our history belongs to us. It
won't be written, from now on, by anybody else but
us."*

*This family saga was gleaned from the driftwood of
history. The people I have tried to show to be of flesh
and blood came of a tightly knit community of Russian-German ancestry.*

Ingrid Rimland

Prologue

The year is 1989. It's been two hundred years since our Russian-German ancestors first pioneered the steppe, five decades since the war began that Erika experienced as a child. The sky is smooth. A few white clouds slide by; next to me sits a wooden stranger; below sprawls Wichita; and not an hour's drive from Wichita lies Mennotown, where I am heading now. I nibble on a cracker like a squirrel. In Malibu, near Hollywood, that's where you find the thinnest people in the world.

I think: "In yet another hour, I will be hiding all my thoughts."

No matter how much time goes by, it happens every time. To face my relatives takes effort. No matter what my upper hand, I still seek their esteem.

For many years, my relatives and I lived on two different planets, between us, lumbering with righteous wrath, their Elder, Archibald. One day I wrote to them. I even sent a picture.

"A movie star! Almost!" cried Josephine, an unrepentant motion picture buff, still awed by Hollywood.

A movie star? Not quite. To tell the truth, not even close to where I really live. Nobody knows. At times, not even I am sure. Bygones are buried deep.

Now there is *Left and Right.* It changed the Midwest land-scape. When it hit all the screens, my good friend Josephine, had she been still alive, would have rushed down to see it, and after-wards she would have surely said: "Oh, I cried, I cried. It was lovely."

I am so proud of Mennotown that I can hardly stand it, al-though it isn't often that I admit to that. Its stars keep on spar-kling like jewels. Every carrot is grown and consumed on the spot. My folks rise early and plow deep. They are like that—their feet deep in their furrows. They know the earth must breathe.

And yet, how often have they let their enemies choose their own enemies to decimate their kin? Their sense of history is like an unkempt garden.

When I saw Josie last, she was as frail and delicate as a No-vember leaf, one of the oldest citizens of Kansas. But that did not stop her; she still watched every flick—when she was young, she said, they used to call them flickers—with the power to trig-ger her tears. Through thick and thin this woman stayed herself, which wasn't always easy.

Whenever I would visit—as I would often do in later years when time had mellowed strife—she was in seventh heaven. She would move her old wicker chair into the sunshine on the porch where Lizzy's red geraniums still grew, and settle in with many wrinkled smiles: "Now tell me everything. I want to know the smallest morsel. All of it. All! Precisely." She energized herself by learning details of the world I have created for myself—a world she ached to know but never had the chance to see, for the De-pression nullified such plans. *Left and Right* is my tribute to Josie. To her world. To her dreams. To her clan.

To the earth that grew Josie and Jan.

To the kernels that conquered the prairie. To the kernels that brought down The Wall.

One evening, as we were sitting on the porch, just she and I and in the sky a misty moon, she told me that, once Jan was dead, she was all set to go, leave Mennotown behind, take nothing else but Rarey.

She told me of the auction going forward, only in reverse; she told me all about the time the bankers came and took Jan's farm equipment, took off with combine after combine, and even repossessed the brand new harvesters that Jan had planned to ship to Apanlee but somehow never did—and how his good friend, Doctorjay, the lush, the Lutheran, a man few dared to cross, decided in the end he had it with the bankers and ran them off Jan's property.

All that.

That was before the government succeeded finally in confiscating every gun to safeguard, as they say, democracy, which happened just last year.

Here's what I think, but only to myself: in those days, deep in the Depression, it was acceptable to call a thief a thief. Not now. Now we have laws called Hate Laws. They silence everyone.

There, on the porch that Jan built many years ago for his young, sparkling Josie, this matriarch and I had many cozy chats. On the wall on a bent, rusty nail hung her old, wilted suffragette hat. By then, time had so worn her spine that she could barely straighten it, but early, every morning, she took her walk against the wind.

She was like that. She said she would walk, and she did.

Josie liked to squander all her charms and energies on foreigners. She was known to be partial to them. She either liked people or didn't—and it was clear when we first met that she liked me. A lot. If ever there was such a thing in my turbulent life, she gave me a sense of belonging.

The moment I arrived in Mennotown out of the European war, she rose and stood behind my chair. When no one knew quite what to do with me, she knew; she made me popcorn and hot chocolate milk with marshmallows on top. She even made me eat *vareniki* which she herself disliked.

She told me with a wink I thought odd at the time: "Eat. Eat. You can't shame me by eating so little. They are good for your teeth and your gums."

"Have yet another zwieback," Josie said, warm hands on both my shoulders. She took a shine to me. She spent herself on other people, gladly, but only those she liked.

She was so old, by then, nobody knew for sure just what her age might be. But she was ancient; that we knew. She did not keep that secret.

"I've lied so long about my age I really can't remember," said Josie, being Josie. "Can I afford to die? I have this bet with Archie I will outlive him yet."

For years, she told me many times, when I myself locked horns with Archie, she'd cross the street when she saw Archibald. He never managed to catch up with her, no matter how much energy and cunning he put to the pursuit.

When I saw Josie last, the paper claimed she was two years away from being mentioned coast-to-coast by Willard Scott of NBC as one of Kansas' most esteemed, noteworthy centenarians. I have been told she died in peace, which may be her last laugh.

We spent many evenings together, examining the past. Those nights were rich. She gave me her entire life to help my script along. She never told one story when two or three would do. The winds took up the sweetness of the soil and spread it everywhere—the smell of the earth, freshly plowed.

"I was a child," she said. "Jan was a grown-up suitor."

I see Jan Neufeld clearly. That's where he came alive, the man who founded Mennotown, who spread the first grain on the floor and beat out the heads with jointed flails. Josie told me many stories of the angular young man who put his seed into his land and sons and daughters in her womb to make the future grow, who drove his sturdy roots into the soil of Mennotown so that America could prosper in the Lord.

And may He rest Jan's bones.

Old Josie told me that, when she arrived from the Ukraine—a child herself, about my age when I arrived out of the rubble of Berlin almost six decades later—she took off her shoes and walked barefoot, so she could feel the warmth of Kansas against the white and frozen wasteland she had left behind.

"And ever since," said Josie, smiling wistfully, "I walked through my life with sand in my shoes. In this town, you behave."

Right. You behave.

There is a script, and you conduct yourself according to that script. If you know what is good for you, you pay attention, verily.

I didn't, in my younger years. I was a hothead then. I would not let them be; there was a lot of friction. But there were also rules, and now I know there would not have been Mennotown, had there not been strict rules.

From Josephine, as she was called reproachfully in her own youth when she broke yet another rule, I learned the details of the early pioneering years—the prairie storms, the buffalo chips, the days when the *Wichita Eagle* was only eight pages and people paid with eggs, as fine a currency as any.

"The year when Jan and I were married," said Josephine, "a haircut cost three pennies. A loaf of bread went from a nickel to a dime."

She came to Kansas as an immigrant from the Ukraine at a time when all travel was still done by surrey. She still remembered clearly when beards went out of fashion but mustaches hung on. She told me of the oxen taking people visiting across the bumpy road to Hillsboro, which was before the flivvers came that calcified the prairie's arteries and forced the yields and stops.

I know all about Jan and his turn-of-the-century flivver. And Little Melly's doilies. And her shenanigans. And how Jan, still engaged to Little Melly, was set to marry her but ended up marrying Josie—who then disgraced herself by having one of the unsettling Finkelsteins arrive and have her likeness drawn, proud as she was of her first child, still snug in her young belly.

The earth moved through the tail of Halley's Comet the year when Josie wore a flowered hat—a scandalous offense. She was the first who rode a bicycle along the dusty streets of Mennotown and showed a rakish ankle. The first, but not the last.

I know the stories about Doctorjay who always smelled of iodine, and his wife, Noralee, who hid behind the apple tree so she could better eavesdrop, and how, once Noralee had passed away, he married Abigail who was a Donoghue and danced atop his nose.

"You went to him with all your woes," said Josephine, "and he knew everything, despite a third grade education. He was a riot, people said. Politically astute."

I know. He voted Roosevelt.

"He had his instincts in his bones," insisted Josephine as she and I sat on the porch and watched the shadows lengthen. "When finally the war was done and Hitler put a bullet to his brain, old Doctorjay, the town's most patriotic motorist, made his horn shriek before he took the intersection, and that's when he ran into one of Lizzy's cows. Smack! Plunk! That's how he killed himself. And wholly within character."

I listened, and I did not say a word, and in good time Old Josie died, and much was left unsaid.

Two years before she passed away, Josie took my hand and led me to the mothball-smell Historical Museum, built on the corner lot where the two country roads converge—one out of Hillsboro, one out of Wichita—replete with holes and ruts that always made Jan's horse rear up and buck as he came courting Josephine.

"Against his mother's wishes. She never would have told you so, but we all knew: she was against our marriage."

I know that story, too, for Lizzy's spirit never left; it lives on in a hundred quilts she stitched to give away to charity; it lives in jams cooked to perfection and in *vareniki* that are prepared just so.

"She was all set to have Jan marry Little Melly who wanted him in the worst way," triumphed Old Josephine. And something fired from within. Still. After all these years. And then, with a small sigh: "Well, life is short. What can you say? Then Little Melly passed on, too. She has been dead for years. God rest her spiteful soul."

She took my hand and showed me Doctorjay's museum, where people long since dead spoke to me many times from dusty documents and rusty tools, their voices quietly intense, embedded in the fabric of this place called Mennotown, so I can tell the younger generation that there are, after all, true absolutes.

That black is black and white is white and that there is no argument.

That thrift is preferable to sloth. That it is better to be diligent than lazy and better to be clean than foul.

Here is a town still stuck in time—old-fashioned people still doing their old-fashioned living behind their checkered gingham drapes, still basking in the joys of patriotic holidays, still rolling out their hospitality, yet sensing dimly that a fiendish and nefarious thing is gnawing at the edges of their heritage with sharp and even teeth.

In *Left and Right,* I said out loud what others were merely thinking. That's why, when it premiered, it packed the movie houses, and even Archie cheered.

Now I put up with Archie, and he puts up with me. We found a truce of sorts. He says I cast spells over people. He claims I have what he calls artistry—one step removed from vanity, which is the sin of sins.

Artistry. That is my job. That is also my passion. I try to write with light, although in Hollywood, belching its moral soot, that isn't always easy.

In Mennotown, by contrast and comparison, there is a place for everything, and everything is order. That is the righteous way. Folkways still have a place in Mennotown, and black is never white.

When I was young and foolish, I was determined not to let that ruin my life—their narrow, well-scrubbed habits, as tidy as tidy can be, the lapse into Low German, the tormenting snippets of gossip. Impatient as I was in those young years for Hollywood, not knowing then from where my own impatience would catch its fire next, I thought I could leave everything behind. Just up and walk away. Just head for Hollywood, its glitter and its lure.

Now I know this: I could no more have stopped myself from writing *Left and Right* than I could keep a cloud from raining.

I know every Aryan proverb by heart.

Don't look at me like that.

I'm nearly biting off my tongue when I hear one more time the corny story of the Holocaust, which is our daily sop. It's Whitey's victuals. There's no relief—not ever.

When it comes to my past and heritage and owning up to it, I am still raw and shy, and with my best foot forward. But I measure myself by my relatives' standards, and not by Hollywood's. Let that be clearly known.

My relatives are like old songs—songs with the smell of hay. I feel their ethnic tap root stir in me and burrow deep and bring up those forgotten nutrients on which my past was grown. It is my past; it still belongs to me—and Hollywood won't wrestle it from me. For I have forebears, too.

They suffered, and they died.

From their portraits they stare down at me with their ancient, blue, pacifist stares, and I know that as long as I still walk with sand in my shoes, I can't be at peace with myself. I need to walk barefoot, like Josie.

I didn't understand all that until I was much older.

For many years, I stayed away, because these people hurt me, particularly Archibald.

"Once a Hun, always a Hun!" he told me many times when

out of earshot of the clan.

It happens every time as I go back, periodically, right after the harvest is safely garnered and just before the colors fade from the last days of fall, to be engulfed with familiarity, to soak up that old smell.

A Hun? Unspoken is the slur he might have used, but didn't. That was his private verdict, and is his verdict still, but what does that fool know?

The man is blind. He is so blind he has to finger everything. He always fingers me: "—and what about the ovens? And what about the Jews?"

Well? What about the Jews?

That question mushrooms suddenly, without the slightest warning, out of the clear blue sky. It stigmatizes instantly. It hobbles every thought.

"Just what did we do wrong," I ask myself, "except to lose the war?" I think he is a milk-and-water moralist. He suspects I won't make it to heaven. I, on the other hand, have been to hell and back.

I walked through my Fatherland's ashes.

When I left Mennotown to try my luck in Hollywood, I took my old, Ukrainian nanny's name for my good luck charm, to be safe, and I packed Lilo's dream.

To be a writer for the screen was one of several dreams that Lilo and I shared when we were teenagers in war-torn Germany. That is galling to Archie—to hear about Lilo. He does not understand that it was Lilo's life, and Lilo's death, that made me what I am. When it comes to my sources, I will take orders from no one, not even Archibald.

While I still lived in Mennotown, I was never myself; I settled for somebody else. I had to leave, for Archie's prayers would have strangled me—for he had come, I knew, and crushed my much-beloved Fatherland and stonily laid Lilo's brave, young life to ashes. He was the one who took his gun and pointed it at Jonathan long after all the bombing stopped. He helped the fellow with the bigger mustache. To his eternal shame.

I, too, will have my reckoning. One day I will return for good, to find that warmth again, that prayer-warmth, deep in that ethnic quilt, bypassing Archibald.

I had no idea I would tap into feelings that strong. When I first started working on my play, I thought that I was a mosquito trying to buzz an elephant. As a producer friend once said: no film in Hollywood can win, unless you break at least five of the Ten Commandments.

Yet *Left and Right* won handsomely, which ought to tell you something. That was no accident.

"Next, I will have to tell them about Erika," I think, but something within shrinks away. It is painful to speak about her. Ever since the world has started calling me by my artistic name, I have forgotten about Erika.

I spent years distancing myself. She's dead now. Tasha lives. She leads a rich and lavish life in Malibu, surrounded by the Jews.

It's still that old, crazed fear.

It's easier to go along with the prevailing attitude, to say with nonchalance: "Yes. Yes. Indeed. There was a devil on the loose in Nazi Germany. He had a tail and hoofs. He was up on the mountain. Me, I was down below."

I need to learn to stand up tall, look Archie straight in his left eye—he lost his right one in an ethnic brawl, way back in World War I because he was a German—and say to him as calmly as I can: "But that's not how it was! You have your facts all wrong!"

That's what I need to say.

I see the trembling cross as it is sliding, slowly, over golden patches. I think: "Way down below, there grows the wheat of Apanlee. Those are the nuggets of which history is made. It's not the Hebrew's gold."

How many of them know? Does anybody care?

There lies the quilt my Russian-German relatives commenced

to stitch with diligence and care when Lizzy landed in the prairie more than a hundred years ago, believing that as long as preachers led the faithful in a hymn, good values couldn't help but triumph over bad. She had her values straight. When she sailed the Atlantic, she brought not just the trunk that held the wheat, she brought her non-stop prayers she uttered in High German, the language of her Lord whom she loved more than life. There were no questions in those days as to identity in ethnic terms; there was firm certainty. It mattered little that her native soil was the Ukraine—her language was the language of the country she called her Fatherland with pride. As she would tell her brood a thousand times: "What if a cat has kittens in the oven? Does that make kittens cookies?"

She was an Aryan woman. Let us remember that. Before she came to Kansas to settle on the soil that would grow bread to feed the world, she packed the following: self-discipline, trustworthiness, thrift, diligence, goodwill, neighborly charity, fidelity and pride. In other words, she packed her bedrock values. She never spent a dollar foolishly. Nobody paid her way. She lived a life with satisfaction guaranteed, and when she died, in the Depression, she knew, and so did the entire state of Kansas, that she had lived correctly.

That needs to be said, too. Her way of life was virginal. She had blue eyes. Blond hair.

There was not one of them who did not have blue eyes. She left her progeny, of whom there are so many now you cannot count them all, and they are blond and blue-eyed.

Their gaze is hooded now, their spirit shackled, sadly.

To this day, they are strong and hardy; they all grew strong on air and hymns and healthy food; and every one of them believes, this in the face of our sappy world, that it is mostly food and singing that sets them still apart.

That's how they've been debased.

That's all it takes, they think—just healthy food and lusty hymns and Faith and proper credit to the Lord. That's why their children go to church like little wooden dolls, in all their finery, to hear and take to heart what Archie has to say.

Judeo-Christianity starts early and runs deep in Mennotown, where bingo is forbidden and nicknames clues to vanity. That's Archie's turf. He guards it with ferocity. When I give lectures and tell audiences that there was once a place called Apanlee, they stare and have nothing to say.

Few youngsters, growing up in Mennotown, still have a martyr's memory. High German is already barely breathing; Low German, in another generation, will be gone.

"How much do you remember?" one of the youngsters asked me recently. To him, my people's past is ancient—our war reduced to "Auschwitz," our struggle vilified, our soldiers demonized.

How much did I forget?

Three weeks lay, for example, between the death of Lilo, my best friend, and when the Allies finally arrived—but I remember nothing of that stretch of time. Not one small morsel. Nothing. I do remember clearly, though, the day when Archie and his Negro friend arrived in prostrate, bombed-out Germany, both chewing Wrigley's Gum.

I don't remember, either, how I came to America.

I know the bullets had stopped flying; the Allies were bent over Germany, quartering my Fatherland as though it were an animal as vicious as they come—and not the place where Heidi lived her clean, strict, dedicated life, and Lilo rode her bicycle.

I loved Lilo a lot. I loved Heidi. I loved Jonathan, too, although shyly.

All three of them are dead.

There's much I don't remember rightly. There's much I won't forget.

Then came the bitter and humiliating time I still remember clearly—the stupefying postwar years. The Nuremberg Trials. The whispers about Morgenthau. There was no food in Germany, defeated and divided. There was no fuel. There was no pride, no

splendor. Those few of us who had survived—by means we knew
not how!—flung our lives against the likes of Archibald like
moths into the flame.

You couldn't buy a button or a needle; the shelves were bare;
the people starved; for weeks, we ate nothing but mushrooms.
That's when my mother curled her toes around her wooden sandals and went to Archibald and said: "Me, too," and Archie
sneered: "We don't owe you a living! There's no free ride for
you!" and Mimi tossed away the last shred of her dignity and
spoke with downcast eyes: "I hope your holidays went well?"

I never understood how she could compromise like that. I
never did, but then, I guess, I blotted out a lot.

When I arrived in Mennotown, I curtsied to my relatives in
honor of my betters. I soon enough found out: nobody did that
here.

"No need to genuflect," said Archibald, while giving me the
evil eye. "This is America. We're equal in America."

Says who?

Blood boils between Archie and me. For years, we passed
each other on the sidewalk without speaking. For years, I feared
and loathed him. Now I no longer fear him.

His God is very old and has a giant ear, like the satellite dish
that sits atop three rusty poles with which he listens in on hire-
lings up on the Hill whom he now either sponsors or subverts
with the help of a muddled but stridently militant pulpit.

These days, he does soul-saving electronically. He will not
ever win me to his ways, old sinner that I am, with little to repent.
He knows that. So do I.

He rubs it in at every opportunity: "We've got to watch you
folks. Your goose will soon be cooked. Why do you look at me
like that—sort of funny?"

In Mennotown you walk into the thick of it—into the attitude
that all the Germans ever did in World War II was turn the Hebrews into cinders. That comes not just from Hollywood; it

flows right from the pulpit. Judeo-Christianity. You can't go wrong if you condemn the Holocaust. It works like a charm, every time.

And yet, I watch Archie with awe. He is setting the churches afire with Faith. He knows how to rally his troops.

"You start with a given," says Archie, who glorifies God while berating the sinners. "And it's this: That it is better to speak truth than lies. That it's better to live clean than dirty."

Precisely.

And what does he offer his folks, I think as the heat floods my face and my stomach knots up and my heart fills with rage, that Heidi's Führer, Lilo's Führer didn't offer his disciples a hundred times over and more? Salvation. Peace. Clean living. Decency.

Self-discipline rather than stupor.

Honesty rather than falsehoods.

Robust harvests in place of sick weeds.

In the name of the Cross, said the Führer. On behalf of a world filled with beauty. On behalf of a world free of filth.

I've heard it said from Jonathan's own lips that if you gazed too deeply in the Führer's eyes, you fainted from his dream.

Why do I tell you this? I have no choice but to be faithful to my nature; that is why. It didn't used to be that way, for Archie crippled me. It's only now that I have come to realize that there is rubble to be cleared away from my own Aryan soul.

It has been many years since I arrived in Mennotown out of the fratricidal war that buried not just flesh but spirit, sitting at Wednesday devotions, fire on my cheeks and cotton in my ears. They claim that I so hated Archibald that I braided my hair counter-clockwise. That I slept in my bed upside down.

When it was clear to Archibald I would not have my soul be fingered, I had to leave, and Archie stayed, and everyone was glad. Maybe old Josie shed a tear or two. She was the only one.

When I left Mennotown, I was in a hurry to get somewhere fast. Five days before my sixteenth birthday, and doubting I could

ever calm myself, I made my thumb point west and hopped onto
a pickup truck and ended up in Hollywood.

Now I reside in
Malibu where I live in a worldly sense, as Archibald would say,
and all the younger folks in Mennotown, the ones that lean toward the Methodists and Presbyterians, are very proud of me.
Not so the oldsters, though, for Archie sees to that. At their
church rummage sales, they buy each other's doilies and give
him every penny. They have their doubts. I am their object of
curiosity.

They know me only through the stories that Archie has invented.

He suspects that I dabble in karma. He is eager to broadcast
the worst. I've heard of an owl that bites off the paws of a mouse
to keep it in its nest, and Archie is like that.

He is free to say what he wants. I am free to deny it, however.

It's very simple, really. It's not historically correct to say it
was the Führer who captivated, magnetized and charmed young
people by the millions—young people such as Jonathan. Or Mimi.
Lilo. Heidi.

For Heidi, it was mostly order. It was large babies with a lot
of energy. And peace. And certainty. And pride. For Heidi, it
was sweet and virginal. Mysterious. She took the Führer like a
lover to her heart because he understood the fabric of her being.

Or take Marleen, the matriarch of Apanlee. The Führer was
her savior, the genuine Messiah. Did that make her a criminal?
She was one of the steppe's richest women, yet she owned but
two dresses—a dress in which to work, and one in which to pray.
She always prayed in German, since her Bible was written that
way. Her family was slaughtered savagely before the Führer came.
The Führer was her god. He was the best her hard and bitter life
brought forth; he gave enormous pride to people beaten to the
ground.

My mother, Mimi. She as well.

She was one of the first, way back in the Ukraine, to practice the Führer salute. To this day, Mimi argues for the Führer; she'll argue to the latest hour that it is wrong to say that it was merely plunder. That it was hate. And spite. And wanting superiority.

"The Jews are like a hydra," claims Mimi, when Archie needles her. "One body, many heads." She argues that she hates it how they nose themselves through Wichita. She says Americans are dense and dumb, wilfully arrogant, ruled by collective ignorance. She says they slave for their exploiters without thinking. My mother knows so little of smooth manners.

She claims that as this country aches for a decisive leader not yet beholden to the usurers, still dragging nation after nation into beggary, the people should remember—if you please!—that, way back in the thirties, at least in Germany, the future walked in light.

"The *Führer's* message is just as relevant today as it was then," says Mimi. "If you ask me—more so, today, than ever. Why did we lose? Because your numbers triumphed over race and reason? Because the Germany we knew and loved was overwhelmed, not overcome? That quantity, not quality, won out?"

I only need to watch the teeming underbelly of America to know that it is so.

"Sure. Sure. The ovens one more time," sneers Archibald.

The war goes on and on. The news reels never stop.

"It has been more than fifty years," claims Mimi, "yet still the Führer's spirit dances across Europe, clad in his fiery robe, igniting brush and shrub."

That's Mimi, who was victimized as well, which is forgotten now. She looks at me, accusingly, and asks:

"Well? Speak your piece. Don't sit there, only listening. Answer me. Speak up. What do you think?"

What do I think? Here's what I think: I think that if salvation ever comes, it has to come with truth. With naked truth inspected with clear eyes.

I know back home, at Apanlee, the Jews and we lived side by side, for centuries. The Jews left us alone, and we left them alone.

We didn't hurt each other. We lived in worlds apart.

But then the Beast sprang from the canyons of New York and started crunching bone. It clawed at our race and swallowed our males, and shortly after I was born, my people had no men.

That, too, must be called genocide.

But then the Führer came. And wondrously, the swastika spelled calm.

And then the trek. The Allied firebombs. The Führer's city, ashes. The voice of Ilya Ehrenburg, the Jewish propagandist, who hectored the Red Army: "Kill! Kill! And kill! No one is innocent. Nobody! Nobody! Neither the living nor yet the unborn."

It was rivers of Aryan blood in the gutters.

What happened to Natasha, for example, is to this day a question mark. She was an Aryan, too—of Russian ancestry. She wasn't even kin. There's no museum squatting in the heart of Washington to mourn for my dear Baba.

So much—so many died. I am one of the last who made it out of Apanlee, and let me tell you, for the record, that there's no guilt in me.

*

I feel the Kansas wind as I am stepping off the plane. The prairie in November lets you breathe. In the Midwest, the seasons write the script; there is a quietness, a stoic gathering about the sharp horizon that shouldn't be confused with calm. A force of nature. Imminent. Preceding an austere but beneficial country rain.

These people hold the fort. They know the year is running out of days. They know about blocking and tackling. They may not know it yet, but all of them perch at the edge of history.

I count on them. They will link arms to cross a stream, their instincts welding them.

The moment Archie spots me at the Baggage Claim, he fixes me with his left eye, steps forward, and turns breezy. "Well, how's it going, Sputnik? All systems set to go?"

We give each other harmless smiles. We act as if we are the fattest relatives.

"Say cheese and smile," winks Archibald, elbows a few reporters, and snaps himself a Polaroid to send to the *Wichita Eagle.*

I relish this small interlude, amid the flash of cameras, on spindly heels, with naked toes, strobe lights exploding in my face, snarling traffic with my autographs. Since *Left and Right* turned out to be an unexpected winner, the media dogs me everywhere.

Next, Archie winks: "Well, look at you! My, my! As gaudy as an Easter egg. They say you have so many clothes that you can change your outfit every day. You'll have yourself being gossiped about. You know that, don't you, Sputnik?"

Against my will, I say: "I buy my things on sale." My mouth is dry. My heart is pounding. I know what will come next, and sure enough:

"Well, have you found yourself a rich and comfortable bachelor as yet?"

That's Archie—he goes for the jugular swiftly.

"There's four mighty fine fellows in my congregation—" says Archie. "You'd have your pick. You could do worse, you know. If you would only take advice, you'd know—"

"Please, Archie. Not again."

I ache with the effort of unspoken words. I feel that old, familiar numbness coming over me but manage to keep silent, while Archie tends an itch atop his cranium.

"—you'd know that if you joined, you'd have your choice of charities, what with—"

"I said please don't—"

"—what with your famous name. What with your fine connections all over Hollywood, you could—"

"I cannot be what you would call a genuine Christian—" I try to interrupt, and Archie finishes his thought:

"—you could do so much good. You could help carve the Kingdom of our Lord Christ Jesus who gave His life from love for sinners just like us—"

We both stare ahead, both very solemn and correct, both knowing that time has blurred nothing.

A billboard warns as we leave Wichita: "Don't trash our town." A deep growl is embedded in that sign. Don't trash America!

Towns smell as people do—some clean, and others dirty. Wichita smells like its slaughter yards on Twenty-First and Market, but Mennotown, I know from visits past, smells clean. It's spic-and-span, this Midwest German town, with smells you take in through both nostrils, lustily, while walking through young pine woods, or between well-scrubbed laundry dried in the morning air, or sitting in a coffee house, depending on which way the wind just happens to be blowing.

I like to visit here. Each year, I visit for a week, but one week is enough.

"Were it not for this man who's sitting next to me," I think, "I wouldn't mind staying a bit." For he knows. And I know. And it is this: He talks about the end result, but nobody questions the path.

The path was everything.

Why was it, for example, I'd really like to know, that this old toady's allies all sported and displayed the pentagrams on their gray, furry caps? That's what I want to know. Americans wore white. The Bolsheviks wore red. On tanks. Planes. Uniforms. But it was Satan's logo.

That's why I still go back, to my own roots, to listen to my past, incomprehensible to most, like a forgotten language.

Each year, when I return, I see that the Midwest has changed a little more. Each year it's darker. Grittier. Each year there's more graffiti.

"That is because the Donoghues have intermixed," says Archie angrily, who reads my thoughts, and steps hard on the gas.

The Donoghues are still considered rabble. Their offspring

are as common and as grimy as the streets of Wichita. They still
lead their scandalous lives. They have all sorts of rights the Midwest farmers never even knew existed, but they complain of
wrongs.

"And where it will end, I cannot begin to imagine," scolds
Archie.

"You wonder," I agree.

His brow is furrowed now. The spittle flies. "They keep on
having children, some good, some bad, but all of them on welfare. No morals there. No discipline. All having different fathers."

"Some colored, Archibald?"

"You're darn right, Sputnik. Right! Unfortunately, that's part
of it. Precisely!" That's still where Archibald, in every other
way a Democrat, all for equality and giving every fellow a fair
shake, tends his big grudge against the bureaucrats. "The Feds
have dough for almost any cause as long as you are intermixed,"
sneers Archie.

"Is that a fact?"

"They keep pushing entitlement modes. They give unwor-
thy people subsidies and loans so they can multiply like rabbits—
"

Right. But if I voice a heresy like that—what with my German accent and with my German past—all of my motives are in
question. He sees no parallels. He holds the Scriptures in one
hand and shakes his index finger at the social order with the other.

"He can afford to hitch his morals to misogyny," I think.
Aloud, I try to say as calmly as I can:

"But if I say, for instance, that keeping one's own ethnic pool
as strong and pure as possible is laudable—"

"You can't say things like that!" scolds Archibald. "That's
Nazi talk. Not to say racist, Sputnik."

"But didn't you just—?"

"You can't say things like that around here. Just you remember that."

"Why not?"

"This is America. We're equal in America."

Which, he thinks, ends the argument.

Next he says this: "I hear that *Left and Right* is going through the roof?"

"That's what they say," I tell him modestly.

"How many zeroes, Sputnik?"

"You'd be amazed to know."

But Archie only sniffs. "A zero here, a zero there, that is the modern way. You can't grow real wealth based on zeroes. It's like I always tell my kids, you've got to practice stewardship. Just practice proper stewardship—"

The Lord gave Archibald his share of sons and daughters, this after Archie finally threw caution to the wind and married Temperance. Now, for my benefit, he counts his offspring's virtues on his fingers. "I taught my children personally that, by themselves, they all add up to nothing. Life's seasoning is Faith."

I know most all of them—all fine and upright citizens, equal to Satan's challenge. Some have preceded him and rest already in eternity; but most are still alive. The carpets in their homes are inches thick. When that old Kansas wind is blowing, they all wear woolen underwear. One opted for a lucrative career in dentistry. A second is a known environmentalist; a third is anti-nuclear, on account of his pacifist roots. One female teaches Anabaptist history. Still yet another, Norah Leigh—born after Noralee died and just before the geezer, Doctorjay, wed Abigail—works as a postal carrier in Mennotown's main office, a job she held for more than forty years. There was some talk about retirement a few years back, but Nora Leigh convinced the government that would be mental cruelty: her life would be curtailed beyond repair if she no longer knew who got his mail from whom.

A few years back, her oldest son ran for Congress on the Moral Majority ticket, but missed election by an inch.

"He lost," claims Archibald, "because he didn't have sufficient visibility, which was the reason why he turned into a televangelist. He is a real Epp that way. He knows the politicians on the Hill are ripe and ready for the Gospel."

A pious Anabaptist zeal runs deep in straight-line Epp descendants. They do not scatter among Lutherans. Or visit arcades or, for that matter, ice cream parlors. Never! Or roll their socks. Or take up hockey as a sport. Or waste their sentiment on nicknames.

The Epps have multiplied and multiplied again. There are so many Epps, by now, you cannot count them all. A fraction only lives in Mennotown; the rest are in chronic retreat—from the world and its wicked temptations. They farm in Grand Forks, Mountain Lake and Freeman, South Dakota; they carry on in Iowa; they frown with disapproval the moment visitors arrive: a faster pace of singing, up there in Winnipeg! They know they must be ever vigilant to spot the mischief of the Fiend. It's vigilance that sets an Epp apart!

"It took two years and some enormously expensive travel to trace the entire Epp family tree," explains the Epp clan patriarch who's sitting next to me. "Percentage-wise, most of our first names start with M. Not mine, of course. I think that's odd. Don't you?"

"Not really. No."

"I do."

The Epps all keep on shedding spirit pollen, all teaching heathens stealthily and patiently how to let go of gods of stone. One grandchild, Archie tells me proudly, is affiliated with a church that has a growing edge in Africa and Indonesia. Another witnesses in Haiti where gospelling is striking sturdy roots. You find Epps everywhere. Not a few live in Minnesota. Some in Brazil. In Canada. You find them even in the high plateaus of Mexico and in the thorny hell of Paraguay where, odd to say, the hottest season is December, the cold comes from the south in June, the moon hangs upside down; palms dot the land like an army of one-legged soldiers, "—and where, or so some people claim, this sadist doctor that the Jews are always after, this Joseph-what's-his-name, is hiding out among old Nazi brass," says

Archie, giving me a sidelong glance.

"Well, are they making headway?"

"It's up to the authorities," grunts Archibald. "They have their own agenda."

I take care to admire the fence posts. I mention the weather, still mild for this time of the year. I also comment on the ruts in the asphalt.

Not that that stifles Archie, who is like a bloodhound that way.

"I hope they catch him soon. I hope they hang him in Jerusalem. Although I must confess: I've had it now. The Hebrews always think they are the navel of the universe. I've had it up to here."

"No kidding."

"Who do they think they are? They kvetch—they don't stop kvetching! Are they the only ones who have a patent on the Wailing Wall? Is that their copyright?"

There is a lightness in my head and ringing in my ears. That's what I'd like to know.

I stare out of the window. This is some country here. I know the neighbors will cook up some mighty meals to put some meat on me.

We drive through fields and yet more fields—some grain, but mostly stubble. While Archie keeps on staring straight ahead, his neck getting ever more mottled, I watch the tractors, throbbing rhythmically, while several long-haired youngsters sit atop with earphones on, sipping Coke through plastic straws while listening to Randy Travis.

"Those kids just shift the levers leisurely and push assorted buttons; the tractors do the work," brags Archibald, while looking at me sideways.

We drive along in silence. Now that we are alone and he is gathering diplomacy, he doesn't call me Sputnik, and I begin to sense just what is troubling him.

He clears his throat. "Our folks are moving with the times.

We are not that old-fashioned."

"I know."

"The media makes us out that way, but we move with the times."

"Well, who believes the media?"

"Right. Well. Ahem. We have a lot of pride in our machinery. Especially our combines. Those babies cut and thresh up to a thousand bushels of winter wheat per day. You might just want to mention that tomorrow."

"All right."

"Why don't you mention that? How up-to-date we are? How we're moving with the times?"

"Why not? I'll be glad to oblige you that way."

"We aren't as dumb as some people think." His voice has turned defiant. "We're modern folks. We're interfaith. I've checked it out. We've got to think global these days."

"I'm glad you think so, Archie."

"Now that the Berlin Wall has fallen, we know it was our wheat the Russians wanted all along," says Archie, coming at me sideways.

"Last time, that was my argument."

He gives me a suspicious look. "Build that up in your keynote, Sputnik. Be inspirational. Uplifting. Give credit where credit is due. That would please many folks."

"All right."

"Oh, that reminds me. That reminds me. There's this reporter from the *Eagle* who asked if he could do an interview. Now that your movie is a hit, I thought we might discuss a slant—"

"Why not?"

"What will you say?"

"What do you mean, what will I say? I'll answer the reporter's questions."

He inches a bit closer. "The other day, I heard an earful."

"Such as?"

"Are you involved with folks who call themselves Revisionists?"

"I read them, if that's what you mean."

At once, he hectors me: "You know that isn't good for you. That's dangerous. That's foolish. That's harmful to your health. Why stir up memories? It will bring your stomach pains back."

"Don't worry about that."

His head doesn't move, just his eye. He clears his throat. "Some papers claim you said that Jewish and conniving go together."

"I never said that, Archie."

"Well, you came close. You better watch it, Sputnik. Some folks will read between the lines. All through that movie script, you kept on dropping hints. About the Jews. And their shenanigans. If I were you, I'd be real careful. Real careful. And I mean careful. Careful is the word."

"All right. I said all right."

"This is America. We don't agree with stuff like that. Nobody doubts the Holocaust. Besides, the Jews—they have their noses everywhere; they know how to follow the stink. They're much too powerful, if you ask me, but on the other hand, we've got to get along. There's this one Jew, for instance, approving every grant—"

"Is that a fact?"

"Around here, we are civilized. We've got to let bygones be bygones. We wouldn't want to have an odious repeat of history, now would we? In this country?"

Those are his exact words. His blustery, insincere face has turned purple, and I see tiny droplets forming underneath his nose.

"Go on."

"Well. Now." He tells the steering wheel: "What can a fellow do? The Catholics revere the rosary; the Lutherans the Trinity; the Jews the Holocaust. You better not mention that stuff. We wouldn't want to spoil the keynote, now, would we? We wouldn't want to get the delegates all hopping mad, now, would we? You can't go wrong with being inspirational and patriotic and leave the Holocaust alone. Just stick to generalities, and all will work out smooth."

"I answer only to myself," I say, but only to myself. It's still that old, crazed fear. He still sees history, I think, through the wrong end of a distorting telescope, where every woe is magnified for them and every hurt that we endured is tiny.

Out loud I say: "Don't worry. Just don't fret. I promise you that I won't breathe a word about the Hebrew Holocaust."

"Right. Right. Let's shut the door forever on that unhappy episode."

"Right. That's my very point."

"I don't like the tone of your voice."

I say between clenched teeth: "Why do we keep on fighting World War II five decades after it was lost for Germany? We lost. And you guys won. So let it be. Just let it be. Let go. Who gains by stirring up the past?"

"Good. Fine. That is my point. Exactly. That puts my mind at ease. I'm glad you think so. Truly!" Now Archie beams with gratitude, deflating. "That's fine. Just fine. That's what I always say."

He starts to chat; he is chummy; one thing leads to another. He is not one of those who want to turn the present back into the past; the past is the past, and the present the present; you can't re-write a single page; some things were not that clear-cut in that war and some of it—well, murky.

I make another bargain with myself while sitting next to Archie: I will speak up. Tell all. One of these days, I will.

But childhood fears run deep, and I have never had the courage which, for instance, my good friend Lilo had.

Now there was bravery. When she and I were young, in war-torn Germany, my cowardice was one long, never-ending nightmare, but Lilo had the touch. She had that inner honor that shone from clear blue eyes. By contrast, even now, I am as fearful as a rabbit, as though the first part of my young life didn't count.

"Look. Over there. That's Jan's and Josie's grandsons, over there. See? You can tell who's a Neufeld, can't you?"

Right. You can't miss a Neufeld. You look at them and know there must be something to those genes that came from Apanlee. They are a clan apart. They are easy to spot by their passionate love for the soil. They aren't afraid to take risks, to experiment, to move into various endeavors. Some strange, persistent streak of genius strains hard to find expression.

One claims a patent on a gadget that attaches to up-to-date threshers. Another won three medals for streamlining the creamery. A third perfected a gate latch for cattle. They prosper, and they multiply. Their tomb stones testify.

"No bloodshed for princes and kings," they have proclaimed for centuries. And if a worldly ruler tried to tax them for their pacifist tradition, they knew precisely what to do: they packed and left and said: "Be this, again, God's will."

Determined every other way, accomplished every other way, time and again, they voted with their feet. Yet, here's my question mark: what do they know of ethnic pride? Its glory, and its cost?

I bite my lip. The town car gives a lurch.

The day has not yet melted into twilight as we glide into Mennotown.

There is a Janzen Court. There is a Harder Street. Sleek taxicabs, controlled by traffic lights, speed along Siemens Avenue, around the rim of Penner Park.

We pass the library that Josie helped to build by raising every penny with huge spaghetti feeds. It bears her husband's name.

Around the corner, to the left, we pass the place where Lizzy's sod house used to be, next to the Women's Shelter, where Little Melly's special cross stitch secrets are still taught.

Jan's steam mill, to the north of Mennotown, is now a modern restaurant, a popular tourist attraction. You can order *vareniki* there, an ethnic specialty, prepared from yellowed recipes that have been handed down from family to family—or so claims the brochure that must have cost a dime, a nickel and a penny.

I know the place; I've dined there many times. Blond, blue-eyed youngsters serve you home-baked bread grown from the winter wheat Peet Neufeld traded from the Tartars—imported to America a century ago. A reproduction of the wheat bin Lizzy brought from the Ukraine hangs prominently on the wall, next to the framed first nickel Lizzy earned, the one she vowed she'd never spend. And didn't.

The town car purrs. It's landmark after landmark, but time has not stood still. Beside the Unemployment Office, the Friesen store still stands, updated and remodeled. Next to it, Express Mail. Not all that many years ago, it was a mirthful Noralee who did her postal clerking there. I never met her, but she lives. She lives in memory. Still shrill. Still undiminished and rotund. Now there was ethnic color!

Ah, Noralee!

She scrubbed the linens every day, way back at Apanlee. By hand, she rinsed her children's diapers in the waterhole of Apanlee; her grandchild owns a chain of Laundromats. Another grandchild runs a grocery store, filled wall to wall with peaches, plums and gooseberries, with labels telling visitors the seeds came all the way from Apanlee, sewn into Noralee's skirt hem to keep it prim across her ankles.

Child-rich but penny-poor, the moment Noralee hit prairie soil, she waylaid Doctorjay, half-Lutheran, half-Christian, the Lord at his periphery because he guzzled so! There is the corner, by that lamp post, where her husband lost his life. It has been almost fifty years since Doctorjay collided with that calf and crushed himself inside his flivver, but this is still remembered and repeated, as are the many juicy tales of Noralee who passed on before he did, whom he forsook, the moment she passed on, for Abigail—who was a Donoghue, if you remember, Sputnik!— a Donoghue, a harlot, and a flirt!

Once every two years—July through August or September, provided the weather is placid—the Elder Archibald takes senior citizens of Mennotown on trips to the Ukraine. That is his hobby now. As a sideline, he smuggles his Bibles. He snaps his Polaroids of the abandoned and neglected steppe where, in the olden days, the tsarist Cossacks roamed and where one princeling, once upon a distant time, was fed a bowl of noodle soup by Jan's and Josie's folks. He checked the story out. A few years back, he talked the Soviet guide into a little detour, and when he found it finally, this place called Apanlee, it disappointed mightily.

"Just crumbling buildings. Broken fences. Dilapidated—floor to ceiling. High weeds between the cobble stones."

"How sad."

"A goat or two, maybe. That's all. That's all that's left. That is God's punishment for straying from the path."

His face, so jovial up to now, has become cold and hard. Now he is chewing on his mustache, overwrought. "Now, Sputnik, tell me this. Why don't we ever learn from history? Now our country is decaying. We should have learned from them. When they went godless over there, at Apanlee, that's how it all began."

"If you say so."

"Now people keep on tossing spitballs here, instead of rolling up their sleeves. Where will it end? Why can't we put an end to all the moral rot?"

He echoes many farmers, aghast at what they see. They have no name for it. They have no frame of reference. Their past has been stolen from them. You can see many crusty oldsters sitting in their rocking chairs, reading their Daily Devotions, turning page after page with huge, wheat-gnarled hands. They are the newly disenfranchised—this in a country they helped build and which is still their home.

There is no doubt that even Mennotown has started its decay in spirit and in fact. The Jensen home, now crumbling at the edges. The brand new grammar school has many classrooms—thirty, forty?—and is connected through an intercom. Neglecting the Three R's, kids learn about such things as birth control and Stay-Away-From-Drugs. The latest horror is the condom push; and worse is yet to come.

"They don't learn hymns and catechism, and prayer is out-lawed," grieves Archibald.

"Well, what's your remedy?"

"Apply the paddle! Use the paddle! That's what I always say."

"I see."

"Our teachers can no longer teach; now they patrol the halls, because twelve-year-old children carry guns. Can you imagine, Sputnik? Guns! We must outlaw all guns. I'm all for gun control. We need some gun control!"

*

So here I am, in Mennotown, on Josie's L-shaped couch, next to a pumpkin of a cousin. The neighborhood is watching Donahue. The relatives make sure they don't miss Donahue, an expert baby kisser.

"The Russians are coming! The Russians are coming!" yells Phil and runs into the audience, coattails flapping, to hand some-body else the microphone. He is a Liberal. He interrupts. He heckles.

"Just what are we afraid of? In Russia, you cannot even pur-chase toilet paper! Their queues are stretching over city blocks! They love our hamburgers and jeans! They're eager to try on democracy for size! Why are we so afraid to lend a helping hand?"

The relatives bob heads. Here is one talk show host who knows his arguments.

"Look at Vietnam," shouts Phil, and waves his microphone and scratches his gray head. "Look at El Salvador. Argentina. Panama. Nicaragua. The Philippines. Everywhere, a thousand quarrels. Why not, instead, adopt a thousand points of light?"

When Phil gets eloquent like that, nobody has a counter-ar-gument.

"Why not, with so much strife, adopt a world-wide policy that's fair to everyone?"

One global village? One strong government? One market

and one currency?

"His point of view, you must admit, is very hard to argue with," says Archibald authoritatively.

The folks nod to that, sagely. A thousand points of light in a revamped, re-ordered universe—they like that phrase a lot. That sounds magnificent.

"In fact, it's practically Biblical," says Archie, looking flushed.

The conversation drifts. The coffee scent is wafting. No matter what the time of day, somewhere there is a coffee pot. A cousin starts to speculate that Phil might be related to the Donoghues of Mennotown, who all vote the Democrat ticket—provided you can get them to the polls, a mighty undertaking. They're still a lazy bunch, one step removed from bums.

"Assuming they can all walk down the primrose path," as Archie puts it archly.

"There is no rousing them to any honest work—"

"They know which side their bread is buttered on, and every one of them—"

"—and every one of them is heading for the trough."

"Entitlements. Up to their dirty ears."

This makes the townsfolk mad. If they would only try—so goes the argument on Josie's L-shaped couch—they could catch the American dream. It's there. Within reach. For the asking.

"They ought to at least try to save a little more to have a nest egg for the future, but do they do it? No."

One Donoghue, for instance, is now in charge of underwriting loans that Washington doles out to subsidize the crop. He throws his weight around, that one. He sits behind his desk—feet up, smirk on his face and polish on his fingernails—and all the farmers have to go to him each fall to finance next year's harvest.

A second Donoghue has found himself a cozy nest in the ranks of Affirmative Action.

A third is busy with the homeless—hotfooting it with special airline vouchers back and forth to Washington, while farmers struggle to buy gas. And several of his older sons, still teenagers, already make a beeline for the loot, romancing with the Blacks.

"Why mongrelize the neighborhood?" is what they want to know. They're all for giving everybody a fair shake, since this is still America. But where does it say we must mix?

Not in their Old World Gospel, still in the Gothic script.

I watch them as they warm their chairs, alone with my own thoughts. In Mennotown, the spotted owl is not important; it's politicians playing re-election games; both pro-life outcomes for the unborn innocents and pro-death punishment for hard-core criminals get thumbs-up signs; free trade is really just the only way to go; embargoing the wheat to stop the Soviets in Afghanistan upsets them mightily.

Sometimes there's benign disagreement between the young folks and the old, but one thing never changes: does anybody really think that anyone could really hurt America? The greatest country in the world? No way!

America. The Gospel is embedded in that word. In Mennotown, the Stars and Stripes have meaning.

It is a pleasant afternoon. It smells of *apfelstrudel.*

"The Hitler days are gone!" yells Phil, and runs into the audience, perspiring at the arm pits. "The Stalin times are gone! The only thing that's left is to clean up our act and do away with prejudice. If there's one lesson we have learned, it's this: We are created equal. We're all created equal."

"An agitated liberal, that's what he is," squirms Mimi, while giving Phil the evil eye. "Look at him, sidling up to Posner!"

The folks just glare at her. The Jews are less than popular in Mennotown, but still, you mind your manners. All Jews, they know, turn their opinions on a dime—to wit, this Posner fellow. Right on your television screen! That one is to be watched! They saw him switch his loyalties according to the breeze; the moment the Berlin Wall came crashing down, what did he do? He cleverly jumped horses in mid-stream, denying he had ever been at heart a Communist, maneuvering himself right next to Donahue with his philosophies.

"They are like that," says Mimi, now taunting Archibald.

"And what, precisely, do you mean by that?"

She starts to count her main points on her fingers. "No principles. No pride. No sense of self. No loyalty to anything or
anyone. Say what you will, Jews just aren't lovable people—"

When she is agitated by her memories of war, my mother
gets like that.

When she and I arrived in Kansas—just barely squeezing
through the cracks, thanks to enduring kinship ties that helped us
with our visas—she had no teeth; the Russians knocked them
out when they knocked Mimi to the ground and had their way
with her.

My mother, Mimi, dug herself out of the ruins of Germany.
She regrets nothing to this day. When she talks of the war and
aftermath, she makes the relatives just cringe, but luckily, there
is no bite to anything she says; she lost her teeth; that's why.

"Our only crime is that we lost a war," claims Mimi now, and
lifts a trembling chin.

I edge a little closer. She is my mother, after all, although I
think of her as Mimi.

When I was born, it took her weeks before she even found a
name. I never really was her child; there was no time; there was
a war; the country blazed in violence. I don't remember ever
sitting next to her, her arms around my shoulders.

"It was a vicious war."

Nobody in that spotless kitchen approves of the atrocities of
war. They're pacifists. Not that appearances would tell. It takes
a trained eye to single out a pacifist today. It's easier with the
ear, for their diphthongs still give them away. They are decidedly against the sword, but they approve of troops sent to the
farthest corners of the world to protect other people's right to
vote themselves a democratic government as well.

They are warm-hearted people with squeaky-clean windows,
clinging to custom, clinging to soil. They keep neat sidewalks;
painted fences; mulberry rows along the streets amid huge fields

of waving grain. In front of every home in Mennotown, you find
a flower garden. Pride in their pristine, peaceful way of life is
what unites the clan.

Each year, when all the work is done, they reunite in Wichita,
renew the Covenant, and give thanks to the Lord and Provider.
This week, the town is full of them, all relatives so well-to-do
they bypass the Ramadas; they look for Sheratons and Hyatts to
showcase their success. They travel with their Samsonites so
packed with double underwear and flannel gowns they don't fit
in the trunks. They don't waste electricity, not even in hotels.

It is that kind of thrifty spirit that has put our astronauts smack
on the moon where you weigh less and can leap high, from where
you can behold the earth the way the good Lord made it—all
blue and blithe and shimmering, just floating in a sable sheen as
evidence of His magnificence and might.

"His favorite place in the entire universe is Kansas," claimed
Archie just the other day, while blessing the Rotarians, express-
ing thus a patriotic sentiment that made those twenty dollar bills
just float into his hat.

"I dare you here and now to find another country equal to
America to live and die in, Mimi," taunts Archie, while Temperance refills his cup.

"And you have no idea," snaps Mimi and works her needle
back and forth into a sock, "how late it is already. How little time
is left."

"Don't be ridiculous."

"It's true. Just wait and see. It's true."

"Aw! Gee! Come on now! Don't be silly."

Those are beguiling times when Archibald has Mimi to tor-
ment and Mimi counters, tit for tat, and people keep on taking
sides, half-laughing and half-furious, until the two run out of
words and oldsters start to nod.

"This country is already faceless. Soon you will wish you
never fought your war—"

She does not finish, knowing that the afternoon is long and

arguments have to be savored to the fullest. Those two have long since made their peace; now she is baptized properly; she'll be in Heaven, too, where he is heading forthwith.

But still, if Archie has an audience, he likes to browbeat her.

My mother, on the other hand—though in her old age she is grateful for the nest that Archibald provided sumptuously when he permitted her to move into the flat where Little Melly used to live—has never learned to yield her memories when Archie launches into one of his tirades regarding her peculiar past.

"My war?" roars Archibald. "Come on! Get outta here! It was your war! It was your Führer's war!"

"Your war! That's what I said. You heard me right. Your war!"

"You were the ones who started it. We had to finish it."

"We did not!"

"Oh, yes you did! You did! We always finish other people's wars. We always have to clean up other people's messes."

"What messes? Are you kidding? When terror struck in Russia and took our men—our sons, our husbands, brothers, fathers!—and not one family was left untouched, where was America?"

"What do you mean, where was America?"

"That's right! Where were you guys? In bed with Joseph Stalin!"

She's gathering her steam. She mentions Prussia. Estonia. Latvia. Lithuania. Pomerania. She talks about Silesia. The Balkan nations. *Ach*! Though she has told the litany of Germany's defeat so many times that everybody knows it backwards, she cannot help herself. She wipes her eyes. She blows her nose. She cries while choking on emotions:

"Sit not in judgment, you! Your ally had the bigger mustache."

She has her memories.

She still remembers how Berlin was quartered and dismembered by the Allies—a bloody quarter thrown to every victor!—while she was hanging on a curtain rod behind some draperies.

Me, too. I huddled down below, in the potato cellar.

I was still small, but I remember clearly how Soviet soldiers came repeatedly and sliced the drapes with bayonets and snapped my mother's moral fiber. It happened yesterday.

I often heard my mother say she wishes she could go and die in Germany. She dreads her resting place, she says, amid uncomprehending strangers. She was there when the Allies let the butt of righteousness fall on her *Landsers'* shoulder blades, and she stood watching, weeping, as they were herded to Siberia with crutches in their armpits and stumps where legs had been.

"The war was done, and you? Don't talk to me of crimes. You handed innocents to Russia by the millions," cries Mimi. "Talk about ethnic cleansing!"

"Whatever do you mean?"

"At point of gun, you threw your kinfolk to the wolves. Your flesh and blood! Your relatives! That isn't taught in any of your schools.   All that is still a well-kept secret! A whole civilization died, because of you! Americans! and the world isn't any the wiser—"

And Archibald, maliciously: "Maybe you had it coming?"

I think: "Here's where his nasty character comes out. Now's when he shows his colors."

"We are now writing 1989," says Mimi, her old eyes bright with pain, her tea cup rattling in her hand, "and still that war goes on."

She's right. That war has never stopped.   It chokes the television set. It clogs the radio. It spills buckets of slime in the paper. It spells rape of the mind, spirit and soul.

My mother was still young when she was driven out of Apanlee with bleeding heart and empty hands, caught between blazing guns of two determined dictators. Their cannons, equally, spat smoke and shells and flames across the plains of the Ukraine. She still sees all those refugees as they poured westwards, westwards, in the direction of the sinking sun through all that ice and snow, a milling, stumbling horde. Her fingers fly; her breath comes in short gasps. "If Germany had won the war, instead of losing it because you were too dense to recognize the enemy that had you dancing to his tune, who would harp on and on about the Holocaust?"

"Look. There she goes again!"

"There isn't one of us who hasn't suffered, too. But do we bleed our neighbors? Are we moored to the Wailing Wall? Do we insist on having shrines at taxpayers' expense for a disastrous war fought half a world away?"

For Mimi, with one foot already in the grave, the wounds of that war fester on. "What Holocaust?" she wants to know, and her old, beaten, wrinkled face takes on defiance and despair. She claims she knows of not one single case of setting fire to a synagogue and burning up the Jews—at which point Archie finds a bit of wood with which to poke his teeth.

He loosens a soft belch. "You can't deny the chimneys."

There is an awkward silence in the room, and everybody looks at Mimi.

"Dreamed up in Hollywood! Trademarked in Israel. Made in America."

"Ha! Listen to who's telling!"

"How often will you send your boys as cannon fodder just so the Jews can once again put diamonds in their pockets?"

I read their faces easily. While everybody digs into the *apfelstrudel,* I watch as Archibald is working up a steam because he senses there is still some mileage left in Mimi.

"And not a child in school today," cries Mimi, "is taught the truth about what really happened. That innocents were sacrificed like cattle!"

But Archie bristles at the thought, and he is not alone. The relatives think proudly of their war—and, more so, of the aftermath. That's when the real business of recovery began, while they were rehabilitating Europe.

"You've got to grant us that! Thanks to the Marshall Plan, we rehabilitated Europe! The speed with which the country turned to rehabilitating Europe was astounding."

And to what end? That is their question mark. This unrepentant Russian-German relative—along with others of her kind whom Mennotown went to such lengths to rescue from the rubble—is still a die-hard anti-Communist, one step removed from Nazi.

The truth be put where it belongs: she never did repent. Not Mimi.

My mother could have gone to night school when she first came to Mennotown, at taxpayers expense, to be re-educated—realigned politically. The opportunities were there. But no. She simply shrugged; she never even took out papers to become a proper citizen. That still goads Archibald. He glares at her. She swallows hard, shrinks back into her cushions, and speaks so softly it is hard to understand that, thank you, never mind, don't waste your time, she has a Fatherland to last her to her grave.

I listen to that, too, while keeping to myself.

My mother and her Kansas relatives cannot see eye to eye on anything pertaining to the war. The cousins sit there, munching popcorn after popcorn, with downcast eyes and hardened heart, wearing their Sunday best and trying not to muss it.

"What in the name of common sense did you see in your Führer?" baits Archie.

"Well, he was basically a dreamer of big dreams," says Mimi, still defiant, lifting a trembling chin. The relatives inspect the ceiling as though they have never seen it before.

She tells them one more time. She says he touched the sky. She says he shook the earth.

"Had not the cripple Roosevelt been jealous of the rebirth of Germany," says Mimi, "there would have been no way the Führer would have lost. Had not his cotery of Rosenmans, Kuhns, Loebs and Morgenthaus been jealous of the success of Germany, the Führer would have won!"

"Don't be ridiculous."

"And you'll be next," she tells them with grim satisfaction. "Ha!"

"And all your sappy talk about the greatest country in the world won't get you anywhere as long as you can't recognize what's being done to children. Your children! Your own children! In public schools. Out in the streets. In the arcades. In gang wars. Via television. These things are not mere accidents. It's planned. It's systematic wreckage. Destruction of your race. America, beset by predatory aliens subverting every law—"

That's Mimi. That's her sentiment. When she flails at her windmills, a show which only Archibald can trigger to full passion, she speaks against the guffaws in the parlor. My heart just aches for her. She has no teeth—the Russians knocked them out.

The years crept over Mimi. Her shoulders ache. Her spine caved in. Her eyes are now too dim to see the headlines, but she knows from her own experience who's who.

What's what.

She knows. My mother knows that it is still the Jews who are bedeviling the world in any way they can.

"She still thinks," whispers Temperance in the kitchen and helps herself to yet another slice of pie, "that Communism was a Jewish plot."

"They're all like that," nods Susan, a cousin thrice removed, born just before the Vietnam war. "You can't reform a Nazi." She, too, has often wondered why it is that foreigners will spread themselves all over other people's kitchens and then start arguing about those murky things the Allied armies settled half a century ago with gallows and with guns.

Right after Nuremberg, my mother came to Mennotown, so weak that she could barely crawl, with me in tow, her only living relative. She simply curled her frozen toes around her wooden clogs, crept through the rubble of Berlin, and said to some official: "I have some relatives in Kansas."

She found a law somebody dusted off, and one day, there she was, in shock that she had made it, sitting primly on a chair in Josie's sunny kitchen, me next to her, and next to me three tattered cardboard boxes containing our worldly goods—all that was left of Apanlee.

"Well, there you are, you two," said Josephine that day. "I better call the relatives. They'll want to take a look."

In the first postwar years in Mennotown, Displaced Persons were roundly disliked, and some of that rubbed off on me in my own teenage years. Some people tried to feel compassion for that dilapidated batch of refugees that Archie helped dig out from Berlin's blackened rubble, but it was hard if not impossible: their underthings were ragged; remorse was non-existent; the trusted Faith was not for them; to heal and to conceal them in the patchwork quilt of ethnic unity was quite an undertaking.

Still, blood is blood; you don't disown a kinsman. So we were taken in.

A phone call brought them all together in a hurry. Among them was Archie, pretending we had never met. Of course I did the same. A cat dislikes a dog.

That day, old Josie cautioned with a smile: "Watch out for Archibald. All you can do, dear child, is to lay low. Just duck and keep the lowest profile possible."

She smiled when she said that. She stroked my hair and smiled.

They say it was the first time since the White House telegram arrived, informing her that Rarey had been killed, that Josie found a smile.

I'll say it here and now: My mother has a point. She did survive the trek, the fury of the elements, but not without a price. There are deep scars in Mimi, as in a million of her generation.

She spent a lifetime waiting. Though she escaped, she left behind a child, its eyelashes coated with ice; she left behind her mother, dying, wrapped in a torn and frozen *Landser's* coat. She left behind one husband in the tomb that was Siberia, another lying in his blood that seeped along the sidewalk of Berlin.

She sees Jews as a dangerous, underground power. They talk too fast and wave their arms, and their one aim—nursed over centuries—is to control the world.

"Is that another of your silly jokes?" says Archie, winking slyly, while settling down to an enormous supper. He has a grand-niece, Sissie, who lives in Winnipeg and cleans and cooks for Jews. He points that out with pride that there's no racial prejudice in his own family.

"Not one small speck. Not even a faint whiff."

He says they treat her well, despite the Holocaust. He says she treats them likewise. It is well known in Mennotown that many Jewish families who chose America after the war prefer to use unmarried German relatives as maids, for almost all the European Jews speak broken German, and almost all the Kansas relatives do, too.

"Our Sissie, for example, works for four Jewish bachelors. She says they are just wonderful to her. Despite the Holocaust." He scans the parlor, a triumphant man. Who says that there is anti-Semitism in the midst of Mennotown? He even did a presentation on that topic in a synagogue for Jews, explaining how the Brethren, which is his congregation, were far and wide the only ones in the possession of the Truth, but generous with converts to a fault. He went so far as to invite the rabbis to visit him in turn and tell their point of view. They never did, alas. He wonders what he might have said that might have been offending.

But Mimi, stubbornly: "But don't you wish they would stop kvetching on and on about the Holocaust?"

"Shhh! Not so loud!" whispers somebody, fiercely, and Mimi shrinks into her cross-stitched cushions and licks her lower lip.

"You weren't there," says Mimi.

"Excuse me, but I was," says Archibald.

Those were his glory days. He is proud he was there when Ivan met Joe by the Elbe. He likes to reminisce about the times when he and his young buddies celebrated all night long because the Hun had finally been whipped. He still remembers how they climbed up on trees and poles so they could better see the Soviet trampling on the Nazi flag and spitting on the swastika.

Did she forget the many CARE parcels that kept her alive right after the war? Did she forget her Nescafe? Her cakes of soap? Her cereal?

Compared to war-torn Europe, America was full of gold, like King Tut's tomb, and he was sent to share. He, Archie, was in charge of the entire loathsome business of digging deep into the blackened rubble and finding the survivors of the war. That's what he did; he dug. That's why he came; he shared. The Elder Archie volunteered to go to Germany to help the dregs of war, expecting a country in sackcloth and ashes. And where was his reward?

That's still his question mark.

He saw first-hand how all those Huns climbed from the rubble—this was before the Marshall Plan—to pass their buckets filled with stone and ash and mortar bits from hand to hand in long, humiliating lines.

"I stayed just long enough," he tells the munching people in the kitchen who heard this story many times but listen nonetheless the way you listen to a melody that touches a rhapsodic chord, "to watch how they were caught, these so-called Führer sympathizers, grabbed by the ears like rabbits in the fields, packed into cattle cars—" He said it then. He says it now. He looks around triumphantly. "—along with the dregs of the pitiful Wehrmacht. They had it coming. All of them. They got what they had coming."

America dispensing righteous wrath on Nazi Germany is still a memory that warms his preacher belly like a flame.

"My generation had no men," says Mimi softly, still on Josie's couch, her life now winding down.

I know that story, too. The splendid warriors of my mother's youth who hurled themselves against the Bolsheviks to stop the Antichrist—they froze to death at Stalingrad; they perished in the forests of Siberia and in the coal mines of Kolyma; they died like beasts of woe in Stalin's dungeon pits. No letter ever came out of the silence of the grave.

"They died like dogs," said Mimi. "When all was said and done, there was nobody left. A woman of my generation never had a chance to lead a normal life. To love a man. To raise a healthy family."

"Not true," says Temperance, and putters about in the kitchen. "You had a suitor once."

"Sure. Hannele from Hillsboro?" sighs Mimi.

"And what was wrong with Hannele?" asks Temperance, hands on her hefty hips. "He buttons himself properly. He has a spotless past. He owns three hundred acres. He is quite popular."

That must have been right after we arrived. When Hannele saw Mimi, he had been widowed fourteen years, he said that she would do, now was the time, he was a modest man and not that picky-picky. He studied everything about my mother, thoroughly, and realized her only earthly goods were just three cardboard boxes. But Hannele came courting, nonetheless. He laid a stubborn siege.

She smiled a toothless smile. "I'd rather not," said Mimi.

Still, he came several Sundays in a row, in an old, bucking Buick that had a handle missing. He was one of those fellows who, a little short of breath but long on doggedness, can't force big words across his lips but knows how to let go of little rolling yodels when an Oktoberfest arrives. His hair was neatly brushed and parted with cold water, and he wore shoes with shiny double buckles.

He told my mother all about himself. He gave her the width of his sleeves, the breadth of his shoulders. He held strong views on evolution, excessive sports, lipstick, Jehovah's Witnesses and other moral pitfalls.

"We are made for each other," he told her and patted the spot next to him.

That was the only time I saw my mother cry.

She knew a man's love once. His name was Jonathan.

When Hitler's torch lights flickered, she was still young and beautiful. She felt the warmth of one short summer in her hair.

But then the years slipped by. Her eyes lost their luster; her step lost its bounce. Her hair turned gray, then white. Now she has rheumatism churning in her bones, and death is just around the corner. But to this day, she still remembers Jonathan.

"As I look back," she told me once, "it seems to me that only hours passed. Do you remember him? I see him vividly." Those thoughts are born of loneliness and sorrow. Most of the time, she keeps them to herself.

Yes, I remember Jonathan. His love was like a touch of wing, in service to ideals he thought could never be destroyed. Will-power. Strength. Devotion. Work. Tenacity. Pride and self-confidence. All that.

"He fought," says Mimi stubbornly, "because he thought the Soviet monster could be smitten. He loved his Fatherland, a country strong and beautiful, a land like any other land on earth that sent her sons to war—"

In Josie's spotless kitchen, she pleads with passion and conviction that Germany is surely entitled, is she not, to rest her heroes in their far-flung graves—without insults and sneers?

But Archie slurps his coffee noisily and tries to change the subject. All that is theoretical. Where Jonathan lies buried, nobody ever knew.

*

The night is cool and moonlit. The freshly fallen snow outside is delicate as lace. Around me it is dark and still, and I am glad that I am finally alone.

I always sleep in Rarey's room, dressed for the night in one of Josie's flannel gowns. I like to be alone with Rarey. I am more intimate with Rarey than I could ever be with people still alive. He, too, rests in eternity, where I will be tomorrow, where Josie dwells, no doubt. Her Bible tells me so. It's sitting on the night stand. In her old age, she started reading it, which pleased the relatives.

I pick it up, and it falls open to the passages she loved. Though her own Faith was off-beat to the end, she loved the poetry inherent in the Scriptures as caught in that exquisite mixture of sadness and relief. And here it says, as if I didn't know: "For man that is born of a woman is of few days, and full of trouble."

That is the message that is woven in my genes.

"He comes forth like a flower," says Josie's chancy Faith, with which I, of another generation and of another world, can easily identify, never having felt the certitude that marks the simpleton. "He flees like a shadow and does not continue."

All flesh is grass, says Josie's Faith, and all its loveliness is like the flower of the field. The grass withers, the flower fades, because the breath of the Lord blows upon it; surely the people are grass. The grass withers, the flower fades, but the word of our God stands forever.

As for man, his days are like grass; as a flower of the field, so he flourishes. For the wind passes over it, and it is gone, and its own place remembers it no more.

How much did Rarey know of Apanlee that gave him life—and death?

The room is given over to his memory. For Rarey Neufeld, Josie's last-born, much-beloved son, eternity began in a sharp burst of light the U.S. government went to some pains describing.

She should be proud, the letter said; the nation grieved with her; her young son gave his life, regrettably—but in a blaze of glory while straining for the sun.

What nobler sacrifice?

It happened in the last days of the war. The city of Berlin lay way below, defeated and collapsed, convulsing in its death throes. Death, said the telegram, was instantaneous, while what was left of his young life sailed through the April clouds and fell into a tulip bed.

That's how young Rarey died—in someone's tulip bed.

The Air Force, Josie told me in that brittle voice of hers that cracked each time she spoke of her lost son, wrapped Rarey in a silken flag, and buried him for just a little while on a small plot that gently sloped toward a river. The air that day, the letter claimed that came after the telegram, was thick and sweet with spring.

Not so when he came home to Arlington, the stars and stripes wrapped all around his casket so that his comrades had to fumble for the handle. The heavens wept that day.

"All day long," Josie told me once while doing almost all the talking, sipping tea, explaining that the European war had been a necessary evil, fought honorably, won by the strength of righteous wrath, "it rained in a light drizzle. I guess the angels cried."

I guess they did. The angels must have cried. He was an Aryan. He fought a *Bruderkrieg*—a fratricidal war

His medals, ribbons, watch and billfold, scores of old newspaper clippings, old postcards, the death certificate replete with Presidential seal and listing hometown, serial number, rank—all that is still preserved and dusted every week. Even his army jacket. The one he wore before he fell into the rubble of Berlin and landed in a tulip bed.

Said Josephine: "The honor guard shot thrice into the leaden sky—" And Josie flinched, each time, she told me decades later, while sipping tea and dabbing at her eyes, "—as though the bullets struck my heart, but I must tell you this. It's odd but true. I never felt so proud."

"A sad and rainy day," said Josephine, while telling me about the son she sacrificed to let what she called the Four Freedoms reign.

He must have believed it was so. He had been told this would be his last mission; his duty was to to rid the world of Hitler's shadow, to smash the loathsome city. He could still see the flotsam of the great migrations, still struggling on through all the rubble, cluttering the Führer's Autobahn. He held his wing tips steady. He nosed his airplane up and tried to fly out of the pall of dust and smoke—straight up into the sun. The war was almost done; he was just about done with the barbarians; he could go home and raise a child. His first.

He reached for his binoculars and peered down at the cratered landscape. His thoughts were drifting; he was glad; he was not meant to be a soldier; he of a clan of pacifists; he saw his wife; he saw his baby boy; his heart was light and free. He plunged, released his bombs, pulled up into a climb and knew that his comrades stood by the Elbe, waiting for the Russian bear—and at this moment, down below, it happened.

I saw it; I was there.

As he descended carefully, he may have realized he came into some anti-aircraft fire. Maybe. And maybe not. I often think of that. He may have vaguely realized that someone, down below, was nipping at his silver wings with a well-oiled and swinging ack-ack gun—and that, on any other day he might have been more cautious!—but on this day, his thoughts were with his wife and child, for word had come. At last.

"The war was over. Finally. The Führer's dream was dead."

When Josie told me that, one sunny afternoon that baked the prairie soil, a burly youth, born six months after World War II, named after a forgotten forebear who traded, so the story goes, those first blessed kernels from the Tartars that feed the world today, materialized out of the kitchen and sat beside her silently and gently stroked her hand.

"The angels cried. The angels cried. The angels cried," young Peet consoled his grandmother, as though it were a litany. "Remember how it rained? One of those good old country rains that drench the land so that the earth renews?"

I know that kind of rain. There's nothing like it. Nothing.

I will tell you a secret. It doesn't even have a name, but it exists. Believe me it exists. The force of nature can't be stopped. It rises from the earth. It's gathering at the horizon. It will arrive and drench America; for she is parched for rain. The leaves and the grass have stopped growing. The fields lie sapless. Barren. Thirsting. The soil—Jan's soil, Peet's soil—cannot renew until it rains again.

Now between wakefulness and sleep, I finally face up to Erika—as she was then; not as she is today. It is as though I see a double feature—first one side, then the other.

First I see Rarey, young and kind and full of life and nothing but goodwill and certitude. Then I see Lilo, likewise.

And there is Erika, still without words, still non-descript. Right in the middle. Scared.

In California, I hardly ever think of Erika, as busy as I am. But here, in Rarey's room, she comes alive as though by magic— a slim, young thirteen-year-old girl in Hitler uniform perched next to a small anti-aircraft gun, right on a Berlin rooftop, and at her side a wounded man. With SS epaulets.

Her name was Erika. His name was Jonathan. Both came from Apanlee, where duty was writ large.

He was a German soldier, a convert to the Mystic Cross—the cult of Blood and Soil and Race. It was a cult as arbitrary, all-embracing, monolithic, absolute, authoritarian as Archie ever could have wished. She was an honor student, one of those tiny timid females caught in the Führer's war, all thumbs and toes, still much too babyish—but that would change; she was resolved that it would change, consumed as she was in those last sad days of war with a raw will to live, to fight against the cowardice that was the dragon of her youth, and has been ever since.

True. Erika survived. The war was over, and she lived. All life was ashes, but she lived. Not that it mattered, but she lived. How? On numb feet across a dead city, that's how.

She survived because she had hidden herself in the ashcan the psychic had spoken about. She crouched in that ashcan, hour after hour, while all around her, roof by roof and house by house, a city flew apart.

The stars kept raining bombs. The guns belched ceaselessly. The ashcan was dented all over.

Then it grew light. The noise died down. The hissing and sputtering stopped. The shelling fell off around dawn. The airplanes that had tried to blow all life to smithereens miraculously vanished. The sun came out—a bloody ball three times its size, monstrously magnified by all the dust and smoke.

Berlin was Ghost City, writ large.

With hands that were trembling with terror and chill, she lifted the lid and crawled out.

It hurt to walk. It hurt to sit. It hurt to breathe in air. The streets were lit with fire, the sky was crimson still, the trees stood beheaded and the neighbors were dead. She guessed it might be Tuesday—scrap day! to go from door to door collecting papers, clothes, bones, helmets—anything!—to help the Führer's war along, but one quick glance sufficed to know that that was foolish, verily! as useless as her ration vouchers dated yesterday.

What fighting there still was had now dispersed into the side streets and small alleys. She sensed a breathing spell.

She sat down at the rim of a bomb crater, half-filled with dirty water. A main line must have broken; the water still gurgled and seeped. Something was floating there, but luckily face down.

She looked around. The streets were foul with refuse. A coward had unfurled a banner from the window, and it was white, the color of surrender. That gave her a brief jolt, but she composed herself.

She carefully sidestepped the carcass of a burned-out bus and came upon a weeping toddler who reached for her and clung to her—a snot-smeared child with sunken eyes, no older than three years. He was a trying sight. His soles were charred, and that was sad. She wondered what to do. She hesitated, undecided, then bent to him and lifted him into a suitcase, spilling things. She freed herself from his small fists still clutching at her skirt as though they were two burrs. Though he whimpered and sniveled and wouldn't let go, she patted him briefly and walked.

She rallied all her strength still left to find the street where Heidi lived. It, too, was black with death.

Her chest felt tight and prickly as she kept looking hard.

Stalled trucks and burnt-out automobiles lined the street and blocked her way; she scrambled, dazed and blinded, across all obstacles, some of them smoking faintly. As she stood, contemplating her next step, a tank came barreling around the corner, and she ducked just in time. She watched it crush the tulips. That's when it came to her that this was Heidi's house that took the bomb smack on the roof. She knew it by the tulips.

She found the mail box next. Some giant fist had crushed it flat, but Heidi's name was legible. She stood silent, not even surprised.

Small fires were eating away at the rafters, creating black gaps in the rubble. There was a deep hole where the cellar had been; small wisps curled from the ashes.

She didn't weep. There was no point in weeping over Heidi who would remain in that rubble forever. She simply sat down, in the ashes.

She would never feel young again. Ever. There might be a tomorrow still, but yesterday was gone. Her former self was gone. It had died, exhausted from hurting.

She sat there for the longest time until a soft thing nudged at her, and that was Lilo's pet. He had no tail and only three legs, and his left eye was hanging by a sinew.

"Well, Winston Churchill. It's all over now," she said to Lilo's pet, amazed she still had words.

The mutt gave a whimpering sound.

A veil of dust hung in the air. The cloud of ashes was so thick the sun could not break through. The world she had known lay in smoldering ruins, but she was hungry; she would eat. She kept looking for something to eat, and she found it before it was noon: a bone that looked like a thigh bone. The fire had gnawed off the flesh. She didn't know if it was man or beast, but she would take her chances. She took a brick and crushed it. She slurped the marrow, raw.

Now there was sweet contentment in her belly.

She decided to check up on Lilo. Somebody had to check,

and so she did; she checked. The pet helped some; he whimpered and hobbled, three-legged.

Lilo lay where she had fallen, a soldier for the cause. She lay supine and very still, her young lips pale and slack. Her sooty face was gray. Her blond, fat braids were singed. Someone had violated her in death; had rammed a flag pole's sharpened end from in between her legs into her twisted body with such force that it stuck out where Lilo's lusty heart had beaten for the future. Yesterday.

Was that a shock? Well, yes and no.

Her knees were buckling, but she looked. Her eyes were blurring, but she looked. And then she did something that came by itself. Her arm shot out; she stood straight; she gave Lilo the Führer salute.

Her name was Erika. That was the timid girl I knew, so many years ago.

She is no longer part of me; I have disowned her to survive; but once upon a distant time, I knew her well indeed. She gave Lilo the Führer salute. It was the only thing still left to do, the most natural thing in the world. It wasn't that she felt the need to be dramatic; or blasphemous; or obstinate; there was no irony in that; she wasn't trying to say anything or make heroic gestures. She stood in a world bereft of all landmarks, and gave over her heart to the wind.

That's how I still see Erika—this after all these years—saluting her brave and defiant and beautiful friend who blew a lot of bubbles each morning as she brushed her teeth, who dreamed the day would come when she would shine on celluloid, who had a whole life to look forward to, who always scolded Erika:

"Where is your spirit, girl? It's for the Fatherland—" and whom the Allies killed.

The firing fell off around noon. Cheap cotton flags, with pentagrams, the logo of the Antichrist, stitched onto them by hand, appeared and fluttered down from blackened, gutted windows.

Two were still left. Alive.

A soldier and a girl were left, alone, atop a bombed-out edifice, the moon-lit night around them, while down below, Berlin lay in its death throes. He knew his wound was mortal, but there were calm and fealty in his face; he had one last devoted little comrade, next to him, a little girl in Hitler uniform, who did her duty neatly, who carried to him food and drink and what morsels of news she could gather. He had a small transmitter. He broadcast for as long as someone still took messages.

The anguish coming from his wounded leg had thickened his speech and glazed his vision; his leg was badly gangrenous.

She said to him. "In every door, a drunken Russian."

"I know."

By then, she had stopped counting. It happened day by day.

She took that risk; she carried food and drink and news, bypassing monsters wearing pentagrams on furry caps, prowling in search of loot and mayhem, who jeered and ordered her: "*Komm. Komm. Frau, komm.*" Sometimes they saw how young she was, and then they called her *Fräulein.*

They said: "*Komm, Fräulein. Komm.*"

Then they would grab her by her hair and treat her cruelly, and even when she tried to hide herself beneath some blankets, say, or maybe in the straw, depending on the situation, they jabbed at her with pointed bayonets and grabbed her by the ankles and pulled hard. And she would go with them and once again endure.

At night, she would sit, shivering, within the bend of Jonathan's good arm that lay in a warm scoop around her narrow shoulders. He was a man. She was a girl. Love comes in many shades.

The moon was throwing shadows when he said: "I want you to remember that there are absolutes worth knowing. They have nothing to do with the outcome. The outcome can be bought. Or forced. Or swindled. Or connived. But absolutes cannot."

He said to her while giving her his legacy atop a dying city:

"Some win, and others lose. Some die, and others live. The losers are forgotten in defeat; the winners write their history. The winners do their cartwheels; the losers have no voice. And in the end, who counts the medals? Anyone? Will anybody ever read the balance sheet correctly? But always you remember: there is a history worth knowing. The earth has rights. It belongs to the bravest and best."

She took his hand and stroked it. Her fingers felt their way along a scar.

"A dog bit you?"

"No, not a dog. A little girl. A little cousin I once loved. It happened long ago."

She did not ask: "Why are you telling me? As if I didn't know."

She quietly listened as he said: "If you survive, you'll have a mission, Erika. You are a child of gifted fancy. Here's what you must remember, always. There is a story to be told. Don't touch up anything."

She had just finished changing Jonathan's blood-soaked, earth-crusted bandages, when she looked up and saw two men in speckled uniform. One of these men was huge and black. Colossal. Towering. Her hands flew to her lips and she shrank back against the wall, for she had never seen a Negro, ever, not even in a photograph. The other one was gangly, vague, with sanctimonious brows; he looked excitable and edgy in a simmering, smoldering way.

"Gum?" asked the Negro, grinning, chewing, inspecting her with a black glitter in his eyes.

Gum. *Komm*.

She had endured an avalanche of rape. The words were practically identical. He had fat thumbs, fat cheeks; he rolled his l's and r's; his neck was purple and bombastic and he was shifting chewing gum from cheek to cheek while looking for an opportunity to pounce. His hands had vanished, fumbling, in his trousers, but both his thumbs stuck out, and they were wiggling now.

He was the worst of feral beasts out of her many nightmares, but his companion, freckled, weasly, looked vaguely familiar.

"Well, well. This will be a day to remember," said the black paratrooper and nodded in a significant way, while the second, the blond one, leaned forward and said, slightly slurred:

"Well, I'll be damned! Look what we found. A real live Nazi girl."

The C.O. volunteers of Mennotown did not wear guns, and Archie didn't either, but that night, to be safe, Archie had borrowed one as he and his black pal stepped out into the dark to calm their jagged nerves.

It had been a harrowing day.

He had arrived in Germany with all the best intentions, and he was sickened in his soul. One of the first relief cohorts sent overseas to comb through the rubble and pick up survivors, Archie was trying hard; intent on building goodwill with the burlap sacks of Mennotown, setting a splint to a world out of joint. That day, he had worked sixteen hours at a stretch; his head was throbbing with revulsion and fatigue. He, Archie Epp, may not have finished high school, but was he anybody's fool?

He understood one thing: of remorse, there was none. These people, whom he tried to help, were still disciples of the Führer.

He had enlisted, taken pity, packed his bags, forsaking his soft bed in Kansas. And he expected gratitude. Remorse. Contrition. Penitence. And there was none of that.

But prayers must come first, insisted Archibald, reared in the Faith and, hence, affirming Faith and, yes! obedience. Obedience writ large! He was proud of his pacifist mission. He cut the straps to let the losers get an eyeful of the riches of a land that stressed equality and, hence, reaped peace and harmony: dresses and shirts, shoes and socks and sweaters—all items to alleviate the suffering of war. Little Melly's Christian spirit was alive in every patch and stitch; he smelled that in the smell of mothballs; he felt it in his fingertips.

He tried to talk to them. He tried to listen to their stories, but what they told him made no sense at all.

"You're mercenaries for the Beast," said one, and others nodded gravely. They told him even then: "You'll find out soon enough."

They said: "We're innocent. It's you, Americans, who bear the guilt for what will happen next. We tried to finish off the Antichrist. We tried to stem the tide."

They didn't look so innocent to him. "You're criminals," he told them, sparing no one, then or now. "You're scum. The worst. You're hooligans."

They looked at him with glassy, apathetic eyes. It was too much. It was plain overload. His spectacles fogged up. He was sick to death of them all—all famished, sick and weary, with vermin in their hair and hunger in their eyes, still loyal to their Führer. The devil's brood they were, as far as he could tell—this untidy flotsam of war, no doubt flag-waving all the way to prison or, better yet, goose-stepping to Siberia.

Which was just fine with him!

He was building a murderous rage. He needed to cool off. That's when he motioned to his Negro friend who pocketed one gun and handed a second to Archie.

Together, they stepped out into the streets to draw a breath of air, and that is when he spotted it—the shredded parachute still hanging from a tree. And that's when every shred of pacifism went like poof! and Archie knew that, given provocation, he, too, would kill.

He'd kill the Hun! He'd finish off the Hun! Without remorse! With gusto!

This was Archie's murderous moment.

Ever since that rock, hurled hard against his people's ethnic pride, had ripped out his right eye and forced him to his knees, he had kept rage inside. And that's precisely when he heard a strange, suspicious sound, pushed open a burned door, stepped gingerly into the hall, and found those two: the trembling Hitler girl beside the wounded *Landser*. And something snapped in Archie.

His lungs filled up with wrath. He knew that this was it. All guns had fallen silent; peace had already been declared, and there they were, the viper's brood, manning their anti-aircraft gun still pointed at the sky.

A wave of fury flooded Archie's chest with an enormous whoosh! He touched the barrel; it was hot; he could have sworn it was still hot. He could not pry the girl's hands from the barrel.

"Don't move, or I will shoot," he bellowed, which was superfluous because he knew he would—this was his opportunity. It would not slip away. His unit leader had a German wife from Pennsylvania, one of those old and stubborn crusts who stuck to ethnic pride, through thick and thin, against all better evidence. If his commander knew this Nazi riffraff, hiding here, evading justice, were counting on American largesse, he'd botch the opportunity.

"Are you Ameri—" the German soldier said but did not finish what he meant to say, for Archie had his finger on the trigger. It curled around the bolt.

"You bet I am," said Archie. "You bet your blasted swastika I am." He said to her: "You little viper! You! Now move! You heard me! I said move!" while his black buddy lumbered forward clumsily. "Gum? *Fräulein*? Gum?" he asked, for lack of better words.

She saw the huge, black hands still fumbling in the pockets of his trousers. The *Landser* saw it, too; he swung around and felt with his good hand for his own gun, and that's when Archie pulled the trigger. It gave him a sweet rush. The barrel went poof! and the *Landser* fell back and was dead.

The little girl in Hitler uniform was hiccuping.

But Archie wasn't finished yet. He gave her an enormous shove and said in halting German, thick with the diphthongs of four centuries:

"Now, listen, you! You little runt! This war is over, and you lost! You lost! You lost! You lost!"

Yes, Archie, that was you. That was your side. You told it to exhaustion.

Here, now, speaks Erika.

Chapter 1

What do we know of Erika? This much: her script was set more than four centuries ago. Her ethnic roots go deep into the soil of martyrdom.

Her ancestors were dogged folks of Faith, committed to a restive monk who took his friar's lantern, shone it on the ancient script, and found a zealous God who bade him break with Rome so as to stand apart.

Confessing to be born-again in olden days risked being broken on the rack, torched at the stake, imprisoned, branded, drowned—for little mercy did the Holy Roman Empire have for those who felt they needed to profess their sovereign pledge to God.

An outlaw he became, this feisty ancestor of bygone days who spurned monastic rule—an outlaw and a fugitive, dogs on his heels and a high bounty on his head, for years evading persecuting Papists and rapacious overlords with prudent skill and trickery.

He was of peasant origin, this founder of a stubborn sect,

born in a village a few miles inland from a dark and frenzied sea—a man of penetrating mind, of unremitting ardor. He said and wrote, since there was no tomorrow:

"What if they burn our bones to ashes? What if they rip our tongues to shreds? What if they blind our eyes? There is no death blow to our cause. Watch love and brotherhood spread through the efforts of merchants and weavers, and know that, in the end, the peaceful always win—"

You had to be a saint to speak like that in times when European lords wrought chains of war across the land by choice and by necessity. They were unpopular, this small, determined band of rebel pacifists who spread God's message fast and far.

It was a message, they believed, aglow with hidden strength. And so it must have been—for neither torture nor the grievous plights of years of homeless wandering could weaken their impassioned message in the least. Their *Martyr's Mirror* testifies how willingly they suffered for their Faith: it tells of galley slaves who perished on high sea, of foreheads marked with scorching irons so others would refuse them food, tongues torn from throats to stop the spread of heresy—that's how they lived and died.

By the ax they died on Alba's many scaffolds, those first fierce Anabaptist sufferers for Christ—but not before this one, that one had sired yet another child to take the light and keep it burning in a dark and vengeful land.

Nobody silenced them. Nobody could.

Whole generations came and went, and still the Anabaptists spoke, and still they testified while dying by the hundreds by stake, rack, sword—for peace.

For many years, they wandered back and forth along the North Sea coast, for kings and overlords had use for them as drainers of their marshes. They knew of dikes and dams. You glimpse that in their names: Dück. Dyck. Dirk. Dirksen. Derksen. In time, they settled in the swamps of Prussia—for many years, obscure. Just when the first ones settled in the region which became the Polish Corridor, nobody knows for sure. Most were of Frisian and Flemish stock—as written in their blue eyes, blond hair, in their strong and swaying gait, in names like Fröse, Friesen, Riesen.

Despised for their poverty, yet they were envied for their skills and diligence. They took a bitter bread out of the mouths of natives, and hate and jealousy grew strong. They could not trade in various Free Cities. Their children had no rights before the law. For decades, they could not inherit property. Their Elders could not preach at funerals, for fear they would mislead a weakened soul.

Forced thus to stay among themselves by circumstance and feudal rule, their Elders said: "This suits us fine. This way, we need not suffer pagans, fools and sinners."

A haughty mindset blossomed forth.

For centuries, no stranger found his way into this close-knit brotherhood. No new blood came to them. The years of isolation even spawned a special tongue. Go to Nebraska. Kansas. The Dakotas. Winnipeg. Go visit Reedley, in the heart of California. Tucked deep into the orchards, you'll find Low German still.

"No guns and spears. Just Christ," plain folks aver in drawn-out, awkward diphthongs, as centuries ago their founder once proclaimed. And draft boards during war have no more use for them today than kings and overlords had in the past.

"No swords for sons of saints," they say.

"No bloodshed. Ever. Not by our hands," they said for centuries.

They said it long enough, and lived by it with kith and kin, until even hard-headed rulers admitted: "Truly, these are the children of peace who have beaten their swords into plowshares—"

At a time when rich men still powdered their hair and a horse could be bought for three *Pfennig*, a strong-willed Prussian king gazed wistfully across his land, impoverished and battle-torn, and longed to fuse a country. A delta was partitioned. The sect fell to his lot.

"My enterprising citizens," he called them with great pride. He bade his ministers to leave alone his artisans: his weavers, cobblers, lantern tinkers, dikers, millers, farmers.

In turn, they gave him gifts of gratitude: two well-fed oxen, four hundred pounds of butter, a flock of fattened ducks. Not being folks content with doing anything by halves, they also gave him a petition: "Are we still free from mandate to shed precious human blood?"

"There is a kingdom to enlarge," said he.

"We have a separate Lord," was their reply.

He did not mind their God. He minded losing husky, long-legged boys to military service. He taxed them many *Thalers* for military schools. The Elders stood aggrieved, for other lords had drained their pockets with taxation for their wars.

The king's recruiting marshals kept casting greedy eyes upon their strapping sons. Their villages turned into hives of discontent.

Where to? What now? Was there a way out of this festering dilemma?

At just that time, a shrewd and daring princess, born to the humble House of Hesse and married to a half-wit of the House of Romanov, was busily threading her way through a maze of courtly intrigues. Barely had she reached the throne of Russia than she made clever wars with Poland and Turkey. To feed her burning ambition to extend her empire to the shores of the Black Sea, she seized vast patches of steppe from wild, disheveled tribes whom she forced willy-nilly from ancient grazing ground.

"Be gone, ye vermin, ye!" she said, steeped in conviction of her might.

The heathen fought their dispossession hard: the steppe had been theirs for centuries. Blood-thirsty tribes fell upon helpless Russian villages, stole children, calves and horses, and put the torch to property.

The empress, with a will to rule and do it well, fought many a boisterous battle, forcing them eastward and trying to keep them at bay. To make her conquest stick, she needed the bulwark of orderly, civilized souls to keep borders secure and barbarians out. And in her strong, impatient hands lay millions of black, fertile acres.

She released a batch of tempting manifestos, as a cat might litter kittens. She flooded the land of her birth with land scouts, proclaiming:

"Come any, come all! Vast fortunes are yours for the asking along the Black and Caspian Seas. Free land in abundance. Protection by the Crown. Unfettered self-rule. And freedom from conscription."

All this at a time when the pacifist creed bore the yoke of increasing and unfair taxation, when Elder after Elder scowled at the Soldier King repeatedly and told him stubbornly: "No swords for our sons! Not under any guise!" And saw him turn away and frown.

This offer coming from a land called Russia was tempting to people much oppressed. The agents of the empress coined the lure that carried fire: *Lebensraum.* The word is nothing new. Its call is deep in people such as Erika. They hear it constantly.

Small wonder that her forebears cocked their ears and listened carefully and knew: fat, virgin, fertile acres for their kin— so they could grow and prosper in the Lord, and multiply, and fill the earth with blond and blue-eyed children.

The Elders sent their land scouts to investigate. After having seen and sniffed the soil, the sleuths returned with frozen toes but favorable opinions. They told magical tales in the churches of Danzig. In person, they had met the empress and her court.

"Soil. Fat. Black. Virgin acres."

They knew it was God's will that they pack up and cast their lot with Russia. Two hundred years ago these pious people heard the Russian-German Empress say, desiring greatly that the world think well of her:

"No lice. No sloth. No criminals. No Jews."

Thus started Erika's forebears walking a difficult, untrodden path.

The poorer came on foot, the middle class by river barge, the rich and elegant by carriage. By the thousands they came, in the decades that followed—some pushing wheelbarrows, others riding haughtily with servants, guides, and guards. They came because the agents of the crown had talked with honeyed tongues: "A land of opportunities beyond the dreams of men—"

Regrettably, they found there was no paradise. Nothing but tall grass, gray sky, myriads of field mice, and thieving, marauding Tartars who stole cattle, worshipped Allah, and slurped the blood of goats.

Lesser men would have despaired.

They built some hasty dug-outs—pathetic hovels that soon filled with hunger, illness and despair. They shivered through the winter as ice floes drifted down the Dnyeper River, as cold air from Siberia knifed across the barren plains.

The Empress tried to help. The food she sent spoiled on the way. The building lumber disappeared. The money vanished into the pockets of crooked, devious couriers. The pious German pioneers who had arrived in search of *Lebensraum* were much too weak and poor to try to make it back.

How many perished that first year? The archives do not tell.

Some dug in deep, as Peter Neufeld did, a man with expert hands and fierce ambition. He came, and he would stay.

With the help of his young son, he built a crude sod shanty, relying on his skills, his dogged will to live, his rugged perseverance. Others, perhaps more fatalistic, perhaps more trusting in the Lord, stayed in their hooded wagons, from where they prayed to Heaven day and night. Among them was Hans Epp, a self-appointed Elder who had been saved from a mysterious illness and born-again for Christ while still a paltry child.

The Lord, saith he, was good. He gave and took, blessed

always be His name.

A son was born to him beneath the wagon covers.

The baby brought him meager joy: it killed his wife. She stiffened with cold and her spirit departed, despite many *amens* and heartrending wails beseeching the Maker for mercy.

This Elder, however, came amply endowed with the zeal of the righteous. When, in his mix of happiness and grief, he opened his trunk to ready himself for a sermon, he found that someone had stolen his boots. Instead, there were rocks in his pouches. Some pilferer along the way, to cover up his thievery, had put them there to trick him.

For a moment, he stood overwhelmed, thinking of the sweat and pain his wheelbarrow had drained out of his brittle bones as he pushed it along, on foot, all the way from the Vistula plains.

"Be this, as well, God's will," he sighed.

The road had worn the Elder's strength but not his voice or spirit. He could still preach, he could still sing, and he did both, and ringingly—he stood beneath a gray, indifferent sky and preached the first of many sermons.

"Beloved brethren," cried the Elder, bracing himself with shivering arms. "Behold, I may have lost my wife and boots, but I did wash my feet—I washed them thrice, in honor of the Holy Trinity. Thus, I stand clean and willing and obedient before the Romanovs who called me here, before my Lord who will provide. Let us draw lessons from adversity. Let us be thrice as honest. Thrice as clean. Thrice as humble and obedient, so as to set a laudable example and counteract bad luck."

He dug a grave. He swaddled the infant. Each day, he said a triple prayer and sang a triple hymn. The pious flock did likewise.

He had obediently signed a promise to the Crown that for all times to come his people would conduct themselves with dignity, refrain from quarreling and drink, and keep their young from eating green apples. His older sons were fine—each born, bred, baptized properly. But Willy, last in line, turned out to be a sickly child, given to numerous nosebleeds and sniffles.

"Be sure not to venture too far—" he admonished the lad who was begging early to be taken on the road to find the needy and the bedfast while braving winds, storms, rains and often vicious blizzards, "—because of wolves and Tartars, because of Lutherans and Catholics and Jews—" The ardent Elder was so busy gospeling and seeking out assorted sinners to convince them of the errors of their ways that he would sometimes leash his offspring to a tree and then forget him there, finding him at night again, starved silly, shivering and bawling.

As a result young Willy, sad to say, grew featherbrained, but discipline and many timely prayers made of the boy in no time short a qualified, obedient son who bowed his head, crossed all ten fingers willingly, and memorized with halting tongue his father's cast-off sermons, for lo! to let a free tongue reign was boastful—a grave and untoward sin.

At the idle age of nine, Willy Epp experienced his conversion and was thus born again. Early on, he fit himself to a life of holy service, having learned the useful diatribes of conduct early at his father's knobby knees. In later years—in middle life and deep into old age—the Elder Willy never varied either his opinions or his sermons.

"Where weeds grow in abundance," he would thunder, as his father thundered now, "our food will grow as well. There is no steppe dry enough the Lord can't send a cloud—"

The Lord sent clouds. Rains made the mud huts muddier.

The Devil tried in other ways to bring calamities to aggravate the pious clan: typhoid, smallpox, choking sickness, cholera. Oldsters succumbed, but youngsters were born. Horses and cattle were stolen or lost for lack of fences, but cows kept on producing calves, and horses brought forth foals.

To guard against marauders, the brethren settled in tight villages of thirty homesteads each. Every village boasted to the next in tribal, thick Low German: "A butcher. A blacksmith. Two cobblers and three carpenters."

They were racial and proud; they were separate and clannish; yet they were also practical in scope. Every farmer soon had equal access to a midwife, a bonesetter, a clock tuner, a coffin maker, a cartwright, two vigilant Elders flanking each village who told them, instructed by Willy: "There is no steppe dry enough the Lord can't send a cloud—"

And still they came out of the west, in creaking, covered wagons. Every new trek brought precocious love, autonomous and willing to be married. The new arrivals reinforced the Elders' influence, for each young pair was told a dozen times: "Be an example of persistence, decency and order, and teach your children diligence and self-control—"

Some died too soon, but more were readily born—all born to a life blessed with labor, all rising early, working hard, their faces to the sun. They all had freckled noses, cheeks that shone like polished apples, hair thick and straight and bleached as sun-drenched straw.

"The width of Russia," said Peter Neufeld, choked with joy, "is hardly large enough to settle them—" and watched them straddle the beloved steppe with their proverbial silent strength.

Aryan settlements sprang up all over southern Russia, and all of them were pious. Had some proclaimed them coarse and backwards for their simple, traditional ways? Perhaps in bygone days, in the Kingdom of Poland, the Duchy of Prussia, hampered by unwise lords and unfair taxation, with not a plot of land to call their own. Not here. Not now. The days were long and hot. The work was hard and heady. Life was a joyous battle for their children's future and for the coming Kingdom of the Lord.

A boy, before he was twelve years of age, would jump into his trousers to beat the sun, to lead an ox, to pull a plow, to shame a lazy neighbor. A maiden, before she would marry and start dropping baby after baby right into the scented clover, would swing a broom and spin the yarn and milk a stubborn goat with strong and nimble fingers.

In times of peace the skies are clear. The children's eyes are luminous.

Peet, eldest son of Peter Neufeld, grew to early manhood in those pioneering years. He learned from the example of his father, who came with ample testimonials to his fine past and wondrous capabilities.

This man could cure malaria, boils and dizziness, and he could even banish freckles. There was free bird and fish catch in his records. In the Vistula plains, he had wrestled the land from the swamps. Here was a patriarch of wisdom and humor and spirit, not so easily driven to prayers, not so prone to lean on the Lord— not by the weeds as high as his heart nor by the blistering winds; not by the numerous field mice nor by the frequent marauders.

"Look at this tree," he told his son. "See the sap? Spring is but a fortnight coming. We'll seed two crops per year—" The records tell us tersely, furthermore, that he could read with ease and speed—much faster than the Elder Epp, although the latter had, by far, the louder, heartier voice.

"The more pious the farmer, the healthier the crop," the Elder preached with meaning.

"There is no time to lose," said Peter Neufeld, parrying.

"Why hurry in the face of centuries?" the Elder cried with heat.

"The evening will be wiser than the morning."

"Time is not tied to a post. Eternity is but a stone's throw away."

"Let's seed first, then pray hard the seed will sprout and prosper."

"Why not first order your life in the sight of the Cross?"

"Time doesn't stand still. You have to move forward." The sinner paid no heed. Beside him walked his son whose mind leapt over boundaries.

At the bank of a small tributary river, the father said: "Right here."

He put his shovel to the ground. Where others saw nothing but wasteland, his father's heart saw gold.

"The sleep of the steppe has come to an end," he told Peet, who stood, silent, beside him. "A life of abundance is yours, to be drawn with your hands from this earth. This land will yield to you. This soil holds moisture in great volume."

The air was fresh and balmy. Peet's young heart hammered with hard joy.

"The word," his father said, "is *Lebensraum.*"

There was a wooden plow, brought all the way from the Vistula plains. He pulled it from the thickets, along with an unwilling ox.

"Let me," said Peet in soft Low German. "Let us plow deep while sluggards sleep."

Its blade cut into fatty sod as though a knife had cut into the heart of Russia. A father watched. A son stopped short where earth touched sky and fused them to a dim horizon. A haze was lifting from the trees. Peet's bare toes crusted with the earth. His young mind all but reeled.

"Right here," called Peet, while pointing to the place where buttercups and dandelions raised their sassy heads each May, a piece of land next to a languid stream that found its way into the sea. At its mouth, farther down, the Russian town Berdyansk grew sluggishly.

Thus, long before he was a man, or so the chronicles recall, Peet Neufeld spied himself a splendid parcel and called it Apanlee.

Chapter 2

A plow, a rake, a fork, a prayer—such were his tools, such was his start. Perhaps a mare or two. Who knows? On details, the archives are sparse.

We may assume he built a modest home at first. The Crown may have furnished the lumber. He wove twigs and straw into the walls. He sealed the roof with mud and clay to keep the thatch in place.

Perhaps he calculated after rains washed it away repeatedly: "If I attempt to slant the roof just right so that the angle of the raindrops hits the angle of the thatch stuck to the angle of the rafters—" Young Peet possessed a strong and curious mind, forever searching pathways into knowlege.

In time the Empress, charitable to the settlers, passed away. The tsars who took her place knew, one by one, that she had chosen well when, by a lucky stroke of pen, she had settled the devout in the south of her realm, not far from the newly-formed Valley of Jews.

The settlers multiplied and prospered. There was lard in the pantry, food on the table, Faith in tomorrow, joy in today. The meadows filled with fat, complacent cows. The sun sent rays into the thick of leaves and sweetened orchards, one by one.

"Self-rule," they said, "suits us just fine. No mingling with outsiders."

There was no need to keep themselves authentic by government decree, for they carefully governed themselves. More diligent, harmonious citizens could not be found in all of Russia. Their doors all faced the street in unison, each path connecting to the neighbors' paths, measured to equal width and length. Everyone knew everybody, left and right and fore and aft, and watched each other's conduct. As they met after work by the well, at the store or by the fence, they made sure their gossip kept that edge, well-honed and keen enough to guard a proud existence.

First and foremost, it was Willy who ensured a stranger recognized a German villager from lesser men who might have practiced worthless ways. From house to house he went, a tireless servant of God, to hone and sharpen souls and build their ethnic pride: "Stand tall. Speak truth. Bring work and joy to Russia and honor to His Kingdom."

And thus, a German settler was seldom heard to swear, to lie, to cheat, to steal, to foist a fraud upon a fool, covet his neighbor's wife, or entertain a lusty thought—smoke thrice as thick as Russian smoke would billow from his chimney.

While Willy kept his church without a spot or scratch, Peet kept neat count of village council meetings and new arrival charts. Refined and mannerly, he could converse with ease on nearly any topic. He studied maps, committing them to memory for laying out new villages—and soon a gray, despairing landscape became a lush and thriving garden, with Apanlee the hub, and lesser homesteads serving as the spokes.

His neighbors said with pride: "Peet's tongue tips the scales of the tsars."

"The desert shall rejoice and blossom so long as we obey the Lord," the Elder Willy would proclaim, and Peet would hear that and stand tall, in his proud heart such joy and loneliness as is given only to the best of men in rarest times.

He knew: "No brakes on the future. No limits to what we can do. The door is wide open. Our children need only walk through."

"No patchwork for the Lord," said Willy cautiously.

Peet's pride near burst his heart. He stood, a man in a world made for manliness, knowing: "Mine for the asking—cucumbers and cabbage, seeds and pumpkins, squash and watermelons, beans and cherries and apples and pears, horses and cattle, fat flocks of geese, hundreds of serfs, thousands of sheep, and as early as tomorrow—" Here was his chosen country—Russia the Vast, Russia the Bountiful, to be broken, molded and transformed by his plow.

Soon, Russian peasants stood in awe outside the stately gates of Apanlee, this one or that one proclaiming: "The same rain. The same soil. The very same sunshine. How is it possible? Look at the Germans—a separate God?"

Peet gave to the Lord's ever-widening Kingdom, using both hands as a matter of fact—whether it be rubles, time or counsel or tiles as hard and durable as could be found in all of Russia.

"For all eternity," the Empress had declared—that's how Peet longed to build.

Peet drew up plans to build a church, and Willy claimed the pulpit.

Peet made the bricks, which horses carted out of Apanlee in wagon after wagon, and Willy counted them and said: "All brick and mortar to God's praise."

When the new chapel stood completed, Willy said, immensely pleased: "A splendid church, and full of pardoned souls but one—"

Peet smiled and slapped the prodding Elder on the shoulder: "Well, for a start, how would you like to marry me? I am claiming a beautiful woman,"

Peet's chosen was a distant cousin who came visiting from Chortitza. Peet knew at once: "A girl to share my spirit." He saw that Greta was exceptional. She knew how to lengthen the life of a candle, how to shorten the grief of a child. She cooked, scrubbed, swept, washed, knit, and sang like a canary. She dried apples, cherries, pears while stringing pretty chains of peppers. She stone-churned golden slabs of butter with the prettiest, daintiest hands.

As soon as he laid eyes on her, Peet told her, daringly: "Beloved, let us marry just as soon as geese are fat and nights are cool—" His love for her was like a lake without a bottom.

She looked at him and blushed—now what to do with all that happiness except to pluck another chicken for the pot?

"A woman to rise with the sun," the Elder Willy said approvingly, and Peet spoke from the fullness of his heart: "Yes, Apanlee will be a shrine."

Guests poured in from all directions to see the lovely bride. Peet had his prancing horses ribboned, ear to tail. The Elder Willy spoke a somber blessing. His fine-tuned choir sang praise in perfect, four-part harmony.

"A couple straight out of a love song," said the guests, and wiped their eyes. A touching thing, a wedding—it drew tears.

"Good luck, and God's eternal blessings," said Willy.

"The same to you," said Peet, a happy man indeed.

It was a wondrous day, and it was clear to all that these two men, in their respective functions, would manage splendidly to keep the universe from wobbling—Peet corresponding with the tsars, and Willy keeping up the link to the hereafter. The German villages, it was agreed, were in the best of hands—in this life and the next.

But matters festered like a boil when Peet resolved to build a school, for there were many children, all barefoot, all untutored—and more arrived in dusty wagons every day. Peet firmly argued at the council meeting that they must learn to read and write, and to that end, not waiting for an answer, he went away to find a kindly teacher who was, as it turned out, plagued and possessed by a progressive spirit—or so, at least, it seemed to Willy who sensed before a year had passed that things were getting out of hand. His nervous goiter told him there was trouble—and more to come, unless he put a stop to it, and fast.

"Reading, writing, recitation—" Peet stipulated, but Willy added cautiously: "—but only from the Scriptures!"

"By example rather than by rod," objected Peet, but Willy provided the hickory stick.

With cane in hand, the Elder visited one day, and what he saw, he did not like one bit. "Where is the lecture?" the Elder wanted to know. "Who's paying you for silence?"

"My lecture is being applied. I gave it before you came in," the teacher shrugged, and bit his lower lip.

In turn, the Elder glared. This was an idler, clearly.

The room was far too hot. There was a pail of water with a dipper, and now and then a little one would tiptoe for a drink.

"No discipline?"

"No need for discipline," the teacher said, for all the children sat and scribbled, mutely.

"Say! Is it true that you are fond of modern notions?"

"Modern notions?" asked the teacher, leaning back.

"Do you teach the alphabet forwards and backwards?"

"Whatever for? Straightforward is all they need."

"Do you make them recite the Chapters of Luke?"

A hush fell suddenly. The little boys and girls sat, doing slate work silently.

"No, Elder Willy," the teacher said at length. "With due respect, this is a classroom, not a church."

The Elder watched the children for a while, not knowing what to say, against his will impressed—until he saw just what it was they copied: poetry! A waste! A shame! "Why not, instead, copy a hymn?" That would have been prudent. That would have made sense. Hymns needed practice, anyway, until they lodged in memory.

There was a pause. The teacher had nothing to say.

The Elder, for his part, sat by the window, reflecting in anguish, not wanting to seem like a fool by raising an issue he might not be able to see to conclusion. His roving glance fell on an illustrated cover on the teacher's desk, and the boulder deep within turned over in his chest.

"A fairytale!" he all but yelped. "If ever there's a book of lies, this must be it! And left, without the blink of eye, right within reach of trusting little children!"

"There's nothing wrong with fairytales. Myths make a mind grow lush with imagery," the teacher said, his eyes as clear as ice.

The Elder Willy howled: "I didn't ask you for your likes. Or for your views. Did I?"

"I thought I'd offer them to you. To edify your sentiments."

The children ducked. A cannon might have sounded. At long last, the teacher said softly: "—pray let me go on," and the Elder stood tall and said sharply: "You are welcome to leave. This instant. Right now."

And, sucking in his sagging belly, throwing back his mighty mane, he took his cane and, leaving, slammed the door on progress and modernity. He slammed it hard, with all his might. He did not even wait to check on the twenty-six end-of-day Recitation-of-Rules he himself had helped compose. He gave his horse a sharp slap with a hazel switch, thus forcing it into a nervous trot, and took himself straight to the gates of Apanlee to settle an overdue grievance with Peet.

He grabbed Peet Neufeld by the sleeve: "So? Are you satisfied? And do you know what else is going on? All fairy tales are lies!"

Peet laughed and slapped the Elder on the shoulder: "Why worry about unhatched eggs?"

Right then and there, the Elder knew that it was time to strengthen vigil. Give the Devil your pinkie—he'll grab you by both elbows and steer you straight into the pit! One thing would lead to the next. Folk songs. Nicknames. Red dresses with puffed sleeves. Unrestrained laughter on Sundays.

"Let one-armed Penner teach," he demanded. "Why not let the poor cripple be useful? His plow wobbles sadly. A cow on a leash will run havoc with him."

"You can't be serious. He's not equipped to teach. He cannot even read."

"Well, he can learn, and in the meantime—"

"I have heard your complaint," said Peet Neufeld.

"And?"

"We live in the world, and we must understand that world. It is no longer possible to isolate ourselves."

"What kind of talk is this? Whatever do you mean?"

"See here? Look at this box. See all these feeble seedlings? In this small crate there grows a future forest. Withhold the sun and the soil's nourishment from these young roots, and wood will never be as hard and durable as wood is meant to be."

The Elder Willy looked at Peet and sadly shook his head. A bookish man could be as fanciful with thought as the tsars' ballerinas.

Willy brooded hard on ways to remedy the situation at the school without provoking Peet to slacken his donations and blight the work still left to do in the lush vineyards of the Lord. He perspired to find a harmonious solution. But all the while he knew what all the righteous know: uncensored reading leads to unchecked thoughts, more dangerous than bullets.

He knew: temptations spring from books like feathers from a down comforter. Once ripped, you cannot ever put them back. You didn't need a fairy tale to know that right was right, and left was left, and any fool could tell the difference by concentrating on the pounding of his heart.

At last, the Elder could stand it no longer.

He took a key one night and let himself into the classroom. He worked with grim determination into the early morning hours, deciphering laboriously, cutting page after page from great heaps of books, flinging them into the fire he had lit to warm his bunions. When he was finished, there was nothing but shreds at his feet, nothing but wrath in his bones!

"So there!" he said, and heaved a sigh. "Have we need of the world?"

The teacher found an envelope beneath his door before the villagers could rise, catch notice, and protest. In a swirl of dust, he was gone.

Proud of his victory, the Elder added two lame sisters to his choir.

Peet started skipping devotions.

Chapter 3

In years to come, Apanlee became a peerless showcase farm.
Peet harvested on double summer fallow, first plowing shallow and then deep. He loosened the soil now this way, then that—harrowing, seeding, watching and learning.

He crossed Dutch and Frisian cattle and gave away their calves. He bred cattle red of color, full of udder, sleek with glossy sheen, so that the women of his village stood enamored, just staring at the splendid beasts.

Peet widened his attic, dug trenches around trees, and planted windbreaks everywhere to stem the force of gale. From Peet, the settlers learned how to improve their wooden latches; their wives and daughters learned the secrets of *vareniki* from Greta.

Peet traded secrets with the Tartars. One sunny afternoon, he came home with a small sack of special seed. From it, by trial and error, experimenting patiently, he grew a stronger type of grain. In the early years of pioneering, seeding, harvesting and threshing still were done by hand, and that was slow, that took too many hours—and time, to Peet, seemed priceless. His bril-

liant sap of genius ran strong, in need of outlet, compelling him
to set his teeth against the special needs of time. He could tell
how his life, by the hour, diminished—how late it was already,
how much yet to be done.

"Time is not hitched to a post," he often said to Greta, the
apple of his eye.

"You are carving the future," said she.

There was no end to Peet's inventions. He started drawing
wheels and swivels, and soon there stood a brand new outfit in
the threshing shed of Apanlee, with every bolt in place and every
hinge well-oiled.

"That's progress, Greta. Wealth."

Her eyes met his in loving understanding. He reached for her
and, in broad daylight, with all the neighbors looking on, he
stroked across her golden hair and watched her cheeks turn red
and lush as poppies.

For such a man of force and vision, Greta was the perfect
mate. She knit his socks and mittens. Nobody baked zwieback
as fluffy as Greta's. Nobody rolled *vareniki* her way.

She drew lava currents from Peet's heart; the midwife soon
drew baby after baby from her body. She gave him three sons,
one after the other. He, for his part, bestowed on them the names
of Emperors: Peter. Alexander. Nicholas.

He stood, his heart ablaze with pride, atop his loaded granaries. With both his hands, he dug into his riches. Such was the
bounty of those summers. Such was the dowry of his love.

A man with strength enough to pound an anvil, at night he sat
alone, quill twirling in his fingers, sifting through the numbers
that summed his success, composing careful letters to the tsars.
His study, even then, became a widely whispered legend. The
luxuries he owned are mentioned to this day: a desk with an
enormous writing surface, a divan of brocade, an open fireplace,
a gold ink blotter, sped to him by courtly courier as a special
present from the tsars, a fancy box of sealing wax, a window
wide enough to give a panoramic view of Apanlee.

A lover of print, Peet Neufeld read many a book to sharpen his judgment, tracing down page after page with sensitive hands, searching for secrets embedded in letters.

"A genius," declared the Crown, and gave Peet land and yet more land to plow and seed and harvest.

"A man who hears out any serf in any tongue," the Russian peasants said, to whom he brought the alphabet for those who longed to read.

It was a trying time for Willy—how to keep his tongue in check, yet prudent counsel handy without imperiling Peet's generous donations to the church.

Willy drew his knowledge solely from the proddings of the Holy Spirit. He watched Peet's ruminative fervor with ambivalence and worry. He who delved deep, not into mysteries of growth and progress but rather into shameful scandals in the lives of erring souls, saw danger in Peet's path.

Not to be outdone by Peet, the Elder Willy kept on widening his influence and strengthening his mark. The Lord kept adding to his flock, for babies came from everywhere, filling cradle after cradle. They still arrived in dusty covered wagons. Fat midwives fished them from a well. Storks dropped them through the chimneys from the gables. A fairy put them, swaddled head to toe, beneath the Christmas trees.

The Elder Willy smiled with glee. His sway solidified, as did his Sunday sermons.

Willy, too, was married. Thrice. He lived three-score-and-ten, and as the Bible promised, the Lord gave him his share. Between three wives and a long life, he had more sons and daughters than he could comfortably count—not that he didn't try.

His first wife, Margarete, bore seven, but three did not survive their infancy. One son, regrettably, was mad. Then Margarete passed on; Willy married her sister, Maria, a widow with five children of her own. The middle one, whose name was Anne Elizabeth, had been already nicknamed carelessly, and people called her Lizzy. He did his best, posthaste, to point out the anomaly.

Maria would have none of it:

"It's Lizzy," said Maria, heaving, for she was fat and always out of breath. "Say what you will. It's Lizzy."

Maria was the envy of the neighborhood, although the midwife fretted. She sat on double chairs and alternated feet so as to balance weight. Not normally defiant, Maria turned skittish soon after, for she was expecting again. She leaned her elbows on the sill at intermittent intervals to study passersby.

"Let her have just a little bit of vanity," she said. "What harm can come of that?"

He did not argue back; she had a bloated belly. He knew she was excitable. For quite a while, he kept the little girl within his sight, watching warily out of the corner of his eye.

But not for long; he realized to his relief that he could trust this child. Where Lizzy walked, the violets nodded. She was a smiling, friendly youngster, born around 1844. She had a sweet, accommodating nature; she hardly ever cried.

Matilda, his third wife, was twenty years younger than Willy and therefore outlived him by many a year and several additional children, thus adding to a crowded household already nebulous with kin. But all that happened later. For now, Matilda still sang in somebody else's choir; he hardly noticed her. He was still married to Maria when, suddenly, misfortune struck and she succumbed in shrieking terror when Willy's Sunday horse stepped on a twig, reared unexpectedly, and kicked her in her belly.

Sadly, Maria died. Her son was born, regardless

Little Lizzy, barely six years old, was not yet practiced well enough to iron Willy's Sunday trousers to a truly royal sheen in honor of the tearful funeral, but she was old enough to baby-sit, as it turned out, for Willy tossed the newborn enterprisingly into her lap and told her curtly: "He's yours. His name is Claas. You watch him at all times."

Thus, Lizzy learned mothering early.

Across his second wife's grave, Willy expertly spotted his third.

Matilda was a providential choice, with a low forehead and a curious light in her watery, wide-open eyes. He looked her over carefully. He knew that she was made for him.

Matilda had a pointed tongue, useful in helping him minister to people slipping from the path prescribed by tradition and Scriptures. He liked that very much. She hailed from a village where revivals were strong while untoward laughter was scarce. He liked that even more. Her short and stubby fingers could milk the fattest goat. He liked that best of all.

Willy showed her every corner of his house. He led her to the well along the path his grieving orphaned boys and girls had raked into a fancy pattern to show obedience. He told Matilda: "Here's the barn. Here is the chicken house. Here is the summer kitchen."

He took her to the parlor where all the offspring sat, lined up along a bench like sparrows on a fence. He said to them: "She is your mother now."

They stared at her and hung their heads in memory of their departed mother. Matilda sat on a chair and said nothing.

He knew that he had chosen well when, early the next morning, he heard Matilda sweeping through the house with broom and feather duster, scolding the children heartily. They scattered to their duties as they should.

Born the year that saw the flies come out in flocks, Claas Epp was from the start a sorely troubled youngster, a child with a cleft in his soul.

His first breath turned his mother's face to ashes. Even at birth, his forehead was knotted with anguish. His head was too large. His bones were too soft. The midwife took one look at him and said to Willy Epp: "Why bother?"

The Russian peasants cried: "Let's call a priest and christen him before it is too late." Against the greatest odds, explicit prayers pulled him through. Somehow, Claas managed to survive.

"It looks as if he'll live," Matilda said to Willy. She had no time for him; she, too, was glad for Lizzy's dimpled arms and turned to other chores.

Before too long, Claas stood up on wobbly knees. He suffered from repeated hiccups. That he formed words at all was seen as a decided miracle. His speech was as disorderly as grounds left in a coffee pot.

He had a mind as violent as a September storm, excitable and anguished long before he left the cradle. As he grew up, he took great pains to hide his hands, his eyes and his thoughts. The only remedy that seemed to help and calm his ragged nerves was the balm of the Good Word. He took up preaching early.

One of the first of three more children born to Willy and Matilda was a girl named Noralee. In contrast to Claas, Noralee grew as a weed grows, as rapidly as her surroundings permitted.

She was a useful, level-headed child, soon helping Lizzy soothe the wild gaze in one of her half-brothers' eyes.

"You! Do not look at me like that!" Matilda yelled at times, made fretful by the chores that came with a household of too many children and too little space for herself. "It's not as if I have two heads."

Claas tucked his head between his shoulder blades. He was odd in his infancy and would grow odder still.

This mattered not to Noralee. She loved Claas well enough in small and peevish ways, though it would never do to show affection openly. She lunged to pull his hair to cover up her feelings. He hid, shivering, under her bed, remaining there all afternoon, curled up and shaking badly. No matter how Matilda tried to poke him back into the sunlight with her broom, he huddled in the dark.

"Odd as a Buddha's tooth," Matilda said to Willy.

"What do you mean by that?"

"He slaps himself, day-in, day-out. He acts as if he's sitting on a bee. And on the coldest day, he's wet with perspiration."

"Just grab him by both earlobes," said Willy to his wife. "As soon as I find time, I'll cure him with some private talks."

"You will?"

"I will. If all else fails, a handful of gray salt."

"Salt?"

"Salt. You heard me. Salt. Salt cures most any itch."

With a sly look, he gazed at young Matilda.

"Why, poison ivy on your thoughts!"

He took his hat. He put it on just so. He even pushed it down his ears a little, at a sassy angle, before he took himself into a slipshod village where modernism tried to grow—where he tried hard to forestall drinking, dancing, dominoes and general buffoonery.

All that took place while Peet and Greta still reigned at Apanlee. You would have thought life lay before them like a meadow, so happy were those two.

When visitors arrived, they paused in awe and wonder at the gates of Apanlee: "Just look how blessedly the Germans live—"

Perfection blossomed everywhere. There was no end to wonderment. Large mulberry trees led up to a generous entrance and stairway. To the left and right lay three straight rows of flower beds, filled board to board with roses, marigolds and pansies. To the back of the main house stretched an expansive orchard, its branches bent with fruit, replete with scratching hens and roosters, hissing geese and quacking ducks.

So much wealth! So many riches!

Along the walls of the front hall hung an impressive row of portraits of the Romanovs. Sun rays caught themselves in polished floors and in imported mirrors as well as in the silver sheen of samovars that kept on humming day and night so as to offer tea to countless guests who kept arriving at the gates. Rose jam for nobles and Tartars alike! Ironed lace on Greta Neufeld's pillows! Windows buffed to brilliance with a special cotton cloth! Curtains starched with snow-white flour!

Enormous brick stoves everywhere in winter—all spreading warmth and comfort to the farthest corner of the mansion, no matter how the Russian night might shudder, how loud the steppe winds kept howling through the stiffened orchards in the night. A clock of solemn chimes and heavy weights, brought all the way from the Vistula plains, sat in a corner and kept ticking. Peet wound it every morning with an enormous ornamental key.

"Time is not hitched to a post," he would say with that faraway look in his eyes.

"That's right," said Willy, never one to miss an opportunity to press a timely point, and added cautiously: "Abhorred of God is anyone who loves geometry—"

He was returning from a funeral where he had delivered an uplifting sermon and had received a strengthening meal. "Peet, don't you think it's time at last to re-aquaint yourself with the Good Lord?"

"We aren't strangers, Willy," said Peet with confidence. He smiled contentedly. There was warmth in his belly, good will in his heart. He gloried in his sheaves, lined up as if with rulers.

They bantered often, back and forth, in wary understanding of each other. Each heard the pounding of the stone that whet the scythe as if it were the bells of Jericho.

Peet bought up land and yet more land. The church did likewise, not to be outdone.

The end result was many spin-off daughter colonies. The settlers all bought soil as if there might come shortages tomorrow. Rows of neat homes emerged like carrot seeds that started sprouting caps.

How different a way of life was this compared to life in Russian huts where poverty and ignorance stared out of blinded windows.

When snow lay thick and there was leisure, Peet would go visiting to prod the Russian populace. "Why that foul pig beneath the oven bench? Why bedbugs in those ridges?"

The serfs would listen most attentively, with their backs against a mud stove and frozen feet against a calf. Not one of them would anger at his chiding. They liked him much; they let him plead with them on lazy winter days to wash their beards with kerosene to rid themselves of lice.

"A saint," was the verdict. Both serfs and peasants showed respect. "With a handshake like a thunderclap. A man to be judged by his friends. A teacher worthy of our imitation. And not a kopeck does he owe to anyone—"

Talented and venturesome and prosperous already well beyond the needs of mortal men, Peet kept on adding rubles to his coffers. While others still wove linen, he specialized in silk. He bred a special breed of sheep, whose wool and juicy cuts of lamb he sold to noble families whom he would often go to visit while traveling first rate, a bear skin cover tucked around his knees.

He told colorful stories to Greta of life in the City of Peter and Paul. She never tired learning of how princelings lived and how the Cossacks drew their sabers. "Men drink their tea from glasses," said Greta to Matilda, "and women use small cups—"

"With Greta's honey," Matilda told her jealous neighbors. The neighbors stared, struck dumb.

"That's vanity," her husband said.

Matilda rolled her eyes. She echoed all his thoughts.

The years revealed that Willy was a perfect branch off the pious tree. No different than his father, he visited the sick, married young love, baptized the willing, buried the dead—and still had energy enough to track down erring souls. For his work, he took a modest fee—seven kopecks for a wedding, twice as much for birth and death.

Peet, in turn, recorded all village statistics—keeping charts and graphs and figures of how fast the settlements grew. There was a goose at Apanlee, kept pampered for this very purpose—to yield the quills that Peet kept wearing out.

"I'll see you in church? Next Sunday, Peet Neufeld? A day to thank God for your myriad goods—?"

"Oh, Willy. Please. Just leave me be."

"You know that too much human aspiration is a sin. It says

so in the Bible."

It was not easy work, the Elder knew, to censor sinners, impose penalties, bring down the haughty, reprimand the lax. "Just give the Holy Ghost a chance. Just think about it. Will you?"

"Your sermons, Willy, just do not reach my heart."

"I'll lengthen them. With singing. Come Sunday, I'll be preaching on the parable of the Red Sea—"

Peet was a man with an abiding patience. "Let me correct one small misunderstanding, now that you mention it. The Red Sea isn't red."

"It's red," said Willy firmly. "The Lord makes no mistakes."

Let no one laugh at him—he had his own defenses. He aimed many a tailor-made sermon at Peet, hinting broadly of the camel and the needle's eye of which the Gospel spoke.

Peet had become a very wealthy man. His stables grew. His borders widened. He had so much money his kopecks tore holes in his trousers—hence vainly embroidered suspenders of late!

To spy on Greta was Matilda's practiced specialty. Nothing escaped the stab of her eyes. The lash of her tongue was amazing.

One sunny Easter morning, Matilda's jaw dropped to her collarbone. Parked by the gates of Apanlee stood—what? Did she see right? A scarlet livery with silken yellow tassels!

"The tsarevich!"

With a thud, her wooden sandals flew into a corner. "Good gracious Lord," Matilda all but yelped, and ran along the village road on barefoot soles to spread the message far and wide: "A princeling has arrived to drink a cup of tea at Apanlee—"

Windows flew open. Children climbed fences. Peasants everywhere knelt in the dust as though felled by a powerful blow. Assorted serfs held up their progeny.

Bless them, our little ones! Such honor! Such indulgence! Bless us, our little father!

"Thousands of acres," Peet told the royal guest who stretched his weary legs. "Eight thousand sheep. Four hundred horses. Large herds of cross-bred cattle—"

"How many villages?"

Peet spread a hand-drawn map. His heart grew soft with pride. "More than five dozen German towns. See here? That's where it all began. Here's Halbstadt. And here's Chortitza." Once a bald, dry, desolate steppe—now town after town after town! Gnadenfeld. Field of Grace. Lichtenau. Meadow's Light. Rosenort. Place of Roses. "Since the peasants trip over our names, each village is given a number—"

"I call that Prussian thoroughness—" the princeling said and smiled.

"We sweep the streets. We punish sloth. We have the means, collectively, to put a wayward fire out. And in the very middle of each village, a place of honor is accorded our dead—"

"What's next?"

"An orphan's bank. A home for the old and weary."

"A man with an eye for the future?"

"We are links in a chain," Peet replied.

The wind carried songs. The apple blossoms scattered. A man could swing his scythe all day and barely make a dent.

"What is your key?" the princeling asked. "What is the secret, pray?"

"I'll tell you," Peet replied, eyes crinkling with his pride. "My people all rise early. My people plow the dew."

He knew: year after year, the soil would yield rich grain. More and more land would be broken and seeded. The sheaves would fall in golden swaths. Prosperity would widen homes and sharpen plows and bring another crop of healthy, blue-eyed children. Year after year, his silent, sturdy progeny would carve a larger kingdom from the land.

"My children," said Peet Neufeld, "will carve a pathway to the stars. Through hard work. Diligence. Thrift. Application. Competition. Science."

"No excuses for sniffles and toothaches?"

"None. Take my word for it."

And Greta took the princeling shyly by the sleeve to give a happy woman's point of view:

"—a modern butter churn. A coffee grinder. An automatic candle snuffer. Five matching iron kettles. A wooden kneading trough—" and, blushing crimson, next: "—a charcoal warmer for my feet—"

"I am in awe," the royal guest declared and sipped his steaming tea. "Are those real fireflies, Peet Neufeld, that keep on dancing in your eyes?"

His beard trimmed to a perfect angle, Peet smiled right back into the kindly eyes, a daring and progressive man and unafraid to brace his heart with words: "This time, a daughter, so we hope. We have three sons already."

For dinner, they ate Greta's noodle soup and chicken meat with zwieback.

"Subjects any country would be proud to call its own," the princeling said before he climbed up on his carriage to depart. "We of the House of Romanov are very proud of you."

"We honor you with all our hearts."

"The House of Romanov will stand behind you like a mountain."

"We have two masters only. The Lord above. And you."

"Peet Neufeld, see that sun? As long as it hangs in the sky, we of the House of Romanov vouch for protection. Always."

Peet said: "I'll sleep on that."

With words gleaned from his Prussian nanny, the tsarevich shook hands with Peet before the princely entourage disappeared around the corner in a steady, even trot. The children waved until the distance blurred the horses and the strong steppe wind diffused the sounds of rolling wheels.

Peet noted in his diary that night: "For now and all eternity we're guaranteed self-rule."

That's what the princeling said. He said: *"Ich wünsch Euch wohl—"* In gratitude, Peet founded yet another Aryan town and called it Alexanderwohl.

Chapter 4

As Noralee grew up and into early womanhood, she learned to bend the rules to suit her robust nature.

Not that she lacked good will. She did not mind to stand corrected; she, too, bent gladly to other folks' superior knowledge, much as a willow bends to wind—but she would make a flying leap away, this long before she had good cause, whenever a chastising Elder appeared.

Through her mother, Matilda, nee Friesen, Noralee derived from sturdy but non-descript stock. Face to feet, that's how the Friesens slept, and at right angles to the window, to take advantage of the earthy smell that wafted from the fields. That's why they were as numerous, as common and as brash as buttercups in meadows—quite unlike Lizzy, who nestled her face in the crook of her arm, who would have fainted, too, had she not been too scared to faint the moment a stranger appeared.

Noralee was known for bold and hardy ways; she could not be dismayed. Fat arms akimbo, that's how she handled life.

Lizzy, by contrast—as fluid as water. You touched her, and

she started rippling, all eager to adjust.

"All right! All right!" wailed Noralee when scolded for a child's trespasses, and then forgot her promises. She missed no opportunity; she dove for Claas, guns blazing:

"Asleep again?" shrieked Noralee. "Claas? Claas? Asleep again? Will you be found asleep when the Lord's trumpets blow?" She had a voice that carried far.

"Sleep helps him calm his headaches," begged Lizzy, and stroked her brother's sweaty brow. She mediated constantly. "Noralee, now leave him be! Will you please leave him be?"

"Wake up! Wake up! Wake up and watch the lightning!"

"He is afraid," begged Lizzy, while cringing at such cruelty. It was her chore for many years to keep his tormentors at bay.

While every other healthy child would revel in the riches of the harvest, Claas Epp would sit behind the barns of Apanlee, shivering and sneezing, wailing that the itch of wheat beards did him in. Napping was Claas's favorite pastime long before he grew into long trousers.

Peet, watching from the window, told Greta, yielding to disquiet: "That child is ill of spirit."

"He makes himself an easy target. Somebody always shoves him from behind to coax that eerie whine."

"Yes. You're right. He's different. He's odd."

Both watched the boy with worry as he leaned helplessly against a tree, his throbbing temples cradled in both hands, as he listened to the wind that sat in the Apanlee mulberry trees, howling in a low and mournful voice.

"He's shivering as though he's lying in a grave," said Greta, addled greatly. "And yet he laughs; he can't stop laughing. Whatever might it be?"

Nobody had an answer.

The herbalists were flustered. The midwife hid herself. Three bonesetters, consulted as a last resort, predicted to a voice: "There's trouble brewing somewhere. His fingernails are blue."

Matilda had her hands full with the skittish boy. She marshaled her home antidotes. She rummaged thoroughly among the row of labeled bottles on her shelves, mix-matching this and that.

"Try this," she said. "Try that." She punctured both his nostrils. She pricked a blister with a needle she dunked in honey first.

It made no difference. Nothing did. Claas's headaches only worsened.

She decided a kitten might help. She put it in a basket and handed it to him: "Be sure to feed it every day. And keep its milk dish clean."

"I will," Claas promised her with lowered lashes, but it died from his fervent caresses.

And then there was The Voice. The Voice hissed in his ears. It gave him arguments. It told him he must seek out sinners to convince them of the errors of their ways—this long before he grew a set of proper preacher's whiskers.

Of all the weird afflictions that plagued this boy possessed by evil spirits, the thunderstorms of muggy summers were the worst, when lightning flashed within his overheated mind.

"Let us ask God for mercy for all sinners! Mercy! Mercy! For all sinners!"

He jumped at every thunderclap, and Noralee, who relished drama from the cradle, kept jumping, too, this for good measure, thus helping Claas holler for Jesus. She did not mind a relative who was already practicing his sermons on the rabbits.

Not so young Lizzy, though. Had she known how to seal Claas's ears with beeswax to keep The Voice away, she, Lizzy, would have tried.

In a blind surge of love she summoned every counter-argument she knew to make Claas see that lightning never struck the righteous. But even she knew early: there was no way to keep The Voice from Claas.

The little boy heard something dreadful yet compelling within the rolling sounds. When thunder started tormenting his sparking brain, he would dash through the streets and leap-frog, unconstrained, into the nearest cellar.

All was not well. Even his pets behaved as though he made them drunk and spooked.

"Where's Claas," Matilda kept after Lizzy. "Are you watching your brother? Where is he? Have you paid attention to him?"

"I locked him in the barn. Along with three pieces of sugar."

"Be sure to check."

"I threw the chain. No way can he get out," explained Lizzy, who was willing to lavish attention, but Claas did not invite attention; no matter what she tried to do, the recalcitrant youngster sucked in his breath and strained backwards.

Matilda took her worries to her husband. "What might be the solution?"

The Elder took his prayers to the Lord who told him he should tell his wife that she should try to counteract her step-son's maladies with salted cucumbers.

"I'll watch him," offered Noralee. "I'll watch him twice as hard. I'll watch him through the keyhole."

The day the Gypsies arrived, he escaped. A loose nail in the board, an unlatched side door, the lure of the forbidden, whichever it was—before Matilda looked up from her washboard, the child with the wild eyes was up and was gone! Astute neighbors spotted him gingerly putting one toe in front of the other, and—just in the nick of time!—snatched him away from witchery.

"Claas! The rooster should get you and shred you!" scolded Matilda.

"Suck on a watermelon rind!" the Elder Willy cried.

"A jealous spider stung him," wailed sundry herbalists. "Ah, yes. That must be it."

Matilda, who was hoping against hope she might lose her troubling stepson to measles, knew then there would be no relief. The household was crowded already with too many children, and she was expecting again.

"Foreshadowing again?" asked Greta archly, too.

No matter what her vigilance, her bread knife disappeared. Her knitting came unraveled. Her flower pots turned upside down.

It stared her in the face; she could not help her feelings.

She did not like the child. His eyebrows arched unevenly. Thin hair grew on his fingers. She watched him stray about the halls of Apanlee and frighten cats and dogs.

She took her worries to her oldest son, on whose advice she leaned. They were of like mind in most matters.

"He acts just a water beetle," she said to Alexander. "The way his mind keeps darting to the surface for some air, then bottoming again—"

Her son was proud to be a marginal believer. "When he was born, the moon might have emitted strange rays."

He might as well have spoken in Kirghize. Consensus rapidly solidified. Claas was in trouble from the start, like mildew wafting from a hole.

Before long, Claas was speaking in several tongues.

His sister, Lizzy, tried to shush him, terrified. She held him by both hands, to help his eyes to focus.

"Hush! Hush!" cried Lizzy, overcome. She cherished charity within her heart for anything or anybody small enough to curl up in her lap, yet when it came to Claas, she found her patience running thin. Something deep in this troubled child cried out for mothering and soothing, but what that was she was too young to know.

She felt that she was fighting gravity on stilts: tears welling in her eyes, she dared not delve too deeply. The little boy called forth in her raw feelings she did not like and tried her best to quell.

She tried to soothe him with a heated brick against his aching belly, but when she reached for him, he arched and pushed back, hard.

Odd as a Buddha's tooth.

"Odd as a Buddha's tooth," the neighbors passed the chant.

"That one will grow to be a vagrant," predicted every herbalist the family consulted.

"Or worse," said Willy from the door. "He might become a Lutheran."

"Oh, anything but that!" cried Lizzy, mortified.

Young Lizzy often visited at Apanlee to fortify herself with common sense when overwhelmed by prophesy and being prodded to perfection, the fare in her stepfather's house. She was a softly rounded youngster, warm, appetizing, fragrant like zwieback dough, with not a single pimple. She lived on a mysterious inner warmth.

She, too, came from an earnest peasant clan maternally, all liberally sprinkled with freckles. On both her father's and her mother's side, she was entwined with the more bounteous Harders, Friesens, Wiebes—a breed of stoic, somber farmers, attuned to the needs of the earth.

While visiting at Apanlee, young Lizzy cheered herself with sips of Greta's tea.

She spoke up in a timid voice. "I'd rather be here than at home." She knew she was deserving to be chastised and flooded herself with her shame.

Greta opted for Christian mercy. A troubled relative, no matter what the urgency, was certainly no pleasure to behold.

"Let me speak freely, Lizzy. You ask: what ails your little brother? Nobody seems to know. There is no point in speculating. Just stay away from him."

Young Lizzy hung her flaxen head. She, too, wished for a rosy brother; she hurt on Claas's behalf. His speech was slurred and blurred. He was the butt of everybody's jokes.

She knew he focused his veiled eyes on his surroundings and read a strong revulsion. If anyone as much as looked at Claas askew, blood bubbled from his nose.

The neighbors watched with anxious, knowing eyes. Was it too late to counteract the spell? To this day, many people think the Gypsies were at fault.

In early spring, small bands of Gypsies pitched their tents and caused vexation in the German villages. Dogs sneezed and couldn't stop. Cows yielded bloody milk. Roosters lapsed into silence, and ganders showed no interest in geese.

The churches stood aggrieved. Soon, there were loud complaints from everywhere. Who was at fault? The deacons huddled daily.

"Misfortune," warned the Elder Willy, "will strike abundantly."

He opened his mouth to say more, but no strengthening sermon came forth. The air reeked of decay. With scraggly, wind-blown wings, the village stork sat hunched atop his gable, nursing a badly broken beak.

The vagrants' chants, their heathen songs and spicy smells and mesmerizing thimbles cast wicked spells on any man or beast. A poisonous light tinged the horizon. Sleep evaded the Elder at night. He tossed and turned and tried to throw off feelings of foreboding. He was convinced the heathen Gypsy band had cast the evil eye.

Take now: he gave the pitch of a song, and it did not catch. He cleared his throat and muttered hoarsely: "Lot's descendants have arrived—"

The congregation ducked. In a matter as fearsome as this, they took his word on Faith. They knew they could trust his opinion.

"Let us now bow our heads and pray—"

"The Devil's kin!" That's what the Elder thundered. The congregation paid attention sluggishly.

The Gypsies all had burning eyes and raven hair. They spoke a language no one understood and no one cared to try.

They studied stars and predicted disaster. They put forth foul scents; they nodded to hail; they sat in hordes along the embankment within the shelter belt of the Apanlee mulberry trees, waiting for mischief to happen.

No fences, no prayers, no snarling dogs kept them away.

The Elder Willy fought the heathen with a vengeance. He dogged them hard, with knives in his lungs; they were quicker, more cunning, than he.

By the time he arrived with a broom or a shoemaker's knee strap, they had already grazed an unsuspecting village—clothespins stolen, dreams dissected, fortunes told and even worse. Behind his back, to spite him, they spread their wares to trade in miracles and cures.

Lilac tea for stomach aches.

Goose grease for a broken smile.

Amulets against the treacheries of love.

No matter how the Elder tongue-lashed, no matter how he prayed high in his attic, on his knees, beseeching God to cleanse the German streets and make the Gypsies leave, they stayed, a noisy nuisance, predictable and slatternly as April sparrows.

One Gypsy tossed a lizard backwards and proclaimed: "I see a shadow where no shadow should be—"

That was a potent hex. A light, gray mist hung low.

It would take many prayers and lavish offerings to Willy's special Orphan Fund until it wore away.

It might have helped speed matters, produced an antidote against the darker powers of the Fiend if those from Apanlee with all their influence, their might and moneyed pockets had deigned to join the praying congregation.

But no. Peet Neufeld only pulled the Good Book from his shelf to point a righteous finger: "In my father's house are many mansions. In God's garden we find many different fruits—"

"I take my bearings from the Holy Spirit," argued Willy.

Peet spoke, an open disbeliever: "A shadow does not make a mountain."

"Some may think that," said the Elder. "And others, Peet, do not."

Peet's glance stopped further arguments, so Willy took his hat and shook his head and left.

Peet's serfs were busy harrowing. The soil had thawed out early. Daisies popped up everywhere. Acacia trees exploded into clouds of snowy clusters, and insects crawled into the hearts of blooms with spindly legs to suck the honeyed dew.

Soon, workers turned the cut grass over to free the scent of earth and sun, and little girls and boys would stand and wait for Peet until he scooped them up and hoisted them atop the ladder wagons that slowly rolled the fodder for his mares into the stalls of Apanlee before the thunders came.

"All right now! Lizzy! Claas! Stop shrieking, Noralee!"

He liked to swing the squealing children, one by one, by their strong arms and legs atop the pile of hay that shook, collapsing, burying their laughter. The earth's smell, fresh and pungent, lodged sweetly in Peet's nostrils and dizzied him a bit.

Anticipating fatherhood and, therefore, of a mellow mood, Peet touched it gently with his fingertips to feel its fragrant warmth. His head swam with his happiness and with the feel of coming harvests. He grabbed a pitchfork eagerly to help disperse the dung—he knew it was a year so good, so rich and right, that the black soil would yield its gold straight out of fairyland.

A fortnight after, to Greta and Peet their last child, a daughter, was born. By then, Peet's beard was woven through with silver, and Greta, it was noted, looked perplexed. They were no longer young; the pregnancy was a surprise, although those two were intertwined as though they were Adam and Eve. Fat smoke kept billowing from Apanlee's twelve chimneys as if to advertise the ancient laws of love.

Matilda doubled as a midwife. While waiting for the baby to be born, she kept on fishing for her *schlorren* and rolling up her sleeves. Matilda could sense it; in fact, she could tell: it was there, the awaited misfortune—like the lapping of water under an oar.

"It might be twins," said Peet. Matilda held her breath. She knew: when a man is afraid in his heart, he sees double.

Greta, meanwhile, took soothing walks among her stately trees. Often, Peet would watch her from afar, still shy before the miracle, and feed Claas Epp sweet lumps of sugar from his pockets to calm his sparking brain.

Peet had gone out into the fields to check the serfs who stacked the shocks of grain when labor pangs began in earnest to hammer Greta's spine. He could tell the birthing had begun when he saw the Elder Willy, white of face and stiff with fear, wave his arms at him.

He brought his plow to a sharp, sudden halt. He ran, cutting through meadows and orchards, flinging himself across fences, on the steps of Apanlee all but colliding with Matilda.

"It's time? It's not too late?"

Matilda shushed him curtly. Matilda slammed the door. Her face was taut and hard.

For quite a while, Peet stood in the hallway, waiting. He looked like a horse that was thrown on its side. He sat, alone, by the cistern. All afternoon. Waiting. Matilda sat judgmentally and frowning at the end of Greta's bed.

To aid in the difficult birth, the servants threw open all windows.

That night, Peet ate a meal in silence. It took too long. It was too hard. He wiped a sweaty brow. The infant was his; he never knew humility; the archives point that out. He had three sons; his heart yearned for a daughter. He had resolved to name her Katharina, in honor of the settlers' royal benefactress—long dead and gone but still remembered with much love.

Matilda lit three extra lamps. She poured water from a kettle. She put a match to the straw in the hearth.

In the end, a mite of a girl-child came forth.

"A stem too weak to hold that wobbling head," Matilda said to Peet. Claas, hanging on Matilda's skirts, sucked in his breath through his teeth.

Peet inspected the newborn, mist in his eyes and lead in his soul. He spread his hand for measurement—the infant reached from thumb to little finger. He held the stirring thing within his callused palm and for some dark and brooding reason withheld the royal name. Instead, he named her Olga.

Why Olga? Had Peet lost his mind?

Not a soul within sight who approved!

The German Bible and the German-friendly Romanovs provided ample choices—or why not make a spinster happy, or an aunt? Why challenge fate? Why not be modest and obedient? Did Peet not understand the hidden warning—that, in the end, the good Lord always evened up a score?

"She will not live," announced Matilda, and blew the tears from her red nose.

Peet said: "She will. She must!" Peet looked, Matilda later told her husband, shivering, just like an animal that growled and bared its fangs.

"I read between the lines," said Willy, who went gospeling.

Peet turned on him in such a rage that Willy backed away: "All right. All right. So what if she lives? So what if she dies?"

Peet stared at him with palpable dislike. "She'll live," he said again.

Olga lived, for Peet imported foreign doctors. Greta wept and wrung her hands. The Elders watched and prayed.

The servants kept the newborn in a drawer, beseeching their icons, putting heated bricks around her tiny limbs to give her added warmth. The herbalists sliced onions near her eyes to make her weep and help her gain her hold on life's assorted sorrows. They wrapped worn socks around her throat to help her ease her grasp of air. They put cobwebs on her forehead; they sprinkled holy water on her scalp. All seemed in vain; she almost died; she might as well have died.

One wintry afternoon, the tiny life convulsed. Limp and listless, it lay afterwards in its richly tasseled cradle. The rudest Catholics took off their hats to cross themselves in fear.

Chapter 5

A dreadful thing had happened to Peet's little girl who bore a worldly name. The next few years revealed: she could not hear; she could not speak.

"She will not live," wept Greta.

Peet said again: "She will. She must."

"Poor child," Matilda mourned. "If she survives at all, what might be waiting for her?" All night long, candles flickered. The servants were mingling their tears.

Peet's hair turned white with worry: he watched the moon cast crooked rays across his daughter's anguished face as she lay limp within her pillows, worn with her twitchings, transparent and wan. He, who in olden days had never spoken caustically to any man or animal, now walked around in search of faults, in search of sloth and thievery, swinging a stick to mete out swift justice as he alone saw fit. Whereas in by-gone days he might have searched for patient words for anyone in any language, now he no longer answered twice. His servants saw him lean against a plow and struggle for composure.

"All that while in the lap of plenty," the loyal servants said, adorning their saints with additional glitter on behalf of the whimpering baby. They fed it sour cream and sugared tea to put some dimples on its body, but even that was difficult. Matilda predicted the worst. Peet, yielding to his stubborn streak, kept trying this and that.

Lizzy, in her gentle ways, came up with a solution. She walked up to the silent child one sunny afternoon and told her simply: "Here. Just take my hand."

The deaf-mute reached for her, and Lizzy smiled and added: "I'll lend you the use of my tongue."

Hence, Lizzy spent much time at Apanlee with Olga and her brothers. Although she would not have admitted it, not even to herself, she much preferred the scented child as company to Claas's. There hung about this little girl the fragrant smell of honey that Greta now lavished on her.

At first, the silent youngster seemed oblivious to what had chanced on her. She skipped along the neighbor path like any other child, making friends in time not just with Lizzy and her siblings but other young folk of her age.

Only, they in sturdy wooden sandals—she in tiny pointed shoes.

They in heavy woven skirts and trousers—she in a delicate rustle of crocheted lace.

They with chitchat, song and laughter. She in thoughtful silence, always. Growing deeper with the years.

"No grass will grow beneath her feet," the servants told each other. The serfs drew the sign of the cross at her sight.

With practiced patience, Willy looked for prayer loopholes, letting the Gospel fall open to where it was written: "Do not be deceived, God is not mocked. For whatever a man soweth, that he will also reap." Not that it made much difference, for offering the Gospel's balm to Peet was pouring mercury on glass.

"Though Jesus shed his blood for any sinner," said Willy to Matilda, "Peet just won't let himself be saved."

"Remember that the girl was born the year the Gypsies tossed a lizard backwards," sighed Matilda.

"A year like any other year," said Peet, a stubborn man, disdaining any possible surrender. "It's not the Gypsies' fault. It isn't anybody's fault if nature goes awry."

"It's our Savior's finger, and pointing straight at you."

But Peet was Peet. His skull was thick. The hurt sat deep. An old scar on his cheek flared hotly.

"—a princely child. A diamond. The Emperor of Russia might well have bounced her on his knees—"

"Your spirit, thornier than a rosebush," the Elder Willy pointed out. "If you would only pray—"

"Prayer," said Peet Neufeld coldly, "is just like sailing over dry and barren land."

The Elder Willy Epp sermonized to iron and to stone. Peet shunned all Christian comfort: mid-week devotions, the kiss of peace, foot washing for the sake of harmony to bind the villages together. God's wrath had struck down Apanlee at last.

Claas's tantrums cast sharp shadows. Even his sister Noralee, as sturdy as they came, a child who would have faced the Antichrist bare-handed, kept Claas away with her ear-splitting shrieks.

Lizzy wept many a frustrated tear, quaking at the sight of cruelty, when she discovered that her brother tormented the muted child much as a cat might bait a birdling.

Claas teased and tickled Olga until she shrank in tears into the shadows, refusing to come out.

One morning Greta told the boy: "Now leave. That's it. And don't come back tomorrow."

Willy gave Claas a brisk lashing. "For your sins," he told the boy. "Now ask the Lord to let you start a brand new ledger."

Claas fell into an eery laughter; on the heels of that laughter, he broke into tears.

"My sins," he said to Lizzy sobbingly that night, "have a peculiar smell."

Lizzy's eyes filled up with ready tears. "I'll help you scrub," she promised.

She took him to the waterhole to wash away the odor. He slipped and fell, head-first. In panic, Lizzy reached for him to put him on his feet—and found his teeth embedded in her wrist.

At midpoint in the nineteenth century a Jew of German origin holed up within an English tenement to write a big, fat tome about the have-nots and the haves. A quarter century would come and pass before the German pacifists—who had come eagerly to the Ukraine to sow the grain and build the Kingdom for the Lord— were forced to take their *Wanderstab* again in search of peace and land, and would end up in Kansas.

Yet fifty years would pass before a female firebrand named Carrie Nation would sweep her caravan through Wichita and one of Claas's offspring, Josephine, would swing the rebel's torch.

No one could have known then.

The benchmarks stayed simple as the shadows grew long: life took them from autumn to autumn.

Each year, there came persistent mists at first, then came the plodding rains that brought the angry winds. Nobody paid attention.

As children do, they played at hide-and-seek within the stooks of grain that stood like little huts about the fields of Apanlee. If there was gloom among the serfs—or famine, illness, misery outside the gates of Apanlee and its devout surroundings—that fell beyond their scope; they were not bred to question.

Such were the early childhood days of Lizzy, Olga, Claas and Noralee.

They were still young enough, those four, for scrubbing, one by one, each Saturday in the communal tub—still small enough so that their foot soles didn't touch the floor as they sat in their church pews, enveloped in the ancient prophecies.

They were of a sufficient age, but only barely, to feel grief swell their little hearts until they thought that they would suffocate when, without warning, suddenly, Peet Neufeld passed away.

Peet Neufeld was felled by the Lord as if cut from this earth by the blade of his very own scythe.

Here's how that came to pass.

One drowsy summer afternoon, Greta stood on her porch to supervise the serfs who packed cold meat, boiled eggs, a jar of sour cream, a couple of pieces of bacon.

"Be sure not to stay out too long in the fields," she told her husband worriedly.

The night before, he paid but small attention to the *vareniki* she had so lovingly prepared. "Eat," she had urged her husband, but Peet just shook his head.

Before they went to bed, he groped his way along the wall as though there were no candle. She saw that one of his suspenders trailed behind him, and she rushed up to him and pulled them off and quickly hugged him.

Hard.

He turned to her and smiled a wistful smile: "A dog must get used to a cat. A man must get used to old age."

"Old age? Why, look at you, Peet Neufeld. Whatever do you mean?"

"Old age," he told her slowly, "is like beholding the tide of the sea. You see it coming at you, but you can't grasp the boundless power that will erode the soil beneath your feet."

He seldom talked to her in poetry. She told him in a sudden burst of worry: "Go see the bonesetter. Don't put it off. Make sure that your bones are aligned."

"It isn't my bones. Ask a bald man what happened to his hair."

She smiled a mischievous smile. "Old age is like shaving the beard but still leaving the mustache," she told him.

He took her hand. "Why, Greta," he said tenderly. "Who raised you to such images?"

"You did. My thoughts are your thoughts. My life is your life. I count on growing old with you. I do not need to tell you."

She knew that such love as they shared could not be diminished by old age. Old age came to all. It came calling as surely as Willy came calling each New Year's Day to bring the update on the Truth and trade it for ten rubles.

Peet told her, speaking slowly: "I'm tired. *Hundemüde.* It was a hot and muggy day."

Now Greta looked out of the window. "He's leap-frogging still."

"Claas is?"

"His mind—like a rickety bridge."

"In shallow waters there's no mystery," said Peet. "Let us give thanks, instead, for Lizzy—"

He loved the little female. That Lizzy Epp, by then, belonged to Apanlee was clear to everyone. Through the open windows drifted melodies his little favorite rehearsed with nimble fingers on a flute a servant had chiseled for her.

Greta nodded eagerly, well-practiced in reading Peet's mind. "Yes, you are right. All of your sons are fond of her."

"But I would say that she loves Nicky best."

"You're right.   There's harmony between those two."

"To think of her as passing on my progeny is comforting. Like putting hot feet in cold water—"

"I am afraid tomorrow will be hotter than today," said Greta. "The rye will suffer grievously—" But when she turned around, she saw Peet slumped beside his chair.

"Peet," she cried out. "Oh, Peet. Oh, my beloved."

He mumbled in a puzzled voice: "It's weeds? It's weeds that pierce through grain—?"

He never spoke again. He waged a brief but valiant struggle, and somehow lived on through the night. It was a breezy, brittle night. In the morning, the clouds moved slowly over the horizon, although it didn't come to storms. Before another day was gone, a muggy wave washed over Apanlee, but Peet passed on to meet his Maker while yet the air was crisp, the skies still blue and smooth.

Greta watched his face in silent concentration, to read what might be written there as he preceded her into eternity. "At least he didn't suffer," she said, submitting, when all was said and done, yet loath to yield him to the preachers. "His death was swift and fair."

Woe and despair washed over her, for she had loved him much. She knew the Lord would surely console tomorrow, but little did that comfort her today.

She pulled her wedding locket from her neck and wound it through Peet's stiffened fingers. With trembling hands, she stopped his clock. She felt as though stabbed by a sharpened stiletto.

"Reclaimed by the Lord and his forebears," she announced to serfs and free servants alike.

She sent her eldest, Alexander, to lift the gleaming scythe. Her second, Nicky, took the heavy hammer from the rafters and nailed the metal to the roof. Peter, still young enough to give free reign to tears without redress for excess grief, which would have been unseemly, bent down with a choked sob and hoisted the child with the paralyzed tongue.

"Draw the black cloth across the blade," cried all the serfs in unison. "To forestall ill-matched luck—"

The neighbors told each other, nodding: "A beacon light for others is no more—"

The *Voice of Peace* proclaimed: "Departed from our midst— a brilliant, daring man."

The tsar sent a dispatch: "A man of the soil. A Moses to his people."

"Vainglorious yet, and at the very rim of grave," said Willy to Matilda, for Peet had stipulated in his will: "Be sure to bury me beneath a slab of broken marble, for my work is not yet done."

Matilda blew from her nose the salty tears the excitement of funerals brought. "Well. There he lies," said she. Pallbearers did their duties gravely. The murmur of preliminary prayers faded.

The Elder Willy bared his head. "For a thousand years in Your sight are like yesterday when it is past—" He grasped Peet's

Bible forcefully. It was a heavy book, replete with silver clasps, that had so often lain between them on the bench when he and Peet had been young boys, disputing passages. "Hear ye! Hear ye! I shall teach ye the fear."

The mourners listened silently. The Elder Willy looked around and drew on the crusading zeal that served him well at such an opportunity. He let the Holy Book fall open, and there it was, in black and white, the passage he was struggling to compose.

"Likewise, ye younger folks. Be clothed with due humility, for God resists the proud, but gives grace to the humble—" The Elder's glance was full of caustic meaning. It slammed on Peet's untested progeny: "Therefore, humble yourselves under the mighty hand of God, that He may exalt you in due time. Be sober. Vigilant. Because the Devil walks about you like a roaring lion, seeking whom he may devour—"

Matilda cast quick, furtive glances. The Jews. The Jews. She had already spotted several at Peet's ambitious funeral. Peet had befriended them—a people more tenacious than weeds. Matilda kept them in the corner of her eye. A wrathful God it was, Matilda knew, intent on retribution.

"Break their teeth in their mouths, oh my Lord," shouted Willy. "Break out the fangs of the young lions, oh Lord—"

The prayers made the Hebrews pull yarmulkes.

"Unless you practice vigilance, He who controls the firmaments shall take you all away. He plucks you out of your own dwelling place, and uproots you from the land of the living—"

By contrast, Peet's descendants sat, constrained and orderly and silent—a crop of blue-eyed, flaxen children, their toes lined up in unison, their shoulders straightened out. They listened to the Elder's words as he dispensed both solace and support, safeguarding them with admonition. Both were appropriate at funerals. He who had lived an unbeliever had also died an unbeliever—now it was time to plow the soil Peet Neufeld left behind.

Matilda savored funerals. You could no more have kept Matilda from a gaping grave than you could keep a goose in spring from heading north. She throve on the solemnity that called for many handkerchiefs.

She cast arch glances at the casket: preserved and dressed up like a Pharaoh! Her temples throbbed with ecstasy. She took it all in, with a lump in her throat but an eye for the smallest detail. She felt ready to faint; she was as sweaty as a water pump, but she made sure that she missed not a thing.

Here's what the archives say: Peet Neufeld had himself the most majestic funeral of the decade.

Both rich and poor were there. Hundreds arrived in closed and open carriages, drawn to the somber spectacle by strapping horses attired in beautiful harness, white ribbons in their forelocks, tails swishing in the wind.

The poor came in bark sandals or barefoot; the nobles in convoys of splendor and sparkle, to pay their last respect. They sat upright, the haughty Russian nobles, deep in their black upholstery, their lackeys stiff behind them, staring straight ahead.

From the Valley of Jews arrived many untoward mourners, clutching their pink handkerchiefs, grieving with the grieving. They nodded to each other, gesticulating unrestrained: "He will be missed. He will be greatly missed."

Matilda spotted Moshe, the yarn-and-button peddler. She watched him deftly from the corner of her eye.

She knew he was a huckster, and maybe even worse. No matter what he sold, he fetched the highest price. His spools of thread were skimpy; they didn't last six aprons. She knew whereof she spoke: she'd checked them out, and double-checked. She had all her strategies pat.

Next time he'd appear and try to strike his bargains—why, she would slam the door. She would hide in the pantry, or else in the potato cellar.

She knew all about Jews, which was plenty. They talked so fast it made a Christian dizzy. They fasted for no reason. They always criticized the Throne. For centuries, the tsars had dealt with them by making them bleed at their noses.

Now Moshe turned his jagged profile and leaned into her face: "Who is that little girl?"

"Hush," hissed Matilda, glaring at the Jew. "The prayers aren't finished!"

The Hebrew's face fell into several added folds: "I'm sorry. See? I'm sorry."

Faint shame stirred in Matilda. This was a funeral that called for courtesy. "Her name is Olga," whispered she.

"Peet's daughter?"

"Yes. The Lord saw fit to punish."

"How so?"

"He sealed her ears. He froze her tongue. She cannot hear. She cannot speak. She cannot, therefore, understand—"

Claas scowled and started chewing on his nails. Matilda couldn't finish, for Claas let out a whoop.

"Our shields and swords for naught," shrieked Claas. "Our shields and swords for naught!"

"Will you be quiet?" Matilda cried, resolved to box his ears. "What's gotten into you?"

Claas kept on hollering while pointing at the Jews: "Scatter them by their power and bring them down, oh Lord, our shield—"

Matilda threw up her hands in despair, and Willy, forgetting to finish the Psalter, cried angrily: "Will you stop dancing, Claas? What is it now? What ails you, son? Are you in need of the outhouse?"

"Oh, Lord, do not be far from me," shouted Claas. "Stir up Thyself! Awake to my vindication!"

"He likes to have the center stage," Matilda told the Hebrew who nodded and fell back.

Matilda gave Claas a withering look and shifted cleverly: "Some people are like that."

"That boy needs help," said Moshe.

"You're telling me?"

Matilda lurched like a train about to start moving but caught herself and swallowed resolutely what she had meant to say. This was Peet's funeral and not her quilting bee. These were Peet's friends, not hers.

"Perhaps next time I visit—"

She watched the son of Judah with cold eyes. The beard tax had been implemented long ago, but still he flaunted hair. Now he was combing through his fuzz with long and shaking fingers.

"There's ferment in his mind."

Matilda sighed. Some Jews wrote poetry as well. All bragged about their forebear, Abraham. And, worst of all, they spurned the Lord Christ Jesus who had cried out despairingly: "Jerusalem! Jerusalem!"

She knew Peet had indulged the Jews, despite her husband's direst warnings. In turn, they so adored Peet Neufeld they would have had their cannons fired here and now, had they not found themselves surrounded to a man by people of a pacifist tradition.

"Now pay attention. Will you?" Matilda counseled primly. If Peet chose of his own free will to walk among the heretics, he should not be surprised that now they saw him to his grave, which was what brought them here.

The Jew repeated stubbornly. "The boy needs help. I know a learned doctor in Berdjansk—"

"Some people can't be helped," said Matilda. "Some people never learn."

"Some, on the other hand," said he, his eye on the mute girl, "would like to learn but can't."

"Can't hear a sound. Can't say a single word," replied Matilda, shifting her focus deftly.

The peddler, in distress, combed through his beard with all ten shaking fingers and then reached out and, one by one, unfurled the little girl's cramped fingers.

"Your father told me once about his secret wish," the peddler said to her, "that you be educated properly."

The youngster looked at him with swimming eyes as if she understood. She stood, a frail but ramrod child, and nodded to his words.

Matilda, nearest witness to the odd discourse, felt suddenly as if someone had laced her bulk into a stiff corset. She gave a toothy smile. She looked around to marshal assistance from Willy, but Willy was preoccupied: he thumbed through the Book to look for some Biblical slaughter.

"If you permit, I'll bring you books—"

Matilda felt her neck perspiring: this was a genuine emergency. From where to marshall help? Print from a city yet? Across from her sat Jacob, her husband's favorite deacon. He had a soft and nasal voice, but even so, he always packed the church.

She tried to beckon him. "Quick, Jacob! Quick!" But Jacob paid no heed, wrapped as he was in prayers. There was no energy in him. If he could sit, he sat.

The son of Judah said: "You can take in? You can't put out?"

The deaf-mute nodded silently. Two tears collected in the corners of her eyes.

"You understand, don't you?"

She nodded to that, too.

The Hebrew took a stick and carved a sign into the soil. They say it had six corners.

"That's where we'll meet. Each year, I'll come and check on you."

Matilda did not know if she should laugh or cry. To have the Hebrews' ruses claim a child this young—and silent yet!—at such a vulnerable moment, was just like drinking vodka, and on an empty stomach.

"To Him be the glory and the dominion forever and ever," said Willy, winding down.

Lizzy was there; she would always remember. She knew it was a sermon and a funeral nobody would forget.

Her steady eyes on Nicky's down-cast face, she whispered lovingly: "He heals the broken-hearted, and binds up every wound. Here is my handkerchief."

"I know," said Nicky slowly. His eyes met hers; they were glazed as if from a frost. To his right sat his mother, as lifeless as the ashes the serfs raked from the stove. To his left, his two brothers sat. The Jews from the Valley stood sharply apart, as did the Catholics, as did the Lutherans. With a triumphant thud, the Elder snapped his Bible shut and looked around: "—let us return Thy servant to the earth—"

The morning was still young. All shades of light pushed hues of splendor through the ripening Apanlee orchards.

The grass was fresh and sweet. The sun was warming all.

"Amen," chorused to a voice all those who lived, and who could hope to die, at Apanlee. After a moment of absolute quiet, Matilda sank into a swoon.

"Amen. Amen." said the Catholics. The Lutherans. The servants next, and finally the serfs.

"Amen!" said the Jews as well. Their turn came last. They were the first to leave.

They shuffled through the ranks and disappeared, gesticulating to each other. On the horizon hung billowy clouds. A breeze stroked the carpet of grain as a lover might stroke the hair of a beautiful woman.

Between church and school, Peet lay buried. The slant-eyed Tartars wept.

Chapter 6

The years slid into ice and snow. The road to certain spinsterhood was tedious.

Had Olga been just anyone's afflicted child, she would have grown into a modest spinster to sigh her life away by the window, knitting socks or stitching pillow slips while steeped in resignation. But she was still a child of Apanlee, and so they came and went, the marriageable males.

Many suitors tried their luck—from Orloff, from Sagradowka, from Alexanderwohl and Tiegenhagen and Samara. They came and left, and she could not be wooed. She merely twisted trembling fingers through her braids and hung her golden head.

Matilda hid behind curtains. Her triple-chin wobbled with grief. Why did the female scatterbrain so foolishly disdain this sober and clean-shaven fellow whose only flaw was that he squinted, or that meek cousin from the daughter settlement Grossliebenthal, who was so overcome with Apanlee he could not say a word?

And then, a truth emerged at last—a truth so utterly beyond belief that it sent tremors through the villages. Matilda, earning extra cash by sewing and darning for others while carrying gossip between them, ran speedily from home to home as fast as her slippery *schlorren* permitted:

"—the peddler's son," she said, and fanned herself in agony.

Terror came with bat-like wings. The neighborhood trembled and shivered.

The overlords of yore became vociferous when anyone mentioned the Jews, for more than one tsar had punished their wiles and ripped open their nostrils for mischief. For this and many other reasons, the Jews were not esteemed in the vicinity of Apanlee, and for good cause: their Sundays came on Saturdays. They scoffed at honest work. They practiced usury. They changed their names at every whim, a fundamental trait. They licked their young with narrow tongues to make them just like them.

You kept them at arm's length.

A daring Jew had, many years ago, tried brazenly to move into a German village, but lightning struck his horse.

Moshe was the only Jew the settlers knew first-hand and from repeated contacts, because each year he drifted into German homes right after the harvest was reaped—to sharpen knives for hog-killing days, sell buttons and ribbons, let children pull his sidelocks, hold still while being teased for merriment, and otherwise make himself useful. If nothing else, you bought a needle and some thread and had a little fun.

He was a friendly, wizened fellow who pulled his cart or sled through the entire neighborhood and did nobody harm. But who he was and where he lived, nobody knew or cared to know. It never did occur to them that he might have a family—that he might have a son.

Now, on an early winter morning, there walked into the halls of Apanlee this curly Hebrew sprout, wooden *Koffer* opened wide:

"This blue ribbon, *Fräulein* Neufeld? Or perhaps this heart-shaped box? For your embroidery yarn?"

Many years have passed since all this happened, but the legend has survived, still as vivid and revealing as though it happened yesterday. Four generations later, its details still live on.

Large snow flakes, goes the story, melted in the Hebrew's corkscrew hair. He smiled, and Olga reddened. He did not say a word. He merely reached for her. His hands were blue with cold.

In silence, Olga took his icy fingers and led him to the *samovar.*

"A cup of tea," she would have said, with lowered lashes, had she but had the use of tongue. But she was mute; the Lord had silenced her. Instead, she looked at him, compelled to read his lips.

"A cup of tea?" he said to her, instead, while drawing on the easy charm a worldly man could summon.

She nodded, an expert at guessing.

He studied her while deepening his smile. "That would be marvelous. A cup of tea is just what this poor, frozen body needs." Might she not need to have her scissors sharpened? And how about that special skein of yarn?

She shook her head. Her eyes hung on his lips.

He chatted idle conversation as he warmed himself by the fire. He told her, though she couldn't hear, would not have understood in any case, that he was studying to revamp Russia's laws in need of overhaul, home for an early New Year's break. He was a *weltkind,* said the Jew. He palavered as though she might answer.

She leaned a little closer.

"Might I persuade you, then, to try this silver thimble?"

She blushed at that, slowly and painfully, and drew her fingers to her lips in a gesture of quiet resignation.

He understood at once. There was no shock. There was no hesitation: his father might have told him.

He kept on speaking softly, leaning close: "If I should stroke your hair, will you be very angry?"

She stared at him, within the tingle of a sweet anticipation she had not known could stir her hungry heart. She who had never heard the sound of rolling thunder began to hear the hum of water, the drops of icicles as they fell in a clatter from the roof, the crackle of flames, the untoward roar of her blood. His hands beheld the city's sweet temptation—multi-colored ribbons, heady perfumes, sweet-smelling soaps, silken embroidery yarn.

"What can I do for you?" the serpent asked the girl.

She understood. It was a piercing moment.

"A red one, please," said Greta sharply, entering, and watched the Jew braid fire through her daughter's golden hair.

While Apanlee slept soundly, and while Peet's haughty bones were crumbling on the hill, the intruder kept wooing the fool-hardy maiden. The neighborhood hung from the fences.

"Look at your people's wounded pride!" Matilda cried, for Greta was, as much as anyone, against the ill-matched union. She was a human being, too; she told the neighborhood. She couldn't help her feelings. In fact, it broke her heart: the fool girl had her brothers wrapped around her little finger. Her brothers could have put a stop to it; they could have tried, wept Greta, according to Matilda, who stood with flaring nostrils, but didn't. Didn't even try!

Nobody fooled Matilda. She knew, and she predicted: heartache would follow heartache.

From her window she watched, then bolted for the nearest neighbor: "Bearded and booted! Believe it or not!"

The neighbors all cried to a voice: "How could you keep this news from us? We'll never forgive you, Matilda."

"Left-handed, too," Matilda hissed, and fanned herself in agony.

The liaison caused a sensation. Not even once within the oldest oldster's living memory had any Jew been brash enough to beleaguer the tightly-knit clan. And that was true not only of the pacifists, who had good reason to be sovereign and to remain aloof. The Lutherans, the Catholics felt that way, too. Exactly.

No Jews! Not under any guise!

And for good cause: the Good Book told them so.

The Hebrews had scourged Him; but not before He drove them from their temple; their history of usury was documented in the Bible, where every word was true. The tsars, who were as fair as any sovereigns, refused to have Jews in the army. Vandals would often sack the Hebrews' fields and put their matches to the synagogues. But did it change them? No.

Was there a way to make an honest Christian out of an ingrained Jew?

No.

"Ribbons, red sashes, the works," cried Matilda. 'And what will follow next, the good Lord only knows."

All summer long, the Jew came courting, clad in his Sabbath best, sporting a handlebar mustache, triumphantly curled at both ends. He and the silent girl sat openly together on the steps of Apanlee. He talked and talked and talked. A light shone through her face. Her laughter came in merry bubbles. She knew the herbalists were baffled. She did not care one whit.

His fancy for her silent tongue made everyone conclude he was a fortune hunter. In fact, so eager was the Jew for Apanlee that he had blisters on both heels. Each time he came to visit, he loitered over dinner, said please and *dankeschön,* and Olga shed her bashfulness entirely and laughed out loud at what his curving smile conveyed. She radiated happiness, leafing through books that excited the skin, all the while smelling of mothballs and clover.

Gossip ran rampant. The icons themselves shed their tears.

It turned out that the clan of Apanlee—though not, at first, without some apprehension—was tolerant of curls. The brothers watched their silent sister take to love as if to benediction. If she was happy—and she was!— what more could any brother ask? That was their attitude.

They caught Matilda by her flapping apron strings and threat-

ened her in vain: "Will you keep quiet, for once? You hem seams
but rip reputations!"

Matilda shook them off expertly and kept up a running account.

The brothers caught the Elder Willy by the elbow to read him
the *Leviticus.*

"If you can't make her shut her mouth, we shall re-think our
next donation to the church—"

"As if it were that easy," the Elder Willy snorted. He knew
whereof he spoke. The Elder Willy agonized so much at what he
saw rushed straight at Apanlee, he was a man near tears.

And with good cause. It was an ancient law that centuries
had wrought: why mix and match with foreign blood? Why
throw away a righteous life? Why not leave sleeping dogs alone?
Why choose on purpose to be disobedient?

"A Hebrew?" Willy cried, enraged. "Each one of them infested with the democratic spirit."

Not that it mattered; by then nothing mattered; the two were
entwined with each other. Malicious gossip flew from door to
door. Idle rumors? Empty tales? If you had eyes, you saw.

The aberration ran its course. Greta resigned herself to the
inevitable while dabbing at her eyes with a soft prayer shawl she
had received from some potential relatives she didn't even know.
Still, she kept hope alive.

"It will wear off. He will be gone by Christmas."

"He tempts," Matilda said, exuding protest from all pores.
"He argues, and she listens."

And it was true; the sparrows chirped that from the roof.
The deaf-mute wished the Jew would never cease to speak, for
now she listened with her heart and understood the currents of
another human being. He made her lively and vivacious; he made
her laugh; he made her glow. Her twitchings disappeared. In
broad daylight they met. In full view of all. By the Apanlee
watering hole.

"He loves her much," said even Nicky, by then so blinded by his love for his own chosen, Lizzy, that he was not as vigilant as he might otherwise have been.

"He does," said Lizzy, glowing, a romantic. "It is her life. She is a lonely girl. He will surround her with protection. He loves her very much indeed. He promised he will love and cherish and protect her."

By winter, they were gone. Together. Absorbed into the Valley of Jews.

She never did come home again. There was no wedding. Ever. There was not even a betrothal the Elders might have blessed. She left, and that was that. There was no steady address. What those two did to earn an honest living remained a shrouded mystery.

"Gone to that hovel hatching sin," said Willy, shaking but relieved.

The tales grew fanciful and twisted: that he wrote ornamental essays passed on in subterranean ways; that she worked as a bottle washer to help her lover pay for ink; that he surrounded her with barbs of jealousy; that she was wasting slowly of a sad and broken heart.

No wayward child of any settler's had ever caused such grief.

She sent back greetings now and then: a pound of *Halvah* for her mother, a blouse for a beloved servant, a special book to lift her brothers' hearts.

One day came word that she had died in childbirth. You drew your own conclusions.

Her brothers hitched their haughtiest horse. It walked with wooden knee-caps beneath the windswept sky, one hoof before the other. For three days they were gone; when they came back, they brought to Apanlee a mewling, stirring bundle that Noralee and Lizzy kept warm within their sheepskins, alternating, close to their pounding hearts.

"He is a darling baby," said Lizzy in defiance and stared her neighbors down.

"And potty-trained already," bragged Noralee as well, for she was practical.

You couldn't fool the pessimists. Had Peet still lived—had he not died and thereby spared himself this mockery—why, Peet would now forever have to watch this child, his daughter's erring soul, walk bent and hunched and twisted.

One might have thought the curly-headed hunchback child would have been a decided irritant at Apanlee. But tellingly, he wasn't. It was as if a thorn had been at last withdrawn from smarting flesh: at long last, healing could begin.

Now that the foolish girl was dead, peace and calm rolled over Apanlee once more and covered all harsh feelings, as if it were an ocean. The credit for this transformation fell to Lizzy.

She pierced her blue gaze deep into the baby's onyx eyes and said: "Now, hush. He's mine. I shall take care of him."

She named the hunchback infant Benjamin to make it clear to all that he was much beloved. In teasing mockery, she called him Uncle Benny, thus putting sturdy handles on his brittle childhood, describing him as if he had a titled birthright to the wealth of Apanlee written clearly on his furrowed little brow. She stood in awe of little Uncle Benny, for he was wise and ancient even in the cradle.

Lizzy was the first to see that there was something set about this little changeling—something old and penetrating and mature—ill-suited to the knoll he had to carry on his back. Throughout his life, his spine would cause him pain. She kept propping him up with plump pillows.

"Don't stand when you can sit. Don't strain when you can rest. You hear me, Uncle Benny?"

She did what she was born to do. She mothered where she could.

She mediated, too, for Greta sorrowed privately and needed time to nestle her emotions: "He is a stranger, is he not? Don't you agree he is?"

"Hush," Lizzy said. "So what?" Was any baby smarter? As

far as Lizzy was concerned, the little hunchback was a mild and gracious child with many winning ways.

Next, Lizzy made it her campaign to help her neighbors understand that this misshapen child was not at fault that his parents had grievously erred. "He's ours," Lizzy said. "That's it. That is the alpha and omega."

And once the folks of Apanlee accepted Uncle Benny and bracketed him firmly, the neighbors followed slowly. The wagging tongues grew tired, wagging less. Those oldsters with long memories now kept them to themselves.

It was soon evident to all that Uncle Benny would grow up to be a poet and a dreamer. Nobody raised a hand to put a stop to it. To punish him for dreaming would have been just like pulling petals from a daisy.

The little strangeling dreamed such useless dreams as only artists dream. He was a verbal child. The words his stricken mother had so sadly lacked sat crowded on his tongue. It was as though he had been born atop a dictionary. He saw a sunset and broke into rhyme the way a normal child might catch the measles. A dandelion caught his dark, ironic eyes, and lo! a common weed became a tiny sun. He was like that. Astonishing.

Or take a boysenberry, for example. The scandal child would gaze at it and study it in silent concentration as though it had a soul. He held it cradled in his palm and even moved it closer to the window so he could study it some more—and it transformed; it turned into a crimson droplet, such as you drew if carelessly you plucked a rose and overlooked its thorns.

The boisterous serfs, including everybody in their salty curses as they bemoaned their lot in life—freed now from servitude by a progressive tsar, but sunk in debt that would take generations to repay—did not leave little Uncle Benny to his own devices.

"Hey, you! You little oddball, you!" they shouted lustily.

They might have meant no harm. They tried to strengthen him for life's predestined sorrows. Toward that end, they called him many hurtful names.

They often took him with them to the fields to harden him and nullify the smothering that Lizzy openly lavished on him. They scooped him up and dropped him deep into the scented hay and roared when he was spooked.

They tickled his feet. They told him bawdy stories. He flinched. He blushed, recoiling from all levity.

The servants tried to harden him with fire water, but he just gagged and shook himself—a source of consternation.

For without pointing one small, spindly finger, this little boy had power over all who came in touch with him. The tooth pullers learned to send word to put wax in his ears before they arrived with their pliers. He could not bear to see a creature suffer, be it a worm, be it a king. He was that delicate.

Take Nicky, for example.

Young Nicky was as vigorous a man as all the sturdy roots of Apanlee produced, with goodwill and with energy to spare. He owned a lucky pole; he caught fat fish when others caught small minnows.

Up the porch he raced, his bounty jerking on a copper string. "Look how they bit! Look how they bit!" he would shout joyously, and Uncle Benny, barely toddling, would throw thin arms around his uncle's knees and heave.

That's all it took. Not one small word.

"All right. All right," said Nicky.

He could have squashed the little oddling with his thumb. Instead, he hung his head in shame as though an Elder had scolded him harshly, and threw his catch, alive, right back into the waterhole of Apanlee.

He catered to the youngster's every whim. He never flicked his hissing leather whip across his stallion's back when Uncle-Benny rode with him on visits in the neighborhood. He clicked his tongue, instead. He clicked it until it was sore.

His Uncle Alexander even—he with the roar of a Siberian boar when he felt angered for moot cause!—he took his piglets to the market furtively, waiting patiently until the frail child was asleep, head on his arms, arms on the table! then sneaking down the steps of Apanlee as though he were a thief.

Not even Noralee felt uninhibited enough to stretch a chicken neck to fill her Sunday pot. Such was the cripple's clout.

"What can you do?" asked Noralee. "He has that touch. He's magic."

She said that to her brother, Claas. By then, Claas preached with regularity.

Claas did not necessarily agree. He would shush Uncle Benny with a broom and otherwise make fun of him, but even he made sure the little hunchback took his nap before he gave the dog a blister on the sly with Greta's smoking iron.

So. Was there acrimony?

Well, yes and no. Perhaps in the beginning. It's wrong to say they didn't try. As Uncle Benny grew out of his infancy, there might have been some teasing but very little malice. The clan kept shielding him.

For all his body frailty, his mind and personality grew supple. He might have shivered at the taunts—he drew on a mysterious inner well. He nursed some odd ideas.

"What does the Bible say?" he pointed out, a steely dwarf who did not grow, regardless of the quality of Apanlee's *vareniki*. "The man who owns two mules should surely give up one."

He did exactly as he pleased, and things that pleased him very much indeed made nearly everybody squirm. He crooked his small left finger while sipping lemon tea.

He kept up an uncanny rapport with a bird.

Somebody overheard him beg, as though he were a girl whom Lizzy might have tried to teach, while showing off her knitting skills: "Will you please show me how?"

And she? She put her arm around his hump and led him to the window.

"Why not?" asked Lizzy, unawares.

She said to Noralee: "Where is the harm? Sewing and knitting will relax his spine."

Her sister's jaw just fell agape. She watched the hunchback wrap the thread around mid-finger, thumb and pinkie and settle back with ease as though the call for soil and progeny was absent in his loins.

"Take two, skip one," said Uncle Benny, while smiling a beatific smile.

Some things were hard to understand. Some things were better left untouched. Some were unnatural,

No words sufficed in any case to help you comprehend, decided Noralee. But when, a few days later, she caught a bully poking fun at Uncle Benny and his soft, gentle ways, this sturdy maid of German stock just planted chunky legs into his path and told him fiercely:

"You idiot you! You hairy freak! Now all I need to make me happy is your corpse."

Thus even Noralee, who did not waste her time on subtleties because they made her stomach queasy, took to the oddly verbal child. She grew as fond of Uncle Benny as though he were a kitten, crushed accidentally beneath a horse's hoof.

"Don't stand when you can sit," she scolded him as well, as she had heard her sister do. She added of her own accord: "Look at your skinny hen's legs! As if they can carry your weight!"

She wished that she could get him to admit—just once!— that it was wise to holler for assistance when those two spindly sticks gave out. "If you need help, just holler, Uncle Benny! Holler! We'll help you anytime."

She often found herself staring at him in alarm. He spoke High German. Low German. Russian. Ukrainian. When he leaped thus from tongue to tongue, it left her mind a-blur.

"Is that a human being?" asked Noralee, perplexed.

"You wonder," Lizzy smiled. "He is incredible at analyzing pros and cons of every known issue. He knows the Psalter Book by rote."

"The only thing he cannot do," said Noralee, "is help a cow give birth to an unruly calf."

"What for?" shrugged Lizzy, nonchalant. A task where she excelled.

Had it been up to Noralee, she would have fattened him. She held her breath when she watched Uncle Benny. Within his soul, she sensed the silence of the forest. He had no appetite at all— she couldn't get him to her table to finish three *vareniki*, no matter how much care she took, preparing them just so.

When she bent down to pick him up to carry him over a puddle, she feared that she might crack his bones; he was that delicate. She ran to stuff newspapers inside his shirt to break the force of gusts that whistled from Siberia.

If he was lost—which happened now and then, sleep-walking as he did through life, the little oddity!—she was the one who searched for him among the bushes.

She found him. She shook him. She stood him upright, and she dusted him off.

"He's getting stronger," argued Noralee, not making any secret of the fact that she was hooked, by then, on Uncle Benny's notions.

"Sure. Health permitting. Health permitting," said Matilda, slurping her soup like a satisfied cat. Matilda was a pessimist. "I keep my fingers crossed. He might develop water in his lungs."

Matilda watched him learn to read before his eyes were level with the shelf on which he kept his library. Was this tomorrow's man? He read so many books, he burned holes in the bottoms of his trousers.

Reading was not something on which Matilda wasted energy. Deciphering a church hymn was a decided undertaking.

"America: A country so enormous that you can lose yourself," he read to her, instead.

"His thoughts contain more sparkle than the most fantastic rumors," thought Noralee admiringly.

She never tired watching him as he built splendor on the sands of shifting thought. Fine words fell from his rosy, chiseled lips like pretty, fragile petals.

It was true: he had butterfly hands. His skin was free of pores—whereas she, Noralee, was pockmarked. Ear to ear.

She pondered gravely, being Willy's daughter: did Uncle Benny pray?

If so, the odds were: on one knee!

No matter, she decided loyally.

And yet. A tiny, unacknowledged part of her stood back.

"Our Motherland is running out of soil," wrote Uncle Benny soon thereafter, as though he were the Count of Petersburg instead of just a twelve-year-old still lacking any whiskers.

"What's that supposed to mean?"

"Soon we'll become the envy and the target of our poorer Russian neighbors—"

"What nonsense, Uncle Benny."

Noralee gnawed on her lower lip and probed a brittle tooth. When he started a book, he finished it, too. She studied him in silence: a human lexicon, sunk deep into his grandfather's abandoned chair, behind him the eyes of benevolent tsars. She knew he read voraciously. He kept himself informed.

"We must share our wealth, or we will bleed," said Uncle Benny gently.

She listened in amazement. His pointed fingertips lay on the pulse of history through papers that he ordered from Odessa.

"He looks," said Noralee to Lizzy, "like everybody's favorite aunt."

"He does. Does he not?" agreed Lizzy. "He is left-handed, true. But he's brimful of clever ideas."

Nothing so impressed Noralee as someone else's clever ideas. Here was a growing youngster who spoke and wrote as though he were a highly paid professor instead of just a tolerated loner in a warm niche at Apanlee. He examined his issues the way she examined a sock to look for a hole.

"See this?" he asked. "Read what it says here, Noralee. And give me your opinion."

He spoke to her as if she were a man instead of still a maid, unwed, though looking, looking everywhere.

"You read it to me, Uncle Benny."

"Just try."

"No. No. You read it, Uncle Benny."

"Insulation from outside control?"

He might as well have spoken Greek. She shouted at him: "So?" She often shouted in his ear as though he couldn't hear. She watched him carefully.

"Protection from racial invasion?"

When he used words like that, it helped her to remember that he was just a relative by proxy.

Her eyes would wander in astonishment across the images he etched with words across her heart as if with diamond on a pane. He talked philosophy. He spoke of betterment. He kept a copy of the tsarist promise—the royal manifesto securing rights, assuring privileges to every German settler, from the cradle to the grave—in a sealed box within his reach. He often rolled it out and studied it and let her take a peek. It was a letter with large dots and fancy flourishes, a stiff and brittle document.

"See? Jesus Christ, too, was a devoted revolutionary," said the young cripple softly.

She listened, enthralled, willing to learn. She nodded to everything, quite overwhelmed.

That he was of discerning eye and of superior intellect was clear to all who met him. Few friends he had, beyond his loving kin, but many reluctant admirers.

Chapter 7

Years hence, the Elder Willy vouchsafed Lizzy's nickname, admitting that it did no harm. He even took some pride, when land grew scarce and parlors crowded, in seeing Lizzy make a tip-top choice for one of Apanlee's descendants who had a nickname, too.

As mentioned in the chronicles, this Nicky, christened Nicholas, the middle son of Peet and Greta Neufeld, was the young man who married Lizzy Epp before he organized the exodus to Kansas, and it was Nicky Neufeld who, while on the journey to America, drowned unexpectedly.

But that was yet to come.

Meanwhile, the years passed by. While emigration ferment ate its way into the farthest settlements, Uncle Benny snuggled quietly into the quilts of Apanlee.

Then came the decade during which the Elder Willy split the church in half as though he swung a cleaver. The sudden lure of virgin acres in a far land with a melodious name, America—nothing yet but utter wilderness and sky!—had much to do with that.

The Elder Willy had grown old. His knees gave out;   no longer could he track down sinners, as he had done in olden days, but that did not stop him from trying. Everywhere he looked, and every place he checked, modernity crept in—his people planted their cucumbers sideways in harsh defiance of tradition. It didn't matter any more to most if he, their worried Elder, in anger stomped his foot or not. His eyes and ears could not be everywhere; the Fiend ensnared his lambs. No longer did his congregation members ask permission for printer's ink from Petersburg. Young people nursed outlandish thoughts.

"Like standing by a thawing river, watching the ice break into chunks," the Elder fretted to himself. To stay on top, you needed second sight.

The Elder Willy roared: "Let us, therefore, seek out a brand new wilderness to keep ourselves apart!"

The Lord would come with thunderbolts and fire darts, he threatened and cajoled. "Sifting the wheat!" shouted Willy. "Discarding the chaff!"

The angels would come swooping down, he thundered from the pulpit, to demolish the world and its wicked. Rapture was near, he discovered with the help of scriptural numerology. "Messiah will arrive—and soon! Get on your knees, meanwhile! Repent and purify!"

Did many listen? No.

"We're talking *Lebensraum!*" they shouted back at him, their beards straight in the air.

"Now Nicky has caught the America fever," said Lizzy to her sister.

"That, too, will pass," said Noralee, and for a while, it did.

The Kansas land scouts came and went. The seasons rotated. The sun took its turn with the moon. It would be several years before the Iron Chancellor made Germany an empire, before the man was born who would preach to the milling Russian masses the doctrine of a violent revolution. But even so. The watchword, even then, was *Lebensraum.*

Land hunger drove them long before the man was born who, claimed the Hebrews later, stained the good word with blood. The wonder child of Apanlee would live and die before the yellow patches with the star of David would brand his kin as traitors. Much time would pass before the rubber stamp marked "J" would empty the Valley of Jews.

Fate crept through many decades. It wove its tentacles throughout the soil, tenacious like crabgrass.

Three hundred German families had come with the first wave of wagons to the land ordained for the grain by the tsars. By the time Napoleon invaded the steppe and failed—for his audacity forced, stumbling backwards, bloodied, through the snow!—there lived eight thousand sturdy, flaxen people on the Russian soil, their handshakes firm as ever.

Their families were large indeed. The push was to the East.

And since both tsars and God decreed that all who could, should propagate—and since by strict imperial edict the homesteads could not be partitioned—it was no wonder that, in decades hence, their offspring kept on gobbling up the land.

"All homesteads undivided to the youngest," the tsars had posited, in fact. "Let the older ones fend for themselves." And they all multiplied, and prospered strongly in the Lord, and kept on swallowing fat acres.

When, midway through the century, a lenient tsar set free the Russian serfs and gave them their own scattered strips of land— but in the process saddled them with debts to tie them to their former owners more harshly than before—you found these German-looking, German-speaking settlers entrenched in tightly-knit communities as far away as Orenburg, Am Trakt, Samara, Sagradowka, Memrick.

They looked alike. They thought alike. They dreamed alike. They all had straight hair and blue eyes, long legs, strong necks, thick wrists. They all observed the rules by which they had been reared.

They clung to identical values.

In their communities, God had a place of honor, the tsars their undivided loyalty. They all upheld their forebears' tested laws. Their Elders had the wisdom of interpreters. You did not fool them, lie to them, question them or fail to carry out their orders.

The Elders saw to it, in turn, that all the settlers spoke alike—in a forced and stilted High German in school and in church, in sprawling diphthongs while at home or at their frequent *vespas*.

Time passed. The apple blossoms scattered.

And while some tardy settlers still arrived out of the West to seek their fortunes in the steppe, some who had lived in Russia for many fruitful years now started pulling out their sturdy roots in painful, sudden ways, daring to brave the great waters in search for additional soil.

Uncle Benny sensed the anguish embedded in this yen for *Lebensraum.* He had his printer's ink to help the clan decide in which direction lay its fortune, and though his whiskers sprouted sparsely if at all, many sought him out for sage and prudent counsel.

Take Noralee.

It had not once occurred to her until—while listening to Uncle Benny, and overhearing Nicky tell of America where people born to lesser wealth and status could carve a future for themselves—she realized she had some options, too.

At every opportunity, she sought out Uncle Benny for some additional enlightenment.

"America or not? Am I a fool, or what?"

"Tell me. Why do you want to leave?"

"My own shed, filled with hay?"

"Certainly."

"My own cow, giving milk so rich in cream I need only ladle it right off the rim?"

"True. Chances are that's true."

She and Lizzy often raced each other to the stalls of Apanlee—no greater joy than seeing fresh milk frothing in the pails, and seeing who squeezed more from a beleaguered cow. Her head sat level on her shoulders. "How many liters, Uncle Benny?"

"Nine hundred liters *per annum.*"

"No! Nine hundred? Did you say nine hundred liters?"

"You heard me. Nine hundred liters."

She bit her nails in her impatience. Such prospects were almost too much.

Uncle Benny stayed his patient glance on her. He never laughed at her when she asked silly questions. He treated her with an extravagant respect, as if she were a land scout coming for advice instead of just a struggling maid—unmarried still despite relentless efforts!—who scrubbed the sheets of Apanlee until her shoulders flared and blisters formed on both her water-shriveled hands.

Uncle Benny pulled a map and pointed a thin finger. "See here? Right in the center of America." He leaned back in his chair and asked in a low voice: "Noralee, now tell me carefully. Why do you want to leave?"

"Does barley grow in America?

"Yes."

"Rye?"

"Yes."

"Oats?"

"Buckwheat, lentils, peas, hemp — everything."

"Well, then. It is decided." Noralee leaned back in her chair and spoke firmly: "I opt for the untrodden land." She thought her lungs would burst, her heart explode with excitement. "One cow is worth nine hundred liters?"

The changeling with his chiseled words and his affinity for history spoke slowly: "Here. See? I'm underlining it with my red pencil."

"You know I have weak eyes. I can't read anthing that small."

"Lebensraum," said Uncle Benny, fond of his double-jointed words. "That is the issue. Isn't it?"

"So?"

She listened while he talked, explaining things to her. He never lost his patience. She listened with stunned joy while he kept analyzing pros and cons of staying versus leaving.

"It tears apart large families," said Uncle Benny slowly as if he were a scholar teaching school in Petersburg, buffered by enormous wages, instead of just a budding bachelor wrapped in a blanket on cold days with pillows all around him. "It drains our villages of needed strength. Bakers, cobblers, tailors, carpenters—everybody's leaving!"

"Yes. Everybody wants to go."

"There must be better ways."

She couldn't think of any.

By his window in Peet's study, the young cripple spent his pensive afternoons sitting on embroidered cushions, sipping tea, nursing a malaise deep within his fragile spine, composing complicated editorials. "Cows find their pastures here as there," he wrote. "The key is land reform. The watchword is equality."

Noralee, who stopped by visiting as often as she could, gave him a sidelong glance. She opened her mouth to say something blunt and snapped it shut again.

"A cow," she pointed out at last, "is the beginning of a herd."

That was but one of Noralee's ideas. She devoted herself to her favorite task: to look for a man of her own. If she could snare herself a husband, then she could travel to America as well. All she needed was a man—a thought so novel and so mesmerizing that it would startle her at night.

Before too many years had passed, the Elder Willy was the one who shouted loudest: *"Lebensraum! Lebensraum! To set ourselves apart!"*

When many years ago his father settled in the steppe to baptize in rivers and lakes, cheap land had been there for the asking. The Elder Willy could have laid claim to his share of good soil for his numerous young, had agrarian riches been part of his uppermost aim.

Instead, it was the grain of Faith he chose to sow into the hearts of needy youth—important work, he knew, to be contin-

ued by his sons and his sons' sons and their sons' sons as well.
Now children grew faster than income!

Though he was old, the Elder Willy was no fool. He knew it
was wiser to join than defy. He heard the shout for *Lebensraum*,
right in his living room.

Between three fruitful females, he had produced so many offspring he knew not how to count them. They all needed soil.
They strained at the seams of time-tested values with their eyes
on the cities of Babel. As land shrank more and more, the Elder
Willy knew with ever-deeper certainty that it was time to leave.

When Willy resolved to splinter the church, the pressure for
land was exploding the homesteads around him. There was no
choice, the Elder Willy thundered: the congregation must be split
and purified. How else to keep control?

"We've moved before, and move we will again. Be this, again,
God's will."

It was a controversial decade. It brought with it much heartache and added to the conflict that tore not just the settlements
but close-knit families apart.

"And, meanwhile," said the cautious ones, "there is the covenant. We came here to strengthen the tsars. In turn, we were
given a scroll. The tsars have kept their word. Dare we do less?
We owe them loyalty."

It seemed at first God did not like the split—the walls caved
in, the choir ran out of tunes, the weekly offerings were meager.

"It's us," the Elder shouted heartily, though already on faltering knees, "against the wicked world!"

Finding souls who needed purifying was like working on a
clearing. His voice still counted at revivals. He mixed the message for new land with rules for stricter living: *verboten* to eat
horse meat; *verboten* also slapstick jokes, silk suspenders, fire
water, dominoes.

The fires of renewal proved spectacular.

The new church's followers increased in numbers. They
jumped and shouted in their joy at having been reclaimed from

Satan's claws just in the nick of time.

They called themselves The Brethren so as to stand apart. The Brethren shunned debts, dancing, gambling, hail insurance, excessive Sunday laughter. They railed against the gatherings of the unmarried. They warned against the mischief of the Catholics, Lutherans and Jews.

Nicky Neufeld was a handsome youth with rippling arms and strength to spare who listened keenly to the pros and cons of leaving versus staying. At sunset time, when all work stopped and workers went to find the straw on which to rest their bones, he went to consult with the land scouts.

"Now tell me more about America," said Nicky eagerly. "Good soil and gentle hills?"

Nicky was as peaceful and as stately as the legendary Oak of Chortitza, a gentle animation sparkling ever from his eyes. Of stories of America he could not have his fill.

"Just where, precisely, is America?" teased Lizzy.

He looked at her with longing: what might it take to nuzzle that pink ear?

"Near Pennsylvania," he told her promptly, winking.

She looked at him and read his thoughts, producing pretty blushes. He looked at her and puffed his pipe. He noticed with a wildly pounding heart how suddenly the autumn breeze blew freely through her blouse.

Why not? The sun shone here as there.

"Cows, here as there," said Lizzy, while pouring her chamomile tea. She was content. Whatever Nicky wanted would be her pleasure, too. She gave him ample leeway; she was a willing female.

He brushed against her accidentally. She laughed and fed him sugared apples. They were young, healthy and in love.

Both took their time. There was no rush. He courted her in proper fashion, observing every single rule.

They looked each other over. She matched his kinfolk's expectations and still had room to spare. He matched her inner qualities, her stepfather in piety, her long departed mother's relatives in values, her forebears in self-discipline and drive.

He knew of her: thrift and frugality. Home remedies. Clairvoyance when it came to zwieback recipes.

She knew he had a sixth sense for the grain.

Nicky fenced a patch of grain and spared it at the harvest. Each day he checked, until he saw the strongest kernels separating from the sheaves. With careful hands, he stroked across the tips so that they sowed themselves. A patient man, he did that five years running until the wheat was amber gold.

"Those are God's kernels, selected by Him," he told Lizzy.

"Yes, Nicky. You are right." She echoed every word.

She realized that she would have to stay away from Apanlee until an Elder tied the matrimonial knot empowering the future. She saw her Nicky coming down the winding road, replete with hat and new galoshes, to have a chat with Willy.

And everyone knew why.

The time had come to wed. It was a happy time. The seasons did the rest. The two of them were made for one another other as if poured from a uniform mold.

When the cherry orchards turned to snow, the Elder Willy gave his blessing to the union. That day, he was uncommonly verbose. He told them that just as the Cossacks buttressed their beloved tsars with bayonets, so would the Holy Ghost sustain and buttress Lizzy and her chosen and shield them from all harm.

They had four children in five years—a splendid first-born they named Jan, along with three nondescript girls.

Being in her husband's arms, confided Lizzy once to Noralee—she, still not wed but looking hard, looking simply everywhere!—was just like sleeping on fresh hay. Her heart was as full as a river about to run over its banks.

Noralee could only reply, overwhelmed: "Lucky you. Oh, lucky you."

She knew, a realistic maiden: God in His bounty would provide, though with her pockmarks and her freckles—who could tell?—she might end up with someone limping on both sides and with a lisp to boot.

"No matter," she decided.

That was Noralee's favorite phrase. Long before she grew into a ripened woman with round shoulders and wide hips, excellent with needlework and knitting, it dawned on Noralee that she herself need not stay all her life within the backwaters of Apanlee, watching Lizzy preen herself having *vespa* with the Russian nobles, a napkin on her knees. If she could get herself a husband, she, too, could travel to America—a country without rules and hardly any borders.

America! A country without tsars!

The scouts kept seeking out their targets, filling ledger after ledger carefully with age, date, well-established rules.

Who could have resisted? Not she.

"Faith will be the pied piper's weapon," said Uncle Benny softly. "Obedience his tool."

She pondered that as well. She knew that Uncle Benny was obedient, considerate, and never spoke a lie. She treated him with reverence; he did the same for her.

"The messenger who rides on Faith," said Uncle Benny next to Noralee—his willing audience always, no matter what the season—"will take the golden hopes of men and leave but mounds of ashes."

"For everything, there is a precedent in history," frail Uncle Benny pointed out.

"A precedent?"

"A prior reason."

"Huh?"

It was comforting to be told there was a reason for the things she did not understand and had no wish to know.

He spent another patient Sunday afternoon on intellectual betterment. She listened. She absorbed. But as often as not, she would shrug. "You read too much," she told him.

"I'm strong," she said. By contrast, he? As fragile as an egg.
A breeze could topple him.

With deep and heaving sighs, she kept surmising he might
grow into a pale and sickly man who then would light his pipe
three times a day—no doubt to prove his manliness!—a learned
man with rosy fingers and always in the public eye, with total
recall of the smallest detail. And she was right. All her predic-
tions would come true. But that was yet to come.

Had Uncle Benny lived to see clairvoyance to conclusion, he
might have warned in finely crafted editorials: "Beware! Beware not of the clarity of reason, but of the cat's soles that are
faith's."

He would have said, to those who stayed, as well as those
who left in droves: "Look, here as there, a land of opportunity.
As long as we're willing to share."

The fragile cripple born to the sturdy clan of Apanlee would
live and die and never see the cross of destiny that hooked its
barbs into the hearts of modest men by shouting: "*Lebensraum!*"
He of the alien blood—some oldsters had long memories!—would
never hear the voice that sprang atop the crest of global sentiment to hammer souls of sober men into a searing blaze:
Lebensraum!

And yet. He sensed that blood would flow like water.

Why did he speak to Noralee? Because she listened. She
absorbed. She always heard him out with open ear. She patted
his shoulder, nestling him into a corner. She scurried for several
additional pillows.

"Stay out of the draft, Uncle Benny," she cautioned.

Chapter 8

So much is lost of history. Of Nicky, the archives tell but little—only that he saw the light of life two decades after Waterloo. It would appear he was a man of iron health—a swimmer even, so the archives claim—but it was Nicky, sadly, whom the Lord, inscrutably aggrieved, would wash into the ocean.

Why was He aggravated with so kind a man, so good a man? To this day, no one knows.

It seems to many, even now, as they leaf through their history, the Lord should have approved. They claim that Nicky should have lived, a farmer's son, one of the best that Apanlee brought forth, devoid of any quirks. He should have brought his wheat to Kansas: for it was Nicky Neufeld who, one rain-washed Saturday, hammered six hefty boards into a trunk to hold the hardened grain.

Nicky Neufeld, they will say, stood out above and from his brothers by his progressive spirit. All three wore beards, and all three kept them trimmed to allow for breezy thought, but Nicky's beard was not just trimmed—he kept his face hair angled sharply.

"Help me decide, my dear," said Nicky to his wife. "America

or not?" He fancied many modern notions, such as permitting women equal say.

"Christ walks before us everywhere," said Lizzy evenly, a sweet, compliant woman.

"You're certain, Lizzy? It's for good. We're never coming back."

"Yes, Nicky. I am certain. We take along our fathers' Faith. With us travels Christ the Redeemer."

"There will not be instant success."

"I count not on instant success. I'll travel on horseback, by donkey or on foot."

Beholding Nicky, famished for soil, she was sure that the Kingdom of God would realize itself—no less there than here. What did she want? Whatever he wanted. Land. Peace. A flock of well-scrubbed children—like everybody else.

She knew the land of Apanlee, passed on to Alexander, could not be sliced asunder. Peter, too, was packing now, having claimed a homestead in the East where pious daughter colonies were sprouting from the soil like mushrooms after rain.

Only natural, therefore, that Nicky, third in line for Apanlee, hankering to carve a landed kingdom for himself, would be the first of many men who started eyeing the blank spaces on the map that boasted but a single settlement one might have called a city.

Wichita.

Lizzy's heart grew lighter than a feather. Her trust in her Lord and her love knew no bounds. In that way, she resembled the Biblical Ruth—a genuine Biblical female. To her, the lure of foreign soil was not an alien thought.

"Get thee out of thy country," her Bible had instructed her, this with the help of Willy. "And from thy kindred, and from thy father's house, unto a land that I will shew thee. And I will make of thee a great nation."

"Your land will be my land," said she, eyes brimming over readily. "Your joy will be my joy."

America—a country so enormous that from New York to

California took longer than to cross the ocean twice as wide and dangerous to boot. Let him not think she was not well-informed. Her children would need land. She would not be a mother who would rely on table-tapping.

Before the decade ran its course, the Elder Willy told the congregation firmly: "The world is drifting deeper into sin. A new start in a wasteland, far from all wicked influence, is what we need to keep ourselves apart."

Dreadful news had trickled down out of St. Petersburg: The tsarist manifesto that had pledged ethnic sovereignty and freedom from conscription was splintering like glass.

The treachery came as a blow. Word flew from mouth to mouth: "The *Wanderstab* again?"

An Elder was dispatched in haste to learn how far the tsarist promise stretched. He spied himself a civil servant and waylaid him in the palatial garden.

"The gun and sword for pacifists?" the Elder probed, his hat in hand, his dogged German diphthongs crowding on his tongue.

The underling had a beaked look and spoke with a decided sneer: "What's this? How long have you been here? Three generations? Four? And still, you haven't mingled? And still, you don't speak Russian?"

"We have a royal document securing separate schools—"

"A sad mistake. A turn of speech. Watch me. I spit on it. I tear it into pieces and throw it to the winds"

The Elder cried, enraged: "But that is treachery! That's blasphemy! We'll leave! We'll go!"

To that, the bureaucrat replied, unmoved: "So go. What's it to us? You have ten years to leave—"

The churches were packed, with standing room only. The breach of trust cut deep. No prayers could settle the conflict. The faithful prayed repeatedly for guidance and direction. The future still remained for most of them a gaping question mark.

It was, the chronicles recall, a time of push and pull. It tipped the scales for many. Had someone said: "Democracy!" it would have had no meaning.

This much they sensed, however: in faraway America, life would be just like gravity reversed. The top layers would fall to the bottom; the bottom would rise to the top.

Old Willy still had energy to spare for storm-tossed village council meetings, where farming opportunities across the waters were debated with much heat. He was always the first to arrive at such meetings, the last to shut the door. Old Willy made sure he missed nothing. Old Willy was there to be heard.

"Facts are facts," the land-hungry settlers would outshout each other. "Children grow faster than gains. Our families are huge. Our income trifling by comparison—"

The Elder climbed on chairs and tables: "So let us leave for our Faith—"

"No. Let us stay to honor promises—"

"Conditions will improve—"

"No. No! And triple no!"

Leave? Stay? Impassioned speeches filled the air. Why not pack up and go and plow the land no farmer's hand had touched? The church pews shook. The tide of hunger for new land rose mightily, seeped into every home. Soon, it was said in the *Herald of Truth,* the publication of the Brethren: "We pity the next generation."

"The home of the wolf, the badger, and the eagle," said some and shook their heads. But others spoke persuasively: "Vast corn fields ripe for harvests, and pastures populous with herds."

"—let's look at Turkestan—"

"—the distant Amur regions—"

"—New Zealand—"

"—better yet, America—"

A few cried out: "America? The land of pitch black cannibals?" But many others had it pat: a land where milk and honey flowed.

In his endeavors for new soil, the Elder Willy had two aides who challenged his resolve. They treated him as though he were a human wishbone, by pulling this way and that way.

One was a deacon, Jacob by name, a widower with water in his lungs, who was a distant relative. Jacob was timid as a hare. The other one was Claas, his son, who had more zeal than sense.

"No need for haste! No need for haste!" intoned the Deacon Jacob. He often repeated himself.

He, too, had felt the population pressure keenly, down in the churning marrow of his bones, having borne his share of landless grief, his offspring tumbling round him, puppies, full of fuss and agitation, with little space to roam. Who knew what lay in wait across the storm-tossed waters? He coughed and wiped a cold, damp brow.

"But haste is all that matters!" shouted Claas who, as he grew to manhood, thumbed through his Bible more and more, eager to frighten, to flay and to scold. Ever since his childhood days, there had been people asking him to testify to visions. Claas was besieged with visions. Fiery tongues leaped from his lips straight at the congregation.

Claas Epp bestirred himself to an odd ministry. He next reversed direction as though he were a crab.

He, too, had caught America fever. He was convinced, however, that he should travel East.

He staked out his disciples.

Juxtaposed to all the status, wealth and elegance of Apanlee lived many landless families, fanning out in every direction, living in small huts at the outskirts of the village. The *Anwohner Tracts*, they were called - where folks lived on the margin.

Each morning, long before the roosters crowed, the Apanlee folks took generous pitchers of milk to the *Anwohner Tracts*. And where did Noralee still live, as though she were a serf? In a hut in the *Anwohner Tracts*.

Noralee scrubbed all the sheets and tablecloths at Apanlee, rinsing them in sparkling water, while Lizzy entertained the land scouts. Lavishly. If that was not enough to get your dander up, then what?

"And all I need," she told her sister, "is a husband."

"You need a husband," echoed Lizzy, who spoke from happiness.

In her stepsister, Noralee found a natural ally. Ever since their infant days, those two had looked upon each other with approval and delight.

"I'll take the plunge," cried Noralee. "I have a plan. I have a strategy. Just wait. Just wait and see."

She, too, would find gold. Or glory. Or both. She knew such luck as Lizzy had did not strike twice within one family. And since she knew she was not likely to be wed to one of fortune's favorite sons, her eyes shrewdly settled on Jacob.

She rolled her eyes with meaning. A man was a man, she concluded, even someone who was cackling like a spinster when she unleashed a skillful rumor. The rumors Noralee let fly all had a clever purpose. All had to do with land—land, land and yet more land, as fat as bacon slices! Since Lizzy started dreaming of America, that's what she wanted also. When *Lebensraum* took hold of Noralee—this inbred urge for soil and progeny—she could no longer be content that she had every right on earth to use the outskirt pastures, all part of Apanlee, for plucking dandelions for her goats. She longed to have a cow. And once she had a cow— why, she could beat her sister's butterballs!

When she arrived at that conclusion, she realized that she had reached a major turning point.

That she had staked the Deacon Jacob out romantically was not a secret to his ducks.

"You're bold enough for both," teased Nicky, smiling slyly.

The Deacon Jacob gasped and wheezed and coughed, not nearly as sure of himself. "Meanwhile, pray," was his advice to Noralee, who did, but not as often as he wished.

Jacob's approach to problems big and small was one of patience, reticence and prayer. He said his prayers carefully, leaving wide loopholes either way. Thus He could use his prayers, or else reject them, verily, as He alone saw fit.

The Deacon Jacob knew the need for land, an anguished issue, verily! was much too large for his forbearing brain.

"Should we depart? Should we remain?" he muttered on his knees before he used the chamber pot, for he slept better on an empty bladder.

He coughed behind his hand, while glancing helplessly about when, by and by, it dawned on him that Noralee laid siege with greatest care.

She started listing all her assets. "I never loiter over breakfast. My boiled eggs are perfection. When washing meat, I do not throw the water out. I feed it to the carrots."

He pondered that, while she stood waiting. Smiling.

"You do?" said Jacob in the end.

"I'll boil your mildewed shirts in milk."

"That's wasteful," muttered Jacob, mildly scolding.

She was a female on her toes. "In sour milk, that is."

By contrast, Jacob was a pessimist. He brushed that off. "It might not work. It might not work."

She looked at him with speculating eyes. "That iron rust on your frayed cuffs? Why, it will disappear as if by magic with just five drops of vinegar."

"But why—"

"I am an expert at removing iron rusts from trousers." She stood, ballooning with ambition. "Is that a burn on your left thumb? Why, here is melted soap."

"The solemn days have not yet passed," said Jacob, a stern widower.

"He is much older than you are," sighed Lizzy, thinking of her sister's rotund energy as contrasted by Jacob's slow, evasive shuffle.

"That's not the worst of it," confided Noralee. "In need of constant prodding. But no matter." Noralee blew forcefully into her tea so that the droplets sprayed. "He has produced six children, has he not? You draw your own conclusions."

"I have grave doubts, regardless," said Lizzy carefully, a pink glow on her cheeks.

Noralee had made up her mind. Concessions blended in her ample bosom as milk and coffee blend. For herself, she preferred the taste of raw onion, but she could adjust; she would adapt. She was resolved she would not end up in the brine of life just like a pickled gherkin.

She stalked Jacob from picnic to picnic. "The American kopecks," she gossiped, "lie in the gutter. The American Jews hide their gold in their teeth."

"What? What?" he asked.

"You heard me."

"Are you sure? Hey? Are you sure?"

He nearly drove her mad. If she but said "America," his glance would slide away.

She was determined, though, for since she clearly lacked the choices Lizzy had, she, Noralee, would settle placidly for what she herself could get.

Her sister and her sister's husband kept her buoyant in her efforts. "Any progress to report yet, Noralee?"

"I hope so. I sinserely hope so." Noralee flicked invisible specks of dust off her freckled arms.

"Well, don't give up. Just look at it this way," said Nicky. "In the end, it will be easier to say yes than to say no."

Noralee was sniffling with the overflow of her frustrating struggle. "Once the big tree is felled, it is easy to work with the offshoots?"

"You guessed my thoughts, Noralee."

"If I knew it would work, I would act." She didn't even blush.

She knew that love before marriage was like stripping the bark from a tree. But an imperfect plot was better than no plot; that's why she said: "No matter."

And meanwhile, why not build some castles in the air? It was incumbent upon her to seize an opportunity.

She had clear eyes about that sort of thing. She would just move from rung to rung. She would not die unloved and unwed. With no discernible bloodline between her kinfolk and Jacob's to chance a harelip for a child, she saw no bars for what she had in mind.

The Deacon Jacob never had a chance. Her need was like a timeless wave that kept on pounding at a crumbling shore.

He didn't much discourage her pursuit; in fact, it flattered him to see her so determined. He knew she had her eye not just on him but on America as well, although he felt ambivalence on both accounts and said as much to Nicky.

"Just take the plunge," urged Nicky. "And leave the rest to her."

The scouts that Nicky had sent forth some time ago were more believable than ever. They had brought back a box of soil, some grass, a folded newspaper out of a prairie town.

Now Noralee kept crumbling both between her eager fingers: "A land where milk and honey flow?"

She scouted for additional detail and had more talks with Uncle Benny, all with eye-opening results.

A country full of unbelievers—bald as a shorn sheep's fleece. No roads or tracks. No bells to warn of an approaching troika. No priests to walk their icons for the peasants.

But boots instead of wooden shoes.

Travel without passports.

And best of all: for everyone, no matter whom, a cow with velvet eyes.

No wonder Noralee thrilled to assorted possibilities. She practiced saying: "Wichita."

Enthusiasm for this town called Wichita just made her spittle flow.

Chapter 9

To get the Deacon Jacob to propose turned out to be a major undertaking. He would no more reveal his feelings than his enameled chamber pot. But circumstance and serendipity played into reticence. The mourning period had passed; he had his choice of willing females; there were at least three waiting spinsters singing hallelujah in his choir.

"So—emigration, yes or no?" probed Noralee. She carefully sprinkled her goose path with sand.

As Jacob went about his tasks, side-stepping various booby traps this eager female set for him, the stories he picked up about America were not at all alluring.

He dreaded Noralee. If marry he must, then marry he would, but why should it be Noralee—what with her thirst for land across the murky waters? The moment Noralee spoke of America, the trees around him spun.

"Let's leave! Let's leave!" urged she.

He did not want to go. He did not even want to marry, truth be told, although his orphans needed somebody to tie them to their chores.

"Stay in the country of your birth—" intoned the Deacon Jacob timidly, thus counteracting Biblically.

Beneath her smoking lamp, she kept on hatching strategies. She peered into his faded eyes. "Here. Try my kitchen kvas."

He had a nose bleed as a last resort. An optimist would have despaired.

"The river, full of fish," the Elder Willy counseled Noralee. "And all you need is patience and a fishing rod, my child."

She and the Elder Willy saw eye to eye on emigration matters. As far as her own father was concerned, marrying a strong-willed daughter with a hunger for the soil across the ocean to an authenticated preacher—although, regrettably, a man with porous lungs and an effacing smile—moved matters in desirable directions while keeping close control.

"The river, a mere trickle," mourned Noralee, and rolled her eyes dramatically.

"No progress yet?"

"No progress whatsoever," lamented Noralee.

When she carried all those buckets on a yoke to scrub the linen piles of Apanlee, she moved with the purposeful ease of a dignified cow.

"I'll help you," promised even Lizzy.

Next time she saw the Deacon Jacob standing by the waterhole, wrapped in thoughts or prayers or both, she gave her sibling a firm shove.

Noralee took two determined steps and pointed out the obvious: "Remember the story? Adam and Eve?"

The Deacon Jacob stiffened at the brazen effort: "What? What?" Her need intensified the whistle in his lungs. He plucked a many-colored handkerchief that she had given him at Christmas and mopped his wrinkled brow. His rib cage rattled faintly. "What did you say? Whatever did you say?"

She was near howling, by that time, with injury and pride but decided to swallow her gall.

"Feed him a peacock tongue," laughed Nicky, a merciless

man. "Or better yet, why not train Jacob's horse?"

Wise counsel she couldn't ignore.

She started feeding it each morning at the gate of Apanlee, where she did all her laundry chores. She even swept the droppings up to keep the path free for romance. She thought of everything.

It happened as predicted—the deacon's horse stopped dead one wind-blown morning and would not move a hoof while waiting for the feed. The deacon pulled and pushed. The hoar was hanging from his ears.

"Come in. Come in. Here's my warm laundry room," coaxed Noralee. "It's cold. Here, let me thaw you out."

He blushed the color of a lobster. A droplet started thawing from his nose.

"I can't imagine—can you?— what caused that horse to stop? Right by your gate?"

"I can't imagine either," lied Noralee, and didn't even blush.

"Coincidence, no doubt," Lizzy brought up the rear.

Trapped helplessly between two scheming females, the deacon finally caved in. "To tell the truth, my feet are cold. In fact, I barely feel my toes."

"Here, put your bunions in my soapy water."

Noralee pulled off his boots as if expecting to find buried treasures. She lowered his feet into the suds as though lowering them into a well.

"I work like a demon," she told him. "Look at my hands. See all those calluses?"

He saw. He stared. He knew that it was touch and go.

She watched him with her hungry eyes. "How are your ducks?"

"Ducks? Ducks? What ducks?"

To get him to declare himself was worse than stepping on a log afloat in turgid waters. She set her chin. She had made up her mind. She knew the day would come when she would cross that ocean to make a life belonging to herself. "I know that you have ducks that are neglected badly. Now, I hold ducks in high esteem."

"My ducks are fine. Just fine."

Relentless, that was Noralee. "Your geese? How are your geese?"

"My geese are fine. As well."

She overlooked the glister on his upper lip. "Your goats?"

"What? What?"

"You heard me." What could he do, poor bachelor, beside her washboard, trapped, his feet deep in her bucket? She whispered in his ear: "You would be marrying a touch-me not—"

The Deacon Jacob jumped as if a twig had snapped beneath his soles.

"I need more time," wailed Jacob, his blue toes stuck in suds. What happened next is left for anyone to guess.

It dawned on Jacob, by and large, that Noralee, defying the astonished faces of the congregation, had sprung a trap on him.

When he proposed, perplexed at what had happened, she looked as smug as a successful pickpocket—and he, as sheepish and as pleased as if he had been caught, not accidentally with Noralee—who just forgot herself, that morning, in her laundry room, as later she would tell the congregation, her face aflame with memory—but with a scheming and notorious lady of the night.

However, he was honest with himself. He was a man. She was a willing maiden. His geese needed feeding. His shirts needed buttons. His children all had runny noses and needed laundered handkerchiefs.

That's how and why it was that Jacob married Noralee.

Soon afterward, she found herself engulfed in combat with a feather.

"America or not?"

"Let's pray for guidance," shuffled Jacob. He coughed behind his hand and uttered mild objections one could read either way.

She glared at him. Her hands turned into fists. Had she not been a pacifist, she would have struck him. Hard. "Give me one solid counter-argument. One cow: nine hundred liters."

"That can't be true. It can't."

"Just think of it. Nine hundred liters."

"Impossible," gasped he.

"One cow. Nine hundred liters."

She told her wheezing husband morning, noon and night: "I opt for the untrodden land."

Not much had changed for Jacob except that, now, the warmth of matrimony pressed nightly to his buttocks. As he had done before, he preached in all the places Willy laid out for him, earning extra kopecks as a cobbler on the side while trying to make up his mind.

He turned white and gave a shudder when she but said: America.

She parceled out her finest reasons. "We could compete with Apanlee."

"That would be vanity."

"A goat and a pig, that's all that we possess." By then, Noralee was close to uncontrolled shrieks. "Young and old are dreaming of America. Why not us, too? We could upgrade to cows."

Jacob worried more and more that he was falling prey to vanity. He was a humble man.

At Apanlee, there was no end to wealth. The flail and threshing floors had long since disappeared; from far away, the Russian peasants came to weigh their newborn children and watch how old-fashioned windmills converted to steam. Nobody boasted such power.

"Our home," she argued heatedly, "the smallest hut in the entire village. Merely a bench, a table and two chairs."

"We're simple folks. Why pretend?"

"Your children! Look at them!" howled a frustrated Noralee. "Don't they deserve a chance?"

She cut down his resistance like sheaves. She gathered footing to strengthen her cause. On the bench that ran along the oven
sat all six of them, all barely fed sufficiently with cabbage, carrots and potatoes she grew with Jacob's patient help.

"Whenever I peel a potato, I have to plant the skin! Is that a
way of life? You tell me! You give me one good reason!"

He peered at her across the turnips on the table: "Here is a
radish, Noralee. Sniff it. It might clear your nose."

"Where did it grow?" she wept in frustration. "On a patch
the size of a postage stamp—"

"I call it your fine kitchen garden," scolded Jacob.

"In America, rich and poor can mingle absolutely everywhere.
The rich sink to the bottom. The poor rise to the top."

"Do not indulge in senseless dreams. I beg of you. I beg
you."

"What do we own? The oldest hens in the entire village.
Across the waters, we'd have a chicken coop that's larger than a
barn."

She cried, a stubborn woman: "Before I die, I want to feed
my family a Christmas pudding filled with raisins."

Her aging husband shook his head. "Your vanity! You look
like a bloodthirsty eagle."

In her father, Noralee found a natural ally. She swarmed all
over him. She poured her grief across his prayer book.

He knew whereof she spoke. America was beckoning—had
he been but a decade younger, he might have gone! He would
have gone! He would have set a fine example! But by now, he
had reached the Biblical age.

Noralee made Willy sit down and total them up, the descendants that sprang from his loins and survived: eleven boys and
girls in all, sixty-three grandchildren, even a few great-grand-
sons. All hungered for the land. All had the qualities that guaranteed survival. All daughters married fruitfully as proof of a
pious existence.

"And all you do," the Elder argued with his deacon son-in-law on Noralee's behalf, "is pick the gold that is already lying in the gutter."

Jacob kept slurping his soup. He touched neither tea nor tobacco.

"I have big dreams," howled Noralee. "Look at your sons! What if the tsar starts drafting them? Will you stand by and watch your sons kill other fathers' sons? Think! Think of all the open spaces. "

"What spaces? Full of weeds and thistles."

"Flat acres, Jacob. Cheap!"

"Sure. Cold winds blowing over them?"

"I'm frostbitten now. I'll wear two of everything."

"We barely have the money for the tickets—"

"I'll travel steerage, Jacob! Steerage!"

"I haven't finished learning Russian."

"I do not care," shrieked Noralee, a full-blown traitor, verily! "if in America the birds chirp English, too!"

"It's now or never," decided Noralee. Lizzy and Nicky were packing already, about to leave and never to return.

She focused all her energies. She would not stay behind. She took her husband by the hand and led him to the children's chambers and said to him: "You can't squeeze in a hand. If one more comes, that's it."

"If one more comes," saith he, backed finally into a corner, "I promise that we'll go. "

That's what it took. She had his word. She waited for a rainy afternoon, waylaid him skillfully, threw every bolt, hooked every chain, and dropped her underskirt.

The Deacon Jacob looked around and felt a choking sob: The front yard crowded, fence to fence, as if it were a funeral. He watched all his meager possessions diminish. Piece after piece was borne away; only a few odd items remained.

"A chair," the auctioneer kept hectoring. "A chest. A hoe. Two buckets with good handles. An authentic grandfather clock—" Soon, he was hoarse from shouting.

"—with copper weights!" Noralee triumphantly finished his sentence.

What could not be sold, she had promised to give to the poor.

"A button box!" yelled Noralee. "An old hand grinder for your oats! Two mittens and a spare."

She was in soaring spirits. She had finished the tasks for the voyage: packing her two dozen trunks, wrapping all of Jacob's children's clothes into bundles and tying them, cross-wise, while triple-checking every knot.

"Left and right, we wish you luck!" the neighbors said to Noralee, who ballooned with importance and rapture. The goats were gone, the cow was gone, pulled straight from the pasture and driven away. She rattled her coins in her can.

A fear gripped Jacob then and there. He started shaking like a leaf whirled up within a hurricane. He whispered: "Noralee, there's something wrong with me."

She burst into cruel laughter. "Too late. Say what you will. Too late."

Perspiring copiously, he sat down on a pile of discarded burlap, observing how she made the most of every good-bye. "Imagine. Imagine all the possibilities," she cried, a woman without mercy. "One cow! Nine hundred-twenty liters!"

He collapsed on a mountain of blankets and pillows.

She didn't even notice. She was pushing her valuables into a sack, beset by a crowd of curious onlookers who had gathered in front of her hut.

He tried to rouse himself. The trees spun, round and round.

At supper time, he tried to force himself to eat. A bit of gravy dribbled on his collar. He wheezed: "I don't feel well. Let's reconsider."

She pushed him down and called him names, intoxicated with the immigration spirit.

Before she left to find a new life in America, she dressed the Deacon Jacob for the coffin.

"Of long-standing consumption," the herbalists declared.

She knew a deeper truth.

There is a faded picture, dug up out of somebody's attic. It shows Noralee as she was at her best. She sits triumphant, looking straight ahead, surrounded by six children, not one of them her own. She has a ramrod spine. She keeps her hands demurely in her lap, but there's a sparkle in her eyes.

"No matter," the glitter in her young gaze seems to say. "You salvage what you can."

In this old, faded photograph, she has a slightly rounding belly, and if you check the calendar against the ship list and the birth of her first son, born in the sod near Wichita, a boy whom she would bravely christen Dewey, it being an untested name, you might surmise that Noralee took with her half around the world a prematurely stirring child, her first and Jacob's last, that kicked at her with pious foot soles all the way to Kansas.

Chapter 10

The Lord, propelled by a mysterious anger, tore Nicky from his destiny and swept him out into the heaving sea—much as Claas Epp, when angered for moot cause, would tear a page from an offending book and fling it in the fire. His widow never had a funeral's somber comfort to come to terms with loss.

After the accident, the Elders told her, hovering: "Out of all evil cometh forth good." She must cling to her Faith, said the preachers.

It took many tears, but of course she complied. She had no other recourse. Her life and love, the caring father of her children, was gone forevermore, washed overboard by a ferocious storm that tried to rip the ship apart and lashed still at the sails. Now she was all alone.

So this was death? This was the end? She felt betrayed and wronged. No relatives to gather in full strength? No preacher at her husband's coffin to remind her she would follow? Just this? A watery grave for the sweetest of life she had known?

She longed to see her Nicky laid to rest in his beloved earth's warm bosom, next to his father, Peet—both of them one with the soil. For days on end, the wind kept whipping at the waves, as if to pulverize their foam. The captain petitioned for prayers—a rough, foggy voyage, contrary winds all the way.

When finally the pitching ceased, and there were solid planks beneath her feet again—although they hadn't yet reached shore— this preacher, that one would quietly sit next to her, affirming: "Do not despair, for you are yet in God's good hands."

She was helpless with shock. The limitless world she had hoped to share with her husband had turned into a frightening abyss—worse yet, there was no turning back. The steps behind her had been washed away.

"It takes Faith, in the face of disaster," said her friends and companions.

She nodded, but it didn't help. It would be days until her inner storm subsided. At last, a rainbow perched on the horizon, a magnificent, colorful arch.

She thought she had already shed the last of many tears, but now they welled again. She was alone, sailing on a swaying ship bound for a destiny that had no name, a widow with four little children, their faces plump with tears.

"The Lord is mad," wailed Noralee, but Lizzy shook her head.

"No, Noralee. It's not the Lord." She concluded with shivering sinews: the Devil.

She knew from previous training—knew all of it deep in a cold and silent corner of her brain—that it was not the Lord her Master who tried with both His hands to rip the ship apart.

"Why?" shrieked her sister. "Why? Good Lord, just tell me why!"

"I think I know," said Lizzy in the end. She cast a shy glance at the bin. That's what it was—God's kernels. The Devil wanted Nicky's wheat. The emigrant barge, packed seam to seam with eager seekers of new soil, swayed in the wind, a dark and helpless petal. And since the Devil could not cleave his malice unto the golden nuggets still safely in the bin—the Lord had aided her in holding on to it with all her strength while many other crates washed overboard!—he took her love instead. There was no other explanation. It was a thought, she realized with a small jolt, with the strong, sharp aroma of mint.

When at last the storm subsided, Lizzy sat atop her salvaged bin of grain, her skirts spread over it. She listened patiently to her son's anguished prayers, having gently silenced the tumultuous voices of the girls. She spread her blankets on the floor and watched the young fall into slumber. She stared into the night, in her ears the roll of the sea, in her nostrils the salt of the water.

"He's dead," she thought, but could not grasp the thought. "He's gone, and I am all alone."

She had expected to grow old and limp in Nicky's strong, protective arms. Behind her slept the ship—above her, a distant and glittering ceiling. A chill sat in her marrow. A full moon kept its stealthy pace. At home, the hours struck mindnight— here it was just after nine. How could one gain a head start on the future by turning back the clock?

"Mama," a small voice spoke behind her.

"Yes, Jan?"

"It's you and me, Mama."

At first, she scarcely heard the words. She said mechanically: "Yes, dearest. Yes. I know."

"Mama, if you will let me help—"

She touched her son's warm hand. "I know."

Jan stroked his mother's knee. They sat together wordlessly. At last he said: "You aren't crying any more, Mama?"

"My tears have all been shed."

Her lids were dry as paper, but in her heart sat dread, a cold and clammy toad. She knew eternity was good to all who walked the straight and narrow path: Nicky's place in heaven was assured. That wasn't it; she didn't grieve as those who had no hope because they knew the Savior not. The meaning she searched for was deeper than that, more involved.

"You have your Faith, Mama."

She nodded at the familiar comfort. Nicky's young life had

passed into eternity, a bright and shining star. She knew as well that death held all the answers, but little solace was that now when grief churned deep within her with a surging power all its own.

"Yes, that I do. I thank you for affirming." She dared not ask to understand eternity, for fear of seeming forward. She heard her young son mutter: "Thou who feedeth the fowls in the air, and clotheth with beauty the lilies, hath surely not forsaken me." She cupped her first-born's face and felt a tear squeeze slowly through her fingers.

"Clouds give us rain so grain can grow—"

"I know."

"Storms drive the roots of oak trees deep—"

She heard her husband's favorite proverb as though he sat beside her.

"Why aren't you asleep?"

"I can't sleep either, Mama." Her young son took a struggling breath: "Behind the blackest clouds hide countless twinkling stars—"

She looked at him with gratitude. The words he spoke had long been anchors for her folk. She knew that she must live by them, the proven, tested proverbs of her creed, but in her clammy heart she knew as well: "He's gone, he's dead, and I am all alone."

"Jan, listen—"

He took her hand into his own in a proprietary manner: "I will make sure you have the finest home. The lushest land. The strongest trees." And, with a small and tender smile: "The fattest cows, Mama."

She bonded with her son that night. She loved all of her children more than life, but now she knew she would look up to Jan.

The storms were not yet done. Again, the ship began careening, a nutshell on a crest.

Swollen with new life—and too much food consumed in the excitement of the voyage—Noralee thought that she would surely die. She wrapped herself around a handy railing and spit up peas, pork, bits of stock fish—and someone young and strong, smelling of hoeing and plowing, was carefully holding her head.

"Hold on, now, Noralee. Hold on!"

The ship was upright now, then leaning on its side, creaking in its joints. Bags and suitcases, bundles and baskets kept sliding up and down the planks.

"Hold onto me, Noralee! Hold on! There, now! Good girl!"

She wept with shame that this young male she scarcely knew had seen her retch as though she were a glutton. His fingertips cradled her temples. She couldn't help but see, albeit through her tears: here came an opportunity. Here stood a young but hardy fellow, not in the least put off by nature's purging ways. So why not ride the crest of drama, since there was nothing else to do? She felt her armpits going wet with nausea. "I'm dying! Am I dying?"

He peppered her with many questions. "Do you feel better now? Just one more heave? Good girl!"

He laughed until his whiskers shook—and she? She heaved once more and leaned against him shakily and knew she had come home.

His blue eyes matched her own. She knew that he would be her man, that he would forge her rules.

'Here. Try my fire water."

She took a sip straight from his flask. Strong stuff! It made her tongue sting and her throat contract. It was like biting heartily into a pickled gherkin.

"Ah! Ah! That's good! What is it?"

"It's vodka, little goose. Here. Swallow hard. There now! Another heave? Don't you feel better now?"

"I think so," Noralee agreed, and knew she was in love.

She understood, of course, the interest that lay beneath his charity. She was not deceived—no silly cuckoo she. Yet all the same, a surge of youth and opportunity rushed to her fingertips and toes, which seemed improper and untimely, as though Jacob had never existed.

"I thank you. Right from the bottom of my heart," said Noralee, now mindful of her manners.

The stranger was a godsend from the start. He brought her youth and strength. Death had stood for so long behind her aging husband—and when it came, at last, she did what any woman would have done: she splashed his face with water—did that help him? No. He passed away, obligingly, amid his many pills and bottles.

This youth beside her, twice her size and solid as the old oak tree of Chortitza, now said to her, repeatedly: "Here. Have another sip."

"If you won't tell the Elders," she giggled shakily.

"If you won't either," said the man, and clasped her to himself.

She wasn't anybody's fool; she knew she voyaged to a country thick with intellectuals and Jews. She forced a lump of nausea down once more and told the young man resolutely: "You look familiar to me."

"I do?"

She leaned toward him gingerly. She calculated quickly. Six children slept beneath the bow on plain plank beds, and her belly was arching again. This man looked young enough to have his pick—she'd better be prepared. Just as a town must have a railroad, so, too, a girl must have a man.

"You do. Where are you from?"

"From Alexanderwohl."

"What is your name, if I may ask?"

"My name is Johann Janzen. But everybody calls me Doctorjay, for I set broken bones."

"I'm pleased to meet you, Doctorjay," said Noralee, still struggling for composure. "I take it that you know of Apanlee? I come from the vicinity."

So what if his nose ended in a pimple? Her knees knocked together a bit.

Throughout some fifty years of married life, Noralee would never cease to feel for Doctorjay an ardent admiration.

He came and helped when she needed it most. He stood and watched her cleanse herself; he did not back away. This was the fondest memory she cherished from the voyage: that sturdy, wholesome hand, those tufts of hair on hardy farmer's knuckles, that reached for her and steered her to the railing.

"Doctorjay, I'm glad you helped me with that flask," she told him now, resolved to make the most of luck and opportunity.

"It's good stuff, isn't it?" he smiled.

"But don't you think you better hide it? Now?" The Elders had sharp eyes. "We'll both be punished, in this world and the next."

"I'll empty it first to your health," he said gallantly, bending an elbow, on his lips a merry laugh.

"A Brethren you are?" She better make sure.

He chuckled. "Well. No. Not exactly."

"You're not?" Her eyes were round as saucers.

"Not quite."

"If you don't go to church, I'll read you the *Leviticus*. With laxity, I can be sterner than a preacher."

"I am a German of the Lutheran persuasion."

She pondered that a bit, while he kept watching her alertly.

"So what," she told herself. "There's always a chance to convert." This was a friend of merit. Here was a man with the familiar look, the homely smell she craved. He made her heart pound like a hammer.

"Once born a Lutheran, always a Lutheran. Is that the truth or not?"

Was that an answer or a question? Was he now teasing her? She kept surveying him beneath her lowered lashes. She liked things cut and crisp.

"I go to church," he said while guessing at her thoughts, "like everybody else."

"Is that a fact?"

She pondered carefully. Chances were he said his prayers;

and chances were, he had no fear of bathing. The waves that rocked the ship were rocking them both. "I am a widow, don't you know?"

"Here is my arm. Hang onto me," he laughed.

She grabbed it resolutely. Too soon, she guessed, he would find out about the children that were now hers to raise until they scattered—though, luckily, they slumbered at this moment and could not interfere. Had they been romping underfoot, she might have lost this opportunity.

"Well, then?" she pushed coquettishly. She tilted her chin just a bit. Life was a game of chess. So what if her belly was rounding!

"Doctorjay, tell me the truth. Have I not seen your face before?"

"I might just be your long-lost kin," he told her softly, pressing his advantage, while yielding to the pitching and the heaving of the ship. "You might have seen me. Off and on, I worked at Apanlee. A field hand, you might say."

"Could be."

He pulled in a gulp of smoke and blew it artfully back through his nostrils. "To me, you look familiar, too. You look as though you have been raised on sour cream and cherries."

When she heard that, she was convinced that she had died and gone to heaven. Sheer poetry!

"That is a comely coat you wear," said he, a lavish man, and laughed so that his belly shook. "One of these days, I'd like to help you with your buttons."

Impertinence! Audacity! The ship was pitching her from one horizon to the other. "What's this? Amusing me with flattery? Where are your manners, Doctorjay? You assume that a woman comes easy?"

"He suits me well in all respects," she reported to Lizzy at once.

"I'm glad, Noralee," said her sorrowing sister, her thoughts still far away. "He seems a very nice man."

"He is. I know that for a fact."

She was resolved to settle into marriage just as a fox might settle, having found a hollow tree. She leaned upon the railing, adding softly: "He may not look it, to be sure, and may not even act it, Lizzy, but I know deep down in my heart he is a very pious man."

"That is just wonderful," said Lizzy.

"When he accepts our Lord and Savior, he will surrender all that's Lutheran."

"Has he proposed already?"

"Not yet. Not yet."

"He is a little younger than you are?

"A mere ten years."

"Ten years? Now, listen, Noralee—"

"If you must know—eleven."

"Eleven!"

"So what?" said Noralee. "My aim is, first and last, to please."

Her sister probed: "How old is Doctorjay? Speak up and tell the truth."

"Eighteen."

"What? You are almost twice his age!"

"That's right. Eighteen. Not that it matters, Lizzy. I know that he sets bones, pulls teeth and bleaches freckles. And charges a set fee."

Before she settled down with Doctorjay, she set herself to the compelling task of helping Lizzy cut her mourning time in half. Doctorjay, who never left her side, was of enormous aid in that endeavor from the start, for Lizzy's benefit dispensing healing counsel: "After you are done with grieving, Lizzy, you will be plump and rosy once again."

"Oh, never! Never!" Lizzy sorrowed, numbed head to foot with shock but sensing his good will.

"Oh, yes. You will," said Doctorjay. "You have the courage of a soldier. I never saw a braver woman."

Both Noralee and Doctorjay would tell her every day: "We've

stormed heaven with our prayers. If even half are answered, you have some miracles in store."

They never left her side. They sat with her throughout the voyage, exchanging little pleasantries. They walked her back and forth to make sure melancholy didn't settle in her joints.

Assorted Elders bolstered this crusade, studying their prayer books to arrive at timely solutions: "And meanwhile, Lizzy dear, the ancient Faith. The tested rules. Your Savior is your shield."

No, she was not alone. The pious passengers all stood behind her with a tender constancy so she could ripen in her Faith and walk from doubt to certainty.

Yet she was human, too.

"I know that Sundays will be hardest," Lizzy whispered wretchedly, though bolstered from all sides.

"We'll all come visiting early and stay throughout the day," said Doctorjay.

"You will?"

"Of course. Come Sunday in America—why, you can do whatever strikes your fancy. Stay in bed. Nurse a headache. Eat all the pickles that you want. That is America for you. No matter what the distance, Lizzy—we'll all come early and stay late. Good neighbors here as there."

She smiled a wistful smile that stole into his heart. She might be senseless with her loss—she spared no pains to make herself agreeable. "I want your promise, Doctorjay, that you and Noralee will homestead next to me."

He blurted out, his ears aflame, a daring man who overstepped ten thousand boundaries: "I promise you. Here is my handshake, Lizzy."

"A stroke of luck," she said, a genial woman, "put you right in my way."

His heart leaped to his lips: "Fair weather or foul, I'll always be your friend." He stared at her, enthralled. That was America for you! This woman came from Apanlee where he had been an extra hand at the potato harvest. "You don't mean half of what you say?"

"Of course I do." Such joy careening in his head! Now he began to understand: democracy! That was the secret code—as robust as the scent of the earth after plowing.

She spoke with firm simplicity. "Where we are going, Doctorjay, there will be need of friends."

He answered in a sweeping bow. His heartbeat—in a whirl! Not for ten thousand kingdoms would he have traded in this moment. He knew not what to say.

She watched him thoughtfully. She knew, a refined woman: a bond had formed between her and this common man with pockmarks on his cheeks and all the grime of Russia still clinging to his heels.

He sensed it, too. It hushed him. His blood sang in three octaves when he stood next to Noralee, but Lizzy touched him in a way no woman ever touched his heart before or ever would again. Had he not been so clumsy, he would have kissed her shadow. Before her dainty feet he spread his fleshy heart.

"You are a fine diplomatist," instead he muttered awkwardly, the ocean's salt drops stinging his eyes and his nose.

She turned and tensed her shoulders, her gaze on the emerald sea. He took off his hat, then put it on again. He couldn't speak for several hours; he was that overcome.

Noralee beamed her approval at the exchange that started mending Lizzy's grief. There was no jealousy in her. Her sister was no rival to her hopes. A blind man would have seen why Doctorjay had chosen Noralee.

She noticed even on the ship that he, in deference to her superior age, had camouflaged his youth, in case she noticed and objected, by stiffening his mustache with a special kind of wax that he had cleverly invented.

"Here's to your health, dear Noralee. Longevity, of course," he told her, smiling slyly.

She asked no further proof.

He gave her lively, penetrating looks. He looked as though he carried firecrackers in his pockets.

"Where we are going, Noralee, open loving is freely allowed. I have that from good sources."

"Why, poison oak itch on both nostrils!" she giggled, overcome. "What are you hinting at? I do not understand."

Of course she understood. She collected her wits just in time.

She knew the treasure that he coveted; might he be bold enough to strip before his wife? The thought was too dreadful to finish. Her pulse was throbbing with all sorts of possibilities. Here was a bold and daring man who stood, enraptured, at her elbow. Both understood each other perfectly, for what he valued in a horse, he also valued in a woman—those tell-tale shivers rippling down her spine, collecting in his palm.

Chapter 11

Missy, nicknamed Little Melly, was barely six years old in 1874. She was the third of Jacob's six young orphans whom Noralee had taken over to be raised in trusted Faith when Jacob passed to his reward. She stood as close to Jan, a boy twelve years of age, as modesty allowed.

Protectively, he put both arms around her slender frame so that she wouldn't slip in her excitement and fall into the sea.

"See? See?"

"I see. I see," she echoed happily, as wholesome as baked apple.

Both watched with eager eyes. Straight chimneys rose as if by magic. The sun shone bright and clear. The ship coursed forward like an arrow. The sailors scurried up the masts. The water foamed with spring.

Jan was in all respects a sprout of Apanlee—his dreams came early, lingered long. Wheels within wheels were turning in his mind.

"I have it from good sources that, in America, most anything is possible."

When he touched Little Melly's hair—as he did even on the ship, for he was generous with touch—the sun was sparkling in his eyes.   When Little Melly smiled at Jan—right through the gap where baby teeth had been—the timbre of the harpsichords chimed in: "Here is the key. It will open the door to my heart."

She leaned against him gingerly: with Jan, most anything was possible—although real miracles were rare.

Let no one call it puppy love. The uninformed might say: mere children. Minor minions. She knew that she would marry Jan—she who had known him since the cradle. She had the proper qualities. She knew how to blend in harmoniously.

Whatever he wished to learn on a subject, he found out. What she wished to remember, he taught her.

The time-worn rules had carved their faces so that they looked like siblings. Behind them stood the weight of centuries. The ancient Faith ran in their blood. It wrote the script; some things were understood as though they had been carved on slabs of rock that Moses brought down Sinai. There was a master plan.

They were each other's shadow.

Now she sighed softly, stirring against him, knowing in the center of her being that this boy—freckled skin, red hair and penetrating eyes—would always be smack in the center of her world.

Little Melly's aim in life was first and last to please. Even on the ship as it reached shore and dropped its anchor, Little Melly knew with certainty that, come what may, she would grow up and melt into the noble duties. She would perfect the qualities a woman must possess—foremost thrift, patience and embroidery. Her wisdom issued from the Bible.

Jan knew that he would grow into a man of potent strength who, duties done, would then sleep sound, in his nostrils the scent of the bountiful earth.

Under her guidance, his prayers would reach high perfection. As judged by his approval, so would her *pfeffernüsse*.

Little Melly was, of course, a Brethren child and, therefore, born and bred to peace and to conformity, and she was pious to the backbone. Behind Jan stood his ancestry, known for its friction with the Elders and for some views of certain risk. But you could tell: she would not let him run from church to church; she would grow up to memorize the points of dispute between the Brethren and the Lutherans pertaining to the Trinity and help him see them, too. She would point out to him at every opportunity: "See? See those markers all around you?" He might test this and that, since Peet's agnostic spirit peeked out from his blue stare in flashes, but in the end, he would give in.

She knew it. He did, too.

Together, they made an astonishing couple. Their faces bore a message, etched there by centuries: not reckless with tradition are we.

Tradition was what walked ashore! Tradition walked ashore as though it wore silvery spurs.

"This is my land," cried Doctorjay with stark emotion. "Lord God, this is my land."

And Noralee! She gasped with reverence. She rolled her round, blue eyes. She fell in with the shouts of fellow passengers: "America! America!"

She would have taken off her shoes, had she not known her left sock had a hole—a small one, to be sure, but woefully at a strategic point where no one could have missed it.

"Don't yelp," said Doctorjay, a gallant man, protective of her image.

She quickly checked her voice but cheered the coast no less enthusiastically by clapping. She knew that everything was difficult in the beginning, but He would hold her upright in her Faith, and in the meantime, she would do her share—day-in, day-out— just give her a small chance!

"Goodness only knows what might be on your mind," she told the man who held her elbow firmly and guided her ashore in blinding daylight as though she were a queen and he a nobleman. "Let's say you were to marry me the moment we arrive?"

"That thought has crossed my mind," replied the Lutheran, while warming to the challenge.

She arched away from him in coy retaliation. "Why, Doctorjay! Why, thumbscrews on your thoughts!"

She was no fool. She read his eager blood.

"We'll leave the future up to Providence," he told her teasingly. "Let things evolve. As you so often say, the Lord shall be in charge."

She had no quarrel with that thought. The Lord would always be in charge, but she would help; she had ambitious plans. She knew of Lizzy's pledge to own the fattest cow. She knew that Lizzy's son had plans to grow from just a single calf a model, exemplary herd. She was a woman generous of heart; she would leave raising cows to Lizzy who needed every benefit to help her past her grief.

Let Lizzy have her cows! She, Noralee, would concentrate on fowl.

She would make sure she owned the fattest geese, the plumpest ducks, the hardiest chickens, all housed securely in the sturdiest chicken coop.

That was a decade that saw many walk to shore down swaying board walks, children and baggage in hand, throwing their bundles and bedding. Some couples carried hassocks between them. Some hefted their belongings on their shoulders, or pulled them with a rope.

Noralee headed the throng, Doctorjay at her side. She was so eager for the future she nearly lost a shoe.

She funneled her children through customs, willingly moving when given a shove. She opened her mouth and stuck out her tongue to let it be inspected for diseases.

"A clean bill of health, Doctorjay."

"Same here! Same here, Noralee!"

"Not married yet?" asked the official, catching the romantic drift.

"Not yet," said Noralee. "But he pulls teeth. Sets bones.

And charges a set fee."

"Name?"

"Janzen."

"Spell it."

"Whichever way you please," said Doctorjay, accommodatingly. "It matters not to me."

"Well, let me help you, then. Your name is Jensen now!" Plunk! went the rubber stamp.

The bonesetter stared at his new name, enthralled, then threw his knapsack with aplomb across a rusted railing and, steering Noralee along two narrow planks, with ringing voice commenced to sing:

"A mighty fortress is our God—"

When he did that, all her worries fell away. The dread of disapproval melted. Lutheran or not, he was a pious man; he knew the hymns; the deacons would not be aghast.

"—a bulwark never failing—" boomed Doctorjay, as loudly as he could, thus warding off the hazards of America.

She started beaming radiantly, as though she owned a factory of beams.

"Our helper He, amid the flood, of mortal ills prevailing," sang Noralee, in harmony, thus nullifying Satan's plots.

"For still our ancient foe
doth seek to work us woe—"

Their voices became magnets. The fellow passengers joined in. They formed a circle all around her and the Lutheran: the Lord must have His bidding:

"The prince of darkness grim,
We tremble not for him.
His rage we can endure,
for lo, his doom is sure:
One little word shall fell him."

Ah, but how good it felt to sing that ancient song, united, to a voice! Their voices blended swiftly and rose straight to the clouds.

"That word above all earthly powers,
No thanks to them, abideth.

The Spirit and the gifts are ours
Through Him who with us sideth."

It would take many hymns, they knew. It would take grit. Endurance. Vigor. It would take vigilance.

"Let goods and kindred go,
This mortal life also.
The body they may kill;
God's truth abideth still—
His kingdom is for-ehe-he-ver!"

It would take stamina to cling together as an ethnic group amid the Witches' Sabbath that whirled around them now, while somewhere, in the distance, there played a Russian *balalaika*.

How odd it was to speak and not be understood!

The new arrivals peered about them timidly but nonetheless with curious glances. The city swarmed with Yiddish-speaking characters—as many as hairs on a dog—with beards like bee-hives, prominent noses, their gestures unrestrained.

Two foppish men swung hips as though they were mere women.

A panhandler feigned a decided limp.

A slut leaned haughtily against a post and courted customers.

They stood and struggled to believe. No manners in America? No Cossacks to keep order?

Life here seemed raw and crude. They felt a lively horror. No doubt the law was broad! The people pushed and shoved. The glut of ash cans cluttered all the sidewalks, overflowing. Where could you cut a broom to sweep? How could you counteract the lure of the forbidden?

The Russian-German immigrants side-stepped the city's refuse by going single-file, one close on the heels of another, while choraling their antidotes:

"Did we in our own strength confide,
Our striving would be losing;
Were not the right man on our side,
The man of God's own choosing."

"Dost ask who that may be?
Christ Jesus, it is He.
Lord Sabaoth His name,
From age to age the same,
And He must win the ba-ha-hattle."

Thus were the ethnic demarcation lines drawn early. They were uncompromising, even then—even a man like Doctorjay, a field hand only yesterday who, nonetheless, stood firmly in his *schlorren,* who had arrived, his need for land an exclamation mark, who was a Lutheran and would remain a Lutheran despite ten dozen well-planned sieges in coming years by both his wife and the persistent Brethren deacons. All knew that it would take the Narrow Path. The Ancient Faith. The stubborn conduct taken in with mother's milk and sculpted carefully by timeless generations.

"—and though this world with devils filled,
Should threaten to undo us,
We will not fear, for God hath willed
His truth to triumph through us—"

"Look! Look!" squealed Little Melly.

"It's just a Negro, kid." The customs official spoke kindly. "He really won't do you no harm."

"He's black! He's black as the night!" shrieked the child.

"A skin disorder," the all-knowing bonesetter said.

Little Melly ran howling for cover.

Chapter 12

The Santa Fe agents, furtive men with speedy tongues, had promised Nicky through the scouts while still at Apanlee: "Cheap acres. Free homes. Free passes to buyers of land." Loudly had they praised this stretch of land and that, while Nicky sat, entranced, believing every word. "A fortune can be earned," these men had bragged, about them the fumes of tobacco, "with hard work, diligence and thrift."

A bait it was—this claim of milk and honey!

Now they were long gone, and so was Lizzy's money; she had only two dollars left, in a jar. Here she sat, on a dented pail, in the middle of a pancake land so level that her glance could not attach to anything—afloat in a sea made of weeds.

"What will the future hold? Why did we come?" She gasped with agitation.

"To seek a new life, Mother," said Jan, and gently stroked her knee. "To break the prairie sod."

Unbidden tears collected in her nose. "A life of toil and trouble."

She started pouring out her woes; of them, there was no end. She needed a hatchet, a spade and a hoe. She had none. No field hand. No credit. When the creaking of the cartwheels died away, she was left in a rickety, ramshackle hut.

"We'll make it. Don't you fret."

She saw nothing but high reeds and sky. The grass was a layer of felt. A man whose name was Donoghue—a crook with an elastic conscience!—had traded his debts in exchange for the roof that was hers now, but did her no good; it sagged like an old mattress in the middle, and it already needing thatching.

"Yes, Mother." Jan dug his toes into the soil. "But look at it this way: Once it starts raining—and it will!—the weeding will be easy. No stones to cart away."

"A thief! Took to his heels," she said to her son, suppressing her panic. "Before I had a chance to think it over and tell him that I changed my mind—before I said, we'll turn around; to-morrow we'll go back—"

"We can't go back. We've come to stay. We'll do the best we can."

She dropped her head. "But how will we survive?"

It was a shack, no more, this edifice she must call home—just walls of sod, with spiders everywhere, and cracks in every corner. Scraggly doves had flown in through a broken window, nesting inside, leaving messes on the sills.

"In Wichita they pay a nickel for a gopher's tail. I've already set five traps. That's going to give us some cash. We'll buy a dozen chickens. they can feed on the bugs in the grass."

"Once we have chickens —"

"—why, we'll have eggs."

"And once we have eggs—"

"—we'll trade them for money."

"And once we have money—"

"I'll buy you a cow."

A cow? She tried to smile, but her heart was a boulder—a boulder the size of a mountain. At Apanlee, she could have called a hundred cows her own and never given it a thought. No one had ever claimed she was a lavish dreamer—but this? One cow? One single gloomy cow?

"The fattest cow around, Mama."

She longed to pull him to her bosom but knew it was too late. His childhood, too, went overboard that dark and stormy night. She thought her heart would break as she beheld his future. Behind a broken kitchen window, nothing lay but little drifts of brittle leaves—nothing but a home for foxes, badgers, prairie hens and meadow larks! This place was to harbor her kin? A wretched sod house, dug down several feet, windows flush against the soil? Could this ever be a home, thin-walled, smelly, drafty, naught but old newspapers to stick in the cracks?

Her voice gave way. "No end to empty space—"

"We'll make it, Mama. Be assured."

"We cannot even buy a spade—"

"In ten years' time," her son said, guessing at her thoughts, "you'll have five hundred cows."

"But how—"

"I'll find a way. I heard talk of miracle reapers this morning." His forearms were covered with scratches. "A mere few years, Mama. That's all we need. You'll see."

She said with a small sob: "No streets. No lights. No borders."

The wind blew with fat cheeks and swept debris around the house. It tore open the door and whirled some shreds of paper she had stuck in the cracks. She flinched as if struck in the face.

"Let's call it Mennotown—" He knelt at her knees and took her fingertips with gentle hands. "It's the end of autumn. Everything looks desolate. It will be different once spring is here again." He spoke comfortingly: "Sunflowers grow the length of the Santa Fe trail—"

"Dry and barren. Desolate."

"Rich land. Good soil. Wheat sells for fifty cents a bushel. I dug three feet and found no change in moisture. We'll use the rails to beat out and sharpen our plows."

"Nary a forsaken soul for many miles on end."

"No gossip," her son said, suppressing a small smile. "No quarrelsome neighbors. Not counting Noralee."

She could not have enough of his young confidence. "We'll be so lonely here—"

"They'll come. You'll see. They'll flock to us as if we lived at Apanlee. We talked about it yesterday, the other men and I. We'll help each other clean the harvests. From birth to burial, Mama, you know that a farmer always has friends."

She glanced at her son as he knelt before her, looking set and stubborn and resilient in his rugged pants and wooden shoes. She saw it suddenly, the uncanny likeness.

"Your jaw. Your eyes. You look like your grandfather Peet."

Tears filled her own and blurred her vision. She could have stayed at Apanlee. She thought her heart would stop, remembering the ready wealth of Apanlee. Yet even then she knew: the die was cast. The Lord's work must continue. With Peet's and Greta's children's children it would continue, on and on, and with their children's children. She fell silent, thinking of the man whose eyes and deeds still dominated Apanlee. She tried to hide that she was crying, but he saw.

"You have your prayers. You have your ancient hymnbook, Mama, that Uncle Benny gave you—"

Yes, that she did. God's promises were with her still, the German sounds bound in the finest Russian leather, lying atop her precious crate of wheat.

"This is your country now," she said, and dutifully dried her tears. "For your birthday next Sunday, I give you this land—" A mother's heart must break that she had nothing else to give him. She was flushing with painful surrender. "You will be an American," she said, to add a tiny pittance more.

"I thank you, Mother," said the boy. "I'll put your chest of drawers in the middle, between those two small windows over there—"

"Not yet—" A mother's heart might break: the work must still be done. "Where is my gunny sack? Let me gather some buffalo chips for a fire—"

Life must go on. The seasons would rotate. She took a trembling breath. In a shy gesture, she folded her hands on her belly. She was already making plans. She would ask Doctorjay to help her make a cradle from a packing box, for she hoped fervently that this new baby, Nicky's last, born to this waste and stretch of misery not found on any map, would be a child of golden hair and clear blue eyes and dimples in both buttocks.

The story is told of difficult days, wearisome days—of living on the margin.

And yet. A bygone world—the simple warmth of those pioneer years! You hoped for better times much as you hoped for kindness from the seasons—but meanwhile, you made sure. Your homestead—bare and poor, but clean! Your lifestyle—stainless likewise.

Blessed were those days when life was stark but orderly and those who sowed with tears—as Lizzy did in the beginning, though not for long; she came of hardy stock!—knew they would reap with joy.

The harvests brought together strangers and made them loyal friends. Lizzy's gates creaked back and forth as people came to visit from afar. Both she and Noralee vied for congenial neighbors and courted them with zwieback—the Friesens, the Ensens, the Reimers, the Dycks—all bringing their spindles, their grandfather clocks, all clutching their boxes and bedding, settling around them on farms with good soil.

They all were remarkable people.

In the decade to come, thousands arrived in their eddying throngs, to lay claim to the warmth that was Kansas. They came in pious droves, driving off the Indians, settling firmly with their wooden spoons and samovars and Bibles.

"A haughty, stubborn sect," wrote the *Emporia Gazette*, "have set their faces westwards." The locomotives slipped and stalled on locusts; the pious creed moved on. By midnight, the locusts were gone; the pioneers would stay.

Proud children of pioneer stock, their skirts and their trousers

un-ironed, their voices blending well, they all flocked to the promised land, and where they settled, one by one, they multiplied
and prospered. They staked their land claims, side by side, thus
forging ever stronger kinship ties that bound them more firmly
than wheat twine.

They dug a hole and sniffed the soil and crumbled it between
their fingers. They drew their lots out of a pail and settled in
their little villages, made of adobe blocks and twigs. Abhorring
war, they all made sure their children would do likewise. They
promised they would rotate crops as they had done in Russia.

"Let's watch," wrote the *Emporia Gazette*, "how they give
our prairie a dressing of wheat—"

"Fat soil," they said. "We'll work like ants and bees."

But no one was deceived. It was a bleak beginning yet, somehow, life went on.

"It's time to plow," said Jan. "Before we do, let's bow our
heads and pray." Jan was the kind that saw God face to face, the
kind who plucked His beard. Strong prayers would force rain. If
rain delayed, the fault was in the prayers.

"Yes. Let's."

Conversing with the Lord, by contrast, was balmy ritual for
Lizzy, the wellspring of renewal, not needing further thought.

Her Faith was the ritualized Faith of her clan.

"He maketh lightning for the rain," she read each evening.
"He bringeth wind out of his treasuries. Meanwhile, we are what
we are. We do what we can."

She stood within a wondrous spell, with her confinement
drawing near. Her son was ever at her side and ever within call.

She was of the old school, resisting hardship with proper deportment. Though she could barely walk, she pushed her shoulder to the wheel and shoved, like everybody else. She would let
no one know that still, at night, she lay awake, crying softly to
herself while dreaming of the safe and warm world known as
Apanlee, hidden from view, as though in perpetual haze.

"Fat awns, the size of my finger," Jan told his mother confidently. "I bet you. You'll see. I dreamed of a bountiful harvest last night."

"I dreamed about it, too," said Lizzy loyally. "A sea of rolling wheat."

"He'll send us rain. You'll see."

"He will," she echoed faithfully. How could the Lord refuse? Why, with an outstretched arm, He would bless Nicky's wheat and help Jan bind the sheaves.

A dry heat settled on the prairie. The rains refused to come.

The wind blew every cloud past the horizon. The water pump stood sweaty, and still—it did not rain.

Jan's oxen, stubborn beasts of tedious speed, pulled doggedly. His plow tore deep into the earth. His toes sat squarely and possessively within fat strips of broken crust, preparing confidently for his first harvest.

When a belated prairie preacher chanced, his book of devotions pinned under his arm, that was a sign from heaven. Any preacher was seen as a treat—you helped him fortify his voice as he beseeched the Lord to let the seasons march agreeably. The people watched, intrigued and mesmerized, as he climbed eagerly onto a make-shift table so he could better check on how the faithful bowed their heads.

"Thou causeth the grass for the cattle," he shouted.

They helped him chorus to a voice: "Thou bringeth forth fruit from the earth."

The sun burned the buffalo grass to a crisp. The sky hung pale and milky. The wind blew with fat cheeks. And still, it didn't rain.

More prayers, therefore! More!

It took a week and lots of shouting, but in the end, the wails won out. The prayers won the struggle.

The sky dropped down near the earth, a gray, comforting blanket. The bushes stirred. The roosters scurried for cover. Soft, scented drops began to fall. Creeks and rivers filled to overflowing.

"Now strew your wheat, Mama. Like so. One handful in alternate rows."

She threw gold, just as far as she could. For bounty would come, she was sure. It had to come. It was promised to her. This was not just Faith; it was also a matter of logic. If this grain spoiled, there was none to replace it. The only thing between her and disaster was Faith.

Hence, Lizzy filled herself with Faith. She practically ballooned with Faith.

"The worst is surely behind me, Lord?" she prayed. "The rest is up to you?" Blue smoke curled jauntily toward the sky as Lizzy sped her Faith to heaven. Nobody caught her napping.

She kept reminding Him at every opportunity that the price had already been paid when her husband washed into the ocean. Each day was a new test.

She rose early. She watched the sun rise over her hut.

"Let Thy work appear in Thy servants," she prayed. "Establish the work of our hands."

And she was right. Faith saved the seed. The earth shone like a polished rock. Sweet birdsong filled the heavens. After the long-awaited rain, each carefully selected grain struck tender root that week. She watched how Nicky's grain broke sod with green and pointed tips.

Chapter 13

By late summer, the grain stood so high that it brushed across Jan's broadening chest. He glowed with health and strength. He harvested with care. He swung the scythe with careful strokes, then threshed with flails by candlelight while Little Melly watched. She was his loyal shadow. She seldom spoke a word. Jan scooped her up and put her on a bed of straw left over from the threshing.

"Don't wake her, Mom," he said to Lizzy. "She can go home tomorrow."

Already she belonged. He found an extra blanket with which to cover her.

He climbed into the loft. It was awkward to sleep amid spiders and beams, but Jan preferred his solitude; it was no longer proper to share the sleeping quarters with his sisters and his mother as he had done before they reached the plains.

"We're winning. Aren't we?" he called down from above.

"Yes, son," said Lizzy softly. "Good night, dear. We're winning. I dream of double winter window frames."

Her trust in Jan was absolute. She knew that he slept soundly always, a hard day's work cooling and solidifying in his bones, like molten gold.

She didn't sleep as well. For many nights, she tossed and turned. She listened to the Santa Fe that rumbled through the night.

Her neighbor down the winding road, a widower named Herbert Krahn, who owned a pair of oxen, traded a week of help for Lizzy's mending skills so Jan could take the harvest all the way to Wichita.

"Yoo-hoo!" her helpful neighbor yelled.

"Yoo-hoo!" Jan shouted back and laughed and waved his cap.

"Don't be so forward, son," said Lizzy, coloring.

"Mama, he waved at you," was her son's sly reply.

"You are mistaken. Surely."

"He offered help."

"He did?"

"He did."

"I wonder why he did."

"I can't imagine, Mama."

At dusk, when all the work was done, Herbert would often discuss the odd, fickle weather with Jan. His thoughts were slow but thorough. Words fell between long, awkward pauses. He had huge hands, a ruddy face, a tranquil personality. "If all you need is extra help, just ask," he offered, avoiding Lizzy's eyes.

"He offered help," Jan said, when yet another week was gone. "Did you notice the twine where buttons should have been?"

"You say he offered help?"

"He did. He surely did."

"How did he say it? Be specific."

"He spoke in generalities. He said he would be glad to help."

"Well, if he did, he did."

"That's right, he did," said Jan, and said no more, knowing when to keep his counsel.

Herbert came to mend a pail. He came to bring a greeting from someone who passed by. Soon, he found several additional excuses.

"I praise your charitable qualities," said Herbert shyly, meaning Lizzy, watching Jan.

When a prairie fox sneaked into Lizzy's chicken coop, she wept with anger and vexation while picking the bloody feathers up off the floor. That was the night when Herbert sat up, stealthily—all through the night! a second and a third!—and caught the thief, just as she knew he would. Barehanded, he throttled the fox, proudly handing Lizzy the carcass while wiping his hands on his trousers.

She flung it in the bushes and wiped her hands and laughed.

"No family?" she asked.

"All grown," said Herbert slowly. "All grown, and farming east and north."

He sat and watched an ant. She joined him on the steps. He puffed his pipe. She offered he could stay for dinner. He helped with this and that, avoiding Lizzy's eyes.

Herbert was a model citizen. If someone needed help, his name was on all lips. The dogs rushed out to greet him.

She urged him on at every opportunity: "Eat. Eat. Now eat before that dish gets cold and loses all its flavor."

In gratitude, he fixed her broken water pump and made it good as new.

Soon, she grew used to him. He sharpened hoes and fixed a spade and dug deep holes to plant some trees to give her added shade.

Thanks to his ingenuity, she owned six tripod chairs, a bench, a table, and a rack for seven pots and pans. She was the envy of her neighbors.

"Your peppernuts. Magnificent," said Herbert.

"It wasn't my own recipe." She spoke with downcast lashes. "I borrowed it. That's all."

"Well. All the same. They're excellent."

If she as much as turned around, he laid on lavish praise. That made her beam. Yes, she stood proud. Proud and accomplished, that was Lizzy. Her walls soon glistened with white paint. Her floors were laid with packed mud, mixed with enough chopped straw as binder, then sprinkled with water, swept three times a day. She had a home now, poor but clean. Less and less, she thought of Apanlee.

Such love as came to her and Herbert Krahn while doing virgin homesteading came gently. It felt like a hummingbird's wing. She barely noticed it.

"It is too soon," said Lizzy to her son who wrestled with the sheaves and gave her pensive looks. Her heart was quiet, embedded in ashes; it cried out not for Herbert as it cried out for Nicky, who was dead.

"Marriage to a good and honest man," said her expedient sister, borrowing her words as though she still sat next to Uncle Benny, "is like a fanciful daguerreotype inserted in a frame."

Lizzy tried to hide her feelings from her sister, but in her heart she knew: she needed Herbert Krahn. He needed Lizzy Neufeld. Why not? she asked herself.

She asked around. The things she learned were heartening.

He was a careful penny-pincher, his debts already paid. He was a good, kind, helpful man; he would make an excellent father. Jan needed help—he liked Herb; Herb liked the boy. Jan planned a new barn at a sharp angle to the house, just like the barn at Apanlee. "What do you think?" asked Jan.

"I think you ought to use the lumber from the Santa Fe," said Herbert. At every opportunity, he gave advice and counsel. There was goodwill between them. The girls were girls—too young to have an opinion.

As often as was needed, Herb lent a helping hand. He was as peaceful as a vessel that rode at anchor at a port. Together, he and Jan made many detailed sketches. They talked of this and that.

Much work was waiting to be done. Next week, the plan was to start stacking sheaves. Then came the threshing. Next came the sacking of the grain—most destined for the mills in Wichita, a little kept back for the horses.

Lizzy pushed on forward: there was no denying the obvious. Everything she saw and all she checked confirmed the wisdom of her course. She needed a man to honor and obey. He needed a wife. A wife was the crown of her husband.

As soon as Noralee surmised what Lizzy contemplated, she barely smothered several piercing shrieks—she was that jubilant.

"It is too soon," begged Lizzy, scarlet. "Hold back on gossip, please."

Noralee's eyes opened wide with the excitement of it all. "It's never too soon, Lizzy! Never!"

"Oh, hush," said Lizzy. "What are you saying? Whatever do you mean?"

"I saw you pat his horse."

"I stroked a fly away. That's all. Please. Mention that to no one."

Not in the least was her sister deceived. "There's Greta Unruh waiting. She has her eye on him."

"Greta? No! You must be mistaken. Not Greta! Surely not!"

"You draw your own conclusions."

Lizzy might as well have tried to stop a mountain spring, for Noralee, brimful and practically propelled with joyful tidings, could hold still no longer. She ran to tell Greta. Then Neta. Next Holly. And Susie and Katie and Nan.

Lizzy sat, guiltily peeling potatoes. Caution was called for. If she wasn't careful, she might become fodder for gossips to feast on for weeks!

The neighborhood watched with approval as Herbert's eyes kept searching for Lizzy as she moved carefully from field to field. She kept her skirt tucked up above her ankles so she could reap with ease. The smell of prairie honey clung to her. Her plaits hung down her back. His heart rolled in his chest as if on tiny bearings.

Unspoken hope was in the air. She moved sedately within his thoughtful glance. She knew she could depend on Herb to do exactly what was right, to think precisely what was proper.

And she was right; he looked at her and knew: "As soon as she has given birth, she will be slender as a girl."

She tucked her blouse around her waist. She gathered strings of twine and started tying sheaves, thirty bundles to a stook. Jan proudly led the horses. The girls brought up the rear.

"Why are you watching me like that?" she whispered, agonized.

Her spine was fire; her lids felt dry and hot. She took off her scarf and wiped her sweaty brow. The wind played with small wisps of hair, and Herbert saw, and Herbert flushed.

"I'm sorry. Truly sorry."

"Why don't you stay for supper? I'll treat you to some boiled potatoes."

Next time he came to visit, he came an hour early—his beard combed out, clad in his Sunday best.

"Just passing by," he told her awkwardly.

She was busily weeding her pumpkins. "You're welcome anytime," she said. Without looking at him, she gave him her hand. He held it in his own as though her hand was made of porcelain.

He squeezed her fingers carefully. "Your pole beans, in flower already?"

"I guess they are," said Lizzy.

She did not even know, at first, that what she felt was love. The love she had once shared with Nicky had been like glowing metal pouring from a smelter. This, here and now, was different. Calm. It didn't blur her vision.

Jan was as good as his word. His very first harvest bought

Lizzy a cow. She was a splendid beast. Her name was Caroline.

Caroline arrived one foggy morning on a long, frayed rope. She settled placidly into the meadow by the river, where Doctorjay's brown mare grazed with her filly, but only after Jan pulled her for applause the length and breadth of Mennotown.

Lizzy put in Caroline her pride. When she beheld the foaming pails, sheer poetry leaped to her mind.

"Now you'll be the hub of everything again," said Noralee, while biting down her envy. It was hard to compete against Lizzy. Her milk buckets gave her prestige.

So what if Lizzy beat the cream into soft butterballs? was Noralee's next thought. She owned six dozen hens, one fatter than the other. She would just concentrate on eggs.

Everything came easier after Caroline. Caroline was special from the start, chewing cud sedately, calving every spring as though she watched the calendar, worth years of milk and butter.

As a result, Lizzy's hospitality exceeded even Apanlee's. She and her wooden bucket became synonymous with popularity. The neighbors would gather each Sunday—all loved to eat and drink. Their waistlines grew bigger and bigger.

Lizzy loved Caroline dearly, and taught her girls to cherish her as well. They always took a crust along before they settled down, with many pealing giggles, to squeeze the surplus milk from Caroline. To milk a cow with nimble fingers was the prerequisite to cross-embroidery. Once cross-embroidery was mastered, next followed shadow-stitch.

"You better grab Herb while you can," said Noralee to Lizzy. Now that she herself was spherical with her own pregnancy, out of the matrimonial race herself—albeit only temporarily!—from the sidelines she looked out for Lizzy.

The grapevine was her specialty. She snooped. She tattled. She busybodied everyone. It was almost a calling; she knew how to fine-tune a rumor.

And nothing so elated Noralee as following up rumors of romance. She knew how to read between lines. She knew when to prick up her ears.

"It's rumored," tattled Noralee, "that Greta plans a thatching breakfast. Draw your conclusions, Lizzy."

Lizzy laughed shrilly at this, for no discernible reason. "Oh, really?"

"Yes. Really. As I said, now is the time to draw your own conclusions."

"When?"

Noralee bristled with zeal and impatience. "I don't know when. What does it matter, Lizzy?"

If there was a romantic claim, why not secure it quickly? With undiminished fervor she, for one, believed in following a lead.

"Why take unnecessary risks?"

"Whatever do you mean?"

"Your roof might need re-thatching," mused Noralee. "Let's see now. Who could help? Could Herbert help? If I were you, I'd ask."

"Not yet," said Lizzy modestly. Noralee kept on wringing her hands.

When the first pig was fattened to the point of bursting, Jan told his mother slyly: "Look at that cat washing its face—"

Lizzy colored gently. "Steps creak when stepped upon—"

"Before the week is out, there will be a surprise—"

She busied herself with a broom. She swept the floors three times a day. She dusted all the sills. She scrubbed the threshold thrice, although rain fell outside. She felt so restive lately she could not sit or stand.

When she saw Herbert coming, she rushed to fetch a cup. "Here, Herbert. Drink. A cup of coffee first. To fortify yourself."

He started stepping up his praise: "Fine coffee, Lizzy. Milky. Hot. Magnificent."

She looked at him and thought: "The length and width of Kansas, there is no kinder man."

He shifted awkwardly. She blushed a pretty pink.

"Ground wheat," she whispered, out of breath. "I roasted it just so."

That gave him confidence. "I better start." With measured movements, he took the lantern from the hook. "Where is the knife?"

Her face went white with tension. This was the part she dreaded most. She said, a quiver in her voice: "Right there. Right on that shelf. Jan took it to the rails and sharpened it for you."

"Well, then," said he. "It must be done."

"What must be done," said Lizzy, bravely, "must be done."

The pig was ripe. The pig must go. She knew the procedure: a heavy blow to dull the pain, the piercing blade into the throat, the bleeding off into the sand, the gurgling of the dying creature. She had no choice. Jan was too young. Here was a man to do the task. Why not?

With whitened knuckles, she listened to the desperate squealing. There! It was over! Praise the Lord!

She stepped forward eagerly. She took one leg, and Herbert took one leg. "*Hau ruck!* "

Together, she and Herbert dragged the carcass from the bloody puddle closer to the scalding water for the scraping of the hair. She helped him lift it up: "*Hau ruck! Hau ruck!*"

Her cheeks caught fire as her hand brushed against Herbert's fingers.

"A splendid beast," said he.

She bit her lip. She helped him fasten hind ends to the rafters. No longer something that had lived; it was a white and naked chunk of pork.

She stood there, watching with possessive pride, as Herbert disemboweled the unlucky pig with a clean sweep of blade. Warm and slippery and steaming, the entrails tumbled out. She stepped up with a bucket and caught them with quick expertise, while Herbert started carving down the spine with effortless, masterly strokes.

By noon, the carcass was cut up, the fat trimmed away to the bone. Curled sausages rested in buckets. Noralee let the casings slip expertly through her fingers, trading knowing glances with her neighbor, Greta Unruh. Greta was related to the Quirings and the Edigers who lived just to the north of Hillsboro.

"We'll have a wedding soon," predicted Noralee with glee. "Poor Greta! Not a chance." As she pierced every sausage with a sharp, long darning needle, she kept watching Lizzy from the corner of her eye.

"You said it. Greta looks defeated."

"Look. Now she sprinkles salt. And he is sprinkling pepper."

"So what?" poor Greta said. She came of hardy stock. She knew the value of self-discipline, and kept her hurt in check. She did her best to cook these spare ribs to a crisp, while straining hard to catch the salient gossip.

"Watch Herbert help her. See?" said Noralee, by then beside herself, devoid of any mercy.

"I don't need help," lied Greta, the color of a winter beet. "What's it to me? Spare me your sympathy."

She owned raw, hearty knuckles. She dove her arms into the ground-up meat—dove into it, up to her elbows.

"Here, let me help you," Herb said to Lizzy, his fingers in a pot of axle grease. He rubbed the healing ointment deep into her skin, while stroking finger after finger. They stood alone, behind a tree. He spoke the most romantic sentence of his life.

"Here I am, dearest Lizzy. Swaying between hopes and fears."

She read the words that never crossed his lips. She said with lowered lashes: "I have four children, Herbert. I owe two hundred dollars to the Santa Fe."

"A company of patience and of pity."

"And that's not all. Additionally, I owe—" Cold perspiration collected in her arm pits as she remembered all her pressing obligations. A quarter still to Doctorjay, for a sprain that he treated in May. Two dollars to the grocer—three months now overdue. A dollar-fifty in part payment for the lumber bought to finish the new chicken coop. Four dollars for the barrister in Wichita who told her she had better notarize the paper giving her the title to her homestead, lest the dishonest man came back.

"I have an extra mare," said Herbert, crimson, rubbing hard. "I'll offer it in payment. A chance. That's all I need. A chance."

He did not say but knew: "I know your heart as if it were my own. You love me not, you think? What's love?"

She thought: "What's love? A mushroom might grow overnight. A tree takes many summers."

He asked her while the neighbors processed the pig's heart and liver: "Do you consent to be my wife? I would be deeply honored."

That was the key. Those were the words. She took a deep and trembling breath and said without a quiver: "Yes. I do."

At lunch, beneath the makeshift tent, he sat to Lizzy's left. She took his cup in broiling daylight, and filled it to the brim.

She felt at peace. That was as good as love. She did not ask herself if she could make him happy. She knew that she would smother him with kindness and devotion, and he would make himself happy indeed.

When Doctorjay arrived for supper, dangling a lantern, bringing with him half a dozen unexpected but highly welcome visitors to help him celebrate the slaughter of a pig—why, it was crystal clear to all that love had taken hold. By the time the hams hung proudly in the rafters, a wedding date was firmly set.

"We knew it all along," triumphed Noralee.

And she was right. They knew. They were entwining with the soil; they had a homestead now. Their children and their children's children would once again live flush with God's good earth, if only they followed the rules. By the sheen of the sunsets they knew, and by the golden summer rays that played in dappled leaves before the sun slid back into the sod they had resolved to call their own. They knew as all good people know that life's deep joys are tiny to the eye but mighty to the heart. Why, by the sight of swinging sausages they knew!

Chapter 14

When Noralee arrived on her bare plot of land with two old, tired horses, a cart of broken household goods and half a dozen weeping children, not one of them her own, all fever-shot and raw of voice, she was not yet thirty years old.

"I still need an axe, a hammer, a hatchet," she bawled.

"I have a wagon, a plow, a harrow, a hayrake," he offered.

He came to her aid in the dark of the night with a flickering kerosene lamp.

"A poisonous germ," he said, and scratched himself with all five fingers. He brushed the children's throats with turpentine, a tearful and retching endeavor. He smoked out her hut to forestall contagion. She rubbed her cheek against his sleeve. He asked to stay and stoke the fire. They talked of this and that.

He would want children of his own. She had some mileage left. How many years? She double-checked by counting on his fingers. Ten, surely. Twelve? If all went well, fifteen?

"But marriage first," she said to him. "That's it." By then, it was a game.

Before that year flew by and sank into eternity, she lost two young ones to diphtheria. A third succumbed to whooping cough before the frosts arrived to freeze the toxic germ.

This freed her to view Doctorjay from a brand new perspective. Though still of a mistaken Faith, he was respected in the neighborhood. She knew she could rely far more on Doctorjay than ever she had leaned on Jacob, who was now with the Lord Almighty, safely, in a gold-embroidered robe.

"Three little graves," she sighed, "amid the space and vastness of the land, with the cold winds blowing over them and life still going on?"

His thoughts proceeded independently.

Surveillance was her specialty. Doctorjay wasn't exactly the Sheik of Araby—his eyebrows met smack in the middle. His teeth had a gap to the left. But, not to be forgotten, his chest was firm and broad. His need was palpable. Her family was cut in half; she felt saddened as well as relieved.

"As slow and shuffling as his father!" screamed Noralee as loudly as she could; tomorrow she would practice her restraint. She made the most of the occasion, knowing well that Doctorjay stood sentry, outside, in the wind.

Lizzy shushed her birthing sibling soothingly—she was here for as long as was needed, to speak her share of prayers and help mop up the blood.

"Just take it easy! Take it easy!" pleaded Lizzy, drawing on her ingenuity. "Here. Sit between two tripod chairs."

Dewey Epp was slow to come into the world; he kept his mother up for nights on end with his appalling indecision before he finally appeared, his meager buttocks first.

"Well, there you have it. A born preacher!" observed the hardy healer when finally allowed inside. "Already he's wrinkling his nose." He checked the newborn's fingers. He checked the newborn's toes.

"I predict he'll make a Christian out of you," hissed a triumphant Noralee, recovering her breath.

"I doubt that. Given that he looks like Rumpelstilzkin,"

Doctorjay laughed with good humor, then bent to her and tickled her a bit. "Just get a good night's rest." Walking home that night as though his path were mined, he waved his flask, elated, at the clouds.

By then, the sparrows chirped it from the roof: as soon as Doctorjay was mentioned, the deacon widow's heart leaped—just like a brazen lark.

She kept inviting him to chicken fries as often as she could. She liked him well enough and said so openly. It was late October; a chill was in the air; the fire in the hearth was blazing.

"Now, everybody! Elbows off the table!" she hollered.

She let him know she would not let her children grow like savages. If thereby Doctorjay learned some decorum accidentally—why, that was fine with her. They even sang duets together—sad, melancholy songs such as the Cossacks sang in Russia.

"Oh, it is cold! It's blowing cold!" they sang and snuggled by the fire. He struck the tuning fork and held it to his ear, expertly sounding out the pitch. She stood in awe of his resonant voice.

Life was, for Noralee, sheer poetry.

She watched him struggle through the snowdrifts to get to her with remedies when little Dewey suffered from a stubborn bout of diarrhea. He kept on dunking Dewey in the tub to clean him up as if the baby were an apple. He stayed all afternoon and far into the night. He had a lusty streak. He begged, cajoled and pleaded, but Noralee said *nyet*.

This time around, she held the hand. She held onto her currency. More yet, she made it last. She was no mealy-mouth. What else might she have done, a woman, still young and reasonably pretty, all alone? She had it from reliable authority that Doctorjay was still an untried bachelor.

Each Saturday night, Doctorjay hitched up his mare and came clop-clopping up to her door. He could have just as easily walked, but he strove to impress Noralee.

She kept the coffee pot warm. She smothered him with hospitality. She liked him; therefore, she fed him.

He stacked corn husks for her, wall to wall and floor to ceiling. He helped her rule her brood with slaps and hollering. He carried in buckets of snow to melt on the sputtering stove while she prepared the tub.

"I'm not buying the pig in the burlap," he told her.

She placed her cheeks into her pudgy fingers. "Here as there," she let him know, "the safe road to success is paved with proper modesty."

He laughed, not in the least deceived.

So let him laugh; she knew she had the upper hand. She was resolved that he would lead her to the altar just like an ass hitched to her bridle. Let him not think that was unnatural.

A baby was a baby, but not all babies were alike; the newborn had pinched lips and gently flaring nostrils. It was jaundiced, tormented by gas. It had his father's narrow chest, regrettably, but it was far from docile. It spit and choked and burped.

The next time Doctorjay came visiting, together they took stock: she owned a cow; he had an eager bull. She owned a flail; he had a brand new harrow. He owned an extra team of horses and a stack of building lumber; she matched that with an idle cousin she could borrow for a fortnight from up north to help set up a shack. They say there is a lid to every pot. They matched up perfectly.

She went to work expertly.

His Sunday trouser legs had too much slack; she was a whiz at thread and needle. So eager for her flesh was he, she could afford to tease. She scorned all undergarments; that was strategy and practical besides.

"It's not as though you have the manners of a clerk," she told him more than once. "What is that bulging from your pocket? Is that your flask? Again?"

He looked at her approvingly—a female with a healthy appetite and no imaginary ailings. He piled a few additional logs. "I put it to you, Noralee: it'll give you a new lease on life."

"I go so far, no farther," she told him. She could afford to wait. She wasn't caught, this time around, as she had been with Jacob, between the Devil and the deep.

She was robust; he, too. She saw no need to hide from Doctorjay the chipped, enameled chamberpot that she had brought along from Russia. She had to pee; he didn't leave; why fuss? The choice boiled down to chamberpot or outhouse; the snow outside piled four feet high; and Noralee was Noralee.

"Just turn around," she told him, giggling. "And close your eyes and ears." Why not be practical? She pulled the curtains, told Doctorjay to hum a tune, and settled down majestically to obey nature's call.

So it went through the winter. She could not wait to find out everything she missed about the mysteries of sex as Jacob's wife, but still she savored the pursuit.

Doctorjay was a fanciful suitor. When he surveyed her neck or earlobe, goose pimples rose in unexpected places. She reveled in the luxury of power. She read him like an open book, and what she read, right from the start, was better left unsaid.

His need was as old as the Gospel; she was determined to proceed to matrimonial rectitude the proper way this time.

Yet the outcome was never in doubt. She hugged the infant Dewey to her bosom and told her suitor, coyly: "The treasure beyond price is now my highest currency."

"The baby? Still in pain?" the bonesetter inquired.

"Yes. Still in pain. In great pain. A rash formed on his bottom."

"Well. Let me see. And you? What you need, Noralee, is someone to replace your husband."

He was the first who made a solid shift to English.

She tried to be his equal there as well, defecting from the German tongue. "Yes. Life goes on. The sun comes up. A new day starts. Poor Jacob, as I always say. Flat in the earth. Forgotten."

They looked at each other, suppressing smiles. He found in her eyes what he sought. She knew he made good money.

"Come here," he told her boldly. "By now, you should be hitched."

"You should be, too. To an obedient wife."

"Whatever for?" he teased.

"It's a democracy," said Noralee. "That's why."

"Look. Lots of snow outside," said Noralee, inventively, searching for dampness amid Dewey's diapers.

He offered an opinion: snow could be either shoveled or endured.

Yes, said the widow. That was true.

"A dog is barking. Listen," he added, hopefully.

"It makes you scared to think that we are all alone."

He shifted in his seat, his blue eyes small and merry. "It's lonely, isn't it?"

"You can say that again."

"Come here," he said. "Sit by my side. Sit down by my side, Noralee. Put your two feet on this fine brick I warmed especially for you—or, better yet, right in my lap. There's something we have to discuss."

Sharp joy came in a rush. His appetite was palpable. He would not run away.

"I know all your wishes," she teased. She watched him with attentive eyes. She wasn't blind; he had his faults. But so did she; was anybody perfect? What might he say if he found out that she had burned her Sunday meal? Would he back out if he knew that?

Could be.

With certain things, you stood on quaking ground. She had her fears. She knew that there were ups and downs to almost any marriage.

"Such as?"

She studied him with speculative eyes. This man was popular with everyone: praiseworthy, handsome and robust; nature had been generous. He even held the door for her and let her walk through first. Some people claimed he drank too much, especially on holidays, but so what if he tippled a bit?

And finally, there was the matter of her age. She could practically mother the lad. She came of hardy stock, however; her relatives lived far into the nineties.

"No matter," she decided. Together, they would have their good times and their bad, and she would put a premium on obedience.

Her admiration grew.

The things that Doctorjay could do with herbs; the talent that he had with blisters! In whispers, she filled Lizzy in. Both lost themselves in reveries.

"All but—" said Noralee, while smiling wickedly.

"Oh, that," said Lizzy, squirming, "is understood, of course. He knows that. Doesn't he?"

Well, touch and go, said Noralee, while filling Lizzy in.

Once, when by accident she slipped and dislocated her left ankle, who else but Doctorjay came to her help at once? He was the one who grabbed it, boldly! twisted it, and plunk! the bone slid back into its socket.

"He asked me then and there to just up and surrender my youth."

Lizzy's eyes opened wide: "No! Then and there? Why, Noralee! The outrage!"

"Believe it or not. 'No bill,' said the brute! 'Just a smack on my whiskers. Right on my schmoozer here!'"

"All men are wolves," shuddered Lizzy. The talk confirmed her worst suspicions. But on the other hand, what choice?

"So, yes or no? Did you?"

"Right on his schmoozer."

"No!"

"So?"

"You didn't! Oh, my God!"

"Was there a choice?"

"You had no choice," admitted Lizzy, a pragmatic female. "What might have been the end result, had you gone on to find yourself a haughty doctor practicing in Wichita?"

" A stiff cast and an inflated—"

"—and an inflated bill, that's what!"

"That's right! That's what!" Noralee felt giddy with triumph. "There's only one small problem."

"What's that?"

"See, everything, to him, is like a great, big—"

Lizzy tried hard to catch up with her knitting. "Yes. Hush!" She blushed the color of a strawberry. "It comes with being Lutheran," she whispered.

"—just like a great big carnival."

Silence came after that shocking remark. Next followed some eloquent sighs. There was a price to pay, both knew. When passion struck, what might a Lutheran do?

The widow whispered into Lizzy's ear that she, for one, had every premonition.

"Feed him a gherkin on the sly," advised her sister, mortified. Might Doctorjay insist on making love with the bright sun still hanging in the sky?

One windy afternoon, Doctorjay caught a convenient ride to Wichita and came back with a funny contraption. He called it a velocipede.

"What in the world?" shrieked Noralee. Her eyes just popped; the cat absconded with her tongue. "Why, Doctorjay! What's that? You? Living in the lap of luxury? What's gotten into you!"

"Getting worldly! Getting worldly! " shouted he, pedaling around her thrice before proudly pedaling away, balancing precariously, his gunnysack trousers ballooning.

"Wait! Wait!"

"Make up your mind. Remember the pig in the burlap?"

She was so much in love, by then, the power of her limbs deserted her whenever he was near. Her throat felt dry. Her face caught fire. She looked at Doctorjay and pragmatism settled firmly in her bosom. She squared her chin, resolved to brave the Brethren.

"Oh, well," said Noralee. "So what if he's a Lutheran? The world comes to my door."

Chapter 15

A full-time preacher was as rare as velvet in the early pioneering days, and eager couples waiting to be wed bunched up on part-time preachers' calendars like pussywillows on a stem.

"Next weekend," Noralee announced. "It's all planned properly. And Doctorjay is in for a surprise."

Lizzy peered at her determined sister with suspicion. "But don't you think you better tell him, too?"

The widow blew her nose with sentiment. "He'll find out soon enough."

By then, the winter days were past; the world was carpeted with green; her grief for Jacob's little ones now resting on a hill had all but dissipated. "He won't say no, unless there's water on his brain."

"You aren't rushing things, are you?" asked Herbert laughingly.

She closed her eyes, luxuriating. "Naw! He means business. That I know."

She had rehearsed already. The rest was mere formality.

The splendid double wedding set the trend for many years to come.

The neighborhood women had whitewashed the sod walls with ashes and garnished the gables with wreaths. The backdrop, poor though they were, looked all but palatial, and Herbert plain outdid himself to make sure Lizzy had the spotlight she deserved.

Dozens of close kin attended the festivity, as did the lesser relatives, among them Herbert's father's sister's bedfast wife, one foot already planted in the grave, who almost stole the show with stories of her gout.

The Unruhs and the Ewerts and the Harders arrived from up north with their numerous children, all growing like the grass—silent, tall and lush—every one a jovial farmer, reaping five bushels to the acre, though plowing with slow oxen was a chore.

Doctorjay had canvassed the neighborhood, and friends chipped in—with forks, knives, spoons and coffee cups to help feed the visiting throng. The aunts and uncles helped themselves to extra bellyfuls while Noralee ran back and forth from guest to guest:

"Eat. Eat. Now eat before the food gets cold. Don't shame me by eating so little!"

Herbert was so much in love that he threw caution to the wind: he called upon a Methodist who had a clever eye, and arrived with duffle bag and tripod to get the guests to pose in front of Lizzy's home. That picture still exists.

Lizzy stands beside her husband in a festive, borrowed dress. To her right stands Jan with his three spotless sisters; to her left are four of Herbert's sons and daughters, and all of them are smiling. Noralee, imbued with romantic elan of her own, is standing on a milk pail, bringing up the rear, and next to her stands Doctorjay who grins from ear to ear.

And look at Little Melly in that old, faded photograph—and think what might have been!

Little Melly's radiant smile consumes the crumbling picture.

It is a shy yet lustrous smile—a smile that should have been fanned into passion, that could have extinguished all shadows. That long-forgotten day, still captured in an old daguerrotype, proves that she was a comely girl, her hair a lovely shade.

Misfortune came to Little Melly's love. In years to come, she would oft tell a sad and meager story, fumbling ever with that twisted web of circumstances that stole her happiness and set her on the road, against her will, to spinsterhood.

What lay in store for her, nobody present at that double wedding could have guessed. She was too young to read the sheen in Herbert's eyes, the eagerness in Doctorjay's wide grin—but she was practicing already, one can see that, with marriage in mind. Her cheerful smile told Jan: "I'll marry you when I grow up." The picture captured it, that sparkle in her eyes that told the boy as clearly as a bell: "Wherever you will lead, I'll follow you in confidence."

But Jan? In that old, yellowed photograph the artist Methodist produced, Jan looks as though he is merely suppressing a sneeze.

Noralee sniffled noisily throughout the lengthy sermon the borrowed preacher stuttered forth. She cried as hard at weddings as at funerals; she sang as prettily at each, proud of her lovely voice.

She kept a crafty eye on Doctorjay who nearly burst with sentiment. He had uncorked a bottle, from which he quaffed at intervals. So overcome was Doctorjay with rapture and elation that he kept shouting, patriotically: "Hurray! Hurray! Hurray!.," and tried to climb upon a table to get a better view.

"Hats off! Hats off!" he shouted.

He thought he'd go mad with delight. So overcome was he by his own luck and status that he came close, in fact, asking the Brethren for admission then and there. In fact, he stalked them stealthily throughout an afternoon, and far into the night, yet in the end, he still remained a Lutheran, to everyone's regret—he liked his flask too much.

Had Doctorjay converted to the Brethren, it would have pleased the neighborhood. In fact, in later years it would have mightily pleased Dewey—attending the festivity, in diapers still and, hence, too small to preach against the whiskey flag that emanated pungently from Doctorjay's inebriated nostrils. In years to come, when Dewey settled down to be the mouthpiece of the Lord, he had much catching up to do. But on that afternoon, he was an infant still who lay in a potato crate and chewed upon his fingers.

The Lord smiled on America, and Doctorjay smiled back. He loved America! You had your options here. On meeting either friend or foe, they always paid you notice. No matter where you started out, you could end up in any place you chose.

Day after day slipped away. The calendar kept count. The bake sales never stopped.

Here another brand new flour mill. There a grist mill or brick works. Before you knew it, it was time again for everyone to color Easter eggs with onion skin. Then came summer; sooner, fall. Out came the double underwear. The winter relatives came visiting.

You threw your arms around each aunt and uncle—they did the same to you!—and there were hugs and kisses all around.

Winter days—time for relaxing. Winter nights—long, silent and crisp. The Kansas winter winds blew hard. You gossiped and you shared. The talk was of the common things that gladdened everyone. To the right slept the children, to the left slept the cows. Extra visitors climbed up to the loft, and all across the prairie drifted advent carolings as the beloved Christ Child filtered from the trees and right into the hearts of genuine believers.

New Year. It came and went. The relatives departed. You shouted after them: "Be sure to come visit next year! Come earlier, and stay longer!"

The wind whirled dry snow after them.

All that is gone but not forgotten: those things spelled happiness. Now only memories remain of difficult but richly textured times, those early pioneering years: borscht bubbling aromatically in the terrine, crisp gherkins floating in the brine, cow chips piled clear up to the rafters to keep the sod home toasty, no matter how the prairie wind might howl.

The formula was simple. You worked as hard as the seasons demanded and the markets dictated you should.

Life no bed of roses yet, but nobody complained, and certainly not Noralee. Her husband saw to that. If Noralee compared the life that Doctorjay carved out for her to what she left in Russia, she did so at her peril.

Their diligence paid off. Just yesterday, the homes but lone and wind-blown huts; now, homesteads everywhere you looked— dotting the sea of the prairie. Life was no picnic, then or now, but since you had your Lord, your neighborhood, your quilting bee and your expanding family, you had too much to do to waste your time on dreams.

The swallows were returning once again, obeying an internal clock.

The prairie turned to soft greens and blues and sometimes, briefly, emerald and sapphire.

The sunsets changed from gold to red to purple.

Just as the seed kept multiplying, so did the German families. There were many weddings, which tied, with prayer's twine, the past to present and future.

You managed as you could, and if you dreamed at all, you dreamed of coming harvests. The grain lay shimmering beneath the sun. It still took nearly twenty bushels to buy one pair of boots, and that didn't count extra laces.

Some oldsters died. Young fry were born. The chains of love and kin were there to stay, long after each was bedded in his grave.

Doctorjay increased in importance and status and made hefty money besides.

When an infection swelled Jan's face one windy afternoon,

Doctorjay pulled him aside to counsel him at length. "Your wisdom tooth," said he, already fumbling for his pliers. "You do not need it, Jan. A wisdom tooth is useless."

Jan wiped his brow and smiled a sickly smile.

"It must come out."

"Out?"

"Out."

"When?"

"Now."

Doctorjay did not waste time or energy on mercy. "Now, Little Melly, honey, fetch me my bottle from the hay where I have hidden it. Jan, this will hurt. Here, have a swig. Do just exactly as I say. Here is a chair. Hold on."

Jan took a swallow, shook himself and turned a sickly green: "It's awful, Doctorjay."

"A man gets used to it." In full control, he gave his orders like a general, spread-legged in Lizzy's kitchen. If he said "Out!" then out! He had been born a field hand in the old country; here in America, he had advanced to the admired status of a respected medicus.

"Now, Little Melly! Bolt the door behind you and keep it bolted until this lad can walk again. Now, honey! Don't you cry. Don't worry. He'll survive it."

"Don't worry," Jan said, too, his eyes on Little Melly.

Her eyes filled up with ready tears. He touched her heaving shoulders.

"Don't worry. I'll survive it."

She stored that touch. Endearments were scarce. She was a youngster still. She looked at him, and love shone from her eyes. He looked at her and knew: she will grow up into a strong and lovely girl with water-braided hair.

"I will stay here," she squawked. "And shriek."

"All right," said Doctorjay. "So stay. So shriek. But with your back against the door so he can't bolt the kitchen. Just put your fists up to your ears. Now shriek!"

Jan held on tight, his head careening, while Doctorjay reached for his rusty instrument and started pulling hard. Jan slumped while Little Melly shrieked and Lizzy fell into a swoon. Doctorjay stepped over her and told Jan, who sat up and shivered: "Pay up. You owe me a dime and a nickel."

Jan paid with trembling hands—a bargain, all in all.

As Jan became a man and forged his personality, he bought up land that was cheap. His older sisters, one by one, were marrying compliant husbands and settling where the soil was black.

Their families exploded. They needed more room at the table. Jan planted additional crops.

Though he was still a bachelor, he was soon guiding the community in prudent leadership. When Jan turned up his sleeves, that was the sign for everyone: chip in with your time and your money!

He was his community's pride. He served on a dozen committees. With relatives, he never lost his patience. He was a good provider. Lizzy didn't have to watch her pennies, although she always shopped with care. In Wichita, the Hebrew merchants knew her as a fussy customer.

Lizzy's eyes just shone with love and ownership as she watched Jan plow up the Kansas earth. He laid the sod, expertly, without a break in rhythm, into a straight, long furrow to his left. The heritage of Apanlee was clearly in his bones. Had she been a poetic soul, she would have found the words. The hunchback child she left behind might have done that—not Lizzy.

She didn't need a poem, verily! to plumb the mystery of virgin soil that yielded to Jan's plow.

On snowy winter nights, when work slowed down, Lizzy thought of Apanlee at times, as if that period in her youth had been a hazy dream. Now, winter fostered leisure, and leisure fostered oneness and stability the likes of which she, Lizzy, never could have dreamed while living in the lap of luxury at Apanlee. There rich were rich and poor were poor. Here, everyone was equal. She did not grieve her loss. She came of a genuine pioneer stock. This was America.

Thick snowflakes kept on floating from the clouds. She watched how the prairie moon climbed over the snow-laden roof. She listened to the howling of the winter, hoping for some news stray visitors might bring. Back home, she knew, the winds blew over Apanlee as well, but here, on the prairie, in the oven Herb built, Lizzy's cow chips crackled like rockets.

"A bald land," she had wailed when first she came to tame the prairie plains, and now she knew she loved it. She loved it more than she had ever loved the haughty land of Apanlee.

The only thing that counted in America was that you did your best: You did the best you could. That's what she, Lizzy, did. The glow of her windows? Unmatched.

The starry sky of Apanlee was yesterday; she barely gave those times a thought. Life on the prairie sod was still a harsh and bitter struggle—for man as well as beast—but happiness and certainty were there, deep down where Faith was stored. Outside was locked in winter's depth; inside was certainty. Wet snow lay on her windowsill, clung to her roof, buried fences, blew through the naked branches of the trees. Jan saw to it that she had heaps of cow chips, stacked up in triple rows behind the house. Her daughters, one by one, made sure they did the dishes, alternating peacefully to keep the schedule straight.

And she had Herbert; he had her. She gave him her devotion; he paid her back in kind. What might she want of life she didn't have already? The walls renewed, the gables straight, a horse-drawn pump within her reach—all that spelled prosperity, comfort and bounty. Her armchair sat close to the stove, where Herbert had moved it to give her additional warmth.

While Lizzy waited to give birth to Herb's first prairie child, he carried wood inside for her; he wouldn't even let her stoke the stove; he threw the ashes out.

When Lizzy heard a rumor of the female vote, she merely shook her head: if such an aberration ever came to pass—why, *jemine!* by then she would be dead.

For she sat snug. She was content. Her girls slept in an orderly row. They, too, were safe, and they were warm, and they
were dimpled everywhere, for Herbert saw to it she needn't skimp
on sour cream. He was like that—so generous she could not
think of anything he might withhold from her.

She knew she was cherished, respected and loved.

So would her daughters be, as long as they followed the script
of the creed and the Scriptures the Lord had provided.

Herbert had hoped for a boy, but Lizzy bore only plump daughters. The neighborhood was gratified, for Mennotown was not a
place where females had a waistline as though they competed
with wasps.

Herbert said nothing the first time it happened, though clearly
he longed for that son.

She cast her lashes on her cheeks and hoped he wouldn't
mention gender until the female baby had a chance to nestle in
his heart.

Herb walked on tiptoes for a week as though she had per-
formed a wondrous miracle while merely giving birth. He didn't
track mud in the house. He read every wish from her eyes. He
stifled his voice. He doubled his civility. And though the newborn slept as soundly as any new-born calf embedded in fresh
straw and soon developed a prodigious appetite, he just kept on
tiptoeing gently.

"It's only a girl," she said softly.

"It matters not," said he. His voice was hushed with reverence. "Look at her stubby hands. Look at those arching eyebrows."

"Next time, I'll swallow watermelon rind, and on an empty
stomach," she offered wretchedly.

"My dear. I said it matters not. Look at those darling toes.
They move. They move already. See?"

And Jan as well, who was a doting brother as well as tribal
chief. He took another little sibling to his heart and kept it there
for life.

"Let's call her Daisy," Jan suggested when he first saw the color of his baby sister's hair. But Lizzy was an anxious mother—more so as she matured. Though nicknamed all her life herself and to no obvious peril, the dire warnings of the Elder Willy, now long since dead and gathered to his fathers, were still a warning in her ears. In this world and the next, you followed the general trend.

"A foreign forename? Is that wise? We ought to keep unto ourselves."

"We live now in America," said Jan, for his part getting modern. "We strive not to offend."

She said reluctantly: "It is a pretty name. It makes you think of hay."

Her husband smiled at her, thus kindling a small blush. How well he read her thoughts!

"All right. Why not?" said Lizzy, overcome, but happy, deep inside. The Elders frowned on English names and mentioned certain risks.

The etiquette of Mennotown was marble. If you stuck to the habits that centuries had wrought, then God was on your side. If you trespassed, you stood alone; the deacons looked askance at you; their faces shining like pale moons, while sitting in a row along the wall with thunder on their brows.

But oh! this was America! with bounty beyond words. The overpowering temptation to add a little extra opulence to such a tiny life that smelled so good and clean! Lizzy anxiously cuddled the baby: "You're sure it won't do harm?"

"I checked it with the county clerk. It is a lawful name."

Jan loved his little sister dearly and spoiled her wantonly. She made him laugh; she looked so tranquil and serene as she lay snoozing in her cradle; she would grow up to pots and pans without resistance; she would bake her zwieback to general approval.

"She's perfect," boasted Jan. "I've bought her a parcel already." He bought up land at every opportunity, alert for the right price.

"She'll thank you," promised Lizzy, "as soon as she can speak."

These were the boundaries of joy. She was the luckiest woman in the world to have so fine a son who was so openly protective of his sisters—a son still years away from wearing his mustache upturned at both ends, a sign that he expected female deference and would insist on it.

Like everybody else.

Jan had an instinct for selecting strong, rich soil. His prudent purchases of land increased the homestead limits. He stood atop his wagon, dropping the sheaves into piles, carting them off to the wide-open barn. The Mennotown people looked on.

Herbert's old hat was off to Jan. He trusted and respected his stepson, who knew how to drive vital bargains.

Though Jan deferred to Herb in every other matter, he was the one who saw to it that every penny saved and every dollar set aside, by purchasing, selling and trading, was spent on improving the land.

"Use your own judgment, son," said Herbert many times, a mild man with no need to guard his rightful station at the head of Sunday supper. Trained to obedience from the cradle, Jan had a proper sense of duty. The ways of honoring his elders he always clearly understood.

"That's not for me to say," said Jan when the barn needed widening, the door needed hinges, the cattle buyers needed overwhelming with his mother's hospitality so that they slashed their bargains.

"No. You first. You go first," they kept urging each other when it came time to climb onto the buggy.

You understood the other's point of view. You praised your mother's husband's diligence and gentle manners and frugality, behaving as if polishing a precious stone. In turn, he never humbled you.

"Like father, like son," thought Lizzy, a lump in her throat. A fool might have needed the vote.

While Daisy was still teething, Lizzy waited for her husband's second child, then for his third and, on its heels, his fourth. She named them Hermina, Regina and Lina.

"A lucky clover leaf," said Herbert happily.

She looked at him with misty eyes. What a poetic man!

He was as satisfying as a pot of beans, and just as common-place, but he was gentle always, as gentle as June rain. When she recalled his gentleness, it gave her emotions a twinge. Her feelings kept kneading her heart, as though they were kneading the loaves on her breadboard to feed her growing family. With every passing day, appreciation grew.

When Herb turned fifty years of age, she was so overcome with gratitude she spread an extra tablecloth and lit an extra lamp.

For years, she didn't stop to ask herself: "Am I in love with him?" When she finally did, she gave herself time before she replied.

Her radiant love of yesterday had washed into the ocean; with him had disappeared her youth—a world of light and breezes. The prairie times had schooled her thoroughly in practicality and being down-to-earth.

She had a decent life at Herbert's rugged side—the kind of life that spread her hips and settled on her thighs and thereby signified prosperity, which was the yardstick, after all, by which the neighbors judged.

Herbert had come into her life as though in answer to her prayers. He gave her everything she wanted, needed and con-sumed. She gave him his just due; she gave him her esteem. He turned around and gave her kindness and respect. She matched that with her courtesy, and he, in turn, paid Lizzy back the coin of loyalty and warmth.

Some might have claimed he was a bit plebeian. He kept his elbows frayed. But did that matter? No. He tucked her deep into the feather bed and covered every toe.

Before too many years were gone, she and her second husband walked placidly amid the budding trees, across the beauty of young grasses. She counted her blessings, content. Her daughters—silver voices, all. Just perfect for the choir.

And Jan? The dream of any girl.

She, Lizzy, asked no more. She felt as though she were driving around a blue lake, just marveling at its smooth surface. When Herbert came and knelt by her as she sat scrubbing away at a bucket and made a whistle from a leaf to make her laugh, she knew: "I am so lucky. And so blessed."

She knew with a small shiver: "Before he touches me, he stoops to wash his hands."

Small favor in return to give to him, while she could, the children that he craved. To have as many babies as she could before her body fell as silent as the creek did in December: that was like dropping gold coins in a box.

With Herbert she had seven, and all of them survived.

Each morning, Lizzy thanked the Lord that she had Caroline before she had her prairie girls. Lizzy was as proud of Caroline as if she'd been a relative—instead of just a cow.

She smothered Caroline with dandelions to keep her in top shape. And it paid off. The evidence was there. Each spring, for a small fee, Doctorjay checked out the babies of the entire neighborhood, including Lizzy's brood.

"Fit as a fiddle! Fit as a fiddle!" he shouted, fine sparklets flying from his lips like flying from an anvil.

Concerning doctoring, nobody was his equal. He checked each newborn out from head to toe, smoke curling from his nostrils, while Lizzy stood as close as modesty allowed and beamed.

Who wouldn't have? Resilient babies, all!

All had prodigious appetites. Thank God that she had Caroline—and thanks to Caroline, she had the chubbiest babies of the decade.

"I let them drink all the milk that they want," bragged Lizzy. The cream, of course, was ladled first. The cream she took to Wichita—for cash.

Lizzy started making cheese as an experiment, first wrapping it in clean, wet cloth, then taking it to Wichita to offer at the market. The Wichitans sniffed Lizzy's cheese, rolled slices of it deftly between thumb and finger, licked several slivers carefully, and presto: Lizzy had a business.

Noralee could have just kicked herself: why didn't she think first of all the possibilities of cheese?

She was so cross for having missed her opportunity that all her muscles ached. Now Lizzy didn't need to ask her husband for pin money, though Herbert would have gladly forked it over. So much in love with Lizzy was the man that he indulged her every whim. When she bought sugar, tea, salt, herring, sardines, overshoes and toweling, he didn't say a word. Lizzy went to Wichita to shop at Levi's Wholesales where she could knock the price in half on special rebate days.

She bought as much as sixty yards of gingham, and Herbert? Not a peep. She bought a dozen spools of matching thread, just jingling the change in her purse.

As counterstroke to Lizzy's cheese success, and to augment her own eroding status, Noralee, intent on spicing her own chance, volunteered to be in charge of Mennotown's sparse mail.

When Noralee made of herself a bureaucrat, the government officials made several discreet inquiries: Was Noralee a reader? Could she decipther properly?

It was not easy to become a civil servant, for now it took "criteria".

The bonesetter explained it all. It meant, said he, you couldn't just waltz in; you had to prove yourself. That was a novel thought with which to run a government. But Doctorjay backed Noralee with every resource he could marshall; he would assist; he was strategically located; he owned a store already, on the corner of Maple and Main. There he kept shelves supplied with useful merchandise—straight razors, horse blankets, wheel caps for surreys, harness straps, dishes, pots and pans.

A postal branch, he calculated shrewdly, would draw the most reluctant customers.

Mail came infrequently, but when it came, it had to be distributed, and Noralee bestirred herself to become equal to the task. She took firm control of the mail pouch.

This happened the following spring.

Outgoing mail left once a month, in burlap sacks on the back of one of Doctorjay's retired mares. These letters presented no problem: you aimed them at the basket—plunk!—and bureaucrats were paid to sort them out in Wichita.

Incoming letters, on the other hand, came weekly, and they required ingenuity, which was where Noralee excelled. She sifted them for salient clues. She had to know what was inside before she passed them on, and Noralee had guessing powers in abundance. She practically had second sight.

She sorted through the letters carefully to see which ones to open and inspect. Her rationale was simple: She loved an entertaining story. That's where the tea steam came in handy. It opened every seal.

Her husband chided her at times and poked his elbow in her ribs; she shrugged that off: a fine one, he, to speak! He had his own addiction; now she had hers—a vice no less affording strong euphoria than his alluring flask.

She kibitzed shamelessly. Her eyes just snapped with glee. If Lizzy had her victories—well, so did Noralee. She smilingly watched people buy their groceries while fingering their neighbors' letters and guessing at the content—while, all the while, she knew!

There was no shame in her. Opening somebody else's mail was just like perching on a window sill, as though she were a canary. With her old kettle humming and with her heartbeat in her throat, Noralee felt equal now to almost any challenge.

She studied each letter at length. She read between the lines. The fattest ones she put aside behind her jar that held her garlic salt until she found an afternoon to take them over to Lizzy, for

Lizzy needed news; she wanted to know, too.

Those two had a fine time. They had a headstart on the weeping if someone passed away as far away as Saskatoon, Saskatchewan. If they detected a romance, they broke into small, savage shrieks. At somber news, they clucked their tongues: the church was not deceived.

For years, those two would follow breaking stories. The thing that kept them going was suspense. They waited for the other shoe to drop. And when it did—pure bliss!

Soap operas? Pale, by comparison, compared to prairie melodrama.

Chapter 16

Right after the harvest was in, and the reapers were parked in the sheds, Doctorjay went in search of a Wichita joyfest and found it.

"Where is America?" sang Doctorjay melodically, returning late, while making a beeline for bed.

"Right here. Right here," coaxed Noralee, and steered him by the elbow, not sure if she should laugh or cry.

"Not far from Oregon?" howled Doctorjay while searching for a pillow on which to rest his head.

"Boots off!" hissed Noralee.

He hit the highest note: "In Pennsylvania?" With waves of fiery brandy surging through his veins, the words came by themselves. "I thought it was New Mexico," he hooted lustily, not bothering with pitch and key.

It happened every year, right after the election and just before Thanksgiving. At other patriotic holidays, he practiced his restraint; he settled for the colors of his country in his buttonhole and was content to toast this victory, that celebration, in proper moderation. Two holidays, however, back-to-back, were different. Temptation proved too much. This was his season of indulgence when he pulled out all stops.

"Your antics, the laugh of the town," shrieked Noralee and sprinkled him with vinegar to keep the ants away. "What will the neighbors say?"

"The neighbors? Who? What neighbors?"

"One drink led to another?"

"You guessed it," he admitted peevishly.

Doctorjay stood on his porch and watched how firecrackers lit up the warm Wichita sky in celebration of his chosen country's first centennial.   If you were a real patriot—the kind for which the bonesetter was known—you loved your country's streamers, songs and banners.

"Hip! Hip! Hurray!" he hollered. He hoisted little Dewey onto his shoulders so he could better see the caterpillar band. Did anybody miss the pomp and pageantry of holidays that came with having tsars?

Most anybody, by that time, who could afford to purchase a velocipede, had purchased one and used it to exhaustion; and Doctorjay did too; as often as he could. He pedaled all the way to Wichita, where he could ambush strangers to share a drink and partake in the ways of the world. America was on the move, and he was part of it. Since he had turned his back on monarchy, he couldn't get enough.

More! More! That was his motto. This lust to make friends out of people of uncertain status came over him periodically, like vast and potent waves. The results were strong, radical views.

As hunger follows a meal, no matter how rich, or a baby follows a romp in the hay, no matter how dimpled the last one, so Doctorjay would hit his bottle, broadside and full force, when his passion for handshakes took over. Give him two patriotic holidays where a band played with nary a pause between marches, so loud that all the windows rattled, and Doctorjay would lash his mare into a brisk gallop to take himself to downtown Wichita in his beloved surrey to find an audience.

"What does it take?" he pointed out when several Elders came to scold. "Who helped you build your church?"

"You did," admitted they. "Nobody can deny that. But why don't you attend?"

"I do."

"Once every blue moon."

"I tithe. Do I not tithe?"

He was a solid ten-percenter. He did his tithing with a flourish. He made fat crosses on his calendar, lest he forget the tithing week. In fact, he was next to non-Lutheran that way. Tithing made him feel as though he were a king, instead of just an ordinary healer. One-tenth, and not one penny less, was set aside to please his country and his Lord.

"That's America for you," he said to Noralee. She kept his tithing can right on the kitchen window sill, next to her red geraniums, behind the molars and licorice sticks. She shook it now and then and listened to the clunking. She knew he put his coins smack in the middle of the preacher's hat, right next to Jan's new silver dollars, and here they were. Identical. Each time he did, he stared at them, enthralled. Did not a rooster crow with joy?

"Why is it harder, though, to change my husband than to convert a Tartar?"

It was an argument that went around in circles. It was the flask. It was the blasted bottle. Nothing else set Doctorjay apart from his community. He clung to being Lutheran so he could keep his bottle. His moonshine was the bottom line.

The only sorrow was: he had to drink alone. He thirsted for a mirthful buddy who partook. The deacons waylaid anyone whom Doctorjay tried captivating and recruiting. The roving Elders, at such times, were his decided foes.

The Elders pointed out: "Your habit—even worse than smoking."

That, too. Most folks indulged in pipes, since pipes had a calming effect. Jan's barn, where the entire neighborhood would congregate because the place was wide and warm, was always filled with fumes.

"Say, Jan," coaxed Doctorjay. "A little fire water?" That way, he resembled a donkey. He hankered to round out his pleasures. But Jan just shook him off: "Just leave me out! Could I forget that wisdom tooth? You cured me for all time."

"Just as a favor to a friend?"

"It's not for me," said Jan.

From earliest youth, Jan had his values straight. He spoke with firm conviction. Jan held himself aloof. He was, by then, a model bachelor, held in greater honor than any young man of his day.

By then, progress was everywhere. It could be seen, and heard, and felt. The world was knocking on Mennotown's doors, and with it came temptations. The vanity and fanciness of Eaton's store-bought mittens!

Some people went so far as to predict that soon the horse would be as obsolete as last year's almanac.

Which was, the Elders said, absurd. Was science mad, or what? If you thought that science could antiquate horses, you knew you were building on sand.

There was no doubt, by then: America was turning modern, and Wichita as well. Could Mennotown be far behind? Not with Jan's enterprising spirit, or Lizzy's thrift, or Herbert's eagerness to keep abreast with the times.

Herb went to do a little business with the Jews in Wichita, and bought his wife a Singer. Word spread about the wonder needle. No longer did Herb's Lizzy stitch by hand; she pedaled with her foot; that was extravagant in the extreme, but nonetheless impressive.

Lizzy shared with Noralee the wonders of modernity. Both cut themselves wide, flowing frocks from several printed sugar sacks. Even then, they used Butterick patterns.

They inspected each other—this angle and that!—both of them helpless with giggles. Amazing the bulges a baby could make!

The future grew under their aprons.

After marrying the child-rich widow Noralee, Doctorjay
bought several oxen—replete with yoke and chains—a brake plow
and a brand new axe to get the edge on Herbert. Both strove to
have the highest yield per seed. They were not only neighbors,
they were the best of friends. They sang each other's praises but
competed in livestock as well as in potatoes, leather, wool and
pottery.

They did such things and held such views as did the
neighborhood. Doctorjay looked pained when he learned how
Herb beat him to an oblong parlor, with fancy woodwork and a
clever system of cross-drafts. Now Lizzy's living room had three
large windows, while his had only two. Immediately, Doctorjay
knocked out out a wall, and Noralee caught up with Lizzy's added
status—but not for long, for Lizzy got an indoor pump, next to
her cozy kitchen, which called for added effort.

Lizzy was the perfect model of what prairie life was all
about—combining the old with the new. Accommodation was
her specialty. She improvised and learned from every English-
speaking neighbor.

Lizzy now spoke English to her cats and dogs, though not yet
to her chickens. She switched from *Riebelplatz* to custard pie.
From there it was a tiny step to turkey meat and hot dogs. Next,
spaghetti feeds, a novelty.

There was no end to her inventions to create opulence from
naught—no end to Lizzy's wifely pride. The corners of her
kitchen were fitted out with rough-hewn shelves displaying matching pewter plates in ample order, gifts from her husband's relatives, most of whom farmsteaded north—in the Dakotas, in Nebraska, as far away as Winnipeg.

She and Herb had pooled their household items: five brass
and iron kettles, a skillet, two cleavers, a brand new set of meas-
ures, three funnels, a double set of spoons, along with knives and
forks. Each Friday, Little Melly settled on the porch to scour
them until they shone like jewels.

"Like so?" asked Little Melly, who also strove to be exceptional in all ways big and small.

"No, not like so. Like so," taught Lizzy patiently.

The pots and pans were her domain, but Little Melly stood in line and couldn't wait to trade the school bench for the kitchen, and Lizzy taught her how to pinch *vareniki* with thumb and middle finger so that the cottage cheese did not seep out, another hallowed ritual. Next on the tally for a future wife were tricks of beating sour cream until it clotted into butter. Once that was learned to instinct, in line was shadow stitch.

When Little Melly was laid low with chicken pox and Doctorjay said, shaking a stern finger: "Quarantine!", Jan walked around bereaved as though he'd lost his shadow.

The barley was sprouting already. The yield each year was larger than that of the previous year. Time did not stop; progress marched on; the opportunities were there; inventive people started picking surplus nickels off the street.

Before another year was gone, Doctorjay patented a soothing syrup and called it Doctorjay's Ready Relief. It was a potent tonic. It helped just about everyone for anything at all, and only cost a dime. A sample sat on Noralee's top shelf, next to the molars Doctorjay had harvested and kept in a jar for display.

Doctorjay was a resourceful man; he knew his share of healing secrets. He learned by practicing on shut-ins the things he didn't know. He practiced to his heart's content while everyone held still.

Here are the things he learned. Salt opened boils. Mustard plaster lessened ailments of the liver.   He was a virtuoso, practically, with nasty winter coughs. A baby rash? He happily practiced on Dewey.

"Just grind up some old wheat and brown it on the stove. It will do wonders. Wonders!" he said to Noralee.

He also practiced being a diplomatist, as he would put it coyly.

"A baroness," he said to Lizzy, for example, who visited with Daisy, a prairie dumpling of the finest kind. No wonder Lizzy melted. She smiled at him. He smiled at her. He shuffled and took a deep breath. "A quarter is all that I ask."

"Would June be soon enough?" she said, while coloring a little. "I still owe some small pittance to the grocer."

"Oh, sure. No trouble. None."

"You're sure?"

"Of course. Just pay me whenever you can." That was America for you—giving assistance where it was needed, and credit where credit was due.

In gratitude, she spread the word. From near and far the settlers brought their maladies into the makeshift office he opened as a double in a corner of his barn, behind a tattered blanket on two hooks.

He learned from the Wichita Hebrews: he charged what the market would bear. But he never forgot his own roots; he had the community spirit. He did necks and ankles for free.

Very quickly, Doctorjay turned prosperous. When illness or misfortune struck, you could depend on him to arrive in a flying gallop.

When Herbert Krahn stepped on a rusty nail, Doctorjay announced the perfect remedy: he soaked the puncture first with a parsley brew, then in thick milk to neutralize the poison. The foot healed in no time at all; the money went to Doctorjay; the credit went to Caroline.

By leaps and bounds, his reputation grew.

A bull gored a good neighbor in the buttocks, and Doctorjay put axle grease upon the open wound and then blew wood smoke across the cut. It healed so well, his wife announced, you barely saw the scar.

Doctorjay gloried in the splendor of his role. The deacons praised his stomach bitters right from the Sunday pulpit. The haughtiest neighbor shriveled right before his eyes when he as much as hinted: "That tooth looks dubious to me!"

When the envious Wichita doctors came to spy out the bonesetter's secrets, Doctorjay was ready and waiting for them.

"Here, gentlemen. This way. Come right on in," cried Doctorjay, his whiskers straight up in the air.

The bureaucrats tried bullying: "You practice medicine without a proper license. Last week, you treated a sprained wrist. Did you, or did you not?"

"Huh? Huh? My hearing isn't what it used to be. Just ask around. Ask anyone at all."

"Where did you go to school?"

"Tried once. Can read a little. Have had an aversion to books ever since."

They threatened with the sheriff; they swore they would summon the law.

He pointed out the obvious. He counteracted biblically. Could they tax a quiet prayer? Could they license a handshake? That's all he had done—spoken a prayer and shaken a hand. Like so!

They winced at his grasp and departed with haste—no doubt chain-smoking all the way to Wichita. The Lutheran bonesetter beamed.

A solid beginning was there; the rest was now up to the Lord, and He was generous and fair; the grain had ripened nicely; the yield had been superb. If you held up your end of the bargain, He would do likewise, verily.

Therefore, of sermons, you could never have enough.

They were proud of their new place of worship. By September it had walls. By November the roof was just about finished. It stood without pews—they would come soon. And wooden floors were planned as well—a luxury! Demurely they knelt in a row on the neatly packed mud to give thanks for a chance to do well.

Their victories did not come on a silver platter. Some people might expect that kind of bounty from the sky, but not Doctorjay, nor his neighbors and friends or their ladies.

Life was still hard, but you supported the newly-formed Chamber of Commerce. You put your shoulder to the wheel. You pushed. That was the way to carve yourself a life in Mennotown.

Rains would still wash roofs away; and walls would tumble, mud heaps, onto bedding. In the summer, Lizzy's calves would moan and shuffle with mosquitoes; they lost their tails to frost-bite in the winter.

But still. This was democracy. Still there were freedom, leisure and diversion. Democracy was wonderful and everybody had a chance. Democracy was everywhere in force and leveled all distinctions.

Chapter 17

While on the modern continent, modernity was on the march, there was still Apanlee—as stately as its legendary oak, its Aryan roots deep in the Russian soil, its spreading branches giving shade and comfort to the clan and hideouts for the seasonal sparrows and swallows.

Apanlee was humming like a beehive, warmed into action by the sun, for Uncle Benny, too, albeit getting on in years, had found a bride-to-be and planned on getting married.

That was delightful news. Her name was Dorothy.

She looked as though she stepped out of the pages of a book—a girl in a colorful skirt. The neighborhood watched ardently. The gossip of that year had teeth like needles, but in the end, it was agreed: they had the keys to each other's emotions. He thirsted for knowledge, as always. She consisted of giving and serving. He did not distinguish himself with a plow, and his bones held the damp of the winter, but Dorothy gave him a quiet, mysterious strength; she never left his side.

He still put all his thoughts on paper. Her silence matched his words.

He parted her hair and gave her a kiss on the tip of her nose. She knew all was right with the world.

A love out of a storybook—a little manchild with his forehead always furrowed and his small feet in polished boots went forth and found himself a woman with a thousand golden freckles. To top it off, she was a reader, too—the moon in her novels shone brightly.

The outcome was astonishing to all.

Nobody had expected the exotic oddling to fall in love and marry, like everybody else, much less to follow up with fatherhood, but game was he in ways and means; the clan had sold him short; he did things slowly, day by day—while never losing sight.

The hunchback was, by then, so well-known for his genteel writings that a library in Petersburg was christened after him. He knew how to weigh words, knew how to read between the lines. He had beautiful manners and spoke in a temperate voice. He spoke, and he wrote, and the stubborn refrain?

Revolution.

"The peasant is free," wrote Uncle Benny, while dabbing his forehead with thin, trembling hands. "But what does he own? He is a serf in fact, if not in name. He still wears chains. He has no rights. He is no more than chattel."

He did not say: "Equality." Nobody would have recognized the word. The dread of which he spoke still had no content and no focus, but what the people saw was this: deep in its marrow nested sacrilege. Deep at its core sat Hebrew thought. The swindle and the flimflam. The sidelocks. The yarmulkes.

Consensus was vociferous. The German farmers of that decade, to a body loyal subjects to the tsars, had not the slightest wish to have their status altered. It would have been like cheating on their bargain with the Lord.

Go into any forest, was their convincing argument. Beneath that vast and universal sky, no two trees are alike, and neither, in this world, are we.

All men, on even terms, regardless of the march of history that sorted kernels from the chaff?

"If you ask them: 'What do you want?' they'll tell you: 'More!'" said Alexander angrily.

He did not like the Jews. He was the heir to Apanlee. He echoed wide-held sentiment when it came to the Hebrews. The Jewish hatred of the tsarist sovereignty was known.

Had he had fancy words, which he did not—since Alexander, for his part, read no one's book beyond its first ten pages—he might have told his crippled nephew that parity might be a mandate that looked all right in theory. In poetry. Perhaps in the Beyond.

Not in the German villages. Not in the lush, green fields where status was determined, not by who had the loftiest dreams, but by who grew the finest grain—a grain which, by that time, fed a good part of Russia.

The invalid would not be silenced. "The chains corrode. And what I see is chaos. Anarchy. And mayhem in the streets."

The glitter of the oddling's words! He was half-kin, this little pundit relative of theirs, but he was genial to have around; his heart was above guile. You bent and patted Uncle Benny on the head. "Be sure not to forget your herbs. Here, let me prop you up."

The tsars, still hostile to all reckless change, might listen to the cripple's mediating ways—and his opinions, itching, like woolen underwear, were honored if not heeded—but it was widely understood at Apanlee: go work your fingers to the bone. Leave words to Uncle Benny.

He could put words to thought. He was a stubborn gnome.

"Now is the time to write new rules. The margin for error is small."

There were respectful nods. Not everyone was called by destiny to lend his suntanned arms to bring the kernels in, but nature had its compensations, clearly. It was agreed that Uncle Benny was an oddity but harmless—bred to the sturdy family by accident.

A Christian didn't waiver in his Faith.

Another century would soon begin to test the ancient Faith by heaping hurdle upon hurdle, but oldsters heard the children's prayers, and youngsters paid attention, with care and with due deference, to what their Elders said. Nobody differed with the Elders, for it was they who watched the covenant, struck up a century ago between the German-speaking farmers, the Lord Almighty, and the tsars.

"You render unto Caesar only after you have rendered unto God," said Alexander. "Now, should I close that window, Uncle Benny, so you won't catch the draft?"

Let Uncle Benny scribble or take his pensive walks. So let him craft his ornamental essays on the history of early settlers who coveted the soil. Those soft and rosy hands with flawless fingernails were good for little else.

You never saw the cripple without his pen and paper. By then, his hair had whitened to the color of fir ashes. He liked strong tea and brittle biscuits, and loved to have his blankets warmed.

For his mind, he was widely respected; for his delicate health, he was tenderly coddled as well. Not the worst Tartar of a cousin grudged Uncle Benny his hot water bottle or would have dreamed of sneezing lustily when Uncle Benny napped.

His joints—in constant spasms. His forehead—always knit.

And yet, he fell in love with Dorothy. Stripping corn one hazy summer afternoon, amid the youths of Apanlee, while gathering some anecdotes with which to spruce his paper, Uncle Benny was the lucky bachelor who found the husk with ochre kernels.

"Look what I have here. Look!" he called, and held the ear aloft.

According to an ancient custom, this find was a clear mandate for romance. In a fine mood for merriment, the youngfolk cheered him on and clapped their hands: "Come on, Uncle Benny! Come on! A kiss from the girl of your choice!"

His smart, dark eyes fell on a girl believed to have several admirers.

"Do you permit?" he asked, a shy but faultless suitor, standing first on one frail leg, then shifting to the other.

The girl leaned forward, reddening. What else could she have done?

He reached for her. She did not back away. And as he held her in his arms, the farthest spectators could see: a glow washed over Uncle Benny.

The audience laughed and clapped. "A kiss. A kiss."

His lips touched Dorothy's warm cheek and sent the color to her nape, and afterwards, she stood so close to him she saw herself reflected in the shine of several silver buttons—and Uncle Benny, so the story goes, threw his cane in an arch across the nearest fence and, briefly, walked with a decided bounce, as straight as you and I.

A winter came and went. The gutters started dripping with the changing of the season. Spring cleaning had arrived at Apanlee, a ritual that started with the double window panes and ended with the polishing of the door knobs.

When every tree trunk had received a brand new coat of paint, the woolen underwear was packed, and the stork had completed his nest, Alexander slapped his crippled nephew on the shoulder and told him, man to man:

"We all know how you feel. It's not unnatural." And everybody laughed.

The year was fragrant; the ancient acacias stood clouded in bloom. The snow had long melted; the air smelled of spring and rebirth; the maid-servants polished the windows. Spring sat securely in the trees, and Apanlee would never again be as lovely.

Uncle Benny took his time pursuing Dorothy with the finesse of Apanlee, riding with two splendid horses, their breast harness shiny, their ropes a garish red. He drew a lot of stares and many speculations. He flicked the whip across the horses' ears and just sailed by, a gentle light in his dark eyes, the wind atop his curly hair while on his way—like any other man in love—to take his heart to Dorothy.

The neighborhood took part in the developing romance. The neighbors told each other, laughingly: "Look, Uncle Benny is afire. You better call the fire brigadiers."

There was no malice in their teasing; he was no threat to anyone.

They two were soon detected holding hands beneath the table cloth. And by the time the wheat beards came and went, he and his chosen girl seemed handcuffed to each other, and every spinster was an expert, by September, at guessing this and that.

Love has its ways, they sighed and stared into a misty past. Not since the world began had it been otherwise. The wrinkles in his brow would lessen; that was their sentiment. He was in love, and so was she; they mesmerized each other thoroughly, much to the clan's surprise—though all the while, throughout his courtship even, he kept on writing frantic editorials none at Apanlee had time to read—not while a strong, hot summer drove the harvests.

Russian workers came from miles away—some from as far away as Poltawa—scythes swung across their shoulders.

The menfolk spit into their calluses and then took, singing, to the fields. The women clattered with the dishes in the kitchen; the chickens were already hanging by their legs. But as soon as the kernels were gathered, the villagers rallied, enthralled—it was urgent, no doubt, to start practicing songs, for a wedding was not far away.

". . .*My thoughts are as free*
as wind o'er the ocean
And no one can see
their form or their motion. . ."

No longer did the cripple sit in silence, in discourse with himself. He snapped the reign across his horses' pointed ears, taking off each Sunday morning in clouds of dust that whirled behind him, en route to visit Dorothy, as snatches of the teasing, haunting melody would waft behind him slowly:

". . . no hunter can find them
no trap ever bind them;
my lips may be still
but I think what I will."

It was a happy time for all. He borrowed chiseled words for Dorothy— he loved to hear her sing; she had a lovely voice:

"Though prison enfolds me
its walls cannot hold me
No captive I'll be
While my spirit is free. . ."

Sometimes they sang together on mellow evenings, while neighbors listened pensively to the blows of the flails in the shed. They watched her lean against him cozily, and Uncle Benny's furrowed, melancholy face would soften from her love.

The folks of Apanlee inspected Dorothy, but she passed muster easily. She was a gentle shadow who only raised her voice at intervals: "Let Uncle Benny pass! Let Uncle Benny pass!"

She cooked and baked and scrubbed, with nary a thought for herself. She was busy from dawn until dark. She was an expert with the measles. Her peppernuts, perfection. Her mashed potatoes, without lumps. She never drove a beggar from her gate. Her milk pails, scoured every week, did not fall short on gloss. She easily turned out to be as frugal and as orderly as any girl around, and she was modest, too—the world with all its vanities was not for Dorothy.

"You first. You first," said Dorothy to old and young alike.

She was like that. Demure. She promised everybody many times that she would welcome relatives, no matter how obscure the kin—yes, welcome each and every one of them with open arms and willing smiles, and even if they overstayed and didn't go away.

She was a Catholic, regrettably. A Volga girl, they say. But then, well, wasn't he part Jew?

Some oldsters had long memories.

Some people still recalled with deep and heaving sighs: a sickly child in olden days, packed in protective rugs and furs, hot bricks stuffed all around him. And now, behold: a well-respected publisher. With distressing and upsetting notions.

The tsar had told his ministers: "The Jews are nine-tenths of the trouble."

It didn't loom, but it was there. It was an understanding. Each one of them, infested with the democratic spirit. You better cut an arc.

The Hebrews were the kind who'd fooled the world for centuries.

They ate unhealthy food.

They always traded up and never lost a deal.

They were the kind that made the dunces pull their chestnuts from the fire.

By definition, furthermore, they were non-Christians—no icons on their walls! Why, even Jesus warned: "Jerusalem! Jerusalem!"

Converting them was futile. That's why nobody tried.

"The Jews—in a destructive mood," that was the sentiment, nursed and recycled intermittently through centuries.

That year saw workers' strikes in Kiev, Petersburg and Moscow. Their favored slogan: Liberty. Their battle cry: Equality. Their claim: Fraternity.

Their target: the wealth of the nobles and tsars.

Assorted tsars had tried to bring equality through needed land reform, with dubious results. The serfs had since been freed—but to what thankless end? Child labor was a crime; child loitering, on the increase. The workers in the factories, whose wages had been doubled and doubled yet again, spoke openly of Revolution. The Hebrews carried on in undertones for hours at a time.

"Show me a fire sale," said Alexander, furious, "and there they are, to take advantage of somebody else's tragedy. You have to put up barriers."

He listened sullenly while Uncle Benny told of peasants prick-
ing veins and writing crimson letters, petitioning the tsars. All
people, equal brothers? The world, a giant brotherhood? No
social barriers between a village herdsman and his overlord?

"No wonder," Alexander scolded Uncle Benny while stuffing pillows in the hollow of his back, "that our tsars have many
foes."

"There's worse to come, unless there is a chance for democratic—"

"Oh, hush you, Uncle Benny!"

A fine one, he, to speak! He was a bloodless pundit. He had
been sheltered all his life. He had his bed warmed and his darning done, thanks to the vast abundance that came with Apanlee.

"What do they want? What do the workers want?"

"Well, parity. A chance to share. A chance to partake in the
structure of the government—"

But Alexander merely shrugged his shoulders. In Heaven,
parity was proper, but only after you made room for Christ—a
thought anathema to certain folks who, given their one chance,
had crucified Him wantonly.

He had heard of this social practice called democracy—rule
by collective ignorance. Not here. Not in the plains of Russia.

Alexander did not want to argue with his crippled nephew
whose hobby was philosophy. In the vicinity of Apanlee, where
people born to privilege were raised to duty and example among
their watchful relatives, the concept of equality was as germane
as might have been the moon on a long, sun-drenched day.

"As much against the laws of nature," was Alexander's final
word, "as is a bearded lady."

"If not reform—"

"All right. I heard you out."

"—then bloodshed, Alexander."

"Now, not another word!" said Alexander angrily, a man who
died twelve years before the Lusitania sank, and that was just as
well.

Everyone was greatly pleased and mollified, therefore, when Uncle Benny, if only temporarily, could think of something other than the trouble with the land, its restive peasantry, and stop forecasting pestilence as winter started stripping every tree.

All loved him well enough. They greeted his romantic flowering with outstretched hands and hoped it would lessen his headaches.

"So then? Your living quarters in the right wing or the left?"

They knew that Uncle Benny could no more have changed the well-established order than he could make the month of August come before July.

"Whatever suits you best," said Uncle Benny, a tiny groom but so revered in Russia for words that leashed enormous thought that trains would wait for him. The tsars prized his opinion. Ink foamed from what he said. "I would prefer upstairs. It's quiet there. I won't be underfoot."

A female cousin stroked his hands—those nervous hands that were as delicate as butterflies, that browsed in mildewed papers.

"You will be happy. Finally." She smiled at him, a pleasant and good-natured girl. She put a kindly hand across his burning brow. "We all wish you luck. The servants are spoiling their saints."

Said Uncle Benny softly while dropping a small tear: "Before it is too late."

He was like that. He gloomed and doomed and sorrowed and forewarned.

"Gone are the days," wrote Uncle Benny with ever greater urgency in essay after essay, after searching through old scrolls, "when Faith alone suffices."

Even at the height of his own love affair, that made him shower Dorothy with pretty lyrics as though he showered her with jewels, he was as stubborn as a muzhik when it came to his theories.

The Russian servants pulled threads from Uncle Benny's overcoat, to have a little keepsake and help along his luck. His health was frail and getting worse. His back could not withstand a harvest; his eyes could not withstand the August sun; he barely made it through September; and come the winter storms, the chill crept deep into his marrow and wouldn't go away.

The doctors, to a voice, expressed their bafflement.

But now he had a bride. That would change everything. On a long Easter weekend, they spoke their wedding vows.

The tables stood laden with food; wreaths hung in ribbons from the rafters; the guest list reached into Siberia and Tashkent. You never saw so many cousins all at once!

The vaguest relatives arrived from far away to partake in the drollery. The bridegroom looked so elegant and satisfied with luck that you surmised he thought he was entitled to a ballerina. The elders seated themselves; the young drew into a cluster. Claas Epp, the fieriest preacher of his time, strode forward, took the pulpit, and spoke a double blessing fore and aft to forestall adverse luck.

The bride—as lovely as the morning star. God, was she beautiful! And pure!

Somebody took the bride's white garland: "Surrender now your wreath, for life is but a shadow—"

The barefoot peasants, standing by, wept copiously. "God be with you. The martyrs and saints protect you."

Uncle Benny kept checking the hands of his watch.

"It's late. It's later than you think," said Uncle Benny urgently, and everybody laughed out loud at the well-known refrain that Uncle Benny had been echoing since he had been a little boy who started cracking print.

In the end, the excitement died down; the newlyweds left, behind them the blur of well-wishers.

"Be gone!"

"Be glad!"

"And be happy! Be happy! Be happy!"

Chapter 18

About that time, a bunch of strangers came to Mennotown. They came in from the East, thick with old dust, walking in formation, and wouldn't say from where.

That was the first thing everybody noticed. They weren't neighborly.

From the word go, the Donoghues were trouble. They stayed all summer long, but lifted not one little finger to help bring in the harvests, and even when the wind began to bite in earnest, they gave no sign of leaving. They holed up in a temporary shack, and there they sat and stayed.

Their fences sagged, their hairlines weren't tidy, their nails needed scrubbing and trimming. If something was wobbly, they claimed they lacked hammer and nail. They were notorious for their rages and unreasonable demands. Like locusts they lived even then, devouring things that other people grew.

Even their dogs looked slightly ashamed. Their toes kept on kicking up dust.

It was whispered that jail fever ran in their veins. They talked of an old, missing document that gave them squatters' rights. They were cozy with Wichita's Jews.

At first, the faithful offered guarded welcome.

"Come join us, please," the congregation told the Donoghues. "He shed His blood for everyone. We'll just move over and make room. The church takes every sinner."

"If we don't oversleep," replied the Donoghues.

"We are counting on you," said Lizzy, helplessly, setting up a gentle counter-current while waiting for results.

Lizzy wanted all her neighbors to behave harmoniously, and so she launched herself. To start, she was a gifted cook. She took her husband firmly by the arm and went right in the lion's den to welcome them in person.

"Will you come visit us next Sunday, right after services?" Let them see for themselves! Who owned the shiniest sill? Who owned the finest herds, the fattest geese, the most well-mannered children? A set of perfect strangers to judge who was the winner in a contest that started centuries ago!

"I'll fry my finest rooster," said Noralee as well.

Not that it made a difference. She found out soon enough. To spurn a Sunday supper invitation was an unthinkable rebuff. The Donoghues, ungrateful louts, snubbed Noralee. Repeatedly. And never gave a reason.

"Please come," she begged, refusing to believe: you couldn't set fire to water.

"Do you suppose they could be non-believers?" chimed Lizzy finally, distressed beyond all words.

Nobody ruled that out. Some claimed that they had spied a barrister named Finkelstein, who visited the Donoghues at intervals to try to do a little mischief on the side. The dogs would bark at him.

Still Lizzy, being Lizzy, tried—no one could say she didn't. She was armed with the patience of Job. In later years, she often said she wished she had a dime for every time she tried; she would be a rich woman.

Getting the Donoghues to church grew into a moral crusade. The neighbors, watching from the sidelines, predicting that worse was to come—this long before she, Lizzy, learned about their double-faced shenanigans, the trouble Abigail would cause, the worm in the core of the apple.

Despite repeated efforts, it proved impossible to trace from whence they came. That they were here to stay, of that there seemed no doubt.

"Unhappily," they claimed repeatedly, "the document is lost."

But they were looking. They were searching.

And once they found that missing document and took it to the Hebrew barrister, the fat was in the fire.

In weeks to come, as apprehension and alarm increased, all kinds of aberrations came to light about the Donoghues. Their menfolk slept into the day; their females wore old petticoats on which the lace had frayed. They did not like to be observed. If you tried catching up to them, they quickened their own pace.

They passed for parasites and maybe even worse. They drew no solace from the Bible. Their children ran in rags.

The difference between potatoes planted early and potatoes planted late was a decided mystery to them. They were so poor, because of sloth, they counted on the mushroom season.

Before another year was gone, people told them to their faces what they thought.

The Donoghues, for their part, kept pointing out their squatters' rights; they boasted they had Indian blood; it was the Germans, claimed the Donoghues, who were the real intruders.

Some people grumbled, even then, about their clannish faithfulness and appetite for exclusivity, but they just shrugged that off, for plenty of goodwill was there to enable adjusting. Adapting. Most folks in Mennotown took pride in triple loyalties. In every sod home could be found the picture of the German kaiser and equally the picture of the Russian tsar—but, flanked by both, the current president in Washington, a man who took his baths on

Saturday, like everybody else.

Meanwhile, they built up their community. The German church grew overnight; the building meant to be the German school progressed more slowly. They planned every detail with care, all winter long, with abacus and ruler and many cups of coffee from Lizzy's iron kettle.

"We'll all chip in," they said. "Nobody is excused."

Jan Neufeld was there, from beginning to end, a youth progressive to the hilt. "The railroad," said young Jan, "has plans to move right through our town. The sale of one small parcel will spell a large amount of cash. I'm willing to donate a hefty chunk to speed our youngfolks' schooling. The railroad will donate the lumber."

The settlers looked at him approvingly. Here was a fellow with a purpose. Though he himself had scarcely been to school, he came from Apanlee; he valued education. Each summer bronzed him more; each harvest made him sturdier. The plow no longer jumped out of his hands as it had that first year when he was still a novice plowman.

"We'll search the state from end to end," said Jan, and raised a hand until the visitors grew still: "Now, silence. Everyone! Books. Teachers. Somebody well-equipped to see the future clearly."

The wind whistled softly. The barn filled with tobacco smoke. A train roared by and broke the silence briefly. Trains moved so fast they were a blur; trains never ceased to stun.

The kerosene lamp flickered.

Somebody offered an opinion: grain loaders, surely, were bound to drop in price.

Male neighbors far and wide flocked in for company. Cracking walnuts with a hammer, they'd steer the talk away from Jan's concern for schooling to more immediate matters: the crops, the weather, the still-arriving immigrants the ships pushed through the cold and gray Atlantic.

There was talk of a bicycle shop.

Farmer Ens had made his final payment on his fancy threshing gear.

Farmer Goertzen was busily buying up land in the north.

Herbert's newest neighbor to the right was fortunately German, though not, to everyone's regret, of the true Faith. As yet.

A Methodist? Could be. Or, worse, a Presbyterian? Could be as well. You never knew. You never, never knew.

You were grateful he wasn't a Baptist, for they were serious competition. Some of them even rode the trains to speed from town to town to snare the credulous.

"We need that school," insisted Jan. He did not easily give up. Accosting neighbors left and right, he handed each a pen and said: "Here. On the dotted line."

"Sure. Sure. Why not? Within ten years I might be dead. But in the meantime, why not spend a bit on chalk and blackboard? A pointed ruler? And a bell?" That year, the harvest was so good that even well-known misers felt expansive.

It wasn't that their offspring's schooling didn't matter. It was slow going, though. The seasons marched. The children's nimble hands and feet were needed. Most folks knew that the Bible was the place where you learned everything worth knowing.

Faith, in those early years of pioneering, was writ in large, stiff, Gothic script. The preachers continued to filter the Gospel. The Holy Ghost plowed through the souls of disbelievers.

The Elders did a copious business between the sinners and the Great Beyond, for if you knew what was and would be good for you—not just today but in eternity—when you saw them, you'd better reach into your pockets! The church came first. The school, a distant second.

Building that little red schoolhouse took several additional years.

But in the end, Jan won; he learned to speak firmly and stick out his chin. That chin was his grandfather's chin—some oldsters still remembered.

Thus, on a snowy afternoon, the Mennotown neighbors assembled in Herbert's new barn and voted themselves a committee.

"It's now—or else," insisted Jan, and therefore it was now.

They planned the school, located at the crossroads, right next to the half-finished church. Jan kept on pushing for completion until the men agreed to thatch the roof, ornery weather regardless, with bundling reeds and chinking logs.

Lizzy fired up her quilting bee to buy a black, round stove, a blackboard, and a desk. Lizzy had the community spirit. She volunteered her brand-new, add-on parlor all summer to finish the drive.

"The best is barely good enough," she told the quilting ladies, who nodded solemnly and fanned the flies away, although, by this time, Lizzy had four cross-draft windows, paid for out of her butter fund. But still, the flies crept in. Each Wednesday afternoon, the quilting bee ladies sat, quilting happily within the summer breeze—updating the gossip they'd missed.

When the school stood finished—finally!—they looked around: who might be a fitting teacher?

"Thirty dollars for the year," the school committee had allowed. "Three bins of wheat. Oodles of firewood thrown into the bargain. The right to own a cow. And all the food a poor fellow can swallow—for free."

Johann Wiebe was the first of many prairie teachers—a lanky fellow from up north, straight from the windy plains. He was a meek and gentle man, unsuited for the land, afraid to raise his voice. Blisters formed as easily on his soft palms as bubbles did in Lizzy's zwieback dough. Not yet eighteen when he was signed, he was a serious lad, bookish to the hilt. In years to come, he was the one who cast a timid eye on Lizzy's young Hermine. For now, he did the best he could; he made Hermine, still a child, stop staring dreamily out of the window and start to do her numbers properly, by counting on her fingers.

Before the year was out, he learned that teaching was no bed of roses. One frosty, wind-blown morning, he pushed his hat down on his ears and knocked on Doctorjay's front door. Marshalling all his fortitude, he pointed to Doctorjay's wallet.

"A globe. A map. And certainly a dictionary. These are necessities."

Doctorjay, a man with a heart as wide as a barn, agog with admiration for any fluent reader, reached for his wallet then and there, all set to empty it, but Noralee was quick and caught his fingers just in time.

A dictionary, with print so small that it could ruin your eyesight? A globe that made you think you hung there, in the middle of the universe, with not a hook or safety net to counteract the fear that you might drop into a pit? A map highlighting sinful places, such as California?

"Make do with what you have," she said, and glared with purpose at the door.

"I will, I will," said the young teacher, hastily, and never asked again.

When Noralee, while joining in the quilting bee, spelled out the teacher's plea on behalf of the inquisitive spirit, the ladies, to a body, were equally incensed. Why learn about a world of which they had no part? Such extra frills cost money, and money was still scarce.

School had its place when nature rested up. By bobsled and buggy they came, the clean-scrubbed, flaxen children, when days were slow and snow lay thick outside. Their bashful teacher saw to it that, in the frozen season, there would be ample silent reading, along with writing from dictation, along with careful penmanship.

All winter long, the German youngsters learned their ABCs and other useful matters, and for good reason, too—because more often than the school committee liked, some busybody bureaucrats arrived out of Topeka where government was spreading tentacles like mad.

The bureaucrats asked unbecoming questions:

"Why so much Bible reading in your schools at the expense of other books?"

"Why prayers but no algebra?"

Mennotown thought little of the people in Topeka who kept trying on this governor, that governor as if he were a glove. As far as politics, you knew precisely what was good for you; you held yourself aloof.

"Your absent list is a disgrace," scolded the bureaucrats.

They even threatened fiercely: "One day in jail for every day one of your children misses school—"

Harsh editorials appeared in the *Emporia Gazette* about the German children's schooling. "There is for their curriculum," the worldly write-ups claimed, "no proper explanation."

The papers twisted facts. The scribblers tainted truth. There was an explanation. The harvests interfered.

It wasn't true that the beleaguered settlers didn't try to please the bureaucrats. "A bureaucrat must make a living, too," they said repeatedly. "But how to fight the calendar?"

The farmers huddled in distress. "It's spring," the farmers said. "We need all hands. Nobody is excused."

School? Books? It was well known that too much studying caused water on the brain. School was a fancy luxury for useless winter days; spring was already here and gone; soon every son and daughter would be needed to wrestle in the sheaves.

Year after year, it was the same. As soon as trees dressed up like brides, the schoolhouse doors fell shut.

The straw piles grew.

The horse-drawn drill squeaked fiercely.

The threshing crews arrived.

Somebody's cousin put himself in charge of the entire caravan that hauled the bulging sacks of grain to Wichita. He let the children ride along so they could aggravate the meter maids who ticketed the horses.

Wagon after horse-drawn wagon halted by the elevators in Wichita as the grain flowed to the pit below. Wheat sold, by then, for 70 cents a bushel. There was disturbing talk the price of grain might drop. Speed was, hence, of the essence. You had no choice; the children were recruited; you could not waste their hands. If nothing else, a child could lead a horse aside to find relief at intervals and thus aid calls of nature—in English, if need be.

"As soon as you hear whirring wheels, run! Run and hide in the potato cellar!" Noralee coached Dewey cleverly and kept her truant offspring out of sight of bookish bureaucrats until the dust had settled on the snoopers.

The Donoghues were dropping hints, and Doctorjay became all eyes and ears. He elbowed Lizzy pointedly. "They're whispering about the document again!"

"They do? What document?"

"What document? As if you didn't know!"

"No, I don't know," said Lizzy sharply. "And I don't want to know."

"There's trouble brewing, Lizzy. They are cavorting with this barrister named Finkelstein."

"I paid for it. We had a deal. This land is mine. The law is on my side." A scoundrel had sold her a pigeon-caked hut; he took her coins and ran; should she have given chase?

"Was there a bill of sale?"

"Maybe. I may have put it in my apron. I may have washed that apron."

She acted nonchalant, but deep inside she worried more than she let on. She knew the Donoghues' persistent talk about a squatter claim to prime land in the midst of Mennotown was like a tune that played inside Jan's skull. It was obnoxious, caused much anguish, and wouldn't go away, and even Doctorjay—the only Democrat in a town dependably Republican, a man who customarily took sides with any underdog, who saw it his life's task to help erase class differences—would trumpet heartily into his checkered handkerchief with stress when he heard of this matter. Not even he could warm his heart to any of the Donoghues—excepting, perhaps, Abigail, who was a well-known hussy.

"That one is fun to watch," said Doctorjay, pleased that this female stranger came endowed with curves and loops where you expected them to be on any fetching female.

The rest of them were thin and nervous, and no wonder: their meals were sporadic and meager; their stew was watery and thin.

That was the second feature everybody noticed—their skinniness—particularly Noralee who, by then, carried so much weight she could no longer take a chance on perching on her stool.

Both Noralee and Lizzy thought Abigail alarming. They fussed and worried plenty.

Here was a girl as tricky as a Tartar foe, as tempting as a chunk of meat just turning on the spits. She wore a dress with four contrasting colors and didn't regard herself as a sinner. You watched her. She meant business.

Before the year was out, the girl was the talk of the town. To put it bluntly: Abigail was trouble. And Jan stood in her path.

When Lizzy, filled with dread, consulted Doctorjay to help her think of a deterrent, he cast a jaundiced eye on Little Melly and swallowed just in time what he had meant to say.

"Don't be caught napping, Little Melly," warned Doctorjay, instead, and felt his ears grow crimson with a forbidden thought. "Wake up and smell the tulips."

The girl spoke placidly. "I don't know what you mean. If it is chiefly marriage Abigail is after, then Jan is probably as useless as a flower vendor in July. "

When Little Melly spoke those words, relief went straight into all ten of Lizzy's toes. Jan's course was set. His bride-to-be was waiting.

"You can't allow a horse to drift," said Doctorjay, who knew whereof he spoke.

Chapter 19

Doctorjay and Noralee had a befitting marriage, all in all, despite the spice of many heated arguments the blasted bottle caused.

"Your disgraceful behavior is all over town," lamented Noralee at intervals.

"Nag-nag. More coffee, if you please, madam. Are you still mad at me?"

"I'm even madder now than last year, Doctorjay. Your tongue is spiked. Look at you! Look at your blood-shot eyes! There's only one conclusion."

"It isn't Abigail," he whined, outguessing her, expertly dulling her main arrow.

"The Finkelsteins? Did you cavort with them?"

"Why, Noralee!"

She was a realist. She would have been on guard against most any girl whose name was Abigail—but even more instinctively was she on guard against the clannish Finkelsteins who dealt, ostensibly, in furs.

The Wichita Hebrews—too clever for anyone's comfort!

She knew some facts - specifically, about the Finkelsteins. She carefully fleshed out the rest. Pen wipers, all! Foot scrapers, all! Hatred of cross-stitch was in their blood. They fasted without rhyme or reason—no wonder they were slim; no wonder they got rich.

"I treat all people equally. As an American, I owe that to myself to keep myself informed," claimed Doctorjay, and disappeared in a smart trot in the direction of another celebration that started after sunset and lasted way past midnight. If he ran into friends he hadn't seen in ages, he hung out for several additional rounds. Next thing he knew a song leaped to his tongue and stayed. Next thing that happened was: he started voting Democrat.

In Mennotown, he was the only one who did. His argument was simple. Somebody had to nullify the rising temperance movement, led chiefly by a female firebrand who was lambasting joy.

All this was hard on Noralee. She did her best to close her eyes and help him navigate back to safe shores at such disheveled times.

In time, they struck a compromise. She didn't dwell on his shortcomings—except for the drama that she could extract. He didn't dwell on imperfections either; he took her hollering in stride; he knew she knew that arguing against the flask was much like punching hard into a down comforter—sooner or later, she felt a bit foolish; she started to laugh; and he knew he had won one more round.

She knew her limitations. Her once-slim figure had long disappeared into layers of soft fat. Her eyes began to droop a bit, her hair was thinning out. That he found her attractive, still! was a decided plus.

She scolded, and she yelled—she didn't spurn her drama!—but that was as far as it went. She could have afforded to take a stern view—the Elders urged her to—but she didn't; it wasn't important.

She knew that it would pass. Subtract those few upsetting

times when Doctorjay returned from Wichita so sloshed she would
have gladly strangled him—and she was still in Doctorjay's young
eyes a lavish luxury to snuggle up against when he came home
from having sat all night while waiting for a cow to calve, a boil
to burst, a life to end as nature ran its course. He was a good
provider. They had enough children to sweeten the future—each
one of them, a hearty appetite!—and their harvests were heavy
and lush.

One year became the next—years filled with Faith and certitude—with their beloved church a hub of bustle in the middle,
the homesteads the spokes, one hymn chasing after another. Their
young sat mannerly in church with shining eyes and silent lips,
smelling sweetly of mothballs and wax.

To counteract the fire sap that kept on leading Doctorjay astray,
the moral force in years to come proved to be Dewey Epp. His
last name wasn't really Epp; no one remembered Jacob; he must
have felt a kinship with Old Willy, who had since passed to his
reward. This was the selfsame Dewey Epp, the sallow preacher
boy, whom Doctorjay had raised out of his soggy diapers as though
he were his son. Young Dewey showed his earmarks early. Nobody could say grace at supper time with such hypnotic sing-
song voice.

"Just looking at the little fellow," predicted Doctorjay, "makes
me suspect a sermon's coming on. He'll soon start pilfering my
pockets."

"He's going to accomplish wonders," his wife said hopefully,
while watching her husband digesting his dinner.

"Wonders?"

"Wonders."

"Why wonders, Noralee?"

"Because," said Noralee.

It turned out she was right. In coming years, few sinners
managed to escape the sway of Dewey's dogged sermons. But
until Dewey grew into his preacher trousers and his calling, her
lusty husband did exactly as he pleased, saw whom he liked, slept

where he fell, attended church depending on who preached, ignoring practically every prairie sermonizer, but favoring a few.

He had no quarrel with the Elder Thiessen, for example.

The Elder Thiessen was as bland as gruel without salt. Most people flocked to him because he was a middle-roader. He had no bone to pick with anyone, since he was blind in his left eye and therefore prone to missing flaws two eyes might have noted.

The Elder Thiessen was content to watch the sinners hang their heads and sort out their trespasses. He left them there, no fuss. He made his rounds to speak his prayers for the dead and marry waiting couples. He told the congregation of the birth of God and of the mercies of the crucified Redeemer, and Doctorjay sang lustily to that—a preacher to his liking. He told fine jokes about two skunks who quarreled over whisky, and Doctorjay laughed roaringly and slapped himself with relish on the thighs: "And have you heard the one about three Lutherans, two Presbyterians and a Jew?"

But when the Elder Penner from Fargo, North Dakota, arrived one windy afternoon to pitch his tent and settle down to brimstone, you could not locate Doctorjay—not even with a magnifying glass.

Young Dewey was an odd, peculiar little fellow—a boy with pasty skin, a furrowed brow and wide and flaring nostrils who puckered up his lips to make barbarian noises. Whenever he did that, Little Melly just fled for her life.

It gnawed on Lizzy like a moth chews on a garment: the pious preacher child, her sister's favorite, was greasy to the touch. She did not like the boy. She could not put her finger on the source.

This shocked her to the core.

She said to Herbert finally: "If only he would blow his nose."

Herb brushed away some crumbs and said to Lizzy gently. "Don't be so harsh on your own heart."

"It isn't just his looks," she told herself severely, since she agreed with Herbert. It was better not to examine too closely. But still—the boy was far from handsome. Every time she cut the youngster's hair—for she was excellent with scissors!—she saw that ugly mole growing at the base of his neck.

She kept on hugging her illusions that her unhealthy feelings would pass, for Dewey was, she told herself, a child like any other child, a relative like any other relative, entitled to her loyalty. It was her Christian duty to quench uncharitable thoughts—although the teacher was complaining too, for Dewey Epp was often late to class, slinking in with downcast eyes, using twice his allotment of paper.

"A good, obedient son," claimed Noralee. "He'll grow to be a useful missionary."

"That would be wonderful," said Lizzy, who felt her heart swell with foreboding. She knew the congregation needed full-time preachers sorely to regulate the coming years with threats of hell and promises of Heaven. Why not her sister's son? Of preachers, you could never have enough. This outweighed all the rest—and even she had to admit: Dewey spoke his prayers, always, with a mysterious gravity.

She would catch herself staring at him. About him hung a maddening docility. At best, he was lukewarm about her butter balls—that she could overlook. He greeted guests and took their hats—at least he had some manners. He was as common as sliced turnip—she venerated that, since she lived in America.

But he frightened her geese into hissing at him, and the dogs tore holes in his trousers.

Little Melly came running one morning, in her excitement fanning herself: "Doctorjay! Doctorjay! You are due for a surprise! Dewey says he found the Lord."

"Where did he look for him?" asked Doctorjay and stroked the stubble on his chin.

"Somebody needs to prod your conscience," protested Little Melly with unexpected gusto. "You're overdue yourself to catch up with the Lord." Churchly zeal was one thing she and her little brother had in common.

For Little Melly, the devil was real. He had two hooves, a tail. About him, the odor of brimstone. The devil held full sway in Mennotown, she knew, unless the healer stopped his guzzling; there was no stopping him.

"It's never too soon," chirped Little Melly while wringing her short fingers, "to have a timely update with the Lord."

Doctorjay was still attending church at his convenience, spottily, oblivious of the peril to his soul. Little Melly saw the writing on the wall when she saw Doctorjay take off to Wichita when yet another president had yet another birthday—take off to Wichita upon his trotter, a flag pinned to his saddle as though the village didn't know that this was camouflage. In matters that important, she sided with the elders who stockpiled vehemence for sinners. She put herself, therefore, no matter how demurely, on the hard side of rectitude.

Just being a plain Lutheran, she argued, while heating to the challenge, was simply not enough. She tugged at Doctorjay repeatedly: "Unwilling, still, to admit your being a sinner?"

He peered at her: "What do the gossips say?"

"Let conscience smite you now! You have become an object of suspicion."

"Me? In what way?"

"You tipped your hat to Abigail. What will the neighbors say?"

He kept on searching for a pillow on which to rest his head. "Now, listen, Little Melly. Don't be a worrywart."

"A worrywart? Who? Me?"

According to the gossip of that year, Doctorjay was laughing up his sleeve. Some people shrewdly guessed his secret might be Abigail.

"Well, I for one," said Noralee to Lizzy, reaching for a handle on Doctorjay's evasiveness, "hope fervently with all my heart for a diligent preacher to shed on my husband some helpful additional light."

Lizzy sprang to Doctorjay's defense at once. She offered, squirming gently: "What are you saying? Abigail?"

"You never know," admitted Noralee, enjoying looking gloomy.

"No way," said Lizzy firmly, dismissing all suspicion. She trusted Doctorjay. He was her valued neighbor, who stood by her through thick and thin. An honest man was Doctorjay—he wouldn't pick a berry from someone else's hedge.

"I trust your judgment, Lizzy. You're sure? You're absolutely sure?"

"Pay no attention, Noralee."

Let gossips say what gossips must; from deep and troubling sources came many murky stories. "I close my ears," said Lizzy stoutly, "to every one of them."

He was her friend. The man who led the Prairie Fire Drive was Doctorjay. The one who helped her tally the malingering church volunteers was Doctorjay. "He is an upright Christian, Noralee. You, more than anybody else, should know."

"Yes. True," admitted Noralee, still looking somewhat dubious. "Not easy being Lutheran in Mennotown, these days."

That was one weakness of the Ancient Faith; the rules were a bit lax; most anybody, even Doctorjay, could lay a claim to being genuinely Christian—unless it was your tribulation to have been born a Jew.

Once a month, the sisters would dress up to take themselves to Wichita to bargain with the Hebrews—Lizzy proudly cradling several balls of cheese and Noralee safeguarding half a dozen hens tied firmly by the legs.

"No trouble to hitch up my mare," the prospering bonesetter said. By the angle of his hat you could ascertain success; by the rolls of midriff you could tell the status of his woman.

Brisk gossip shortened the way into town. Updates about the neighborhood, especially the Donoghues, who had the oddest habits, kept everyone in stitches, particularly Noralee. She kept fanning herself with excitement. Her belly shook with mirth.

"A ring? You said a ring? A handshake—not enough?"

"That's what I said. A ring. A wedding ring. Believe you me. Or not."

A wedding ring was vanity, for everybody knew without a ring: just who was married, who was not. Who might be married soon? Who never had a chance? Why waste a ring to advertise the obvious—a thing so widely and so clearly understood? Good money thrown out the window!

It was fun to gossip away. It was fun to spy on your neighbor. They laughed so hard at times, all four of them, that even Doctorjay gasped for a handkerchief.

"Giddap!" yelled Doctorjay, as loudly as he could.

"Giddap," yelled Herbert, too, showing off his baronial horses.

The road to Wichita was dry. The prairie was a yellow sea of flowers. The two proud husbands sat up front, their ladies in the feather seat behind them, filling it from rim to rim. They loved to show themselves. In contrast to the Jews, who had forsaken Him when He gave them a chance to go to Heaven, in contrast to the Donoghues, whose fortunes went from bad to worse, the future smiled on them.

It wasn't just the Jews who lived a world apart. The Donoghues as well caused many heads to shake. The goose bumps wouldn't go away. Their customs were odd, like a blustery Christmas. They still marched Indian-file. They ate their carrots undercooked. Their dogs had an obnoxious bark. Their cats came without whiskers. They kissed each other on both cheeks and championed brotherhood. They talked about that missing document, while twittering with glee.

"They are inviting ruin," decided Lizzy angrily, who did not easily speak ill of either man or beast.

When Noralee tried visiting the Donoghues to find out some specifics, their gate was firmly locked, but when a strong wind gust blew open the door to their hut, she saw an unmade bed. Their turnip patch grew wild. They were a strange, disturbing family; their nearest relatives did not look like a relative at all.

They did not stand within the solid ring of harmony and showed no signs of joining. Most settlers held them in disdain. They had nothing in common with them.

In summary, the Donoghues had been weighed and found wanting.

"It was a lease and not a sale," they claimed while eyeing Lizzy's property. While heading home one hour after midnight, Doctorjay saw several of them shadow-boxing, which was the oddest sight.

"They're up to trouble. Verily!" he said that night to Noralee, who did not pay attention; who feared the wagging tongues about her guzzling husband more than the barley blight.

She scolded Doctorjay repeatedly, and in the voice of August thunder, to no avail at all. What vexed her most of all were his excuses, since she had heard them all. She nearly howled with insult when he retrieved, from thinnest air, the weakest one of all:

"I didn't watch the time. Before I realized it happened, the sun was going down."

"Let go of your flask! That's an order. Remember last week? It took an act of God to get you out of bed. Let me be clear about one thing. I don't need a wandering husband. Explain yourself at once."

The bonesetter put on his widest grin. "Will you believe me this time?"

He had this social talent, which he explained to her. You met a friend. You took a swig and passed around the bottle.

"Before I realized, the time just slipped away."

"What was his name?"

"How should I know? I don't remember names. Should I have asked for his biography?"

"Do you fancy yourself still in your carefree bachelor days? Who was it? Be specific."

"What's in a name? Don't ask me silly questions."

"Was he a she? Out with the truth. Confess." She took her

husband by the shoulders and moved him closer to the light. She shone the beam of scrutiny on him: "Did you, by any chance, run into Abigail?"

"Abigail? Did you say: 'Abigail'?"

"You heard me. Abigail."

She had his number pat. She sat there, sternly, dressed in a long, frayed nightshirt. She had stayed up to wait for him much later than the neighbors knew. "Out with the truth. Confess!"

On detail, he was foggy. He didn't want to be accused of something base without the benefit of memory. He peered at her, suspiciously. "Did anybody see me in her company?"

"Confess!"

"If I had something to confess, I would." Blind to her trembling lower lip, he launched into assault. "You don't have any faults?"

She started blowing steam as though she were a train. "I never ever in my entire life heard such a poor excuse! I hope I never will again! Midnight came. One o'clock. Two o'clock. Where were you, Doctorjay?"

"I told you several times already. I walked along the street and met a long-lost friend. We sat and talked. Updating on old news." He made an expert grab at her and held her, warm and squirming. "You have no foibles, madam?"

She struggled a bit, but he knew her weak places; he had explored them all; her limbs grew leaden; her glance turned soft; these things were overpowering. "You heard me. Where? Where were you?"

He was pleasantly giddy and wanted to share. "In the thick of confetti, that's where."

What was a wife to do? She lent a hand and steered him around corners. Without her help, he would have walked into a wall and, therefore, steer she did. "You are a pretty dreadful sight! The neighborhood is sneering in my face. You, a respected herbalist!"

Doctorjay winked fondly at his wife: an uneven struggle from the beginning. "I tried to leave. Time after time! The time just slipped away. You don't believe your husband?"

"Not always. No."

"Say! Have I ever lied to you?"

"You have. You have. Don't tell me that you haven't. Was it this hussy, Abigail?"

"Naw! There you're wrong. A gentleman approaching sixty."

"No! You don't say."

"He grabbed me by the sleeve to tell me one more lark about the bearded lady. Come. How about a little schmoozy?"

"You're sure it wasn't Abigail?"

"I'm absolutely sure. Most definitely not." While he kept dishing out excuses, systematic as a bank, she jumped, remembering: "The mail pouch, Doctorjay!"

He blinked with shock. "What mail pouch?"

That was the moment when he sobered up. That's when he suddenly remembered with a clarity some people might have called clairvoyance: the loop came loose! The mare jumped at a shadow! "The mail pouch? Plunk! It dropped into the creek."

"No! Doctorjay! How could you!"

He spread both hands, defeated. "Gone. Plunk! No matter how I fished."

Poor Noralee! What would she do for entertainment now? For two long weeks? Until another pouch arrived?

"What? What?" cried Abigail, a master of duplicity, by then well on the road to tragedy. "No. You are wrong. Not Doctorjay! It isn't Doctorjay."

That was believable. A dalliance with a married man was inconceivable and almost unachievable.

As judged from the inflection in her voice, as hinted in her words, Abigail gave added cause for heated speculation. To guess what might come next was favorite entertainment, the daily drama coming in installments. For an entire season, the neighbors kept nodding to each other: I'm as much in the dark as you are.

The rumors didn't quit; they only shifted focus: "It's Abigail and Jan."

All eyes, by then, were firmly on the girl and on the hesitating bachelor who took his time, evasively in many people's estimate, to ask the question nature wanted him to ask.

Little Melly decided to speed up her chances. She pushed one foot in front of the other until she was touching Jan's knee. She kept shifting from left foot to right, aware that the cat had her tongue.

Jan's mind was on the future and on the missing document. He leaned back, forced a worry from his frown and asked. "Yes, Little Melly? What is it this time, honey?"

"Nothing."

"You look as though the roof is falling in?"

"It's nothing. Really. Nothing." Her need was as transparent as the wind. Her face was a geranium.

But Jan was blind that day. "Look, run along," said Jan. "And let me finish this."

Little Melly fled in tears to Lizzy. "What should I do? He never even noticed my starched collar."

"You're not the kind that makes men blush," said Lizzy, quavering. "Just stay close-by. He'll come around. They all do. Trust me."

She knew her son. She knew he would, for he did nothing to discourage speculation. He only said he needed time. He was a man. He wanted the initiative, concluded Lizzy stoutly. In his good time he'd take it.

She gently stroked the girl's soft hair. "Just give him time. He will not run away."

Why, everybody knew, by then: Jan would not run away.

At the next opportunity, she pulled her son aside. "Jan, I'm your mother. Forgive me for speaking my mind. Has she cast a bad spell on you?"

His eyes slid past her anxious glance. He seemed preoccupied. "What are you saying? Who?"

"Who? You ask who? Why, Abigail. I'm speaking about

Abigail."

He crinkled his blue eyes. "Mom! Abigail?"

A lump rose in her throat. Her temples throbbed with tension. She almost died with shame, confessing such a thought. "I must admit it has occurred to me it could be Abigail."

Jan laughed away her fears. "Don't go by gossip, Mom. She isn't kin. You know that."

Her thoughts became like mercury: in keeping with tradition! "I am so glad to hear that, Jan. I'm so relieved that you and Little Melly—"

"Stop worrying."

Relief rushed warmly to her bosom. "If only you and Little Melly—"

"Don't worry, Mom. It's still too soon. She twitters, and she chirps."

"Who? Abigail?'

"No, Mom. We are discussing Little Melly."

"Does she have braids?" asked Lizzy pointedly.

"Who? Little Melly?"

"Abigail."

She knew he laughed at her and at her silly fears. She didn't laugh, however. Discounting Jan, she knew no one who did.

Chapter 20

In Russia, as in America, ancestral customs and folkways were vigilantly watched, experiments with worldly siren songs not treated cavalierly. Their leaders saw to that.

One such was Alexander, Peet's oldest son, a man who, far beyond the boundaries of Apanlee, was recognized as the most imposing estate owner of his day.

The Elders spoke no words that Alexander did not second gladly. Namesake to several tsars, he walked, a king, within his furrows and knew without a doubt: "Faith in the Lord. Obedience to the tsars. And loyalty to blood and kin—that is the only mix of mind and heart that will bring happiness."

He told his sons and daughters speaking from a bursting heart: "Tradition is like granite. He who counts stars has given us a covenant. It will be up to us to hold it in esteem."

It was a message clear and true that rang from every pulpit and found a thousand echoes in everybody's heart. With wealth came obligations, and obligations made more wealth. All knew it; chiefly, he, the head of Apanlee. They were one clan, one blood; they sowed and reaped; they sang and prayed; they counted on the ancient blood of rectitude. Toward the little hunchback, who gently spoke his mind to plead for reason over Faith, their mood was one of benign tolerance.

The spurious child that Alexander's silent sister should have hidden in the woods had grown into a spindly man, still asking that his bed be warmed. The bursting purse of Apanlee kept him in comfort and good standing. Skilled in at least four tongues—Russian, Ukrainian, High German, Low German—he read and read and read.

"Unless you read," ran Uncle Benny's argument, "you cannot be informed. "

Not many farmers did.

Not that they didn't value print. Most everybody kept subscriptions to Uncle Benny's organ, appropriately called the *Voice of Peace*—partly to have sufficient kindling paper for breakfast fires in the morning, partly to keep the little oddling snug and occupied in his exotic world of words, knowing he would never run a blade into the rich and fertile earth.

They were like that; one of their traits was tolerance. In deference to his learned mind, they gladly stepped aside; he had free rein with paper, ink and pen.

His gently chiding editorials are now the stuff of history. They rankled a bit, for they urged the containment of Faith.

On Uncle Benny's throbbing brow sat many a thought that was odd. He saw a saint where a devil might be, and a devil where there was a saint. He sat among them, quietly, a cousin among cousins. His thoughts were far away.

He said to no one in particular: "I wish I did not see so clearly."

Just as the crocuses were breaking, a little girl was born to Uncle Benny and his Dorothy—a child as smooth and perfect as a clover seed, without a single flaw. Her eyes were blue; her hair was fair; but nonetheless, her life was short and sad—much like a Cossack ballad.

Of her, we do not have a single photograph; we only have some moving poems, held fast with shaking pen. We do not even know her name; however, thanks to those few trembling poems a grieving father wrote, we know that she grew up and married young, then sickened, and then died.

The poem said: you could not force the hand of fate. The difference between life and death was luck.

This young girl was as fleeting and as stirring as the wind that sways the crown of trees. That's what the poem said. They say she lived. They say she died. She mattered only insofar as she, in turn, would give birth to a little baby boy around the time the First Great War broke out.

This youngster's name, the hunchback's only kin, was Jonathan.

Pied pipers come in many guises. Claas Epp was one of them.

Whereas many Russian-German settlers still longingly looked westwards across the stormy waters in search of *Lebensraum*, since land was scarce and getting scarcer by the year and decade, Claas stubbornly looked east across the wastes of Tartary .

His ear was always cocked.

He sat, a throbbing ache upon him like a vise, cupping his face with feverish hands, tilting his head this way and that to catch the fleeting Voice.

"I am with you," the Voice told Claas. "Believe. Obey. Do as I say. Apocalypse is near. The trustworthy walk east."

He listened apprehensively. He prayed repeatedly for guidance and direction, finding only small, disjointed answers. All the while, the Voice spoke up. "Have Faith," the Voice told Claas. "Go east in search of bliss. Go west and face damnation."

"Not me!" Claas cried, recoiling. "I am too weak. I fear too much!"

The Voice was unrelenting. "I am with you. Be not afraid. Faith is your trusty arrow."

One sparkling Sunday morning, Claas told his restive congregation: "The Lord has told me in my dreams: 'Lead ye my flock into the sun. The Beast! The Beast! The Antichrist!'"

The congregation hushed.

Claas took a deep and trembling breath. He pounced upon the gullible.

"Don't let yourselves be fooled. Go east and walk into eternal bliss. Go west and face the Fiend."

A mild, obedient girl fell prey to Claas's flickering eyes. This happened at a harvest festival, in the vicinity of Apanlee, where he assisted her in scooping out the juicy hearts of watermelons to boil to a syrupy brew. Her name was Ella Friesen.

Ella hailed from a poor but pious village to the east of Apanlee. She glanced at Claas and wondered: "Who is this man? What is he telling me?"

"I am a messenger of God," he told her broodingly. "That's all you need to know."

He acted as if struck by lightning, suddenly, and she pulled back in fear. He fell to the ground at her feet and kept hugging the earth in convulsions. When he could speak again, he spoke in foreign tongues.

"On curse of future blindness," cried Ella, an untouched girl and therefore strong with wrath. "Thou, Satan! Leave him be!" The blood rushed to her heart. She knelt in the dust by his side, cradling his temples in both of her hands. She tried to calm his demons.

Claas sat up shakily and stared at Ella as a cat stares at a dish of cream. His small eyes glistened greedily.

"Empty your pockets," he told her. "I have to make sure."

She blushed but obeyed since she knew she had nothing to hide.

He took hold of the hem of her dress and inspected the stitches. He let his thumb run through the seams. He added sternly: "Now your clogs. Take off your clogs, Ella."

She blushed a deeper hue but slipped out of her wooden sandals. She stood before him in bare feet, her toes curled inward fearfully.

"I'll wait for you, outside the gate," he said to her, a nervous and perspiring suitor.

She hesitated briefly. The people at the festival watched the exchange, enthralled. She did his bidding, crimson but demure; when it came to the Antichrist, you heeded the Lord's prophets.

Before the year was out, Claas took his hat and went to Ella's parents to ask for Ella's hand. They ignored several warnings from pitying neighbors, for Ella was caught up in Faith.

After his marriage to Ella, Claas grew a shaggy beard. "To resemble Jesus Christ and thereby fool the Fiend," he told her. He knew precisely how to hoodwink Lucifer.

He gave her several pointers. He told her to tread carefully.

Was that a misbegotten dog that kept on snapping at his heels? Was that an ordinary cat that stole along a rainy roof? Others might think so. Claas was not deceived.

He took a rock and hurled it hard, then hid in a cluster of bushes.

"You're hurting? A hot water bottle, Claas?" cried Ella, at a loss.

He cuffed her in response and gave her a black eye.

The coming years revealed that Claas Epp was a man so violent of temper it often came to blows. His congregation grew.

"Have Faith in me," he told his core of staunch disciples. "We must go east. Not west."

His message was beginning to take hold. A timid gathering it was at first—the gullible, the credulous—but then a throng of fierce believers. Claas praised the Lord with lavish tongues for their belief in him.

"You have my word. Faith will sustain you splendidly, " he promised, not the first to discover the key to all mischief.

On wooden clogs, he went from house to house, his ear muffs flapping in the wind, allowing his conviction to grow roots. He climbed on a barrel and shouted to all: "Hear ye! Hear ye! Apocalypse! Apocalypse! Your Judgment day is coming! Your Judgment day is near!" He cried repeatedly: "Go east and walk into eternal life. Salvation to the east! Damnation in the west! Go west and face damnation."

The credulous took up the chant. The throng knelt with their faces to the east and prayed for the illuminating light.

Though many years have passed since, the memories of those hushed years before the global hurricane are still so clear it might have happened yesterday.

Years rich in Faith and grain! Magnificent harvests—five in a row! Majestic revivals—Faith fingering the destitute of self, while shivers trickled down their spines.

The cautious people did not fail to notice: both Claas and Uncle Benny, taking turns, were vying with each other for the congregation's ear while plucking the beard of the Lord. An infant knew the Gospel was not open to dispute, but that's exactly what they did, those two—both of them reckless with philosophies, at loggerheads since boyhood days. They quarreled and they clashed. They bickered and they haggled, though both had better things to do than testing the Old Script. At least that's what the cousins claimed, who took a lively interest.

Curiosity brought many relatives from far away to verify the march of ritual and wheat, and to follow the accelerating dispute of reason versus Faith. Some came to help with the threshing, others for festivities—all eager for their updates, all equal to the feud.

The ancient aunts from Chortitza arrived; the ancient uncles from Großliebenthal—they came to break the bread of Apanlee for one last time before the grave closed over them. Some came for a few days and others came and stayed, for weeks and even months, and there was room for all—it was a clan that spread its branches far and wide with smiles and open arms.

To be a member of a family respected even by the tsarist bureaucrats was ample reason for rejoicing. As raindrops joined each other until there was a creek that turned into a river to flow into the boundless ocean, so did tradition, history and etiquette make for that final push: for us, for every one of us, the gates of eternity, swinging!

Meanwhile, if children misbehaved, you boxed their ears; that settled it. If they repented properly, the verdict was for love.

Before the holidays, haste drove activities, but afterwards, when snow lay deep and nights were long, nobody rushed the gossip; darts flew from quilt to quilt.

Spring knocked again. The meadows—young and green beneath a wind-swept sky.

The pole beans—blooming nicely.

Then summer came. Autumn arrived. The cold rains came and did not go away. While weather-bound, you might have time to read what Uncle Benny had to say about the oddities of Claas and what Claas had to say to nullify his rival's favorite proverbs, but when the sun shone warmly, the anxious cripple's frilly editorials became as useless as the ruffles on his shirt.

"Your essays?" said the people. "They fire the spirit but weigh on the heart. What do you really know?"

The spinsters clucked their tongues. Uncle Benny often spoke as though he were a Christian—a doubtful matter still. He prayed on his left knee, claiming the right one gave him pain. He quoted from the Gospel: "For Faith will make a feast of fat things, a feast of wines on the leas, of fat things full of marrow—"

He read voraciously. When he started a book, he finished it, too. His rosy fingertips lay on the pulse of history through books and papers that he ordered from Odessa. The archives claim that Uncle Benny knew, though no one knew this yet or would have cared to know, that far away, in Germany, a kaiser with a sweeping mustache, a withered arm and a neurotic soul took over from his choking father who died too soon of a malaise that settled in his throat—the Jewish doctors could not help his suffering. He read with interest, furthermore, that far away, at Mayerling, an Austrian prince committed so-called suicide. Even then, there was talk of intrigues. Even then, there were plots aimed at thrones.

"Hath not the potter power over clay?" asked Uncle Benny softly.

He held the Bible on his brittle knees and added: "Faith walks on feathered soles. It crunches living limbs."

Then came the eerie year to Apanlee. From season to season, the birds forgot nesting. The forest stood hushed, while summer lingered past September, but with a queer and ochre light. A chill came out of nowhere next, and dew turned into ice.

When Uncle Benny's turn arrived to read the Devotions at supper, he read with a faltering voice: "Why doest Thou show me iniquity and causeth me to see trouble?"

"Why doest Thou?" repeated the chorus. "Why, Uncle Benny! Your headaches plague you still? Quick! Turn the page to a comforting psalm."

No one took his words to heart. Their little Uncle Benny, whom every female petted lavishly for sentimental reasons, gave fine and upright counsel, but it was known at Apanlee he was a stubborn gnome.

When he was worrying yet one more modern thought, there was no stopping him. The blood rushed to his face. He could not help himself.

"For plundering and violence are before me. There is strife, and contention arises—"

"A troll is sitting on your chest? Here. Let us run for your peppermint drops."

"The curse," urged Uncle Benny, oblivious to his kinfolk's apathy, "devoureth the earth. The joy of the harp ceaseth. All joy is darkened. The mirth of the land is gone. In the city is left desolation, and the gate is smitten with destruction."

The cousins listened sluggishly. The message was well known. All Satan needed was a spark. The dynamite lay ready to explode.

But see? You asked the Holy Ghost to hover as an antidote. You asked for that, and more: protection for the tsars.

That was the nightly ritual. They sang another trembling hymn, attributing all blessings to the righteous majesty of God. The winds carried it over the rooftops. The children started yawning—time to fall into the feather quilts for yet another night after a satisfying day.

But the cripple just wouldn't let go. He spoke up as if under compulsion: "Look at that sunset, Hein. It looks like clotted blood."

The heir to Apanlee, ten years of age, gave a stray mutt a swift, resounding kick.

"Don't do that!" chided Uncle Benny, his voice a little shrill. "For if you hurt a helpless creature, Hein, then Satan stands behind your chair and smirks."

Did Uncle Benny know? Who is to say with certainty? In legend, he lives on. They say he was exceptional. The brittle papers claim he had the gift of the Third Eye. He read Masonic signs. They say he was too smart for his own good; he read too much; to this day it is claimed he dabbled with the devil while drinking scented tea.

As night fell on the roofs of Apanlee, he was the only one, they say, who sensed that, somewhere, deep within the mountains of Georgia, another child with webbed toes and a malicious mood kept pulling spiders from a hole with beeswax.

That year, the April showers sent Claas Epp to bed where he convulsed amid his chills and visions. When he recovered, he shouted hoarsely that the Antichrist had come to earth, roaming the countryside, to snare the gullible. The Voice had told him so. The year was 1889—a hundred years after Peet Neufeld, the German architect of Apanlee, arrived as a young lad from Prussia to claim the soil of Russia, a hundred years before the Berlin Wall came crashing down, thanks to the wheat this gifted Aryan started seeding and perfecting, which Lizzy took to Kansas.

So much of what we see today is ancient—played on a cosmic canvas.

Few knew it then, and even fewer know today that, all the while, nefarious teeth were gnawing at the throne. The evening turned pale; the clouds sank lower still; the relatives prayed fervently.

They were still rich beyond their wildest dreams. They struggled through another lame devotional.

Not one of them would have believed that terror would come clawing at the window panes of Apanlee. It would be yet another quarter century until, both here and there, the fire walk of the Almighty would begin.

Chapter 21

The feathers flew all over Apanlee. At stake was the correct interpretation of reason versus Faith.

"Claas Epp, a charlatan," the *Voice of Peace* declared in ever sharper editorials. "Here's quackery in pious dress. Here's cunning and deception."

While Claas stalked through the villages in search of souls in peril, gathering them everywhere, the pensive cripple sat alone, moored to his window seat, deep in his cushions, up to his eyebrows in tormenting thought.

"All of them sheep, with a wolf for a shepherd," the genteel hunchback of Apanlee wrote. Like the tsar's pampered pundits, he treasured his book marks, flipping through notes, searching for eloquent thought.

"Don't let yourselves be fooled," warned little Uncle Benny. "Do you lack wisdom? Pursue it! Do you lack understanding? Go after it! Value wisdom as silver and understanding as gold."

Had he had feebler gifts, he might have argued less. He read the ghoulish message. He knew what lay in wait. The horses in the stalls of Apanlee reared heads and whinnied without reason. The sky glowed orange, red, and crimson; the clouds hung low;

the soil was badly waterlogged, and even Alexander, impatient with the calendar, decided with a heavy heart that seeding had to wait.

Claas proved himself a match: with withering scorn, he published a book of his own. Point by point and page by page, he simplified, for the convenience of the flock, the complicated prophesies of Daniel.

Before too many moons had passed, he stood and scanned his lists. His boots were thick with dust. He found his strength and rectitude in numbers. His converts sang and prayed in unison while listening to Claas who shouted himself hoarse.

The faithful looked at Uncle Benny scornfully: "What does he know, a lonely bookworm, with tell-tale ink stains always on his fingers? He who has never steered a plow?"

Despite his splitting headaches, Claas was, by then, an asked-for speaker in debates. Wherever he delivered direct messages from Heaven, the faithful flocked from the surrounding villages.

"A man of God," the faithful people said. "One of the prophets, verily, forecast by Revelation."

Claas had his message pat. Not rain nor snow could hinder him from spreading the Lord's word. He hurled the Bible's prophesies, like stones from David's slingshot. From homestead to homestead he went, a dogged spokesman for the Lord, firmly guided by his dreams and visions, a dog-eared songbook in his pockets—a safeguard he kept handy for those few moments of raw panic, when his voice would choke with wrath and with the burden of his calling and constrict his throat with bile.

Each day, he took a stick to ward off dogs, as he went door to door. "Christ will return and slay the Antichrist," he promised fervently.

His eyes emitted wisps of smoke. The church bells pealed. The undecided muttered incantations. The faithful chorused fearfully: "Show us the light. Show us the luminous light."

"Read Revelation!" urged Claas Epp.

"Here is convincing evidence," said many searching souls who listened to Claas Epp and knew: "At his disposal, twelve legions of Angels! The Lord is with him. Here is His prophet. This is His people's Moses. What do God's children have to fear?"

All eyes went to the twisted hunchback, who spoke of reason and restraint before he shrunk into his cushions, while Claas, who spoke of Faith in ringing timbre when not deterred by fits of coughing, won.

The faithful started auctioning off hats, galoshes, sheepskins, dishes. They sold their lanterns, saddles, milk pails, washboards—everything. A caravan was forming east of Apanlee.

"No time to waste," urged Claas. "We don't need much, except God's holy promise."

Ella tied knapsacks and bundles together. She roped bedding, her eyes brimming over with worry. Claas tipped his head in consternation, for she was slow, the children were not dressed as yet for the anticipated taxing road, and time was running out.

He urged her on, impatiently. "Our days are counted on this troubled earth. And though the Lord shall give to Thee the water of affliction, Thine eyes shall see Thy teacher—"

"Yes, you are right, my Lord," wept Ella, brokenly. She had no choice; she followed meekly; she left her life behind; her tailwind, too, was Faith.

Claas grabbed his oldest daughter, Josephine, and hoisted her atop his wagon. "Rise up, Ye women that are at ease," he bellowed angrily.

"Where to?" cried Josephine, who liked to be called Josie.

His glance went like a rake across the youngster's face. "Now, Josephine, your scarf," he told her sternly, watching her with burning eyes. "Shape it. So that the Trinity be pleased."

"Yes, Father," said the child, and bit her lip with mortification, folding the cloth to make a perfect triangle.

Claas watched her, smoldering. He knew right then and there: drop after drop onto a sizzling brick. He knew she must be broken, for she would never bend. He cuffed her with cruel blows. "How you annoy me! Greatly!"

She twisted in the grip of Faith that she saw burning, pinpoint lights, deep in her father's eyes. She was not even ten years old. Faith branded her from infancy. The scar would never heal.

She shrank from the force of his anger. "Whatever do you mean?"

"I know Thy abode, and Thy going out, and Thy coming in, and Thy rage against me—" he chided. "And, therefore," he instructed her, "I put my hook into Thy nose, and my bridle in Thy lips, and I will turn Thee back by the way by which Thou comest, sinner—"

In later years, she would remember always, with that hard lump of ice that would not melt away in any church: she was the only one who struggled hard and long and yet in vain against her father's forceful knuckles.

Many came to see the zealots off.

Claas stalked along the wagons, giving them a last once-over. With trembling lips, he started blessing everything: bolts, screws, a chair, a milking pail, odd household goods. "It's Faith that drives to sacrifice," he told the shivering *Gemeend.*

He looked around triumphantly and saw with satisfaction that Josephine sat, silent and demure, her eyes averted in her lap. His second daughter, Lisabeth, was covered with goose pimples from lingering pneumonia.

The bells tolled mournfully. Thin, misty droplets fell slowly from the sky.

He gave the signal, and the faithful started trekking. This happened on a wet and foggy morning, Claas heading the procession that stretched the length of Apanlee.

They left the cow tied to a tree, the dog still sitting howling on the threshold. Their faces were set east.

By noon, the winds blew hard, pushing the slowly moving caravan. By night, somebody's child was born beneath the wagon covers, a shriveled thing that barely stirred. The waxen mother clung to it with dry and heaving sobs. Claas frowned at her, and she let go. The infant toppled from the wagon. It was the first of many.

That, too, is history. How many of them perished in the weeks and months to come, to this day no one knows.

"A landmark," said Claas Epp, while pointing with his thumb.

On the horizon stood a chain of mountains, very dark and very still. The snow upon them never melted. Cold were Claas' eyes that gazed upon His handiwork. Hard were the words he hurled against the laggards.

He grabbed his ailing daughter by the neck and tried to shake the illness from her body.

"Here, Lisabeth! You're slowing down the caravan!"

"Let go of her," cried Josephine. She lunged at him. He flung her from his side.

"Shave half her head," he ordered, furious. "As punishment."

He knew now that he hated Josephine. What else he said to her, what else she said to him that day, is merely speculation. Of it, she never spoke. She would grow old and brittle, but never touch on that.

Claas was, however, not deceived. She masqueraded as his child; in truth she was The Fiend. He knew she was a child of Lucifer.

He watched her from the corner of his eye. The wisps of smoke intensified. "He writes the script," he said. "You follow. Hear? You daren't disobey!"

She knew that she was done with Faith; he knew it, too. Her lack of Faith caused broken spokes, though he repaired them many times in haste with rusty wire. She drained his energy. She had a way of pouring sand into his thoughts, until he nearly went berserk. At night, her presence kept him up and pacing back and forth, when all his nerve ends shrieked for sleep.

Claas drove the faithful without pity—through oozing dirt, their bedding thick with rain, their sheepskins upturned, cold water sloshing in galoshes. The horses panted hard, in quagmire past their ankles.

He walked ahead, a map with cryptic instructions deep in his water-logged pocket. Rain drops kept pelting on his neck; before another month was gone, low clouds dispersed a drizzling sleet. The road was long and difficult. The air was cold and clammy.

"Return unto me, for I have redeemed Thee—" he chanted with chattering teeth.

The faithful replied to a voice: "Return unto me. Return unto me."

The axles creaked, and spokes fell out of wobbling wheels.

"The earth mourneth and fadeth away," whispered Claas. "But does it matter, verily? I'll help the princes rule."

His daughter, Josie, walked alongside, ice in her heart, her ankles aching. He paid her little heed. The Voice within spoke clearly.

They trekked for many weeks — through barren deserts and over vast plains where Mongol tribes still grazed their meager cattle, a dogged, chill procession, pulling wagon after wagon over yet another hill. The road hardened. The snow deepened. The wind knifed through the caravan.

Claas wiped fat snowflakes from his eyes. The trek crawled on, across vast stretches, empty land, the horses white with hoarfrost. Their heads were drooping. Their flanks were shivering and heaving. The cold was stiffening their gait.

"*Gospodi pomolui,*" muttered the peasants, watching the chariots proceed. "Lord, have mercy on the fools—"

The peasants cowered fearfully.

"Your daughter, dying," Ella wept. "Why can't we stop, my Lord?"

Ella's breath made small puffs in the air. She slid down from the wagon. She sat down in a snowdrift and started to weep.

"A roof, my Lord," begged Ella. "She's dying. Lisabeth is dying. Why can't you see she's dying?"

He watched Ella with seething impatience. "It seems I can't trust anyone." He wasted not his energy. A foolish thing, a woman: she sat and wailed and shook her head until ordered with reluctance to park in yet another hollow.

"A light so bright it takes the color out of everything," he muttered at terse intervals. Absorbed as he was in the struggle of darkness and light, he could hardly be bothered with death.

He tried to lose his oldest daughter, Josie, in the mountains. Not yet a teenager, she trailed the trek, no longer within reach of prayers, cuffs and blows. At night, the sky was her ceiling, her mattress the iron-hard earth.

She mustered her resilience. She walked where the others had walked. She slept when the others slept.

He woke her with swift kicks. He sent her scurrying to gather charred timber to help her mother heat up sugar water. The animals stood trembling, sucking water from the troughs with greedy, slurping sounds.

"Hurry up!" he urged his daughter, furious. "You! Let's get going. Hurry up!" She ducked as he lurched for her shoulders.

He watched her cannily. She was at fault, he knew. He quivered with spasmodic fear. He sent feverish prayers to heaven. He knew that he must crush her soon, as he would crush a ladybug—just crush it with his heel.

She sat there, hunched, beneath his baleful glance. Across from her hunched Ella, made aged by her Faith.

"My jewel. My jewel," wailed Ella, a desperate woman, just rocking on her heel.

By morning, Ella cried: "No breath, my Lord. No breath!" While Ella doubled up in agony and rocked and Claas fell to his knees to pray, it was the living child who said: "Mama. Your daughter died. Now we must bury her."

She watched her mother rummage, weeping, through some bundles. She watched her wrap the thing that lay there, lifeless, a broken doll with spindly fingers.

Claas lent a hand; he dug the grave; he dug with great ferocity.

"Your sister, an angel already," he scolded. "Those are just clods of earth that strike an empty shell." He gave the lifeless child a firm, impatient shove. It tumbled from the wagon and slid into the hole.

He stomped on it to pack the dirt. "Kneel down, I say. And pray."

"No prayers left," said Josephine.

"I'll teach you," said her father, "to obey."

"You won't," said Josephine. "You mark my word. You won't. My tongue is mine. You mark my word."

He stroked the button on his coat in a caressing gesture. "I'll squash you like a louse."

"You won't," she said, a small, defiant child. "You will not smite me. Ever."

He took her by the arm and flung her in the bushes. He left a bruise that would not pale for weeks.

He urged them on, for peril darkened the horizon.

He could see it and feel it, eyes open or shut: the Fiend was gaining distance. He knew because, by then, a cold, dissecting light had crept into his brain.

The clouds were gathering again. The fuel sat, ready to explode. The sole thing needed was a spark. He rubbed his aching chest which, any moment now, would spring into a roaring flame.

"A light so bright it sucks the color out of rainbows—" Claas moaned and wiped a furrowed brow.

The air was thin. His thoughts were strangely heady. He snapped his fingers with impatience. He glanced backwards: there was the ominous shadow again.

"Soon!" gasped Claas Epp, but left that thought unfinished.

He looked around: no sight of Josephine.

He fell asleep. He woke to a deep stillness. Up through his nerve ends rolled tides of sweet balm.

"Today is the day," said The Voice.

Out of a quiet that almost seemed a vacuum, The Voice spoke, to the mournful swaying of the trees. Claas listened with cocked head, and tried to fit the pieces. He caught himself saluting smartly. By noon, he knew with blinding clarity: he was the fourth link in the Trinity. He was the Second Son of God.

Chapter 22

Lizzy often talked of Apanlee as she spent time preparing Little Melly to follow in the footsteps of Jan's forebears. Tying an apron round Little Melly's slender waist, she proudly shared her favorite recipe.

"Here's how we did it, way back home. First, scald three cups of milk. Mix salt and flour. Stir gently. Now add yeast."

"Like so?"

"Like so." No sweeter girl the length and width of Kansas. "Knead smartly on a floured board until the dough feels like a sponge. Keep kneading, honey—keep it up."

"Like so?"

"Yes. Right. See here? Like so. Old Greta used to tell me many times, at Apanlee—"

Soon, Little Melly cooked and baked in Lizzy's cozy kitchen as if it were her own. She ground fat, bursting kernels, ripened to perfection, in Lizzy's brand-new coffee grinder while Lizzy lectured, supervised and lent a hand as needed.

Here was a girl who echoed all her words, who followed all

the rules, a girl who met her betters' expectations, exceptional with needlepoint. She knew the secrets of stuffing goose down pillows so that they wouldn't mildew. She was friends with Caroline as well. Lizzy was so pleased with Little Melly's wifely ways she thought her heart would burst.

"Keep on until small bubbles burst in your hand. And pretty soon, my dear—"

"Like so?"

"Yes. Yes. A little firmer, maybe?"

"A little firmer. Right."

"Add just a table spoon of extra lard. There. Now you have it. See? Like so. Just cover the ball with a cloth. Then let it rise yet one more time. And meanwhile, help me stoke the oven, darling. Remember the first wheat? How bitter it was? And how dark?"

Oh, the pride of snow-white flour, the joy of seeing huge, sweet-smelling loaves cool on clean, starched towels while sending waves of scent into the icy winter air. The rapture—cutting crisp, fat slices from brown loaves!

Lizzy sat in the fierce heart of winter, but safety and comfort were hers, good neighbors were hers, all at her beckon and call. Life was slow, rigid and simple, but even if the snow piled up on Lizzy's window sill and buried Herbert's buggy to the axles, anyone could step into her home at any time of day or night and rest his weary feet.

Lizzy's favorite place was by the parlor window, from where she waved happily to Doctorjay who had, as a precaution against the howling Kansas storm, slung both his muscled legs around the swelling belly of his mare.

"Be sure to stop by for some zwieback," Lizzy called out to him, but the wind snatched the words from her lips.

She knew a friend when she saw one—he was her neighbor and her friend. She was in awe of him; that was mutual. No matter what his weaknesses, she counted on his strength. She watched him plow into the neighborhood, a dogged man, a hardy

man, his belly warmed within, thanks to his hidden flask. He
still set bones, pulled teeth and wrapped splints with hot towels,
for which he charged a quarter or a dime, depending. He did the
Donoghues for free, and that was good enough. She didn't care
he was a Lutheran and would remain a Lutheran. She closed her
ears to all the gossip that made him out beguiled by Abigail.

What kind of bird was Abigail?

The prairie years had welded Noralee and Lizzy. They traded
not just compliments; they traded proven recipes: how apples
changed to vinegar, how peaches could be dried three ways. They
spent their Sunday afternoons together, feet upon a heated brick,
their knitting needles flying, just gossiping away, romanticizing
fulsomely.

"Remember how our parents were excited when Nicky first
came courting you?"

"Remember how you waylaid Jacob?"

"Of course. Remember Jacob's horse?"

"You never gave up, Noralee."

"Of course not. Would you have?"

"Let youngfolk look forward," sighed Lizzy, knitting pensively.

"By contrast," offered Noralee, and clattered with her needles, reflecting on past triumphs, "we oldsters look more and more
back."

By then, she had varicose veins. An ache, an unwanted
stranger, sat deep in her bones. She could no longer do her laundry without resting. The Wichita doctors were baffled.

"Do you suppose, maybe, by spring? Jan does seem a bit
tardy—"

"I hope so. I certainly hope so."

"And high time, too. Don't you agree? Why, just the other
day I heard him say to Doctorjay that it better be sooner—"

"—that it better be sooner than later."

There was a pregnant pause. Then Lizzy squealed: "Could
it, by the remotest chance, be Abigail?"

"What? Abigail? You can't be serious."

"Sometimes I have my doubts."

"Small doubts. But still."

"Don't you?"

"Is Jan a slouch, or what?" wailed Noralee, by then ballooning with frustration at yet another male's snail's pace compared to females' inborn second sight when it concerned what nature wanted them to do harmoniously.

Little Melly had a lap for every baby ever born. She had a sure and certain way with butter churns, an eye for cobwebs, an ear for singing harmony. She knew that Monday was washday, Tuesday was ironing day; on Wednesday, she mended and darned. Her hope chest was filling with doilies.

Whenever Little Melly visited with Lizzy, a mother's heart sang like a nightingale. Here was a girl who sidestepped every quarrel—a girl who was near-faultless now and willing to strive for perfection. In fact, so humble, orderly and frugal was Little Melly that, without the slightest hesitation, first thing each merry morning, she carried the clan's chamber pot outside and emptied it over her roses.

Jan took his time, while Little Melly waited. He liked her well enough. Their lives were linked in love. When Little Melly caught the measles and was put in quarantine, Jan walked around for ten days straight as though he'd lost his shadow.

Why, then, such hesitation?

It seemed just yesterday that Little Melly was still small and tracking Jan from field to field with wide, adoring eyes while nimbly winding dandelion chains, not saying much, just watching him. Intently.

Five years had passed by since. She had advanced to gardening, starting with the proper cultivation of a fuming compost heap. She had all sorts of skills. She knew precisely how to tie the haulms of wheat with strong, sharp twine so that they didn't come apart. Her aprons were a tribute to her sewing skills— washed, starched and ironed to perfection.

As June became July, so, too, a girl became a woman. She looked at Jan and stood on tiptoes, practically. She could already hear the diapers snapping in the breeze. Already she could see Jan's baby children building themselves a fleet of little tractors out of her old, discarded spools.

The seasons drove Jan Neufeld. Although he did not say a word to disturb speculation, he never seemed to drop romantic anchor long enough to come to a full stop.

When Lizzy waylaid him expertly and tried to pin him down so she could mark her calendar for the anticipated feast, he laughed, "Hear! Hear!" and tried to sidestep her.

Another Christmas came and went without a wedding date.

By that time, Lizzy couldn't help herself; the words came by themselves: "Don't think me forward, son. But don't you think it's time?" Small patches of wet snow still lingered in the bushes, but where it had melted, you could already see the shining earth. Jan tested the land, pushing the snow away, searching for kernels of grain.

"Whatever do you mean?"

She stood on quaking ground. She decided on frontal attack. "It isn't Abigail?" she shuddered. "Tell me it isn't Abigail."

"No. It's not Abigail."

"You're sure?"

"Stop fussing about Abigail."

There was no stopping her. She looked upon her son with a profound and all-consuming pride she never knew about herself, but there were parts to Jan's emotions she could not, would not ever understand. Just what did his reluctance mean? Sometimes a mother wondered.

She noticed, for example, that Jan was searching for mirages; he seemed to have that questing bent; he recognized a kindred spirit sometimes even in a Unitarian.

"Jan, when a cow dies on your darling girl," whimpered Lizzy, "she cries as hard as though a relative has died—"

"You're telling me?" said Jan, but would not meet her eyes.

Those were alarming clues. She noticed every one of them, and with a pounding heart. "If only you and Little Melly—"

"Mom, please—"

She does not have a single mole."

"Her blood is cold and thin."

Her hand flew to her lips. She knew her son; she knew his heart beat painfully for causing her this anguish. She thought her own heart might explode—just fly apart with pain. She knew that there were things, romantically, you never touched upon. Yet all the same—like hoar before the snow!

"All that will change once she has given birth to half a dozen babies," she pleaded. She was scarlet of face, yet she knew she must see this through to conclusion. "She doesn't want to put the cart before the horse? Is that it? Jan, if you would only—?"

Jan studied his nails and said nothing.

"How can you judge a meal," cried Lizzy, desperate, "you haven't even tried?"

"Enough."

She reached for him; she almost clung to him, a drowning woman: "What are you saying, Jan? You're young. You are a healthy male. Have you discussed this yet with Doctorjay? If I were you, I wouldn't walk. I'd run."

"Your wedding wouldn't come to grief?" asked Doctorjay as well, and not too subtly, either, in either voice or words. In fact, he near shouted alarm. "Don't back out now! For ages, your wedding has been a foregone conclusion!"

Jan spoke evasively. "What is a year or two?"

"Look at the girl. She'll fit into anyone's pew."

"Do me a favor, Doctorjay." There was a fine edge to Jan's voice. "Let's you and I discuss the weather, shall we? Do you suppose that it will rain?"

"We're talking man to man. Give me one good excuse."

"My reasons are mine. They are private."

The bonesetter grew limp with fear, but then he roused himself; he'd come in a combative mood; he wouldn't leave until he had an answer that would calm down his wife, whose instincts were as raw as radishes. Therefore, he spoke sharply and thrust his chin forward.

"Why wait? What for? It isn't that you have to wait. You can afford the finest feast. Why not get busy now?"

"I am not in the mood."

"Look. I'm just trying to be helpful. I'm your friend. You can tell me. You can confess to me. Is something wrong somewhere?"

Jan shrugged and kicked a rock: "Not that I know of, Doctorjay."

In his distress, the bonesetter was cuffing Jan, whom he respected greatly. "The perfect choice! You hear? Here. Have a swig. I'd put a dollar up to bet that girl is simon-pure." The healer was enormously alarmed. He did not meddle easily in things romantic and emotional, for that was Noralee's domain, but now he moved into his strongest gear: "Now let's discuss your symptoms."

Jan started laughing softly. "There's nothing to discuss."

"Give me details. I want details. Here. Have a swig." He thrust his bottle forward. "Just take a hefty mouthful. Talk will come by itself."

"No. I'm afraid not, Doctorjay."

With trembling fingers, Doctorjay kept pulling on his mustache all the while. "Not much like her beloved Momma?"

Jan turned as silent as the church before the preacher spoke.

"Here. Have a sip. It's just my stomach bitters. If there is something to confess, you'd better do it now."

"There's nothing to confess, much less in need of bitters."

"Well, then?"

"I don't need blinders, Doctorjay. A horse works best with blinders."

The two of them were sitting in the evening breeze, between them a moist silence. At long last, Jan spoke up. "It's very simple, really. I am not sure you'll understand. I'd like a girl with laughter in her eyes. I hunger for a joyous, reckless spirit."

"Don't give me that. Take it from me. They're all alike. Not one of them is different."

"How would I know?"

"What do you want?" cried Doctorjay and felt like throttling Jan. "Just as I've told you many times—I know that for a fact. I've told you that already. I'll vouch for that! I do! And for the record, Jan, one might take Little Melly for a saint, if you want my opinion. She reads your mother's recipes—"

"She reads my mother's recipes," said Jan and faced the healer squarely, " but can she read the secrets of my soul?"

Chapter 23

In the early days of pioneering, patience was a way of life—and that's what Jan and Little Melly needed, patience.

Nobody hurried all too much—you did what you could while the Lord wrote the script. You lived and you died, practicing patience always, until the angels came and scooped you up to sit at the edge of His hem.

And in between, you watched the seasons change.

The men took to the fields. The women did the kitchen chores. The young fry buzzed about the meadows. The oldsters let the good sun warm their creaking bones.

Corn grew two feet; the tassels were already forming. The rye was ripening as well. The chickens laid enthusiastically. A calf became a cow.

You knew that each cow knew its gate. You knew that each child kept a curfew. Thursday was quilting bee day. Friday was volunteer day. On Saturdays, the air was saturated with the smell of rich, fried bacon, which was the proper scent to finish off the week.

Sunday was set aside for leisure, prayer and diversion. Diversion meant getting together with coffee and zwieback—not saying much, just sitting there, quietly, at peace with yourself and the world, content to the tips of your toes, treasuring a sturdy knowledge: that there was joy and certainty in keeping callused hands on plows.

There was rejoicing everywhere as modern machinery came in. Jan's green steam reapers were cutting swaths five feet in width. The wonder and the spectacle of doing things mechanical! Wherever you looked, wherever you turned, breathtaking progress: steely fingers, even teeth that bit into the Kansas earth.

Jan often talked about the future—translated: large-scale farming without animals—a truly shocking thought. He shrugged when preachers voiced their reservations that progress might become affliction if prudent brakes were not applied. He dreamed of travel on wheels without tracks. His mind stretched like a rubber band. His dreams jumped every boundary. He claimed to read the logic of the future—you did not have to argue with machines. They moved without the aid of shouts and whips. They never needed watering. They did the work of fifty men in half the time, and at fantastic savings.

Lizzy, too, was willing to believe whatever Jan believed: that progress was a blessing to behold. But to forsake her loyal livestock altogether? She would have none of that. The future needed brakes. Why would one want to double speed? A horse ran fast enough.

The seasons came and went. The children's voices faded. Large snowflakes floated from the sky. The folks in the Dakotas? Good land and gentle hills—although a Kansas farmer held his own against the best of the Dakotans, anywhere and anytime.

To wit: In Hillsboro, three brand new windmills bearing solid German names. A German restaurant. A street named after ancestors. Another store where you could shop and gossip the old-fashioned way—Low German, naturally—while checking every bargain.

"Next year," Jan told his mother, "I'll build us a more spacious home. A home with red brick tiles."

"How many chimneys, Jan?" Hope rose and fell, much like a breezy curtain.

"Three chimneys. Maybe four?"

That was the best news yet! Both Lizzy and Noralee waddled through clouds. Why would Jan want a larger house, unless he was thinking of children?

"Eat more, honey. Eat! Eat!" urged Lizzy, while stuffing Little Melly as though she were a goose. Let nature have its way! That was her own philosophy. Watching children settle into marriage was much like standing by the window and watching clouds come down in sheets to bring renewal to a parched and dusty earth.

Lizzy started pinching here and saving there; she had enormous aspirations; the stack of cash in her fat cheese account just grew and grew and grew. She'd use it to purchase a full set of dishes to give Little Melly a proper head start.

"Blue rim or red?" she asked.

"I am still undecided. I can't make up my mind."

"Just take your pick. The difference, not even worth quoting. Though next week is a special sale we can't afford to miss—" By this time Lizzy was the matriarch of the foremost family in Mennotown, with honors galore and riches to spare. But when it came to extras from the wishbook catalog, she still relied on discounts.

Yet, even so! A joy to buy what needed to be bought and still have pennies left to spare!

Since Jan kept teasing her about her strict frugality, Lizzy bought herself a brand new coat and gave the old to Abigail. She splurged on thread and gingham. She braved the elders' wrath, since vanity was sin, and after fussing for a week, she went so far as to buy her prairie daughters each a set of Eaton's mittens.

She was in full agreement: the proven way to bounty and abundance was straight and clean and simple: spend just a little less than what you earned—your pennies piling up for you as just reward for good, hard work—and presto! It was absolutely guaranteed: you would come out ahead.

When Lizzy spoke her fears that progress might move faster than was good for Mennotown, Jan laughed and told her not to worry.

"Wheat will double soon in quantity and price," said Jan, and bought a plow with double shares. He bought that plow on time, since he was rich in property but sometimes short on cash. "Progress can never hurt a farmer."

Lizzy did her best to keep her fears and worries to herself, but could not help herself. "It pays to be cautious," she fussed.

"We'll pay it off next year."

"I just don't like to sleep on debt." She knew no one who did.

"Mom, please stop worrying."

Lizzy had a point that made her fuss and fret. His new plow came with a price tag of the kind that made the richest neighbor stop right in the middle of his sentence and lose his train of thought. She didn't know what made her fret—she knew that Jan was right. She quenched her strong misgivings. Jan was so rich, by then, she could whiten his coffee on weekdays. She trusted her son and his judgment; she trusted her husband as well. Both said they had to modernize—and fast!—or else they'd fall behind their more progressive neighbors, the ultimate disgrace.

The world market took a bad turn with low prices for the wheat, but Jan, his instincts on alert, had switched to barley crops before the bad news hit. That year, Jan was decidedly one of the luckiest farmers.

Jan went and bought a grass green cyclone stacker on credit from a bank in downtown Wichita. He signed a pile of papers.

When a large parcel of prime land located north of town went up for sale, Jan bought it for himself. Again he signed, though Lizzy gloomed and doomed. Doing farm business on credit was a frightening risk. The Bible talked about the usurers. Debt stood for the mark of the Beast.

But Jan just smiled and patted Lizzy's hand. "The future beckons, Mom."

When a harness store went out of business in the east, low-traffic end of town, Jan bought that store as well. He bought it for a modest sum; he said he planned to renovate. Again, he used his credit.

He knew a bargain when he saw one. Before the ink was dry, he found another one. He found them everywhere. He signed repeatedly.

Jan bought more plots of land, rich in peat and nutrients. He seeded two to barley and oats and plowed the rest to potatoes. A lucky buy, he claimed. You pushed up the sod; there lay the potatoes—a good three bushels to a square.

For buy he must, he said. Or fall behind forever—play second fiddle to the Friesens and the Harders, who had already bought two glossy Deere tractors on credit from their bank. The money came cheap, and the bankers slapped Jan on both shoulders.

To stem the tide of purchases on time, Lizzy sold six of her finest cows, with Doctorjays's advice and Herbert's help, and let Jan use the slaughter money to pay off what he owed.

Jan's next ambitious project was a mill. The wedding, he explained to Lizzy, had to wait.

For days, he pored over blueprints; her sewing patterns had to yield.

When the mill was finished, the *Wichita Eagle* gave Jan three front page columns full of praise. Lizzy passed around the paper clipping for others to admire.

"Real Progress Comes at Last to Mennotown," the headlines shouted, and there was Jan, sun-bronzed, magnificent, next to the grain that poured from hollow tubes.

Jan filled up his notebook with numbers. The day came when he said: "Why not keep our money at its origin where it will do most good?"

"Whatever do you mean?"

"I have the land," Jan said. "I'll simply build a bank. There is a possibility of partnership. I met some fellows down in Wichita. They offered to put up the cash. I am to give collateral."

Which was as good an argument as any. Some years before, Jan had bought that special corner parcel, next to his parents' property, and set it carefully aside. Now Lizzy saw the purchase came in handy.

While Mennotown slept peacefully, a Hebrew barrister filed paper after paper. Jan's bank was the sensation of the day.

He called it the Mennotown Landesbank. He covered himself with additional glory by opting for burnt brick. The blacksmith shop, the brand new city hall were brick; Jan said he could not fall behind; sod wouldn't do; he must have brick as well.

The deed came with a huge official seal and was composed of fifteen paragraphs in print so small nobody could decipher it, not even in the glaring August sunshine that baked the state of Kansas.

"Mom, safekeep this for me," said Jan, and gave her a brief pat.

She kept it in her sewing box, below her thread and buttons. She even wound a rubber band around to make sure the pages stayed together.

By then, Lizzy was frantic with worry. If progress grew unchecked, the elders thundered from the pulpit, the world would be in trouble—for human beings, being human beings, replete with all delusions, might next decide to ape the birds, attempting to sail through the air!

After a string of fantastic crop years, Jan saw to it that all of Main Street, end to end, was paved with cobblestones, including the church parking lot. Unsparing with the riches he amassed, Jan let the townsfolk benefit; one good deed made room for another.

It was a breeze, thereafter, to sweep up the after-church horse apples the deacons fussed about. Noralee drew triumphant conclusions: "Disarming the preachers, no doubt?"

Jan laughed. "Matchmaking still?"

"Just on my toes. That's all."

"You are an ingrained schemer."

"I'm counting firmly on the ancient laws of love." She surveyed him with female eyes and came away assured. She had his word. It was decidedly not Abigail. No, not for love or money could it be Abigail!

But on the other hand, she was no fool; she drew on past experience in similar predicaments. She kept both eyes wide open. Jan was a man already, shouldering a man's responsibilities. But Little Melly? Still busy filling out her hips.

Jan fixed a steady gaze on her. "Aunt Noralee, what is the rush?"

"You ask what's the rush? How can you say that, Jan?"

"No. You tell me."

"Look at your poor old mother. Her lower lip is quivering."

Indeed it was. And with good cause. The neighbors, all Lizzy's age or younger, had offspring as fluffy as puppies. One son-in-law farmed north in the Dakotas, another farmed in Mountain Lake, a third had moved to Winnipeg where land was rich and cheap, and all their cradles were astir. A neighbor to the right had two. Another, to the left, had four. The one across the street had five already; he might have had seven, had not one died from accidental poisoning, another from the evil germ.

What did she, Lizzy, have to show? An aging bachelor.

Jan was a son of Apanlee, the link that bound her still to Nicky. She often thought of Nicky. It was as if he stood beside her, his questing gaze on her.

Where is the future, Lizzy? Where are the children, Lizzy?

I don't know, Lizzy wailed. I'm at a total loss.

When prodded, Little Melly said, her eyes demurely in her lap: "Jan's wishes? Like wolves in a forest."

Not even a fourth cup of coffee brought the matter any closer to the fore. Little Melly sat there, shadow-stitching, all slender and still and serene. Her breathing was shallow but even.

"Say what you will, it isn't Abigail," said Lizzy forcefully. "I know that for a fact."

"It couldn't possibly be Abigail," said Noralee as well, thus bringing up the rear. "Why, criminy! The very thought! Not Abigail! Why! Abigail?"

"I know. It isn't Abigail."

"Just never mind that hussy."

Both mothers, flanking Little Melly left and right, shed vexing tears into blue-rimmed coffee cups they had recently bought from the wish book.

"You're still a little on the skinny side," decided Lizzy finally.

And Noralee: "You're thin as a rake, Little Melly!"

That must be it. She must be fattened up. They held sage counsel with each other and decided: "He'll want her plump. And of a rosy hue."

"Eat more," urged Noralee. "So something will stick to your ribs."

"More sour cream," urged Lizzy who knew there existed no ailment that Caroline's milk couldn't cure. A bigger slab of mashed potatoes! More dimples, Little Melly!

Lizzy opened her book of devotions: let Abigail remain determined in her folly. She had Jan's word. It wasn't Abigail. Could be that Abigail might fancy Jan a bit—but then, who didn't fancy Jan? So let her fancy him. So let her shower him with arrows of temptation. She might as well be wishing for the moon.

Was there a single maiden in the entire state of Kansas who didn't fancy Jan? Down to the Texas Panhandle and up to both of the Dakotas!

The lazy Donoghues? snarled Noralee as well.

She, too, derived all her opinions from her neighborhood. There was no need to go to Wichita to check a rumor out. Nobody she knew touched the Donoghues. Not even with a ten-foot pole.

She knew enough about the Donoghues to have grave doubts about their course. She questioned their sincerity. She trusted them so far as that was possible. It was clear they were heading for trouble. They still put too much pepper on their food. They weren't equal to the glories of a harvest.

To be anomalous in any way was an offense in matters large or small and, therefore, gossip leaped from lip to lip about the Donoghues. These rumors had it, stubbornly, no matter what the counter-evidence, that Abigail was laying tantalizing traps.

"If that is true, I wish her well," said Little Melly tranquilly, a master of diplomacy. "Who are these people, after all, but drifters out of nowhere?" You snubbed them mildly for their views, but otherwise you let them be. Such was the recommended strategy, though every relative leaned forward in hopes of learning more.

No beads of terror sat on Little Melly's brow. If Abigail entered by one door, Little Melly, soft as a kitten and just as genteel, rose quietly and left by the other.

For her docility, Little Melly won many praising nods. She sat and knit and smiled. The bounds of restraint didn't snap. She loved Jan well enough and said so openly, though girls, not just from Mennotown but all the way to Hillsboro, swarmed over Jan like bees.

Lizzy was scrubbing her buckets to a befitting weekend sheen when Jan sat down on the steps by her side. He told her carefully:

"Mom. Listen hard. I know that this will hurt. But I don't think that I can marry Little Melly. I'm very fond of her. But I don't think I love her."

She would have none of that. "Jan, she loves you. She's loved you since the cradle."

"I know. That makes it hard."

"She's never loved anyone else. You know that. How can you resist such devotion?"

He broke the painful silence. "She's bland as gruel without salt."

"It's only natural," stammered Lizzy, "for a girl to shrink from temptation."

He spoke calmly. "That's not what I'm talking about."

Oh, but it was. Was she born yesterday? She knew him like her shadow. He coveted the earth of Kansas—it seemed he couldn't have his fill. Would he not covet equally the body of a woman?

"Mom, listen—"

She pressed her palms to both her ears. Why talk about the things that nature took for granted? She shook her head, near tears. She spoke into her lap.

"The wedding night," she stammered, scarlet, "will put to rest all doubts." She struggled with the images she knew. He was a man with the desires of a man. She knew he was. He planted trees to break the barrenness of prairie—why not plant children, too? He widened granaries and piggeries and cow barns—why not as well widen a woman's hips to let the future grow? She knew that every tool and every wheel, every plow and yoke and harness stood ready for the coming seeding. So stood Jan's girl, just waiting for his touch.

"The wedding night," said Jan, "is the beginning, Mom. It's not the end. My world is live and lush. Her world is quiet and black."

Time and again, Jan Neufeld postponed plans for his wedding. His excuse was a lame one: his harvests came first.

But in the end, proximity won out. It was a source of boundless joy to their respective families that Jan and Little Melly, after all, announced right after services one merry Sunday morning, that they would tie the knot.

Jan seemed at peace if somewhat somber, while Little Melly walked around, transparent in her dignity. The neighborhood was pleased: these two, the pride of Mennotown, behaved decidedly within the covenant that centuries had wrought.

You could tell by the words in their songs. And how they liked to sing! Jan had a pleasant baritone, and Little Melly harmonized; she hummed; she had a small but lovely voice, and here is what she sang:

"You need not be
At all afraid,
Indeed I love you
Dearly."

Her gaze was fastened on his face. She sang just like a nightingale and—come to think of it!—all nightingales, that year, that brief and wondrous year, sang only for a happy bride-to-be whose name was Little Melly.

"The sooner boys and girls will court," she sang,
"the sooner they will marry."

Soon, other youngfolk joined in, all practicing their tunes to make a perfect choir. Out came the fiddle and guitar:

"The higher up
The cherry tree,
The riper grows
The cherry—"

They sang until they were emptied of songs. They gave over their songs to the night. It was custom to sleep where you fell—the boys in the hay, the girls on the floor in the parlor.

"At last! At last!" shrieked Noralee.

Had she not been rotund, by then—and had not dancing been a sin!—she would have surely danced. She would have surely waltzed through clouds, had she not suffered, more and more, from gout and rheumatism, two ailments that came early.

A boulder rolled from Lizzy's heart as well: the wedding date was firm. She and her sister parlayed possibilities with hushed, excited voices. The egg account, the cheese account were bulging.

Herb spread a glossy coat of paint to spruce up the verandah for the anticipated feast. Lizzy planted white and red geraniums for contrast; they kept cascading over the railing.

"The only task still left to do," said Lizzy, glowingly, "is to throw caution to the wind and order toweling."

That's how it was—within an inch. Within a tiny inch. The town was filling up already with relatives and guests when news came, on a drizzly day, tucked deep into the mail pouch that Doctorjay brought back from Wichita. It was a skinny letter, limp from its voyage out of Russia. It had traveled by land and by water.

It told of Faith gone bad.

And what that letter said, in small script at the bottom part in Uncle Benny's shaky hand, was this: that a small caravan of pious folks from the vicinity of Apanlee—misled, deceived, and decimated beyond words, with no strength left to bury anyone— had wrestled what was left of Faith out of a madman's clutches and now were Kansas-bound.

And nothing would ever again be the same.

Chapter 24

Lizzy's kitchen and parlor were packed—visitors, elbow to elbow!

Whatever had legs had assembled to hear the news first-hand and inspect the bedraggled survivors. Heads swiveling like weather vanes, the neighbors stared with fascination at the few who, tested sorely in their Faith, had come out in the end triumphantly.

Although much time had passed since they themselves had left the safety of the steppe to tame this foreign soil—Russia never more to see, exchanged for a wider horizon—that evening they were all back in thought at Apanlee.

"And Uncle Benny? How fares he? Still thin and frail? No match for Claas's choleric temper?"

Who didn't remember the cripple who sat atop three books so as to reach his food? More yet, had anyone forgotten Claas and the tormenting headaches that plagued him from his childhood, and even made him wrestle demons?

A foolish and misguided man, who even climbed a table, expecting levitation, which, sadly, never came! What vanity! Apostasy! No wonder many perished.

But look at those who survived the mud-spattered, treacherous road! The men kept refilling their pipes and littered the floor with sunflower seeds. The women inspected the children, then scurried for blankets and pillows.

These wracked survivors were the stuff of which church history was made—in numbers now no more than filled a kitchen, whereas hundreds had set out! They had made it safely over mountain chains, sailed clear across the ocean, and now, at last, bore witness to the power of their prayers against Claas' mad, rambling mind: a cuckoo, tumult in his head since the day that he was born! Oh, the folly of misguided Faith!

Doctorjay was in his element. On the sly, he kept patting the flask he had concealed in his ballooning trousers, next to a jar of stomach bitters he kept as antidote. "You all! You might have been wasted! You might have perished from hunger, exposure, or both! He told you that the Rapture was near? Here! Try my elixir!"

Little Melly, that night, was a ministering angel. She was rocking the orphan; she wouldn't let go.

"Now eat and drink! Just eat and drink until your belly hurts, you little darling, you!"

The child could find no words. Her eyes were glass on glass.

"Couldst thou have made it through the wastes of Tartary," chimed Little Melly eagerly, "had He not shone His light on Thee? Had He not lent a helping hand?"

She had eagerly helped Lizzy to put out her finest dishes and to load her table to the edge: eggs, sour cream and bits of tasty cheese, cured pork, fat home-made sausages, preserved apples and peaches, the works.

"Eat now," chirped Little Melly. "Eat all you want. And then admit: as good a slice of bread as any!"

She had been only six years old when she set out for foreign shores—but she, too, still remembered Apanlee, held by a thousand memories. "How are the folks at Apanlee? Can they match our grain? Here. Sample this warm soup, dear child. Have yet another slice of this fine cherry pie. You say your sister died? My. My. How sad. And you helped bury her?"

Jan spoke in warning undertones. "Now, Little Melly. Easy."

"Poor child! Poor child," chimed Little Melly, undeterred. "Your Papa mad. Your Mama in a shallow grave. Your prayers saved you! Did they not? Do witness now, dear child."

"She's tired," said Jan sharply. "Now leave her be. You hear?"

But Little Melly wouldn't hear—she, in her element. She hugged the orphan to herself, her own eyes brimming over. Nothing good enough for these exhausted wayfarers! For an entire month, they had not changed their clothing. Here was water! Here was soap! Here was the ironing board!

"For months and months you trekked? Through ice and snow, you say? No doubt with many prayers?"

She tasted salty tears of pity on her tongue. She added, softly rocking back and forth: "But it was prayers, was it not? How else could you have made it? Just nod, dear child. Just nod."

The girl had clearly lost her tongue. She opened her mouth and closed it again, but not a sound came forth.

"Do witness now. As best you can. We'll fill in the details."

Lizzy, too, held a huge loaf of home-baked bread clutched firmly to her bosom and kept on cutting off fat slices. "Here. Try this, darling child. Do witness, honey. Try. Now is the time to witness."

"That's right. That is exactly right," said Noralee, not one to be left out. "Give credit to the Lord. What was your name again?"

The girl spoke hoarsely: "Josephine."

"Did you not say your name was Josie?"

"I have two names."

"Whyever two? Whatever for?"

The stranger spoke up then. "I use them alternately, befitting the occasion."

"What?"

"It's Josie when I'm happy. When I am sad, it's Josephine."

Noralee dropped both her teaspoon and her jaw. Lizzy cast

her glance into her lap, suppressing a small smile. Doctorjay gave out a hearty guffaw. Jan chuckled softly to himself: a nick-named child, right out of Claas Epp's household?

He took the youngster's hand. "Indulge yourself," he told her soothingly.

Little Melly gently brushed the crumbs from her white shirt. "It's best to settle on one name. It's either Josephine or Josie. Make up your mind. No need to get confused."

"No, Little Melly. Listen—"

"God must be very pleased with you to have spared you when everybody else was left to perish by the road," said Little Melly, her eyes not on the child but on Jan's forehead now. Her voice was velvety.

"God hates me," said the girl with matted hair, regaining her own voice.

"Now, listen, Josephine. Please. Pay attention carefully. God does not hate you, darling. You're special in His eyes. Why else did you survive? In turn, He'll want obedience."

It was as though the young girl ducked a flying object. She shuddered once and closed her eyes. Jan still held her right hand. Now he reached for the other. He spoke in a low voice: "One name or two? What is the difference, really?"

But Little Melly was relentless. "You know that. Don't you, Josephine? That you are special in His eyes? That you now owe the Lord?"

The child took a deep, trembling breath against a wall of anguish. The words came by themselves. "He hates me. That I know."

To put six tiny words to a colossal rage helped instantly. It helped enormously. She said the words again. "He hates me. That I know." She was a little female, with all her instincts raw. Her heart was racing like a hunted beast's, yet all the while, deep inside, shone a light.

That light intensified. That light had warmth.

Into that warmth leaned Jan—young, eager, handsome. Male. "You have two names? Well, and why not? You have two pretty eyes."

The child bit her lip and said nothing. Both hands lay, trembling, in Jan's callused palms. He told her, speaking gently: "You also have a wounded heart. Nobody argues that."

A tremor ran through every limb. "I'm different. I am strong."

Jan said: "I know. I saw that instantly."

Dumbstruck, the folks of Mennotown stared at the brash intruder. Little Melly spoke for them all, her voice a little shrill. "Don't say that, child. That's blasphemy. It wasn't you. It was the Lord. Give credit to the Lord. Your prayers to Him saved you, darling."

"I sent a hundred prayers heavenward," said Josephine, the kind that would go to the scaffold. "And all of them came back."

The wicked tongues, in later years, insisted that it happened then and there. The madman's child dropped all disguise. Could walls but testify! From coffee cup to coffee cup, the common thought was: treason!

Arch-deviltry afoot!

That night destroyed the pleasant fabric of Little Melly's world. It laid a good girl's life to ashes. In the end, the bonesetter cleared thick emotion from his throat. "Tell me. What happened to your arm? Here. Let me take a peek—"

"No! Don't touch me!" All talk hushed instantly before the fear and violence that sprang from her pale face.

"All right! All right! I was just trying to be helpful," stammered Doctorjay. "I won't hurt you. No need to be afraid. I'm just a crusty Lutheran. I doctor in the neighborhood. Here. Easy now. Just let me take a peek—"

"Put first things first," said Dewey Epp, the preacher boy, who watched all this in silence, then hitched up his suspenders before he launched himself.

"God sees the truth. All glory be to Him. I have glad news. If you need cleansing—and you do!—you can be cleansed. And thoroughly. Cleansed right in the blood of our Savior."

"That," said the child, "is nasty language. Verily."

The gasp was uniform. All eyes were widening and staring at the rebel. The shock reverberated in the room, while Little Melly cried, alarmed:

"You mean to tell us you want nothing to do with our Savior?"

"That's what I'm saying. Yes."

"Why not?"

"I just don't see the use."

"Well, then, it's your duty to learn. You and I will have coffee together, first thing in the morning, and practice."

"Look here. Look here," said Jan as though he calmed a trembling foal. "When you are sad or hurt or angry, I'll call you Josephine. When you are happy once again, I'll call you Josie. Right? Is that a deal? Here is my hand. Will you shake hands with me?"

The girl asked, with a cold, chill voice: "Is there a mirror somewhere in the house?"

As if a shot had sounded—without a rifle seen! Indeed, an unseen cannon might have roared.

Little Melly was the first to find her voice again. She swallowed hard. "A mirror? Did you say mirror, child?"

"I'd like to see a mirror."

"I do not own a mirror," said Little Melly sharply. "I don't know anyone who does."

"She's not herself," begged Lizzy wretchedly. "She's plain beside herself with loss of family and friends. Give her a good night's rest. Why don't you tuck her in? A good night's rest will fix her."

"We folks in Mennotown," said Dewey evenly, "do not create ourselves in our own image. See? That would be vanity. And vanity is sin." He drummed now with his knuckles. "Your grasp of our scriptural teachings is frail."

"I have an extra Bible," cried Little Melly, shrilly. "Tomorrow morning—early!—I'll dust it off for her. Her papa mad. Her mama in an unmarked grave. No wonder she's delirious—" She stopped before Jan's glance. It pierced through her, alike to rays that pass through sheets of glass.

So. There it was. Out in the open. Blatant. Nor did it ever go away. It was soon clear to all that Josephine would bring calamity. It was open season on Josie.

When Lizzy said, that night, to break the tension: "Let us now rise and bow our heads—" and Josephine stayed seated, and therefore Jan did, too, nobody said a word.

To preach in coming years the Gospel's healing properties to Josie would be like writing on a hot stove with a candle. The only outcome was more sizzle. Dewey's efforts were in vain; in vain were Little Melly's earnest prayers, proffered up with dimpled hands on Josephine's behalf.

Said Josephine: "I take what suits my fancy. The rest I leave alone."

Those were her very words. They marked her for decades to come. She no more was willing to disguise her nature than she could have changed the color of her eyes.

Those eyes! With flecks in them—like freckles.

Headlong, Jan plunged right into them as though he dived into a gorge. He hung on every word the rebel spoke as though he quaffed the chill, sweet waters of a well.

"I saved myself," she said that night, and many times to come. "By my own strength. I want that understood." She drew a shawl around her shoulders, tightly, and sat there. By herself. The goal she set before herself was freedom. Unwilling she would be, for many years to come, to seek or take advice. She turned her back on Mennotown. She chose the contrary path, and did it with wide-open eyes.

Jan, too. He drew the battle lines as straight as with a ruler.

Some night that was, that hitched such hitherto unseen defiance. Noralee cherished showers of goose bumps; Little Melly kept on gasping audibly; Lizzy could not cease plucking at herself, straightening and straightening her hem. Doctorjay thrust out his chin and growled: "Leave her alone. She's feverish."

She wasn't feverish. She had made up her mind.

Her ragged clothes, all stripped away, were put outside to burn. Her left arm in a sling, she sat, a naked sparrow child, wrapped head to toe in one of Jan's old shirts, that smelled a bit of mothballs. The long sleeves had been folded back; her right hand rested in her lap, her left hand lay in Jan's.

Jan said: "I'll help you. Count on me."

She looked at him with trust and gratitude.

"Whatever I can do, I'll do." Jan sounded as though he were pleading.

She asked in a voice as clipped as a Saturday mustache, while Little Melly's heart stood still: "What will you call me, Jan?"

"I'll call you anything you like. You can be anyone you choose." He added as though at the end of a long conversation: "My little love. Look up at me. Have you no confidence in me? Try to have confidence in me. I want you to have confidence in me."

Their glances locked. The silence that enveloped them was absolute. And in that utter silence that stood between those two, an exclamation point, died Little Melly's hope that she would share Jan's life.

Not that the folks of Mennotown stood idle. Not that they would endure the outrage without a struggle first. The neighborhood stood unified. They marshaled their hymns and their prayers, for kinship was kinship and kinship came first. Beseeching the Lord, they begged for the luminous light. They sang, as they had sung for centuries:

"—*Von der Eh—he..herde reiß mich loß*—"
Mache mei-hei-heinen Glauben groß—"

It was a noble hymn. It had a forceful tune. It made for an unbroken thread.

"*Gib mir ei-hei-heinen treuen Sinn...*"
Nimm mich ga-ha-hanz, mein Jesus, hin—"

The road was clear. The war was on. The rebel did not sing! To spurn a hymn, to say no prayers, was spiritual anemia. It was like having a deficiency disease.

The demon started writhing deep within. A rage, the likes they'd never seen, propelled the rebel forward.

She started screaming, piercingly. "A mirror—a mirror—a mirror!"

She screamed so loudly, gave such shrieks, that for days afterwards she could not find her voice. She shook off Faith. All saw her fling her hymnal right into the fire as if it were a serpent instead of the collection of the finest songs that any church could claim its own—songs that had lived through centuries!

"I said I want a mirror!"

The cross-stitched, nail-pierced hands of Jesus plunged from the wall and clattered to the floor. The windows quivered on their hinges. The dog slunk into darkness, his tail between his legs. "A mirror—a mirror—a mirror!" Utter bedlam reigned in Lizzy's kitchen as they wrestled the child to the floor. Even Doctorjay forsook all caution and disguise, and poured the contents of his hidden flask straight up into her nose.

After she had spent her rage, when her convulsions receded, Jan lifted her and cradled her. She clung to him with her left arm, her broken shoulder heaving.

Jan's open gaze sought Little Melly's eyes. It was as if two sentries crossed their swords.

Chapter 25

"I have no use for superstition," the rebel said in later years. "Faith grows on sluggish minds." She said it sweetly, and she smiled, but no one was deceived.

Defiance ran throughout her nature, a shiny blade of silver. In her burned a bellicose fire the Scriptures only fanned.

Little Melly, by contrast, kept cradling her Faith, though being jilted was the worst, next to the agony of Jesus. Her cousins marveled how she held her little chin high in the air, with vintage saintliness.

"It's not been easy," muttered Little Melly, but added that, for her, reward enough lay in her Faith, the merits of which Josie yet would learn.

Little Melly believed in her Savior and felt sorry for those who did not. Had such a thing been possible, she might have taken out a patent on her Faith.

She stuck close to her young preacher brother. She wrung from Dewey several promises that he would never give up trying to bring the errant stranger back into the fold, not even if it took a trip on camel back to Transylvania. But Dewey needed little urging; the grooves to rein in sinners had been cleaved before Josie came to Mennotown.

"Their kind of love is not my kind of love," said Little Melly haughtily, when she saw Jan and Josie grow enamored with each other as soon as the defiant child grew old enough to put both arms around Jan's neck without the need to stand on tiptoes.

Roughshod across tradition, that was her routine way. To shock her with the threat of family rebuff was hopeless.

For one, she hated visiting her relatives. She did not need the company of people. By choice, she sat alone, ate alone, napped alone, did absolutely everything alone. She could spend an entire Sunday afternoon alone, deep in another book, her fingers in her ears.

All that was almost more than any preacher worth his homilies could bear. Dewey knew he had his work cut out; he was resolved to do what needed to be done, which wasn't always easy. As soon as Josie spied the eager preacher ambling down the twisting trail, the Book of Devotions pinned beneath his arm, she made a dash for safety. If Dewey waylaid her adroitly, she smiled at him in such a way that both his ears grew hot.

He never lost his goal from sight, though that was difficult; once she even tripped him with a broom, for his right eye was swollen shut; a bee had stung him accidentally as he tried sneaking up on Abigail and one of her admirers.

That did not deter Dewey. Whenever he spotted poor Josie, engaged in quiet discourse with herself, he hooked both thumbs into his belt and stood before her, scowling.

"I promise you eternal life," coaxed Dewey. "Scoot over, Josie. Do. I want to talk to you."

"I'd sell you heaven, too, if I could pick your pockets."

But Dewey was not easily deterred. He knew that Josie came from a respected home; the rest was just tenacity and time. Consensus stood behind him like a torch.

"I said scoot over. Didn't I?"

But Josie didn't move. She just turned her back to the wind.

No matter what he said, how vividly he painted all the flames of hell, she tied her neck scarf sideways.

He patted the back of her head. He did that whenever he could. She flinched and moved away. She was her father's daughter. Embedded deep in her quarrelsome core there lay a savagely mistreated youth.

The ultimate insult was this: she would not volunteer for Dewey. She angrily refused to take the nickel can that Dewey handed her.

"I take what suits my nature; the rest I leave alone," said Josephine. She jumped across her radishes and ran.

"Well. Now that you are one of us," said Doctorjay as well, "you might as well adjust."

He was a pragmatist. He was a raw philosopher, and she found that appealing. As she grew up, and into striking womanhood, she liked him well enough.

He loved to amplify the battle-cry of any underdog. He offered his advice. "You can't sweep back an ocean, Josie. I learned that long ago."

A brief smile lit her face. "You did?"

"I did. I did. Have you not noticed, girlie? You haven't watched me hide my whisky flask so I'd not offend?"

"Well, you're a man. For me, it isn't quite as easy."

He scratched his head. "I'm not a learned professor. But I was born with certain wisdom, see? This is a fine community. These people all mean well. The business of grain takes the blessing of God. That is essential fare. That's why the preachers set up tents. If whistling gives you pleasure, go whistle outside Mennotown."

He saved for her the heels of sausages so she could feed stray dogs. She dreamed up airtight alibis for him. Between the two a robust friendship flourished from the start.

Lizzy, Noralee and Little Melly took stock of the developing discord between the slight intruder and the robust community and thought up clever remedies. The task at hand was this: just how to plumb the bottom of what ailed Josie so. That Josie was deeply stricken was clear.

"The root of her rancor lies deep," said the wise. Since she came to Mennotown—name tag dangling from her neck—advice and warnings had rained on her from every side. Not that it made a difference. After a long, painstaking siege, Lizzy lured her temporarily into the Wednesday Quilting Bee, where Josie threw down her needle and started yawning at the walls.

But Lizzy had her antidotes, and so did Little Melly, as did Noralee. Three women, meaning well, kept bolstering the hostile girl with many timely prayers and plenty of advice.

They knew that Josie needed time. Josie needed understanding. Josie needed love. Dewey deftly rounded out the picture: Josie had a desperate need to clear up her rankling business with the Lord.

How else, asked Dewey pointedly, could she partake of life in Mennotown, where everybody strove with all his might to be His faithful servant?

"We hope and pray," said Dewey Epp, responding to the well-known mandate, "that Josie will yet see the light."

"Yes. So we hope and pray."

"Our good Lord is her match."

"Yes. That we know. We know that for a fact."

"Come, darling. Please. No one gets hurt in God's comforting dwelling," begged Lizzy many times, taking turns with both her sister and her niece to bend the prickly relative to proper rites and rules.

"If I do that, what will you promise me?" asked Josie. She sat there, nibbling on an ear of corn. "What will I do in heaven? Knit?"

Little Melly was the first to turn into a pessimist. She couldn't close her eyes to the accumulating evidence: it was slow progress all the way.

Not even at revival time, when preachers left the sinners gasping, as though flattened by a roller, to sob away the last of their transgressions, where might you look for Josie? Velocipeding, verily, the length of Mennotown!

"I just want privacy. I'm not in any contest," said Josie. That was her one refrain.

"Look, Josie dear—"

"Please call me Josephine," said Josie, spear in hand.

But Little Melly didn't easily give up. The faithful, knowing what was good for them and, by extension, Josephine, all streamed into her brother's budding congregation. The bells tolled festively, and Little Melly, who pointedly spurned finery of cloth—in contrast to some folks she knew—marched gingerly ahead of everybody else, come Wednesday prayer services. She always sat, demurely, a little to the back, where she could estimate attendance and help her brother judge the offerings.

She never missed a service. Never. She was the first, arriving early, all gentle smiles and lowered lashes, and was the last to leave.

By contrast, Josephine luxuriated in her clear, translucent nature and shied from all commitments to the Lord. Her spirit ran in all directions; her spirit always broke away. She stood and smiled at everyone. She stood, next to the wisdom teeth that Doctorjay had on display, while sucking on a penny candy. And though in time she kept within herself the anarchy she'd brought from the old country, she started as a thorn in everybody's side, and that's where she dug in.

For one, she was unladylike.

She didn't shriek when startled by a mouse, as Little Melly did, she merely pushed the wayward rodent gently with her foot to give it a chance to escape. When Little Melly shrieked much as a sea gull shrieks—a piercing shriek that brought Jan and his foreman running—why, Josie laughed so hard she had to cross her legs.

Another thing: she had no taste for patient toil. She sneaked forbidden snoozes in the middle of the day.

She read voraciously as well. She'd hide behind a haystack where it was dry and quiet, to curl up with a book. At night, she stuck a candle in a bottle and read until all hours.

She was a wastrel, furthermore, discarding her shoes long before they had holes. She didn't gather crumbs left over from a wedding feast to feed them to the chickens. She didn't even worry over drafts that could have carried measles, mumps and worse. She kept throwing open windows. Though it was only Thursday and lots of chores left to be done, she dipped blithely into her Saturday bath.

A more frivolous creature than Josie was hard to imagine, unless you counted Abigail, a Donoghue, one of a world apart.

Next, Josie stalked the laying hens that strayed. For years, she had no money of her own; she traded eggs she found for postage credit at the store. She used that postage credit to ship clandestine missives back to Russia, addressed to Uncle Benny.

She gobbled Uncle Benny's letters as though they were rare morsels.

Those letters caused a lot of arguments. They were addressed to everyone, for he knew better, certainly, than to waste ink on one small relative alone. By custom and propriety, his meditative missives made the rounds from home to home for many weeks, but always ended up with Josie. She hoarded them. She gently ironed out the creases and then re-read the cripple's careful compositions.

She did that many times. By candlelight.

Since she had never been to school, nobody knew how she had learned to read, but read she did; she gobbled reading, a curious light in her wide-open, unseeing eyes. She drew a secret nourishment from every Uncle Benny letter; they roused her to ideas and perceptions.

Thus she grew up—apart.

She lived an intense inner life, and guarded it that way. She sought out nobody for company and gossip. She did not fit herself into the quilt of Mennotown that centuries had stitched. Come thunderstorms, she didn't pray and wail to ward off punishment; she stood and watched the thunderstorms, alone. For company, she didn't need a soul.

Take Little Melly, for comparison, who stood there, at the ready, just waiting for the nod. She would have gladly served as model; she could have taught her prickly younger cousin how to stir the lye into the grease that made a potent soap with which to wash a future husband's socks.

But was her offer taken up? No chance.

At intervals, the youngster chose the melancholy company of oldsters. They loved to chat with her. With ample time on their gnarled hands as they sat, nodding, by the stove, just waiting to be gathered to their fathers, they welcomed Josephine. Of what she talked with them, for hours at a time, was anybody's guess.

She was fond of an old, diabolical cat.

Worse yet, it was an open secret, before too long, that Josie kept a spurious friendship with the Finkelsteins of Wichita. That race's sins were secret. The tsars had ripped open their nostrils.

"Sometimes," sighed Little Melly, a fine sheen on her face, addressing prayer after prayer against a certain outcome too horrible to contemplate, "I think we aren't good enough for you. Yet man proposes, God disposes. What do you make of that fine motto, Josephine?"

"Just a proverb. Never proven."

If all else failed, she started hiccuping—and that was long before the evidence accumulated that she leaned perilously close to things a Unitarian might believe.

"Come visit us," said Abigail as well, just rocking on her heels, and visit her she did, until there was no way but to step in and put her under house arrest, which is what Lizzy did.

For quite a while, Josie was adrift domestically as well. She had no place to call her own; she wouldn't stay with Noralee where Dewey lay in wait with curfew laws, and there was friction, day and night, with Little Melly's rules. Of needs, she lived with Lizzy for a while—a relative of sorts—but that led to some gossip, for it was clear to all that Jan was partial to her whims.

Jan paid no heed. He was in love. He couldn't bear to leave her side. The neighborhood had ardent eyes; they saw she started looking warm and drowsy as soon as Lizzy lit her lamp so as to fluff the beds.

Jan waited for her patiently while she grew tall and willowy. He gave her ample time to learn the ways of Mennotown he wanted and expected. She still was young, not yet of a sufficient age to be entrusted with full household chores.

"Not even stomach bitters make a difference," lamented Noralee, and cuffed the healer, guffawing.

It was as though a tainted woman, snatched from the meanest streets of Wichita, had smiled at Jan, and Jan had smiled right back.

Sheer sorcery, her eyes!

The sparrows chirped that from the roof: that Josie snared the most fastidious bachelor of Mennotown with her immoral ways. The tempest of her nature soared atop the fire of her tongue, and ambush was the outcome.

After it was clear that, speaking of romance, enormous mischief was afoot, right under Lizzy's roof, it was no longer proper for Jan and Josephine to see each other socially. Hence, she was passed from house to house, much like a straying kitten, until Jan told his mother firmly that he had asked, and Josie had said yes. The day's work done, Jan would ride up the twisting trail to visit Josephine, carefully sidestepping prairie ruts, sidestepping Little Melly, who tried to stem the tide.

Jan knew that Little Melly suffered greatly. His heart was wrung by that.

"I see you as my sister," he told her more than once when she stepped in his path.

"These days, I'm no one in particular to anyone at all," grieved

Little Melly bitterly.

"You, too, will wear a wedding ring," he told her awkwardly.

"Can she stitch a hem? Can she boil an egg?"

Jan flushed with pity for her pain. "So unlike you. The girl who couldn't hurt a fly—a poisoner?"

Little Melly looked at him, and love shone from her eyes. She spoke past her constricted throat. "Jan, seeing you with her is seeing you already in a casket."

"Don't, Missy. Please—"

"If you want me to wait, I'll wait."

"No. It is quite decided."

Much deeper than a well. Much stronger than wheat twine.

"You feel naked with her. Is that it?" Her chest heaved with emotion. She stood and wrung her hands. "It is the fever, isn't it? It is the bestial fever?"

"You wouldn't understand."

"I can't just forget. I can't just pretend that you never existed."

It was a cold and dismal day. Jan stomped his feet to keep his blood from chilling. "Don't feel left out. You know that you are family."

"Me, family? That word chokes in my throat."

She was at her wits' end. She couldn't just force down her rancor. This man whom she loved more than life had raced her with the sheaves. The sun shone then. Now it was winter, chill and dreary.

Her words became sharp icicles she gouged into his heart. "If you ask me, here is the truth. She does not love you equally."

"She's still a child. She will."

"A she-wolf. Mark my word."

"It's cold," he said. "I better go."

"Come in and cuddle by the fire," said Little Melly, reduced to beggary.

But Jan just shook his head and left her standing in the snow, her future as bleak as a factory window, her handkerchief a wad.

"She's worse than Abigail," she shouted after him.

"That is ungracious, Missy," said Jan, and sent the girl who loved him more than anyone on earth just flying to her room to cry herself to sleep.

"Now, Little Melly. Face it. She is Jan's choice," said Doctorjay, not known for subtlety. "He is a normal man. She knows what being female is about."

"His choice? What choice?" Huge tears welled up in Little Melly's eyes. "She has magnetized him. She has mesmerized him. How can those feelings be called normal?"

"If it's his choice, then it's his choice," sighed Lizzy, overcome, and swallowed what she meant to add much as a goose might force down a worm. "I wish it had been you. But, Missy? What to do? What can I say? I'll help you make the best out of a desperate situation."

Here was her reasoning: far better it be Josephine than Abigail. Far better it be a capricious marriage than—God forbid!—an aging bachelor, an injury to nature.

Until the wedding day was set, Lizzy hadn't realized how deep her fear had been that Jan might never marry. Had Jan reneged on marriage altogether—which was what she had feared—why, the entire universe would have come grinding to a halt.

Therefore, not all was lost. Now, the faint scent of honeysuckle kept on wafting through the air.

"So what if she's a little wastrel now?" said Lizzy, out of earshot of the gossips. "Spreading the butter thick?"

"She'll learn." Jan laughed indulgently. "She has a fine and nimble mind. She's swift. She'll learn. There's nothing that Josie can't learn."

And, therefore, Lizzy told herself that she was overjoyed.

She idolized her son and set about to idolize his bride. When she sang Josie's praises throughout the neighborhood, it seemed as though she couldn't do enough.

"What makes me love you so?" Jan asked at times, his love slantways on Josephine—like hot, unbroken sunshine in July.

Josie opened her mouth and closed it again. That's how she went blank, at odd moments.

He didn't expect any answers. His heart was so full that it answered itself. If she tried to reply, he would cut her off.

"No, *Liebling*. No. Don't frown at me. Such a pretty face. Such sparkling eyes. I feel as though I've longed for you a long, long lifetime, Josie."

He poured over Josie whole rivers of love. He kissed her before his own mother.

At once, Lizzy ran and told Noralee, who didn't know if they should laugh or cry. "In front of his mother, he kissed her. I beg of you. Don't tell a soul."

"I won't," swore her sister, herself not a saint, and ran to tell Greta and Susie. "Jan's smitten with Josie," she wailed, and they thought so, too. Here was the drama of the decade; they made the most of it.

Josie loved Jan back, in her own way. When she heard the clop-clop-clop of his retired horse—whose only duty was to take him courting now because it was too old, by then, to pull the plow or be of any use in any other way—a sweet, reluctant warmth stole deep into her heart.

"Why me?" she asked. She sat with him on the front steps, in full view of the moon.

"Whyever not?"

She leaned against him lightly. "I'm vehement in thought and pen."

"I've never known anyone like you."

"Go on."

"What more can I say? You do things in accord with your nature."

"What stops you, then?" asked Josie. The words formed of themselves.

She liked him well enough and tried to make him happy. But there was always that ironic undertone—as if she measured Jan by his surroundings.

Chapter 26

Two weeks before the wedding feast, Jan put his chosen next to him at Sunday *vespa* for all-around inspection. He stood beside her like a rock despite all whisperings in undertones.

Behind her son stood Lizzy. As soon as Lizzy swallowed down her bitter disappointment and reconciled herself to the inevitable—that Jan would marry Josie and not Little Melly—she prayed for Josie every night.

"Give her a sweet and humble mind," she prayed.

"Let her not stare so much into her mirror all the time," she prayed.

"No *Wienerschnitzel*, please!" prayed Lizzy, frugal to the core. "Instead, dear Lord, *vareniki*."

She prayed for Little Melly, too, for this and that—small favors!—but, loyally, the brunt of all of Lizzy's prayers went for Josie. She prayed as hard for Josephine as she had ever prayed for any friend or foe, but Lizzy's prayers, sadly, made no dent: Josie favored *Wienerschnitzel*.

Next, Lizzy pulled her son aside. "Do you suppose she prays at all?"

"I do not ask," Jan told his mother, frowning.

"Perhaps you should?" begged Lizzy timidly, torn sorely between conflicting duties.

Jan's gaze went past his mother's. "She told me once," said Jan, "that prayers were, for her, like sailing over dry and barren land. I've never forgotten she said that."

"Now where," asked Lizzy, frowning, "have I heard that before?" Unable to contain herself, she pointed out: "Now, Little Melly, on the other hand—"

Jan cut his mother off. "Don't. Never in my presence, Mom." What could a mother say?

"The best is barely good enough," bragged Lizzy to her neighbors. She put her pride and energy behind her brooms. She put those brooms to work and made the spiders fly. Chop off the heads of some unlucky rooster; know that a party was on!

The wedding preparations soon wiped out every other thought from Lizzy's buzzing mind. Now that the date was set, her reputation was at stake; Jan's wedding had to be a first-class wedding, the best she could deliver.

She dipped into her cheese account, not skimping on the nickels. The end result was stacks of raisin buns and bread, smooth turkey salad, navy beans, even custard pie to top it off—the works! Just like Americans.

The wedding Lizzy planned was lavish even in the minds of those who could afford to add a worldly touch and brave enough to follow through and copy foreign ways.

That's how Jan wanted it, to please his little Josie.

Lizzy took a map and dotted all the places with red ink: the whole of the United States and Canada, by then, one kith and kin, a huge, tight net of loyal relatives—and she at the hub of it all!

"No matter what, a happy wedding it shall be," she said so often that, at last, Herbert was forced to put a damper on her boasts and tell her, mildly chiding: "Is this a first? In the entire universe?"

She smiled at him. "For me, it is. He is my only son."

In detail, she would show her brand new daughter Josie how all those relatives, all having to be notified, must now be charmed to visit Mennotown where Jan was getting married. Why, anybody doubting that need only come into her kitchen and she would take the time—would find the time!—to spell out all her wedding plans in detail.

"And, meanwhile, Josephine," she cried. "Here. Take this apron, honey. Just tie a knot. Now help me dry that pile of dishes, will you? From now on, I will wash, and you will dry. Be careful with my coffee cups. Don't clatter with the saucers."

In every respect, it was the biggest wedding feast in Kansas any settler could remember, coordinated to perfection. Cousins twice and thrice removed arrived in whistling trains. Relatives and friends came from as far away as Manitoba and Alberta—nieces and nephews, uncles and aunts, *Opas* and *Omas*—all rattling south to Mennotown across the blooming earth.

Herb's married sons and daughters came, the Ensens and the Thiessens who lived in Freeman, South Dakota. His sister's husband's family arrived—the Wiebe clan of good and humble stock, most all of whom had carved their farms out of the grass, near Lincoln, in Nebraska. The Friesens, too, related to both Noralee and Lizzy—the ones who lived near Fargo, North Dakota. The Harder clan from Mountain Lake arrived, all farmers known for their foresight and thrift. The Ungers came and stayed an entire season, watching and learning from Jan how to sack wheat so that neither time nor kernels were lost. The Janzens came as well, a family of legendary moderation, all thirty-four of them, all sitting in their wagon beds and watching carefully how neighbors parked in a straight row before they parked themselves.

Little Melly was there from beginning to end, a silent and suffering shadow. She looked as though struck in the temple.

When Lizzy tried to put her arms around the girl, she merely shook her head.

"I'm going to survive," said Little Melly bravely and in a tone so soft that it was just a whisper, then added, in a breaking voice. "Though how I wish that Doctorjay's old mare would just run over me and end my misery."

In church she sat, her glance demurely in her lap, and didn't move an eyelash. In front of her sat Josephine—a tense but lovely bride, with every hair in place, slicked down with dabs of Lizzy's butter—and let herself be wed.

Right after Jan married Josie, Little Melly fell seriously ill.

No one expected Litte Melly to survive, what with her love in shreds and all hope gone and dead, but Doctorjay marched in one sunny afternoon where she rose feebly on one elbow, rolled up his sleeves, kicked open the drawn shutters, and told her in a voice that ended every argument: "Get well or die!" and Little Melly's fever dropped.

She started eating second breakfasts. Rich food became the balm that healed her broken heart.

"The Lord is my shepherd; I shall not want," prayed Little Melly plaintively, and shortly afterwards became a lifelong born-again with Dewey's expert help.

It was magnificent to watch how she was treated by her fellow citizens, with singular respect. She accepted her lot without grumbling. The folks of Mennotown watched Little Melly reel, then cling to Faith as if it were her lifeline. Jan's love for her went up in flames, much like a brittle Christmas tree, but the hymns did not die on her lips. Except for Doctorjay, when he was soused sufficiently, nobody sang with more feeling.

"*Von der Eh-he-herde reiß mich los,*
   mache mei-hei-heinen Glauben groß—"
sang Little Melly soulfully by giving it her all. She filled the air with sibilants.

That song turned out to be the bane of Josie's appetite, known to be delicate at best. She ate one egg and called that breakfast. When Little Melly launched herself into another drawn-out hymn, Josie launched into a fit. She hated it. She absolutely hated it. Her chest began to heave; her eyes began to blaze; and in those eyes the demons danced as though they craved the tossing of the sea.

The wedding guests had scarcely time to settle their digestion, taxed by the wedding feast, when it was clear to all that serious trouble lay ahead for Jan and his young bride.

Not that there were a lot of bitter words or copious tears; those were not Josie's ways. She just kept rocking in her little wicker chair while making faces at the dog. And everybody knew that when she grudged the jilted spinster girl the comfort of her songs, she was uncharitable in undeserved affluence, while Little Melly, holy-rollering, her eyes blurred with her memories, just sat there, humming to herself between long pauses and deep sighs, while forcing down large gobs of gruel Doctorjay kept prescribing for her.

Little Melly was a martyr whose wounds refused to heal. "Lucky me. Oh, lucky me," claimed Little Melly, spooning. "For now that I am born again, how can I hold a grudge?"

The neighbors sympathized. Whereas Josie hoarded grudges as though there would be shortages tomorrow, there were no grudges whatsoever in Little Melly's heart that the good neighbors could discern. With not a whimper she had laid to rest the biggest grudge of all: that Josie had stolen her wedding.

Romantic suffering clung to Little Melly's shoulders like a thick, gray, clammy mist, but she didn't give herself over to sorrow. Now she identified with any creature's suffering. She kept a little burial plot for all those little birds that Josie's cat kept dragging from the bushes. That cat was definitely of the Devil. Some people saw it crouching and claimed that it laid eggs. From the moment it appeared, the dog kept pinning back his ears.

"Scat, cat! Get out from underfoot!" The world was fast forgetting, but Dewey's saintly sister kept whispering her cues.

For her church, Little Melly developed commendable zeal. Her Lord was on her side; He promised glory if you served Him, chastisement if you slighted Him, and so, when Josie set her cap for Jan, and Jan went blind with love, she didn't reckon with a script already fixed by Providence.

All Little Melly had to do was wait.

"I have my Faith," said Little Melly, "to see me through. To steady me. To deliver me safely to Heaven."

And it was true; she had her safety net. Her Savior stood there, waiting, His doleful eyes on Josephine who did not lean on Him, instead embracing her modernity—not thinking of the aftermath; how sad and also foolish! America was turning modern, and Wichita was, too; and Josie was already dead to shame as far as colors were concerned. Her tulips simply strutted.

When Dewey came collecting, clutching his Happy Hobie jar to be filled for some social benefit—be it a fund-raiser, a picnic or a cookout to help a cause along—there were enormous, swollen pauses. Josie hated tithing. Never gave.

Yet she squandered Jan's money. She bought and bought, however frivolous. No sooner was Jan's money in her purse than it melted in her hands.

Spring chicken, 7 cents a pound!

Wart remover, two dimes a bottle!

Bust cream, along with castor oil, as much as thirty cents!

Whenever fancy beckoned, Josie went out shopping. Jan would laugh and flick her nose, while Lizzy tried with all her might to stem the spendthrift tide with chiding looks and many sighs. In the deepening frowns of her clan, she read doom. She tried to keep harsh words from jumping from her tongue: she didn't say a word when Josie went to buy a grass-green parasol, and then a double belt, and finally a set of sparklers for both ears. There was no end to it.

Lizzy marshaled a frontal attack. "This is America. We're plain folks here. Are you not lovely as you are? Jan seems to think you are."

"Well, I—"

"With your blond hair? With your blue eyes? You don't need adornments to spruce yourself up. Why do you do it, Josie?"

"I guess it makes me happy."

"At least, I should be told the reason."

But Josie only shrugged. She wouldn't say. She didn't even hint. "Please call me Josephine," said Josie.

Thus, she took her rebellion to the edge. The needle of her conscience was askew.

When Dewey came collecting, escorted by two deacons, there was no money left.

"Again?" asked Josephine, pushing a broom around.

"What do you mean, again? What's that supposed to mean?"

"Look how it pours," begged Lizzy, crimson, fast-talking past the preacher visitor who came, expecting courtesy and cash.

"Yes, when it pours, it pours," said Dewey heartily, unwilling to be wearied. One of the youngest prairie preachers, he was, by then, an expert in his field. "Now, Josie. Josephine. Don't you agree it is a good idea to share Jan's fortune with the Lord?"

"An excellent idea."

"Well, then?"

"Jan did already," Josie said. "He gave last week, last month and last year. Right after we married, Jan gave you a whopping donation."

"The Donoghues, as good as penniless," said Dewey pointedly.

"Their hard-luck stories never end."

"They need a hand. Unless we offer them a Christian hand, they won't be mindful of the Christian message. Just yesterday, I happened to pass by their hut. The laundry on their clothesline? Rags. Just rags with holes in them."

"I'll have a talk with Abigail. I'll give her my old dresses. If I decide to help the Donoghues, why first give the money to you?"

"Because," said Dewey righteously, "I am the steward of God's money. I do His handiwork for him. The Donoghues live right next door. At our Lord's behest, they must be born again. There is no point in helping, expecting nothing in return."

"I hear that they are Catholics. And Irish."

"All Irishmen are Catholics. That is precisely why."

"Well, left and right, I wish you luck," said Josie, heartlessly, and steered him by the elbow. She held his coat. She walked him to the door and pushed him out into the rain and even snapped the parlor lock—except, of late, she didn't call a parlor parlor; she called it living room.

She was, to say the very least, extremely un-neighborly.

Jan knew she did not love him equally. She continued to tarnish Jan's reputation. She continued to squander his money.

Jan laughed and drew her on his knees. "Now look at you. Is that a brand new collar scarf? Are you my girl on a flying trapeze?"

She quieted in his presence. "You are as calming to my heart as raindrops hitting on a roof," she told him once, and he had no reply.

There was no end, between those two, to ornamental talk, most of it furnished by Josie.

"You make me drowsy with your love," she told him at another time, and he tucked that away.

Jan lived on very little. He found a lot of sheepish smiles for her modernity. He thought she was the wonder of the universe.

"What is your name?" asked Jan, and gave her a kiss on the tip of her nose.

"My name," said Josephine, "is still disappointingly vague."

"She is a stranger," Lizzy said. She grieved and knew not why.

"She is a child. She means no harm," said Jan, who was no longer half the man he should have been among his friends and relatives.

"A child? Where is the wooden paddle?"

She even went so far as to frequent a carnival the Hebrews brought to Wichita. She was thicker than thieves with the Wichita Jews. She claimed they were an interesting tribe.

There was no reason whatsoever to be so tolerant of whim. Dewey spoke prophetic words to many significant nods: "Jan, hear me out. A woman is like fire. She warms and beautifies. But Jan! Pay heed! Flames have to be contained."

"She'll learn. There is nothing that Josie can't learn." Jan's voice caught in a burr.

Jan was forever looking for excuses, although his young wife spurned the most convenient quilting bee that Lizzy spied for her.

She walked through her first year of marriage as though she wore a peacock feather in her hat; she asked why Jesus was a lamb; she spoke licentious words, like Mississippi, a state just packed with sibilants reminding them of peepee; she overcooked her beans; the rosebush snagged her skirt; a brand new butter churn meant not a thing to her; pie eating contests left her cold. Most telling of all, she denied herself nothing. Jan calmly took out his wallet and forked over the pennies and nickels she craved.

When he did that, she shone her prettiest smile. She knew what it meant to be female. Though Jan had set his jaw and married Josie, in defiance of his town, when she was barely sixteen years of age and he was twice as old, she did not show her gratitude. He gave her all she wanted, needed and admired—and it was not enough.

She left a trail of bitter feelings. No wonder she became the butt of snickering. No wonder she became the object of stern gossip. She said she would not die of overwork. She was sunning herself in the sun.

Not even Lizzy could afford to close her eyes to the accumulating evidence: she wouldn't sing; she wouldn't pray; she did not even cross her sevens. She did precisely as she pleased; Jan let all that pass by. She read, she slept, she walked and sunned herself, no matter what the workload or the season.

Instead of reading poetry, if poetry it might be called, she could have milked a cow.

Lizzy leafed through chapter after chapter of her Bible with Little Melly's help, but decades would roll in like heavy boulders and build a wall no one could penetrate.

Ahead lay grievous years.

Lizzy fetched a cross-stitched apron and proudly shared her favorite recipe.

"Now, let me teach you, Josie. Jan likes his bread just so."

"The kitchen, as I understand the rules, is now my place," said Josie, in a vain attempt to shake off Lizzy's influence, but victory rested with Lizzy.

She was forever after Josie for learning this and that. She was so eager to induct her brand new daughter into the mysteries of rising yeast she launched herself at once.

"First, scald three cups of milk. Mix salt and flour. Now add foam. Knead smartly on a floured board until the dough feels like a sponge. Keep kneading, Josie—keep it up. No, no. Don't push so hard. Be gentle, Josephine. See how I do it? So? Keep on until small bubbles explode in your hand. Be gentle, Josie. So. Like so. I said like so!"

"You said that already," said Josie.

"I did?"

"You did. Why do you repeat yourself? Always?"

They stared at one another. Lizzy was sure that a chicken bone had lodged in her throat.

You couldn't point a finger and say she, Lizzy, didn't try. She plain outdid herself with Josie. She taught her every rule a newly-wed must know. She even tried to spell them out on some white space she spied in an old almanac, but only broke her pencil.

While this was going on, Little Melly smiled seraphic smiles. Her smiles told all. Her prayers were divided equally between her yesterdays and her tomorrows. Her waistline grew thicker and thicker.

In months to come, Lizzy made sure she said to anybody who would listen: "No more obedient relative the length and width of Kansas."

What else could Lizzy say? It would be a shame to spoil illusions.

"Josie and I do the dishes together," cried Lizzy, a warrior on behalf of family.

Ach ja?

"She washes, and I dry."

"If you say so. *Ach ja!*"

It was as if Jan had taken a thorn and pushed it deep into the heart of Mennotown, and here was the result! Since Lizzy clearly didn't have the spine to stomp her foot and make sure rules were followed, the neighbors put their heads together and started making lists.

Don't zigzag. Please walk straight.

Take off your apron when it's Sunday.

Don't nick your coffee cup.

All this was for Jan's benefit. It was discussed at length and seen as a grave matter: just how to help Jan's child-bride run her chores?

For Jan, now proudly married, growing more sedate and solemn in his ways, sat willingly among the portly Elders.

Chapter 27

No sooner had the last of many laggard wedding guests departed and Jan and Josie settled into habit and routine, than Little Melly started circulating the dark rumor as a cat might circle cream.

It was too soon, however, to speak with candor of a fact and not mere supposition. That way, you savored your suspense. That's how you squeezed a rumor.

"I refuse to believe it," said Lizzy.

Her mouth was dry as powder. Her heart was wild with grief. When Little Melly canvassed Lizzy's face, she knew: as good as a public confession.

"You know what people say."

"You speak in riddles," Lizzy muttered, now speaking in a voice that you could barely hear. "I know my son," squawked Lizzy, loyally. "He's for propriety."

Yet all the while, she heard her heart pound with foreboding. If it were true, and all the signs were pointing to that possibility—just mention chicken skin and watch Jan's Josie bolt straight for the dented bucket—the stain would never go away.

"Tell me it isn't true," demanded Little Melly next, while standing in the door and savoring suspense. "So I can tell the neighbors and put their minds at rest."

Lizzy always welcomed Little Melly's company—so on this nippy Wednesday morning as the November leaves kept rustling to the earth. The first chill had set in; the fire was blazing in the hearth, and Lizzy was providing for posterity by knitting little booties. Her needles simply flew.

"Come in. Come in," cried Lizzy, her heart in her voice and her eyes full of tears. "How can I please you? Warm you? Here. Scoot up to the fire."

"Could it be true?" asked Little Melly, eyebrows arched.

The coward spoke in Lizzy. "Whatever do you mean?"

"Just asking. Just asking. That's all."

"Can you come in and stay?"

"For only five minutes," said Little Melly, modestly, settling on the davenport for the remainder of the day.

Now that her dream of sharing life with Jan had come to naught, she was entitled to consideration from the clan. On Lizzy's davenport she had a second cup of coffee, a third, and then a fourth, and only then was she sufficiently prepared to lace her freckled fingers, take a deep breath, and launch herself full force.

"Tell me it isn't true. She is giving rise to serious gossip. Where is she, by the way?"

"Well, snoozing still."

Little Melly inhaled deeply. "It's nine o'clock."

"My, how time flies," sighed Lizzy, one of the world's worst liars.

Little Melly kept fanning herself with excitement. It was her passion and her pastime to get straight to the bottom of the darkest of all rumors. "Let's see now. September. October. November. Do you suppose it's true?"

"What do I know?" wailed Lizzy, martyred thoroughly. "Nobody tells me anything."

"If not you—then, who would?"

Now Lizzy was dabbing her eyes. "She's mum. He's mum. I'm as perplexed as you. Is that a way to treat a family?"

"So marriage was inevitable?"

"I wouldn't go that far—"

"That's what I guessed. From the beginning." That just slipped out. No way to take it back. "Imagine that! And all the while—"

"We cannot say that yet for sure," begged Lizzy, deflecting all arrows, awash with shame and sorrow, —while knowing that this visitor, all arch and coy, all smiles and dimples, a jilted relative who claimed she'd merely come to check a rumor, would be as grim and merciless as nature.

"Just keep the kettle at a boil," suggested Little Melly spitefully. "That's my suggestion, Lizzy. Just keep the kettle on."

"Guess who's expecting now?" Jan told his mother who was picking her way through a huge pile of darning, while Josie lifted her flushed face, stuck out her chin, took a deep breath, and asked: "Expecting what? Expecting guests?"

She favored watermelon rind—the saltier, the better. When invited to help disembowel the Saturday rooster, she vanished.

All that was whispered first to Noralee who took the story to the quilting bee, from where it spread as far as Hillsboro and Hesston, where it caused nonstop talk. The air was thick with wrath.

At intervals, Lizzy was canvassed, drained of the latest news and notified that worse was yet to come.

"No clue if we are right or wrong? Why not prod Doctorjay?"

"No clue. I did already. Yesterday. I prodded Doctorjay."

"Well, what precisely did he say?"

"He said it could be either way."

"No!"

"Yes!"

"*Ach!*"

"He held up his ten fingers, then carefully tucked in his thumb."

"What does that mean? Why does he speak in riddles?"

"He always takes her side."

"The calendar will settle it," said Little Melly firmly, while helping herself to some excellent cheese.

Lizzy knew she stood on quaking ground, but she took Josie's side. "He claims it is a medical curiosity that the first pregnancy could end most anytime. He said not to jump to conclusions."

"Let's settle down and wait." Little Melly let go of her breath. Her knees shook with her victory.

A margin child was verily the worst of all conceivable disasters, next to the agony of Jesus.

The ones for whom suspense proved more than they could bear sat stoutly and judgmentally on Lizzy's porch to get a better profile.

"At the latest, the middle of June—" the neighborhood said, for the matter was still not decided.

The questions grew louder and louder. "If it's earlier than that, then we know."

Poor Lizzy! In the hot seat! Her heart wrung like a dishrag, just hanging on to shreds of dignity, she clung to hospitality: "Here. Take the center cut. Out of the middle, please."

Little Melly was knitting, determined to finish that sock before she ran out of yarn. The knitting needles started dancing gently while she spoke evenly:

"Look, Lizzy, dear. You must speak up. Now is the time to speak your mind before it is too late. Your roof. Your family. Your reputation, Lizzy."

Lizzy, by then, all but sobbed. "But I don't even know if it is true or not. How would I know? And I can't bring myself to ask. How would I ask? What would I say? We don't discuss these matters."

Little Melly's pale eyes held glee and contempt. "Here's how you do it, Lizzy. You sit her down and ask: 'Could it be true? Tell me it isn't true.'"

"How could I possibly—"

"January. February. March," said Little Melly, while counting on her chubby fingers. "Let's see now. *Ach ja.* It's just as Dewey said. My brother said just yesterday—"

This was much worse than what Lizzy had feared. "You mean to say that Dewey knows?"

"You bet he does. Of course he knows. Here's what he said, at Wednesday night Devotions—"

"Right at Devotions? Oh, my God!"

"He said—well, never mind! I won't repeat what Dewey said because, dear Lizzy, dearest Lizzy, if I repeated what he said, then it would break your heart."

After a painful, sleepless night, Lizzy did what Lizzy must and started questioning the newlyweds to pucker the pulsating boil.

"I know it's not my place to ask. But still. Is there not something I should know?"

"Don't speak in riddles, Mom," said Jan, his warm eyes on his bride. "We love each other very much. We're planning a surprise."

She ran and drew the shutters. "What are you saying, Jan? The baby might arrive tomorrow?"

"Jan. Make her stop," said Josephine. She spoke in a low voice.

Jan laughed, completely in the dark. That man had not a clue. "Why? Don't begrudge them their delight. The neighborhood is having fun."

"At my expense."

"It's just a game. It doesn't mean a thing. It's merely entertainment."

She shook as if from a violent fever. "Some game. Please. Make them stop."

"Give them a set of newlyweds, and watch what happens next."

"Jan, make them stop. It hurts."

"This is big gossip, darling." Jan laughed and kept patting

her tummy. "Pay no attention. Just ignore it. It matters not at all. I married you, right? Though the odds were against you? Did I not marry you?"

When she broke into tears, Jan lifted her and cradled her, depositing her carefully, and told her in a trembling voice: "Your eyes, my pet, when you are wronged—like splashes of clear water."

"I'm not your pet."

"Of course you are."

"Why did you, Jan?"

"Why did I what?"

"Why did you marry me?"

"What do you mean? You knew that I would marry you. I had to marry you. The neighborhood? It's just hen party talk."

"But I—"

"Don't give it so much weight. Pay no attention, Josie. Just take yourself out of harm's way. Here. Here's a little something for your bruises."

Jan was that way. No matter how she bruised, he laughed. No matter what she said, he teased and tickled her. He reached into his pockets and fished out the coins that were clanking inside.

"Let Doctorjay take you to town and buy yourself a little something, will you? If there's a need to talk your female apprehensions over with somebody, have a long talk with Doctorjay."

But even Doctorjay turned out to be a traitor. "Jan married you, of course," said Doctorjay, and giggled gleefully, "to save you from disgrace. The way you and your fella carried on—

"He shouldn't have," said Josie. She drew back from the healer whom she liked well enough.

"Heh! You in the family way."

"Don't talk like that. I hate it. It's despicable."

"Huh? What's it now?"

"I said don't talk like that."

"What did I do? It's you who carried on. You tempted him.

And now there's hell to pay."

"There was no need for that," said Josie bitterly.

"No need for what?"

"No need to marry me. Why did Jan marry me?"

"Well, girlie. What a question!"

"I want to know."

"And you in the family way!"

"So what?"

"It's all your fault. You weren't simon-pure. You weren't maidenly."

"It's always women's fault?"

"Of course. Not since Eve tempted Adam has it been otherwise."

Shame came to Josie imperceptibly. At first, she didn't even notice when it came creeping up on her like mildew on an apple.

She was a married woman now, cut off from youth, expected to obey decorum. At first, she sauntered through a Sunday afternoon, flushed rosy with her pregnancy, barefoot and mystified, and gave no thought to muddy toes. She merely wiggled them to tease the cat a bit. But soon that changed. All changed.

To help her preacher brother all the while, Little Melly made herself a solid influence in his congregation by proffering a moral rectitude that amplified conformity. And not a day too soon.

There was a lot to do in general to build His vineyard and strengthen His commandments—primarily by stringent ten-percenting nobody would have dared, excepting Josephine, to challenge then or now. Jan's scandalously spend-thrift wife reflected shamefully on Dewey's tithing goals, a fact that Little Melly pointed out at every opportunity.

"The net result," said Little Melly sprightly, "is lack of harmony."

"That's true. That's true," admitted Lizzy, wretchedly, for Lizzy valued harmony. There was no way around the fact that Josie wasted money. She wouldn't window-shop. She never checked the price of anything, ignoring the fetchingest bargains.

"Toilet soap—3 cakes for 15 cents!" said Little Melly, eyebrows raised.

"A trifling sum," said Lizzy lamely.

"But human nature being human nature," said Little Melly softly, "she'll want to keep that up. Next thing you know she'll want the kind of soap that floats."

"I'll teach her how to stir the lye," decided Lizzy resolutely.

"She'll run through Jan's money like water. I see the writing on the wall. The future is bleak, dearest Lizzy."

"You're still in the dark?" asked Little Melly every day. The burning question squatted on a hundred eager tongues. The neighborhood would often get together for pivotal updates, sharing many cups of coffee, thinking up between them innovative ways in which to offer help and remedy to Jan's young, inexperienced bride.

In Little Melly's narrow life, her friendship for Jan's mother spelled loyalty, writ large. She came over as often as duties permitted. The goose path grew wider and wider. She brought along her knitting to finish a difficult heel.

"I am afraid to ask," wailed Lizzy wretchedly, wide and bewildered eyes on Little Melly. "I am as much in the dark as you are. Worse, even. Trust you me."

"What did I tell you, Lizzy?"

But hoping against hope was Lizzy's specialty. "I always said she was too thin. Maybe she's filling out? Her appetite's improving. I noticed that. I'm glad she's eating now."

"She's never had a balmy stomach."

"And now it's worse. It's even worse. Her stomach has been queasy for a week. One trifling lump in my good mashed potatoes, and there she goes. Off to the outhouse. Running."

"Most people would agree that is unusual." Little Melly fanned herself excitedly with one of Lizzy's cross-stitched napkins, a fine sheen on her face. "Let's see now." She fastened herself on suspense like a shrimp. "Admit it. We might as well know. Where is your calendar? Let's cross off week by week.

That way, we won't forget."

As if Little Melly could ever forget! She was there, at that frolicking wedding, her own glance in her blameless lap.

"Their wedding, the last week of August—" said Lizzy, just sitting there, knitting away but dropping a few stitches.

Little Melly simply let the corners of her mouth drop sadly and fixed her eyes demurely on her shoes. No margin left for pity. Not in a long, long lifetime! "And here it is barely November. And all that hard-earned money, just wasted on a veil."

In weeks to come, triumph was Little Melly's badge. There was none sweeter. None.

She had been set and ready to go to her grave, replete with broken heart, but thanks to Dewey's prayers and lots of sympathy from everyone, she had pulled through and healed herself; in fact, she felt stronger than ever.

It was Josie now, deep in a jam. It was she who would want to plug up her ears with her fingers. She'd want to hide herself away in the crawl space between the ceiling and the roof.

"It's definite!" concluded Little Melly, so loud that Lizzy jumped. "At first, I didn't believe it. I still can't believe it. I can't."

"You were right after all. Oh, my God!"

"I couldn't help myself," said Little Melly, now falling back, exhaling. "I had to bring it up."

"Who could blame you?" asked Lizzy, tears welling in her eyes just like a mountain spring.

"Have you discussed it yet with anyone?"

"Yes. Herbert. Only Herb."

"And Herbert thought so, too?"

Yes. Herbert thought so, too."

Little Melly kept nibbling on a zwieback. "And all the while," said Little Melly silkily, "that hussy acted more and more as though she were descended from some royal line. Just picking herself through a picnic."

Lizzy sighed deeply, defeated. Bad days lay ahead, at cost of

Jan's name and Jan's pride.

"I wouldn't be surprised if the good Lord now snarled her tongue for being such a hypocrite," concluded Little Melly. "That's my opinion, hear? Just my opinion, Lizzy."

She wanted dumplings. Period. She said: "I hate *vareniki*!"

That almost was the straw that broke the camel's back, for Lizzy was now digging in her heels to rescue what was left of domesticity. The dog was whimpering. The cat hid in the bushes. The curtains twitched the length of Main Street, Mennotown— for this was drama, this tug-of-war, to spice the universe a bit!

"Did you hear that? Did you?" cried Noralee whose traits did not include diplomacy. Her belly shook with mirth.

"Now, pay attention, girlie," she counseled Josephine. "You've got to understand some facts. Dumplings won't do. If you don't learn to cook *vareniki* just so, Jan cannot show his face."

There were a hundred nods in unison, while Josie shook her head.

"See, it's like this. You're married now, and anything you do or say will bolster or diminish your husband's reputation. That's how it is. There's nothing you can do. Come Friday night, it's got to be *vareniki*."

"But why?"

"Why? Why, she asks? On account of the leftover curds."

"So?"

"The markets are closed on the weekends. You can't let the curds go to waste."

Jan smiled indulgently when Josephine complained: "Those kitchen raids. Exhausting." In one long breath, it all came out. "I've had it. Up to here! I've had it with *vareniki*!"

"That is exaggerated. Surely!" Jan stretched his legs. He kept on blowing smoke rings. A smile sat on his face.

"I hate *vareniki*. I absolutely hate them! They smell like sour rags."

"Look, they mean well. They want to help, not harm you."

"I'd rather do without."

Jan stroked across her hair and whispered that he loved her. She was his baby bride who still sat on his lap, all arms and legs, all bristling indignation. He started rocking her while sharing private smiles with his surroundings.

"Look. It means nothing whatsoever. It's such a small concession."

"Dumplings?" shrieked Lizzy, horrified, unable to believe her ears.

"Just feed it to the chickens."

"We cannot waste the curds on chickens. And if we let it sit another week, the maggots—"

"Just stop it, please—" begged Josie, tremulous, a fine sheen on her forehead. "I can't. I simply can't. I tried."

"But Jan wants his *vareniki* just so—"

"If Jan wants his *vareniki* just so," cried Little Melly fiercely, "why, lovey! Lovey! All he has to do is ask!"

Little Melly tried her best to help Josie adjust to matrimonial exactitudes in many innovative ways. She, Noralee and Lizzy put their experienced heads together frequently to come up with helpful tips to help her run her household more domestically. They recruited the neighbors as well. The front gate kept creaking and creaking.

"We'll show you, Josephine. We'll teach you how to mix the lye with grease. There's nothing like strong, home-stirred soap. The Hebrews' penny soap is feckless by comparison."

"I like it fine. It's pleasant to the touch."

"It's much too slippery. It's nothing but bubbles and foam."

"But it smells nice and clean."

"Why don't you make your own? There's nothing that beats homemade soap."

"The first step is leftovers."

"You've got to start saving leftovers."

"Save everything. Here is a dripping pan."

"See that big glob of grease right at the bottom of your broiler?"

Josie's neck took on a mottled color. She bent to pet her pet. She took small, shallow breaths.

"Here. Take this spoon. Don't waste your drippings, dear. They smell a bit rancid, but once you stir them in with lye, drippings have awesome powers."

"Lye eats through everything. Jan's socks will smell like new—"

It was too much. It was sheer overload. The child-bride up and bolted for the outhouse, and Little Melly, watching, decided she knew why.

"A margin child?" asked people everywhere, the way you might spit out a fly. The rumor drew concentric circles. It kept the town in tight suspense. It reached as far as Winnipeg, and Lizzy, who never had had any reason to be vague or blurry about anything, now looked for broadening excuses to defend Josephine.

This made for many a sleepless night, for just as soon as she encountered yet another neighbor, she would be pressed to answer: "No clue yet, Lizzy dear?"

"She's skinny like a bean pole, and that is why she shows."

What could poor Lizzy do? The neighbors gave the culprit lots of good, hard stares, but the girl had a mind of her own. Her belly, rounding gently, was being patted constantly. Advice rained down at intervals, and Lizzy tried her best, and more besides, to reform Josephine. She tried to coax her back into her kitchen and to her wifely chores, but when she finally succeeded, it was a pyrrhic victory because Jan's Josie brought her bosom buddy, Abigail, who cooked up spicy casseroles from questionable recipes.

The treason had come from within.

Chapter 28

"It was the Hebrew painting that proved the ultimate insult," said Josephine to Erika before she passed away, all but a centenarian. "That's where it all began."

The decades have not dimmed that story.

The smut you see on television now, the relatives said, wrathfully, while filling in detail, all started with that picture—for Josie, many years ago, threw every caution to the wind and let the Hebrews in her parlor, who, even then, were claiming smut for art and pushing to forsake all modesty.

This portrait story is so vividly embedded in the collective memory of Mennotown that even after all the years that have since passed into eternity, it still is told as though it happened yesterday.

"Let's look for it," said Erika.

They helped her look—in attics and in cellars, in boxes and in bins—and when at last they found it, this after Josie told them to go look yet one more time behind the antique chest that stored the chipped and yellowed knickknack of a discarded century,

Josie's face was awash with emotion.

Old Josie knew her relatives. All their shenanigans.

She knew that one day, when she wasn't vigilant, her mind on something else, the clan had hidden it. But where?

"That was my rebellion to end all rebellions," said Josie who, by then, had outlived all her enemies.

When she said that, her blue eyes, full of roguery and mischief, still sparkled as of old.

Here's how the story goes.

The seams in all her clothes let out as far as they would go, young Josie took a hefty chunk of Jan's good, hard-earned money and had her belly drawn. She chose a shady artist, whose name was Finkelstein - a name which, by itself, spoke volumes.

A blizzard blew this fellow Finkelstein into the middle of her parlor one wintry afternoon—a storm that blew so hard you couldn't see the barn door.

"Come in. Come in," said Josephine to Finkelstein. "A glass of tea? A slice of this fine cherry pie? How can I please you? Warm you?"

He started to unload his easel.

No one knew from whence the Jew had come. Worse, nobody ever found that out. He claimed he was related to rich bankers of dubious repute. His boasting his connections never stopped.

Finkelstein gave Josie chivalrous splashes of color.

"You have good eyes. A carefully cut mouth."

He knew how to flatter and fawn. He made his brushes dance, while Lizzy, Daisy, Noralee and Little Melly did wrathful sentry duty by the door.

"A face too good to waste," the Hebrew said, his tongue between his teeth, his thumb on the palette.

It was as if she took an alien thorn and pushed it deep into the heart of Mennotown, and here was the result! She opened her door to this stranger and let him step into her kitchen, while Jan was busy at the mill. Jan didn't even learn about her wanton deed until his mother took him by the sleeve and whispered it to him.

"She sat for an entire morning," wept Lizzy, mortified, "while with a dozen brushes he kept on stroking every contour of her belly—"

Jan dusted the flour from his trousers. "It's not as though she's hiding a secret disease."

Lizzy was profoundly shocked. "She's showing," shrieked Lizzy, two purple spots high on her cheeks. "She ought to stay inside, concealed from view, knit booties, and wait out her time—"

But Jan looked at his mother steadily and said in a calm voice: "A woman's body is a thing of beauty. That's all she wants to say."

The goslings arched their necks. The chickens spread their wings. The dog rose quietly from the porch and put his paw on Lizzy's knee, as Lizzy bent her face to him to hide from her beloved son how deeply shocked she was.

"It's just a portrait, Mom. It's just a painting. She wants something by which to remember—"

"She's got her wedding photographs! Did Herbert not make sure the picture man took all the pictures at her wedding anyone would ever want to keep? Befitting a family album? She was as pretty then as she will ever be. It's downhill from now on."

It was a clever portrait—so real it caused a sensation. On seeing it, Jan liked the painting. He put much store in it. He even hammered home the nail, above the fireplace.

There hung his Josephine, her eyes not on her toes, demurely, but in some misty distance, her shame beneath her hoops and ruffles for all the world to guess.

"A masterpiece," said Jan, and stopped the flying bullets, thus giving her a kind of freedom that still bewildered everyone.

Throughout her pregnancies, Jan stood behind her chair, warm hands on both her shoulders.

"Now that you've had your way, will we have peace around here, Josie?"

That portrait was, for her, the one triumphant product that issued from that year. She drew from it a hidden strength. It was one of her proudest possessions. She studied it often—the girl in that picture.

"As colorful as anemones," she said to Jan, as though she described a stranger.

How had a complacent clan bred such a rebel as Josie? They tried their best to coax her back into the ethnic quilt, but Josie, by then, ate the wind.

The joyful day arrived when Dewey married Daisy.

Both had been baptized solemnly and, thus, were fit to be a proper couple, well past the age of folly—where Josie stuck as though she were an ant, trapped in a honey pot.

The marriage went as all foresaw, blessed amply by the Lord. The course of time brought many children to this couple, all of whom would remember, this to the very days they died, to hang their heads and close their eyes when asking for God's bounty.

Little Melly saw to that.

Nothing left better to do with her discarded life, Little Melly took herself a narrow room in Dewey's dusty attic, where she unpacked herself and took brisk charge of Dewey's household duties.

Now she and Daisy Epp, two expert, energetic ladies in far more ways than one, set out to bolster Dewey's congregation, of late besieged by Unitarians who had a sinister agenda, it being infiltration into the One True Faith. These two became the Lord's dispatchers, with Dewey the tailwind.

That way, all was not lost. "My Bible. My hymnal. My Book of Devotions," said Little Melly, nudging Daisy, with whom she was on admirable terms. "What more can I expect?"

Whenever she spoke of the Gospel, a flame would blow over her face.

Now that no doubt was left pertaining to the matter of the margin child, it was concluded firmly and judgmentally that Josie had, in fact, in her own youthful folly, abandoned virtue for the urges of a man, ripe with the scents of summer.

There was no way to live it down. No way! Wherever Josie showed her face as her confinement time drew near, the conversation slowed into a trickle.

The menfolk smoked until the air turned blue, and gave her sidelong glances. The ladies, once they found their tongues, kept nodding at the calendar. The gossip never stopped.

Josie didn't take it lying down. She wore her polka-dotted Sunday dress on Saturday.

Cursed with the questing spirit, she said that she was going places—no way to stop her now!—and off she went, to Wichita, sometimes alone, sometimes with Abigail.

The Donoghues, with their limp curtains and lax standards of deportment, were not the worst that could befall Jan's reputation; the Donoghues still marched in single file; they all had itchy hands and cagey eyes, haranguing the entire neighborhood about the missing document. They still lived next to nowhere. They still they gave Jan the evil eye and muttered threats and worse.

But Josie claimed that Abigail had personality. She went so far as to insist there was some beauty even in a spider.

Jan didn't say one word against or for the situation. It was slow going all the way, for Josie's chief trait was her doggedness—pugnacity in matters big or small.

Jan was caught in-between. He had a mother and a wife; he knew the tug of two demanding women, both of whom nestled in his heart. Jan's patience was a rubber band; it stretched and stretched but didn't snap; he never raised his voice.

"What is it, darling? Now?"

Her face was flaming with vexation. "We're baking again! We're cooking again! For two weeks in a row, we've been baking and cooking! Just baking and cooking! Two weeks!"

"Visitors are coming Saturday," Jan pointed out. "Among them, angel child, four worthy cousins we haven't seen for years—"

"Then let them eat salad," hissed Josie. The rhododendrons died of shock!

"They'll be staying for three weeks," beamed Lizzy, giving it her all, for when it came to family, just half-and-half was never good enough.

"Three weeks?" shrieked Josephine.

"Three weeks. That is the minimum."

"I'm out of yeast."

"How could you! Josephine! How could you?" chided Lizzy, abandoning forbearance, now wagging a stern finger. "Did I not teach you only yesterday—"

"She's kidding, Mom! She's only kidding!"

"I'm only trying to be helpful—" sniffled Lizzy, wounded to the core. "She isn't kidding, Jan. Do not deceive yourself."

"Mom, please."

Lizzy kept fishing for a pleated handkerchief with which to dab her eyes. "What will I tell the relatives? Last time I visited in Freeman, North Dakota, I stayed eight weeks. I call that hospitality. She's out of yeast? I'll bet you that she left it in the sun."

"No! I did not!"

"Of course you did. How could you, Josie! Tell me that! How can that be possible? Is there a reason why you left your yeast out in the sun? Now it's lost all its power!"

Taming two turkeys might have been as easy!

As weeks grew into months, Jan looked as if he carried coals between two sticks. Repeatedly, he had to throttle the harvester's motor, dig both his feet into the furrows of his land, and put an arm around his mother and his wife, the two of whom kept on besieging him. "Look, why not have some peace? Let's have some peace around here."

Lizzy stood back and swallowed her rancor. Josie did likewise, but kicking at a clump of earth so that the pieces flew.

Lizzy had a barrel of goodwill, but even she compared. She couldn't help comparing.

Had Jan wed Little Melly and not this Russian thistle, she, Lizzy, might have led a life of leisure—doing little more than darning socks and teaching fancy needlework—instead of lowering the beam of rectitude repeatedly on such a foolish female.

Incredulous, the neighborhood watched anxiously as Lizzy wasted effort to shape Jan's wife into a useful member of her clan, her neighborhood, her township and her church.

"I have but little skill for cheese," claimed Josie next, then threw her parasol into a corner with a smack. That she said before her Hillsboro guests who'd come there to see for themselves.

Had there been a hole nearby, into it Lizzy would have gladly disappeared. Her cheese was not just any cheese. It was her pride and joy. Her cheese account set her apart and brought her extra status, not even mentioning the cash. You did not slander Lizzy's cheese if you knew what was good for you.

Humiliation stinging in her eyes, she said to Josephine, therefore, more sharply than she ever spoke before to any man or beast:

"You're just saying that. To give me a good fright."

"I don't feel well."

"Oh, yes, you do. Of course you do. You just don't know it yet."

Josie couldn't be reformed, it seemed. She didn't iron handkerchiefs. She left the darning in the rain. Her carrot patch died of neglect. She forgot to put oil in her lantern.

Worse yet, she didn't eavesdrop—never. All gossip died inside her.

By contrast, Little Melly managed splendidly in her spare time to keep abreast of everything worth noticing—all the more when Daisy realized, as Little Melly did at once, and Lizzy would soon, too!—that Josephine had stripped her home, one merry afternoon, of every single doily she could find.

"I need the dresser space to write my monthly letters," claimed Josephine, and dumped the doilies in the bottom of a drawer, thereby unleashing a family feud that spread as far as Saskatoon,

Saskatchewan.

Lizzy voiced her enormous disapproval as mildly as she could.

"It is important to each one of us," said Lizzy carefully, "to serve the family harmony. Those doilies on your dresser make many cousins happy."

Josie inspected the tips of her fingers. "I am entitled to some privacy."

Of late, that was her favorite theme—her privacy. All thought revolved around her privacy—that she must have some privacy. She hoarded it; she treasured it, and wasn't that stranger than strange?

When shadows filled the meadows and butterflies stopped dancing in the sun, she took long, lonely walks, all by herself, way down by the rickety bridge. She claimed she had much to say just to herself, all from the surplus of her fantasy.

"It's very cruel, Josephine, to snub your cousins for their pains."

"Sheep run together," Josie said, and buried herself in a book.

Misery washed over Lizzy at Josie's unkind words. "Our cousins are precious to us. We look like one another."

But Josie wouldn't let herself be calmed. Her voice took on a strident pitch. "I need the dresser space to write my private letters, Lizzy. It is the only space I have that I can call my own."

"What? What about the kitchen table?"

"That's where you roll *vareniki*. The surface rocks. Do you want Uncle Benny to chide me for my lettering?"

Here was a potent argument, for Lizzy wanted to impress her long-remembered relatives at Apanlee as much as anyone. And now that Josie was in charge of safeguarding the penmanship of Mennotown, perhaps she merited a few concessions of her own? She liked to correspond. She had an even hand; in fact, her penmanship showed genius. Lizzy knew it was important to send back a perfect envelope to Apanlee. If you didn't, you stood shamed, for all the relatives in Apanlee looked down on you with haughty airs.

Had it not been for Josie's letters and her affinity for Uncle Benny, there would have been dry, dusty spells in news between the families in Mennotown and Apanlee about what happened to the relatives on both sides of the ocean. Folks liked to receive updates from abroad, but writing back was difficult, a chore nobody wanted. You just could hardly think of anything to say.

What was there to report? That the harvests were good? That the children were growing and healthy? That the good Lord supported you as long as you held up your end? Fond as she was of Apanlee, she, Lizzy, had already said all that before. At least a dozen times.

No dearth of newsy items plagued Uncle Benny, by comparison.

The letters coming back from Russia were slippery as silk, a pleasure to the eye and ear, but they lacked the robust scent of the earth as well as the promising waft of Heaven.

"There's vexing discontent in city after city," wrote Uncle Benny, by and by, a chant which Josephine repeated and took on as her own. She claimed he was extremely learned. He wrote the way he talked, his dictionary at his fingertips, still privy to the secrets in the imperial domain. He wrote to Josephine: "Three strikes already. More to come." He wrote: "There's ferment in the populace."

His letters were remarkable, all curls and snarls, especially his J's. She always generously shared with the entire clan the letters she received. But what she wrote to Uncle Benny—her tongue between her teeth, her ears the color of geraniums, sparks flying from her brows—no one could even guess.

Thus, when the doily business puckered to a boil, more lay at stake than privacy for Josie. It had to do with mischief of the kind that people nowadays call liberal and worse—disharmony. already lurking in the corners of her smile, a rupture in the ethnic quilt that did not even have a name in the last days of the expiring century.

It was as Little Melly said: "You draw your own conclusions."

"Does it surprise you? Really?" asked Little Melly, eye-brows raised, and rolled her pale, blue eyes. "Why all that se-crecy? It makes you wonder, doesn't it, just what is going on!"

Lizzy bit her lip until it hurt but didn't say a word. She had her second cup of coffee, her third, and then her fourth, but each was just as bitter as the first.

Next, Little Melly fixed her bluest stare. "Ghost stories filter out of Wichita. Just a few days ago, while waiting at the penny candy store, I heard a Hebrew say—"

"She never likes to be where there are lots of us," grieved Daisy, too, her mother's august daughter. "She bellyflops onto her bed the moment we come visiting—"

"That's what she's like. She's always been a loner. But why does she prefer the Finkelsteins and Solomons?"

"I guess they don't put stock in doilies!"

Lizzy's nose started dripping with sad tears. She couldn't help but notice, since she was human, too, that Little Melly's spinster parlor was loaded up with knickknacks, each one of them atop a fancy masterpiece a relative had stitched. Every spare inch of her sill was covered with daguerreotypes of older, hap-pier days when Daisy, Jan and Little Melly had flown their kites behind the barn. The words came by themselves: "If only Jan and Little Melly—"

'Yes. How I wish that I could rest my weary spirit in a cof-fin—" concluded Little Melly, and Lizzy added, rounding out the sentiment: "—filled with forget-me-nots."

While Josie kept on making faces at herself in the forbidden mirror, Daisy and Little Melly became two bosom buddies, while steaming up the windows with their gossip. Work permitting, they included Lizzy as well as Noralee.

The acid sting of gossip was their weapon. They shared luxu-riant coffee cups, most of all on sluggish winter days, and kept it up and kept it up until another Sunday afternoon was done.

"She may not care for doilies, but she excels at everything," said Lizzy, eagerly, while Little Melly's neck was streaking. "At least her aprons, always crisp. Her braid bands, near perfection." There! Let her daughter and her niece draw from omissions their conclusions as to the pillow slips that weren't changed as often. When Little Melly uttered soft protests about the doilies to keep the rankling matter at the fore, she, Lizzy, picked about her food as if she were a bird.

Next, Little Melly pointed out: "They say it is a good year for the suffragists—"

"She couldn't possibly—"

You could have cut the silence with a knife.

"I tried to ask. Her lips just snapped shut, like a fish. I take that as a no.'

"She wouldn't go that far. I don't believe that for a minute."

"You don't?"

"I don't. She wouldn't undermine Jan's manliness that way."

Deep sigh. "God knows from where that came."

The suffragettes had fantasies. Curiosity might lure Jan's darling into exploring their agenda—but Lizzy knew with certainty that, when it came to suffragettes, Jan's Josie would stop short.

Chapter 29

Ever since the fated coronation, when the slender Russian potentate tripped awkwardly and dropped his scepter with a stony clatter, much evil hearsay spread: "Ill luck. The House of Romanov in danger."

The courtiers tried to nullify the omen, blowing off the dust that gathered on the faces of the icons. The crested tsar knelt humbly and prayed lengthily to quiet the baleful rumors. "Free beer mugs, everyone," he offered afterwards. "With the imperial crest and double-headed eagles baked into the enamel."

The crowd went wild with joy. A panic struck from nowhere. The horses charged and reared; the Cossacks drew their sabers and let their whips fall on the suddenly unruly masses. Many corpses lay about the road. The gutters ran scarlet with blood.

The ministers decreed: the coronation must go on. The music never stopped. The tsar looked at his wife for guidance: to dance or not to dance?

The Empress barely smiled. "We dance," said she, a haughty female, a cold foreigner.

Betrothed to this German princess on the deathbed of his father, the young tsar sought her counsel on every minor matter. "We dance," he told the courtiers, echoing her words.

The couple started twirling—the tsar pale and proud, the Empress chill and beautiful. The noblemen clicked heels and kissed the ladies' hands. The sentries stood in silence behind pillars.

Outside, the dead piled up, with crushed and broken bones, like cord-wood before winter. Survivors sorted through them, weeping. Few of them would forget.

Thousands had knelt like beggars in the snowy streets of St. Petersburg when Nicholas and Alexandra came to power: "Thou shalt make Russia happy. Thy name shall be impressed in our hearts."

The wind howled bitterly. The water in the pails was frozen. A scraggly dog dug somewhere for a bone.

"Greetings, children," called the tsar, repeatedly, and waved to the people below.

Dull though he may have been, intimidated though he may have been, he had been groomed into a pleasant, pleasing ruler who strove to be the best of emperors. He looked splendid in his soldier's uniform, across his chest the blue ribbon of the Order of St. Andrei.

The people waited patiently, lined up on both sides of the street.

"Long live the Romanovs."

"God bless our Little Father."

Each winter might have seemed more difficult than the preceding year, but then the sun came out again; again the earth worms crawled about the surface, warily; once more, the lilacs and the roses were in bloom.

It had been prophesied repeatedly that luck would desert the imperial couple, but their marriage seemed happy enough. They sat on the bench in the imperial gardens, holding hands, telling each other sweet nothings.

In the south, the pacifist people kept seeding and raking and reaping. The wind kept on rustling their sheaves.

In the imperial city built on sand and on the bones of countless serfs, three noble ladies stood on a balcony while peering at
the Winter Palace through lorgnettes.

"A cousin on the throne of England, a cousin on the throne of
Germany, on gracious terms with both. What else can you expect?"

"She tells him only what he wants to hear, considers only
what she whispers in his ear. She thinks of us as savages."

"Let's send her to a nunnery."

"Why not lock her up in a cloister?"

"My little turtledove," the Emperor addressed his wife, expertly drawing on coquettish ardor. "You are my life. You are
my love. Without you, I am nothing."

She called him "pet" and "ducky."

He sparkled with his decorations.

She dressed her daughters in the height of fashion.

The Lord endowed them early with authority; it was their
inborn mandate, both were convinced they carried out His will.
"Now you must learn to stamp your foot," she told him many
times. "You must pound your fist upon the table."

He knew no dreams; he had no visions. No light streamed
from his eyes. In hers, there was a fervent shimmer. If there was
conflict at the core, she might have known; he never knew; it
never troubled him; she saw to that; she kept the beggars with
large sores away from him so that they would not spoil his calm.
She sheltered him; she soothed him; her presence felt like moss
that curled around his toes.

"Hah! Can a fish develop lungs?" the peasants asked, and
shuddered.

The Empress scorned them silently, while her forbearing husband smiled at them and waved at them repeatedly. He promised
them reform.

In gratitude, his subjects bared their heads. A few more years
crawled on.

A minister tore off the last leaf of the Russian calendar, thirteen days behind the calendar of Europe: "The end of an era—at hand."

The noblemen raised vodka glasses and drained them with quick expertise: "Bottoms up! Bottoms up! The past is the past, forgotten already. The future will be set free with machines."

Nine million peasants, by the turn-of-century, were tilling their own land. Five hundred public schools sprawled across Russia. A well-planned strike in a city factory could cause a hated foreman to be fired.

"That's progress," said the tsar, and played another game of dominoes.

His ministers could point to well-kept foundling homes, to special taxes on the gentry's chimneys. Additional concessions yet, demanded by the curly-headed dissidents the universities spewed forth? The Empress was vociferous. The mild tsar shook his head.

He said: "Reform? See here? I sign it with my hand. I seal it with my seal. A special tax on playing cards and mirrors."

He may have said, perhaps, had only he seen clearly: "I am congenial to your cause. I am not sympathetic to your means."

He may have sensed more than he saw, but what he didn't understand, the empress clarified for him: to give in to unwarranted demands would have been just like giving in to women wearing trousers.

"We live on a mean little planet," she told him. He borrowed his opinions from the past.

His martyred grandfather, a man of great restraint and compromise, had started reform in good faith. In all affairs of state, reformers had his heart. They ran their wily words into his ears and left them there to hatch.

What did he gain? A bomb was his reward.

Somebody vaulted out of hiding, threw death, and started racing for his life, and even then some people shouted: "You smell a Jew a *verst* away," for it was widely held that Jews were everywhere where trouble brewed, and in surprising numbers.

Pitched forward on his face, with both legs torn away, the Emperor lay dying in the snowy streets of the beloved city his forebears built to give the tsars a window to the West. The alleys were eerily empty. The snow lay deep that year, and getting deeper.

"Home! Home!" the wounded emperor cried out and, perforated like a sieve by treachery, he sighed, and that was that. Within a fortnight he was dead—another broken cog in the relentless wheels of history. He died a miserable death, but not before he said: "The devil is blacker than even we surmised. Even his eyes have an unnatural color."

It is said he repeated that twice, between clenched teeth, and time has not muffled that rumor.

Around his casket gathered many mourners. Chief among the grieving stood a timid, shaken child—a boy who often saw in his repeated nightmares as he grew up the bloody stumps where legs had been—those limbs the malcontents had shredded with the powder of the Fiend.

The rage and anguish of that day had never left his heart. Nor had his trepidation. It had happened before. It could happen again. "The seed of Abraham," he knew, "sprouts treachery."

He shared his ancient throne's conviction, accumulated over centuries.

His father, who took over, had been a cold, stern man, thickset, parochial to the core, with a loud voice and heavy lids. He rode his country as a foolish man might ride a donkey, facing tailward. The bands around his heart were forged of haughtiness. His servants hunted through the streets in search of the yarmulkes, driving out treason with blows of their fists.

"The Jews are burrowing like moles," he told his son, before he closed his eyes, preparing for eternity. "You must keep them in check."

That was the legacy.

And it was not just Russia. For centuries, all Europe had been full of hatred toward Jews. All thrones detested Jews and kept them far away—except to borrow money.

The Jews tried stealth—no matter. They tried to sneeze quietly—no matter.

"One thought," the monarchies maintained down ages, making sure they passed the message on, from throne to throne, from year to year, "is on the Jewish mind, and that is world control."

The New World Order? Listen. Much older than Methuselah.

When the young Emperor took over the throne, he knew his absolutes: the power of religion rested upon Faith; so, too, the power, might and glory of the Romanovs.

That was the only way.

False friends would urge him, now and then, to open up the prisons of the tsars to let fresh air blow in. In the meantime, for diversion, he tended to his cucumbers, and took leisurely walks in the gardens.

His Cossacks kept crushing revolts. The culprits were sent to Siberia in a cascade of wails and complaints.

The ruling class kept seeking favors and walked away with blessings from the tsar. The peasants toiled to strengthen Mother Russia, whose heart was bleeding at the seams. The stern-faced ancestors in the imperial frames looked on.

"You can't catch birds in flight," a kinky-headed lad said angrily to Uncle Benny, who often rounded out his idle days by visiting the city of the tsars.

"One can, however, try?" suggested Uncle Benny.

The latter was more learned than the former, who was a youngster still, not more than twenty years of age, while Uncle Benny had white hair.

Each produced his note pad to compare. Both felt abiding reverence for ink.

They had no quarrel with the premise: that all should live in brotherhood. They strongly disagreed on this: how brotherhood would come about, when feelings cleaved so deeply between the landed gentry and the poor.

"On one hand, too much wealth, by far," the publisher of Apanlee allowed. "Appalling squalor, poverty, diseases on the other."

"I grant you that. That's not the argument."

"I know. The argument is this: what's fair? You don't breed strength in wooden hovels."

"The people are hungry, illiterate, crafty and cruel."

"To keep them in check, you need more than an arrogant, untrammeled army."

"Gold nuggets in your wagon beds, and silver weighing down your tables?"

"But earned by rightful means. By legal means. There must exist a path between extremes."

The youngster, full of fire: "Not for as long as every tsar believes he is anointed by the Lord. Not for as long as tsars keep telling every bureaucrat: 'Tomorrow is another day.' Without an ax, you cannot chop up wood. Without a match, you cannot light a fire."

"May God forbid! The devil will insert his page, and what will happen then—"

They nodded wisely to each other. They bantered back and forth. The tea house where they sat was clean, well-lit, and warm, but in the streets the icy wind blew horizontally.

"My people never beat their servants," said Uncle Benny gently. "They seldom even scold them. They're just. They're honest and straightforward. They do expect, however, that work be done on time. They do demand that sheaves be bound and streets be swept and rakes and forks be stored in an orderly fashion after the day's work is done."

"So what? What does that mean? Black bread is for the workers. Zwieback is for the rich."

The Revolutionary's face was flaming, filled with impatient anger. "Find me the man," the youth said stormily, "who owns two horses and would surrender one. It simply will not happen."

"My people are convinced they have a covenant—"

"A God who speaks High German?"

"Their ethnic roots have been entwined into a dozen knots with every reigning monarch."

The insurrectionist spoke sharply. "No way to carry out reform without cutting through quivering tissue and spilling a great deal of blood."

"See that old woman over there? See how she sells her doves?"

"All afternoon, I've had my eyes on her. She sits there on her wind-blown corner, hoping against hope that no one will chase her away before she has sold enough birds. Five birds still to sell. The day all but gone." The youth blew circles of blue smoke. "Is hers a life worth living? I know her very well. Each morning, long before the sun comes up, her husband wakes her with a kick. Six children have been born to her; and all of them are dead."

"It's sad. I grant you that. It's sad."

"So millions live and die within appalling poverty and never know their lives might have been different. Will she revolt? Not she."

"Watch me." Uncle Benny hunted in his pockets for some kopecks. He rose and limped across the street to where the woman sat. The youthful radical, while sipping vodka, watched the transaction silently.

The woman narrowed her old eyes. "You want a bird? You need a bird? Which one?"

"That one," said Uncle Benny. "The one with the white, fluffy feathers."

The old woman threw open the cage. "Quick! Grab it! Here! Here's a piece of string."

"I need no string. I want to give it freedom."

"Wastrel! Wastrel!" shrieked the woman. She started cuffing Uncle Benny, pouring forth abuse. The pigeon, unaccustomed to its wings, fluttered clumsily across the street, and settled on a dirty cobblestone. It kept on tipping over, pitching forward finally, first on its beak, then straight into the gutter.

"See what you did? See what you did?" shrieked the street vendor woman. "Why waste a bird? Why waste a bird for nothing?"

With gentle hands, Uncle Benny lifted the pigeon away from the swirl of the sewer and returned it to its cage. "Just keep the kopecks. Here."

A smile broke out across her face. She grinned at him, still half-bewildered and suspicious. "Why waste a bird," she echoed, still perplexed, and slammed the cage for emphasis. "For nothing?"

Chapter 30

Jan thrust Josie into motherhood before she had a chance to savor her virginity and safeguard it as long as possible—the glee of any girl. Their first child was a boy. As all the neighbors had predicted, his birthdate fell into the margin between significance and doubt.

This baby was her heartache from the start. As a toddler, as a kindergartner, the child stayed pale, his fingernails blue, a shy and wispy thing, afflicted with a clumsy tongue. This caused some savage teasings and many speculations.

In fact, some people went so far as to suggest: hardly a boy at all.

When Josie heard that , she picked up a broom and flailed at the chickens like mad.

Little Melly, her virtue still blindingly white, was loath to cease her mischief. She put out lots of double tongues insinuating this and that, but Josie, rising from her first confinement on a pair of wobbly knees but sharp stiletto words, let it be known: She had a baby now. What matter the hard stares?

She took the infant everywhere. She woke herself up with

her nightmares. The little boy was there to stay; in fact, he weaned without a hitch, and even though the boundaries between suspense and certainty were dim, the drone of gossip lessened.

Thanks to a thousand lucky stars, in time he started gaining weight, and Josie, never dull for long, decided to stare back. She never toadied. Never.

"So this is motherhood," said Josie to herself.

Her girlish looks returned; she didn't put on curves; and it was difficult to tell if wedded life agreed with her or not. Wherever Josie went, the baby went as well, but even so, she seemed to all a doubtful, mystifying parent. When the triumphant midwife handed her that firstling, she looked perplexed and baffled.

For weeks after the baby's birth, she slept and slept and slept. She was asleep when Little Melly came tiptoeing into her kitchen to start the yeast for her.

Jan was the first in Mennotown to put in indoor plumbing, but Josie let the faucet drip. She misplaced Jan's best socks; she muttered that she hated liverwurst; she argued that a misty moon caused melancholy and vice versa, and once she even said, regarding Abigail: "She is my one and only friend."

Such things went on for years. Such talk brought dismay to her household.

Lizzy paced the floor and wrung her hands; but Josie sat on the hard kitchen chair or swayed on the balls of her feet, refusing to conform. She once forgot to put away a shovel, and Little Melly stumbled over it and took a serious tumble. Lizzy buried her face in the folds of her apron with shame.

Born out of time and out of place, that was Jan's Josephine. Words came in a furious torrent. Offers to baptize her were in vain. Sermons only brought on hives.

"How does it look, I ask you?" pleaded Lizzy. "Sunday comes, and Sunday goes, and your place in the pew remains empty."

"So?"

"You owe your standing in our villege to your marriage. You must give something back."

"I am still puzzling that one out," said Josie, her eyes two blinded windows.

She took on one of her many disguises. She held her husband in the hollow of her hand; she had a fine time with his money.

It soon came to the fore that the root of all that friction and discord were the opaque and murky Finkelsteins, to whom Josie had taken a shine. Either she liked folks or not, and she liked them. A lot. She lifted her chin, stuck out her tongue, and insisted they were human beings.

When she returned from Wichita, where she would often go—sometimes alone, sometimes alongside Doctorjay, sometimes with Abigail in tow—her eyes still shone like two candles.

From early on, far into old age, there were swarms of Jews about Josie.

Whereas the Donoghues were everywhere, snapping fingers to each other—which could mean anything!—the Finkelsteins were shadowy. Many whispers raced about their odd political connections. When she came back from Wichita, her cheeks were ablaze with excitement. Filled with modernity, she sometimes had the neighborhood in stitches, and often in revolt. The deacons said disaster lurked around the corner, for even then she took to hard ideas like a man. She claimed that Finkelstein ideas made her blood sing and her emotions soar, just like a meadow lark.

Jan sometimes chided Josie, with gentle words and many sighs, but often he did not, for just as soon as he would try to make it clear to her that she should change her ways—that here, in Mennotown, she was an oddity—she'd cut him off:

"I know. I know. They all mean well. The family is friendly."

In the end, Lizzy caught Jan by his sleeve and hissed that she wanted to see him alone. Nobody could blame Lizzy, who might have led a life of leisure, doing little more than darning socks and teaching proper smocking, instead of lowering the beam of rectitude on Jan's young, foolish wife: "When is enough enough?"

Jan's marriage was her cross to bear. Her rocking chair had many cushions, constantly alternated in her woe. Her words came from the heart.

"Jan, be on guard. What is it Josie does in Wichita?"

"She's engaged in enlarging her mind."

"What? How? By getting together with strangers? I'm warning you. There's trouble on the way."

"She says it makes no difference. She claims her name is mud already."

"What's going on with her and Abigail?"

"They study sheet music together."

It was all a bottomless pit. She, Lizzy, kept on rocking, swallowing her tears. She knew in a vague way: it had to do with yearning for a knowledge with no name, or boundaries, or borders. It would become catastrophe. What did the Bible say? Eve was allowed to eat whatever fruit from any tree that grew in the Garden of Eden—except for the tree that grew knowledge.

"You carry that old grudge," said Josie in the end. "He married me. Not her."

Lizzy pressed her lips together and took her time replying, for bearing grudges was most decidedly not a part of Lizzy's arsenal.

"A grudge? What grudge? I don't bear grudges. How can you say that, Josie?"

"I'm smarter. And prettier. And younger."

If these ordeals vexed Josephine, if they caused shame to Lizzy, they did not trouble Jan; he smiled at hearing that his wife forgot to burp the baby; he laughed out loud when he was told that Josie sliced her thumb instead of a cucumber.

"Enjoy yourself as much as possible," he told her many times. He lost his wits to love. His anguish, born of folly, was beginning.

He said it once, he said it many times: "All that she wants, is hers to have. All that is mine to give, is Josie's."

He kept on spoiling her. He kept on pleasing her. He overlooked the Finkelsteins.

"By nightfall, I am always back," claimed Josephine.

When people murmured of the Finkelsteins and what their goals might be, Jan said he trusted Josie. Asked why, he told them rather sharply: "Quite simply—she gave me her word. She is incapable of falsehood."

Pie in the sky, was the verdict. Jan never lost his patience with her foibles.

Josie was his darling baby bride; she was near perfect in his eyes; she bore him the desired son; he tickled both; he searched for their dimples and found them. The first one wasn't even potty trained when she was blossoming again.

Josie had her children with great regularity, each one of them a female—save that first boy, born with a faulty tongue.

Alissa was born. Milly came next. Just as Jan's barns were swelling with wheat bumper crops, so Josie kept swelling with babies. In quick succession next came Tammy, then Betsy and, in the end, Fran. The latter three were born in Wichita, inside a ten-bed hospital, and Josie wore a purple gown that had a tasseled rim.

Her firstling kept on struggling with his tongue. But not until her last—that special child with magic fingers—did Josie savor motherhood.

The family needed more room at the table. Jan planted additional crops.

Each pregnancy deepened a sorrow. Each birth throttled something sharp and vivid within Josie. From baby to baby, she tossed dream after dream to the winds.

Between babies, her stomach was flat, her skin brown and hard. No sooner did another life begin to throb beneath her ruffled skirt than her skin turned gray and mottled; her moods grew dark as night.

"I might as well be one of Lizzy's cows," she once told

Doctorjay. She spoke with a small quaver in her voice. The evening was quiet. A solitary cricket chirped somewhere.

She sat beneath the apple tree, beside the wobbly bridge, from which rich, fertile soil sloped, even, to the river. Trapped once again in motherhood, she waited out her time.

Never one to live her life by halves, Josie signed up for the circulating library; it made the rounds two times a year, in May and in November. May was a busy month, but by November life was quiet; the snow lay deep and covered all the stubble.

The days were bleak. The trees had lost their leaves. The winter storms swept, howlingly, across the frozen Kansas earth, but Josie, by the fire, started glowing.

Those were mysterious times for Josephine.

For weeks on end, before the book cart came, she scoured madly through her kitchen to keep her pots all sweet and clean so Lizzy could not use her undone chores as reason to disturb her solitude and keep her from her reading.

She loved to read at any hour of the day; she curled up beside the the fireplace and was lost to the world and its duties.

"Print is my magic potion," she said to Jan, but of its powers, of the euphoria that came with poignant print, her husband did not have a clue.

He liked to startle her when she sat reading by the fire. He knew she had a way of listening to her surroundings as though she had a butterfly's probes, but he outsmarted her; he played small pranks on her; no matter how his little Josie-girl pricked up her rosy ears, snow deadened roughish noises.

She would plead, anguished: "Please! Don't do that, Jan! I don't like being spooked."

He paid no heed to that. He loved to outwit her. He made sure that she did not hear a sound until he stood behind her suddenly to petrify her with his booming voice and make her drop her book.

"Now, there's a man for you," said Noralee to Doctorjay.

So full of strength and energy was Jan that, every night, when all the work was done, he'd flex his hardened muscles and run three times the length of Mennotown to work off excess spirit.

Doctorjay cast a shrewd glance at Noralee. "What do you mean? What are you saying, woman?"

"Oh, nothing. Nothing. Not a thing."

"Out with the truth."

"Just wondering. That's all."

"Look. Heaven has endowed her with some pretty special gifts," said Doctorjay aggressively, as ever fond of Josie.

"Then why only females?" she wanted to know, her brows arching coyly to drive home her question.

"It's nature's way, I guess."

"By contrast, look at you and me. Is that prosperity, or what?"

Each year made Doctorjay more prosperous. Sometimes he took the teeth he pulled to Wichita to showcase wealth and glory in his status. When Josie took up stenciling and made a sign for him that said he no longer took Sunday appointments, he knew that he'd arrived.

"So. What is new across the violent waters?" he asked, while watching Josephine do final touches with her brush.

"The masses growl, it seems."

He pondered this at length. "The old country always had its share of malcontents."

"Yes. Here as there. The furrows, full of worms. The sparrows scoop them up."

He felt a burning admiration for anybody who could read and write, and Josie did both, like a professor. When she read Uncle Benny's words, she looked as though she were absorbed with beating back an ocean. When she wrote back to Russia, she ornamented every page.

He watched while she worked, absorbed in her task. "And you? Are you growing a little more tranquil?"

She understood at once. She told him in a low and trembling voice while kicking at a rock: "The rumors fly. Right? And isn't that the truth!"

"The rumors fly."

"The rumors have it wrong. One man is quite enough."

"You're sure?"

"I'm sure. Am I the kind that lies?"

"What is it, honey? Tell me."

"I can't."

"One day, it was just me and Abigail out in the fields and not a soul in sight—well, never mind! Believe me, child, I looked her over with great interest. I tried and couldn't either. It's you and Jan. It's me and my old Noralee. That's our universe."

"So, let's just drop it. Shall we?" Her hands were resting in her lap. At last, she spoke. Her voice was low.

"You couldn't be more wrong."

She watched the sun drop into the grain and gave herself over to sadness. The evening was very quiet. Young trees were shooting up across the prairie. She wore a cotton frock, made from a flour sack, cut wide enough around her waist.

He finally said this: "Well, let me tell you what to eat, what not to eat. For breakfast, oatmeal with bacon. For lunch *vareniki* with sour cream. For dinner, bread and *griebenschmalz*. And right before you go to bed, a hard-boiled egg with milk."

"I know. You've told me twenty times already."

"Put garlic in your milk. It's good for your teeth and your gums."

"I hate garlic. You know I hate garlic."

"If you don't watch it, Josie, you'll lose your teeth. You still have pretty teeth. Now let me see. Give me a smile. Give me your prettiest smile."

He saw her trembling lip. He winked at her and tried to humor her. He left her sitting there.

"I'll watch her like the apple of my eye," said Doctorjay to Jan, when he took Josie visiting to Wichita. "I'll watch her carefully. You don't mind? Do you?"

"No. Not at all. Just take her. Squire her around. And bring her back at night."

"I will."

"She never tires of the world that isn't our world," said Jan.

It went without saying that seldom, if ever, did Jan lose patience or control, not even when his wife was quarrelsome beyond the boundaries of any rhyme or reason, not even when she said with gritted teeth while crushing a small cricket with her heel and biting off each word:

"Jan. Please. Please don't talk down to me! Please don't!"

"I didn't know I did."

Her words were as bitter as quinine. "Come spring, there's Caroline, and there goes Josephine, both calving by the calendar."

Jan longed for a second son to help him with the harvests, but Josie kept on birthing girls, ignoring his wishes. She fitted them with paper curls. She kept them all in frills and sashes.

Although her pregnancies were difficult, what counted was: she had wide hips. She had her children with great ease, thus thwarting expectations.

Armed with a ruler, abacus and triangle, Jan went to work to better his town. For month after months, he sat hunched over blueprints, telling the city fathers in the end:

"A larger grammar school. A teacher's college. A picnic park. A modern firehouse."

By then, Jan was by wide acclaim the most esteemed and valued citizen of Mennotown. The village still consisted of one road, but that would change; the town folks said of Jan: "The motorcar is here, and look at Jan! His eye is on a flivver."

The wanton killing of McKinley had pushed Jan's modernizing plans for his community off the front page of the *Wichita Eagle*, but shortly afterward there was a two-page spread that told of Jan's enormous pledge to help expand the church.

One sunny Sunday morning, Jan told his wife: "I feel so grateful for my bounty. I must give something back."

"As if you don't."

"I do. Yet something deep within feels hollow."

"Why, Jan?" she asked, her tongue on the trigger of questions. She shooed a fly from the cheese.

"Why what?"

"Why do you feel that Dewey needs your money? Why don't you take him at his word? The Lord will provide. The Lord always does."

"Don't talk like that. It's not becoming, Josie."

"Well, I don't chew my cud."

"My Faith tells me I must."

"What? Chew your cud?"

"Don't twist my words. You know what I'm saying. You know exactly what I mean. Here's what I mean: my Faith feels like a blanket. It is my heirloom, Josie. It gives me warmth. It gives me peace. I want to frame it properly."

"You must be chill."

Jan could never be angry for long. "And you? Right now you're boiling just beneath your collar," he said with a small laugh.

"Well, practice makes perfect, as Dewey would say."

"There's enough to go around. Let's share our wealth. Let's do it for harmony's sake."

"I feel harmonious. The only thing that gives me hives is Dewey's oily voice."

Jan, awkward with longing, replied: "A life without my church would be as difficult for me as walking with two fallen arches. I'd only like for you to understand. I ask your understanding."

"I continue to blacken your reputation," said Josie, hot from Wichita.

"That isn't it at all."

"Well, then?" She suddenly leaned forward. It was as if she held her breath.

"It's hard to explain," he said slowly. "These days, new prairie towns come cheap. The prairie is astir with growth. All kinds of people come to stay. They aren't us. They're different. Just look at Wichita. It is already straining at the seams. Before too many years are gone, it will be difficult to keep our children from dispersing. They'll want to leave. They will be lured by snare and bait into the shallow waters of modernity. I want them to have roots."

"They have roots aplenty, But where are the leaves?"

"I want them to have soil. And Mennotown is special. There's nothing like it, Josie. This is God's town, God's country. I'd like to keep it that way."

"Sure. Just as soon as that slimer comes jingling—"

"Dewey does wonderful things for the downtrodden, Josie. He needs a larger church. It's proper, Josie. That's the reason."

"He has his fingers in your pocket. And that's where they will stay."

"We do not hurt. The Lord has blessed us lavishly. There is enough for everyone. For him. For you. For our family. For future generations."

"Why is he not accountable for anything he takes from you, yet I must always ask?"

" The wishbook is yours for the asking."

"You always say that I'm a spendthrift. You say that, and you laugh. In Mennotown, that's not a joke. It isn't very funny. Yet when Dewey shows up, hat in hand, you fork over your nickels like hay."

"I don't give anything against my will. It's my church. I built it. I run it. I cherish it. I honor it. It guides me, and it comforts me. How to explain a rainbow to the blind? My church—"

"I have sharp eyes."

"—my church is me. It married me. One day, that church will bury me. That thought gives me great peace."

"Go on."

He gently stroked her tresses. "It makes me feel good. It makes me feel clean. It makes me feel as though I'm running a comb through my hair when I give to the church of my choice. It makes me feel orderly. Proper."

"Worthwhile?"

"Worthwhile. That's the word. That's what I was struggling to say. I feel worthwhile. That's what my church gives me. I stand where I'm supposed to be. That's what my tithing does to me. Dear child, if only you would see—"

"Don't call me child. I've never been a child."

"I want to make up for your childhood, Josie."

"My childhood," Josie said, and there was ice in her blue eyes, "was snuffed out by my father's pious knuckles."

Chapter 31

Dewey's flock increased in numbers as if the Methodists were merely chaff instead of a prodigious nuisance who tried to cut repeatedly into his donation roster, as Little Melly pointed out, she having herself a much-respected influence in matters of the church.

Little Melly, a fervent born-again, felt sorry for those who were not. She was up to the Methodists' shenanigans—they hogged her favorite corner at the fair. She waged an unrelenting war on every Unitarian—they tapped their toes while singing. As for the stiff Episcopalians—she fought their dogma savagely.

Propelled on by the Holy Ghost, she also lit into the libertines. They all seemed to have either colors, flowers, grass or precious metals in their names.

At every opportunity, she squared off with the suffragettes as well, and with good cause—she had strong premonitions, for Josie still half-milked her cows, her mind on something else. Jan's Josie was still blown about by every wind and many an idea.

On Sundays she and Abigail would often disappear; you

wondered where; they didn't say; the neighborhood said spiteful things about them.

"Where to?" asked Little Melly many times, and Josie frowned and shrugged. The summer sun was making flashes in her hair. She had come face to face with Wichita, and that is where she went.

She did so every Sunday afternoon—this long before the nickelodeons arrived. To free herself, she cooked her meals on Saturdays. She acquired three fanciful hats—contraptions as big as the moon, and with streamers. She was bursting with city ideas.

Dewey strove with all his might to turn the tide against modernity. In recognition of his struggle, he was feted from homestead to homestead. His reputation grew by leaps and bounds. He put a part of his abundant energy into nailing down some solid and convincing rules, to wit:

No books that made your heart pound with forbidden longing.

No friendships that the church did not approve.

No songs that smacked of tempo.

No card play. And no dominoes.

Dewey took his mission gravely. He had a pat routine that helped him convert sinners by the score. First he blasted them with fire, then he baptized them with water, and those who didn't dive for cover found true salvation in the Lord.

His pants were too short, his sermons too long, but heaven and hell he precisely defined. The net result was an expanded congregation.

"A masterful sermon, that's all that it takes," was Dewey's firm belief. Not counting Josephine, in Mennotown and its surroundings, the Donoghues were just about the only ones who still remained ungospeled and unchurched.

"What will she think of next?" fussed Lizzy many times, with no doubt left that Josie fancied Finkelstein ideas.

She said so openly. Her parasol was making small dents in the sand. You only had to follow them; you knew which way she headed—down to the Hebrew stores.

"Bust cream, no doubt," predicted Little Melly.

"No!" Lizzy squealed as though she had been stuck with a sharp darning needle. "That's where Jan draws the line."

"You must give him a hint."

There was no time to spare. In every matter moral, Little Melly was her brother's pal. She was in full accord with his philosophy. The disappointment of her youth had made her strong in certitude and filled her with crusading zeal. She had her work cut out.

Now that the Holy Ghost propelled her on, she helped her brother strip away parishioners' transgressions like leaves from the branches of trees.

"I couldn't do without you," said Dewey often, gratefully, acknowledging her skills.

Chit-chatting was her specialty. Just as the raindrops kept the dust from flying, so did her salient gossip keep newfangled novelties in check. It kept his flock from dancing to the tunes of dangerous modernity. No rouge. No see-through sleeves. No ornamental buttons. No flowered drapes on parlor windows. No chrome base bedroom lamps from Sears—such as she spied from the corner of her eye when she sailed by Jan's home.

In the beginning, Dewey and Daisy tried farming on the choice strip of land that Jan had purchased cleverly and set aside as dowry for his sister when Daisy still was small.

"It lies right in the path of progress," Jan said to Daisy lovingly. He was a real patriarch that way—protective of his siblings.

When Jan deeded his land to his sister, he had hoped that one day she and her husband would build there. But that was not to be.

"The railroad has a right-of-way," said Dewey, thoughtfully. "If we sell now, that parcel ought to bring a hefty chunk of cash.

What do you think? We could renew the pews—"

Daisy rocked on peacefully, in front of her a mug. "If you say so. I'm sure that you know best." A cat was purring at her feet. She did not stress herself with matters none of which were women's business: her mind was on red cabbage.

He nodded to himself, immersed in calculations. It was a lovely plot of land; it had nine ancient oak trees growing quietly, and a creek. A brisk breeze blew there in the morning. Across it ran a one-lane dirt trail leading to a bridge where sparrows perched.

That bridge worried Jan; it was narrow and brittle and needed support. Unless the railing was reinforced, and soon, an accident was bound to happen. Jan planned to do the work, but not before convincing City Hall—where bureaucrats and planners talked of widening the roadway. But Josie said, please don't! "It's so romantic there," said Josie, dreamily, and started glowing softly with a forbidden thought.

Once traffic came and ruined the solitude, said Josie, lost in fantasy, it wouldn't be the same.

She didn't say it right out loud, but everybody knew: that's where she went for privacy. That's where she sat, for hours on end, and waited for her mail.

By then, she had lured Doctorjay into her camp. He played into her schemes. He'd meet with Josie, by the brook, down by the wobbly bridge, and hand her this and that.

She needed allies; he, alibis. Those two were mighty cozy with each other. When Doctorjay was done with doctoring and ambling home at leisure on his mare, Annetta, he often stopped the mailman coming out of Wichita to take the bags from him and save him a detour.

Mail always came on Fridays. Friday afternoon was it!

The healer always treated Josephine with courtesy; he didn't punish her with silences when she had overstepped a line. He always spoke to her; he tipped his hat to her. She shone her smiles on him. She was his friend. He was her confidant.

He stood behind her with excuses when she kept birthing girls while Jan was hoping for a second son to carry the family name.

Doctorjay found a champion in Josie. In him, she found a lifelong friend. They kept confiding little secrets to each other. Some people wondered if they had to do with Abigail. He had his eye on Abigail who was a female, by that time, who could best be described with the palms of two hands; that's how he outlined her to Josie.

The two, so different as a rule, were full of mischief when together. The thought of Little Melly, lying in her narrow bed, between her spotless sheets, thinking up assorted schemes to trap them, would render them helpless with giggles.

She backed him up in all his fast and furious stories. She furnished proof that he had spent all night awaiting a delinquent calf's arrival, when, it was later learned, Doctorjay, quite overcome with the felicity of yet another holiday and yet another joyous crowd, had snoozed the night away in Lizzy's cozy barn.

"What do I owe you, Doctorjay?" Josie slid another missive in her neckline.

"Oh, nothing. Nothing. Nothing but your thanks."

"These letters. From another planet," marveled Josie.

He fixed shrewd eyes on her. "I'm glad to be of service."

"You are."

"Out with the truth. It's not the artist? Is it?"

"No. He is just a friend. Don't laugh, but it is mostly Uncle Benny. The fancy of his thoughts!"

That was enough for him. He knew she never lied. She hadn't had the time to be a young and carefree girl, so now she fantasized.

He saw she was no longer sick with emptiness and longing; she was a young and eager girl who waited for surprises. These *tete-a-tetes* down by the bridge, where the meadows lay dappled with daisies, were like a secret pact, although the healer never found out what it was that etched its magic into Josie's heart as though with a sharp diamond.

She smiled. She wouldn't say.

"Giddap, Annetta!" shouted Doctorjay to whom most secrets of the heart were altogether plain. When he appeared and waved another letter, Jan's Josie was beside herself; the bridge would wobble with her joy so that he thought it might collapse from the excitement of a thought that differed from the thoughts of Mennotown. She was the captive of her whimsies and fancies.

Each Friday afternoon she carried on where she left off the week before— and often she would get so feverish that Lizzy had to dip a towel in cold water and lay it on her head, to cool an overheated thought.

Of all her oddities, this was the strangest—her inexplicable affinity for cabalistic Uncle Benny. They carried on a lively correspondence. He wrote to her routinely. She wrote him back at once.

When Uncle Benny visited that way, she shimmered, and she shone. When letters came from Russia, it was as though a window to a gilded palace opened up for just a tiny crack, as though a ray of sunshine briefly caught itself, reflected by a broken piece of glass. Each time it was as if she had received a greeting from a lover, instead of just the half-forgotten invalid of Apanlee.

"He never scolds me. Never!" she said to Doctorjay.

By then, the bonesetter had his own woes; he drank to every holiday. He drank to friendship, peace and understanding. He toasted the Spanish-American War, the death of Queen Victoria, the first of the two meddling Roosevelts—and one long Sunday afternoon that stretched and stretched with nothing else to do, he went so far as toasting Darwin's Theory of Evolution.

"You're heading straight for dipsomania," shrieked Noralee, so mad at him she threw a pail of water at the cat. "The Moabites and Stalactites—"

"She means Amalekites," said Josephine who was the kind, by then, who saw a piece of paper blowing down the street, ran after it, and read it.

The healer hiccuped gently. "Who're they?"

"Don't even ask. Believe me, Doctorjay! They're worse."

"I'll drink to that," said he.

If Josie knew that Doctorjay drank more than might be good for him, she certainly never let on. The bottom line was this: those two worked hand in hand.

The Kansas blizzard winds blew hard. The fire water warmed.

When he felt fortified that way, all chilly on the outside, all mushy on the inside, he knew he could outlast most any crisis, malady or woe.

He introduced her to assorted strangers he met on various detours in Wichita, for Josie needed all the friends and friendships she could get.

She knew where his bottle was hidden. She knew, but didn't tell.

Sly secrets passed between them from the start.

She understood why he felt naked without handshakes. When he passed by her home, she'd coax him inside, plunk him down, right in the middle of her couch, hand him a steaming cup of coffee, then patiently watch over him until he could steady his limbs, quiet his tongue, and properly focus his eyes.

"Time just flew by," he would explain to Noralee when he was late again.

She tried to worm out details. Log rolling would have been easier!

Much as Doctorjay admired and appreciated Josie, there was a complication. She was a woman, with a woman's reluctance to drink. As do all drunks, he itched to fraternize. He craved a bosom buddy to lean against when the trees began to sway.

Among the folks in Mennotown, that was no small objective, not even for a Lutheran as sly as Doctorjay.

He tried to stake out Jan.

"Jan, join me. For the heck of it. No one will ever know."

"No. Thank you, Doctorjay. Some other time, perhaps."

"Just once?"

"No. Thank you just the same."

"Here! Let's sit behind that bush and have ourselves a little something for the bladder."

Quite a few bets were riding on the outcome. The healer had persistence. Jan, for his part, had strength. Conviction. Moral certitude.

But Doctorjay had cunning, in addition. Come yet another holiday, he planned another ambush. "What's just one little tumbler?"

Jan wouldn't hear of it. He would no more have downed a drop of fire water than a lion eaten lettuce, even once. Jan said, with a small shudder: "Remember the pliers? Are you fooling, or what, Doctorjay?"

"All right! If not, then not. Perhaps another time? *Pascholl*, Annetta! Oops! Giddap!"

He clutched the mare's gray neck. He prized the old horse dearly. All through Sedgwick County, most knew her name; most, what she ate. To him, she passed for human. On slow days, he gravely studied her tongue.

Who would have guessed the time would come when Doctorjay would trade Annetta for a flivver?

Because the healer valued Josie, he never told her that he knew why she was sore in every cell of her young life about her offspring's stuttering.

The neighbors knew. The neighbors' stares could make her wince as though she bit a cherry pit into a tooth that had a hidden cavity.

She trembled for her son. She was in a cold sweat.

Her terror even made her tumble out of bed—the night he caught diphtheria and almost choked to death. His throat needed soothing a lot.

We speak now of the margin child, just old enough to go to grammar school, but still blue-veined and timid. The youngster did not in the least resemble Jan, whose voice could shake the rafters.

He was a gentle child; his sisters were robust.

The teacher tied his favored hand, his left, behind his back: in consequence, his p's and t's came in volleys.

It was too much for Josie. She became like a woman possessed.

Come rain or snow, she sent her son to Wichita to have his speech repaired. "You're as good, if not better, than the rest," she told him, and never mind the weather.

The little fellow stooped against the winter wind. Lizzy's heart broke when she saw him standing there, alone, out by the road, a little boy in great, big mittens. Her eyes fogged up with pity, her window fogged up with her breath.

Lizzy tried to think up innovative ways to sabotage the elocution lessons. It was decidedly unwise to make a simple handicap a lifelong liability by fussing over it, yet that's what Josie did. By then, she stood at odds with God, for it was clear to all that only He Who put the burden on this child could likewise take it away. If He did not—and there was little indication that He might—then that could only mean that Josie had not learned her lesson.

But Josie would have none of that philosophy. She would improve the stutterer. She was determined to unfurl her small son's twisted tongue.

She made no secret of the fact that she was visiting the Finkelsteins from time to time who plied her with their theories. "They're just folks," was her refrain. "Like anybody else."

That's what she said when asked. More than that she wouldn't share, even to their questions.

Such as: why did they celebrate their Sundays Saturdays?

Why did they mutilate their boys by snipping at their privates, in caftan and black hat?

Why did they all go fishing for a bargain, some sooner and some later?

Dead or alive, a Jew was still a Jew. Unless your name was Josephine, you stood aloof. Apart.

For years, the age-old evangelical concerns about the usurers the elders fussed about were of no interest to Josie. She sought the Hebrews out to elevate her thoughts, soak up sophistication.

Next, on a whim, she took up bicycling.

"I need a bit of exercise," she said, when Dewey Epp came calling to bring the latest on the Gospel, a tipsy Doctorjay in tow, atop his bicycle, followed by three dogs.

"No, Josie! No!"

"Try racing me!"

While the others looked for chairs on which to settle down for an extended chat, Josie did the ultimate, the absolutely scandalous: she hoisted up her hem—one foot above her ankle—climbed up on Doctorjay's contraption that he had leaned with care against the chicken house, and started weaving down the lane.

"Much better than a skittish horse," cried Josephine, and off she rode, down the leaf-strewn sidewalk. In fact, before her husband had a chance to grab her by her skirt, she wobbled clear across the length of Mennotown.

The healer shouted after her: "Look at her! Watch her go! Yippee!" yelled Doctorjay, and slapped his thigh with gusto.

"You are an oaf," hissed Noralee, and elbowed Doctorjay to stop, but he was in a merry mood that day and wouldn't be denied.

Little Melly could no longer withhold her opinion. She told Lizzy, eyebrows raised, with a small, mocking smile: "She will yet drive Jan to drink or suicide—" but that day, Lizzy snapped: "Now, Little Melly! Hear! That is your last drop of venom!"

Ever after, Little Melly tried to keep her tongue in check, but did not close her ears.

Dewey cornered the Council of Elders. He talked to them at length and gave them firm instructions.

They took his message back to Jan: "It's all your fault. You fan the spark of mutiny. You laugh when you should scold." All that was public knowledge.

Jan shook his head, as much in love as ever.

"She still is young. She'll change. She has always been partial to strangers."

The Elders spoke dire warnings. "She will destroy your Faith."

Jan smiled and leaned back in his favorite chair. He spoke with assurance and measure.

"She's fence-straddling now, and struggling and searching. I don't want to give her a lasting dislike for the Gospel by forcing its teachings too soon."

The Elders repeated their warnings, picked up their hats and nodded their omens, departing, but not before glooming and dooming: "We've looked into this Hebrew business, and cannot see the bottom."

Jan stared after them, at a loss as to how to reply.

It was the age-old argument. Not even the tsar wanted Jews in the army. Even the tsars had police on their heels.

As Jan watched Josephine throughout the years as she kept up her dalliance with the Solomons and Finkelsteins, her quiver always full of arrows, the needle of Jan's conscience jumped with ever greater frequency, as though it were a flea.

Old and young relied on Doctorjay and on his stomach bitters, and when it seemed that Josie went from bad to worse in every respect, Noralee officially dispatched her man to see if he could make a difference.

That day the healer said to Josephine: "Too many eyes are watching you. Why, just last week someone saw you in the branches of an apple tree."

"So? It's just my children's tree house."

"What were you doing there?"

"Who told you? Noralee?"

"She heard it from Betty, who heard it from Nan, who heard it from Susie and Kathy. Slow down a bit. What are you? A peacock? You are spreading your feathers just as wide as you possibly can."

"I only wanted privacy. I have no privacy. I was hiding away in that tree house."

"You. A grown woman."

"I was reading a book. I couldn't put it down, and Lizzy, Noralee, and Little Melly—oh, never mind! Just never mind! They have only themselves to blame for their own cheerless lives. That's what I always say."

"I'm here to help. Whenever you need me."

She gave him a small pat. "I'll remember. Thank you." A book in hand, she was lost to the world and its duties.

"You aren't mad at me, are you?"

"Of course not. You're my friend." She liked him well enough. Regardless of the weather, the season, the time of day or night, you could depend on Doctorjay, whatever the emergency, to be there, at your side, a looming, helpful shadow.

You told him where it hurt. He found a remedy.

When sudden illness struck or death came lurching down the chimney, he was there. He came to lance a boil, to watch the progress of a calf, to help the birth of yet another Donoghue. By contrast, the Wichita doctors were suspect.

He voiced a final thought: "Look. There's a middle way."

"They all follow each other like geese."

"And you are the anomaly?"

"That's right. What's this I heard about a garter snake you put in Little Melly's pocket?"

He took an extra swig and shouted for a handkerchief on which to blow his nose. She had him there. He moved his hairy toes.

"Are these the thanks I get for all my pains?"

By then, his drinking habit had cauterized his stomach. He was welded to his flask; he couldn't do without. He drank outrageously. He quaffed to show his good will; he guzzled to display contempt. He was weaving from picnic to picnic.

When he was tipsy, he started to sing, urging others to join; when he was sloshed, he went so far as to embrace a Donoghue as though they were the best of friends. Drunk, he thought nothing of such aberrations.

Chapter 32

Lizzy had long, lonely cries regarding ominous developments that cast their shadows over Jan's and Josie's marriage bed, now visibly neglected.   She saw the writing on the wall; she was a mother, and a matriarch besides; Jan was the apple of her eye. While Jan was in the fields and needing every hand to keep the harvest going, his wife dressed up and went with Abigail to Wichita.

The two of them. Alone. Bedecked as for a gala.

They never walked the streets on foot, to window-shop; they always took the street car. Why? Just because. Because it made it harder to follow them that way.

Soon, other fearsome rumors coursed. It was a trying time for all, and worse was yet to come, for Josie did precisely as she pleased. Roughshod across tradition, that was her current route.

No hope in shocking her with threats of family rebuff!

Lizzy held her peace with grace; she had no other choice, but she did not lack eyes and ears. She couldn't help compare: poor Little Melly kept no secrets from her clan; she did not sport a dresser without doilies nor spurn *vareniki*; nor did she sashay down each week to Wichita, a place as frightening as Babylon, a city thick with strangers.

In Mennotown that decade, the most important project was to build a bigger church to house the quickly growing, largely German congregation. Jan was picked to head the drive for funds, and he, in turn, enlisted Mennotown's Rotarians.

Becoming a Rotarian was now the ultimate, together with the flivver craze. "Males Only" was the rule. Not even Noralee was let inside to scrub the floor for fear she'd snoop too much and give away male secrets.

"Give me five years," swore Josie, whose specialty were boasts.

"Let's pull together in a common cause," Jan told the fellows, meanwhile, and there was loud applause. He knew the neighbors all approved; all offered to chip in. Jan was a wizard when it came to volunteers; he had a knack for marshaling a lot of willing hands as well as contributions.

Jan and a dozen newly sworn Rotarians stayed up until all hours while planning ways and means. A fine, long remembered meeting it was that ended with a generous gift: a paved parking lot behind the church, entirely at Jan's expense, along with a living allowance for Dewey.

"We cannot let the preacher starve," said Jan, and everybody cheered.

"Where will they live?" Josie wanted to know. A fine film of distaste came over Josie's feelings whenever she shook Dewey's hand. "If Dewey and Daisy decide not to farm, who'll support them in the years to come? You?"

In fact, that had been on Jan's mind. Dewey needed freedom from his daily toil—how else could he pursue his calling in the church?

"You gave Daisy her parcel. Why did she let him sell it? It was excellent soil. Just thirsting for the seed," Josie needled, inspecting a stain on her napkin. "Now he'll be on your pocket.

I thought I'd mention it."

Jan had no reply; there was nothing left to say. He knew she was right, and it rankled.

The townfolks built the preacher's home, replete with pantry and verandah. The project needed barrels full of money. Since Jan was rich in property, but often short on cash, Jan talked at length to several moneylenders, among them Josie's friends.

For several weekends in a row, the Finkelsteins sat snug in Josie's parlor and talked of this and that. Just dibs and dabs. Just stuff about the weather. Jan signed a lot of crackling papers. When Lizzy tried to peek, he shooed her from the door.

While construction still went on, the churchly couple took temporary residence in Lizzy's storage shed. Until the fathers of the church could get together on the books and finalize the enterprise, the place would have to do.

Things took a while; the harvest interfered. Meanwhile Little Melly, majestic in her morning robe, moved in with Lizzy, Jan and Josie.

"For just a month," said she, and stayed almost a year.

An aging spinster long before her time—fine wrinkles in a broad, round face, gray wisps about her temples—Little Melly gloried in the young fry that Dewey and Daisy produced, then handed over to her. Their children were as good as hers, and no one scorned her claim.

Some died in infancy and were efficiently forgotten, but those who lived stood out. Visit Mennotown today—you'll spot them instantly.

First, there's Arnold, well-renowned for his shrewd grocering: he lives a spicy life amid his onions, beets, squash, melons, radishes and mushrooms. Then there's Victor—still alive, but barely. And Douglas, who moved on to settle deep in the Nebraska plains where, to this day, his children and his children's children multiply and prosper.

His younger brother, Simon, is always in the public eye. He never traveled much past Wichita, but still his record shines. This

Simon is a small and simple man, a little daffy in the head, but a fine citizen. To this day, Simon is in charge of the Rotarian festivities in Mennotown, and it is Simon who, just recently, became a Harris Fellow—still in his flapping trousers.

Then there was Cornie, now forgotten, struck by lightning during haying. And Neta, Susie, Lisa. All three of them, when young, looked eagerly for energetic husbands, but only two succeeded. Murriel, pronounced Morell, did not. Her life's main purpose is to spread a lot of Christmas cheer at Christmas, which is what she is doing in Zaire.

All Epps go by two syllables. Except for one: his name is Archibald.

No nephew was nearer Little Melly than Archie. She raised him single-handedly. She spent a lifetime manning Archibald's exhibit booth at fairs to sell her cupcakes and her needlework that kept his Paraguayan leper mission going and helped the poor at home as well, especially the Donoghues.

Which brings us to the Donoghues. In Mennotown, the Donoghues are still regarded with suspicion. That they are loud and boisterous is known. Their backyard, just brambles and weeds. Today as in olden days, their fences are askew. Their windows still are stuffed with rags, their buttons held with wire. And everyone in Mennotown will tell you in detail that the productive land they tried to steal from Lizzy is nowhere near as fertile now as it was then, when Lizzy practiced fallowing. They still talk of the "missing" title that Lizzy must have laundered accidentally. The Donoghues have recently again! engaged a lawyer, a liberal lizard, doubtlessly, to check that old claim out.

"To this day, our grief goes on," the Mennotowners said to Erika who came to probe her roots.

"How so?"

"They say it was a lease and not a sale, no matter what the counterevidence."

The Donoghues still claim it hadn't been a one-shot deal. That paper wasn't signed, the Donoghues insist. That missing document exists, they claim, in someone's dusty attic.

"Rag pickers, every one of them."

"Still counting on the Finkelsteins to help them with their thieving."

"Still feeding on the dole—"

"—rechristened, Affirmative Action."

Dewey railed against the dangers electricity would bring, but electricity was here to stay; modernity won out. It was utilitarian, claimed the utilities; you flipped a switch and all went dark; you didn't have to blow against the flame.

"No telephones," he ordered next while trying to be thorough, but soon he realized that that was a mistake.

Both Noralee and Little Melly would no more have stopped eavesdropping on party lines than they would have quit turning Doctorjay's ballooning trouser pockets inside out, while he kept snoring gently, in hopes of finding clues to augment the excitement of the universe.

When folks began to gossip electrically, their tongues just ran away! Most prairie ladies loved the telephone so much they wished they could have listened with both ears. No housewife worth her yeast supply could be so busy that she didn't strain to catch the latest rumor. When blizzards arrived, and telephone wires oft came tumbing down—why, those were trying times!

Full force came next the flivver craze. At a Rotarian luncheon, Jan stood to make a speech. The audience hushed with reverence.

"The future," said Jan Neufeld, "will be set free with flivvers."

With money from the parcel Daisy brought into the marriage, Dewey was the first to buy himself a motor horse with which to follow weddings, funerals and scandals at ever greater speed. Day by day, he clattered round the countryside in search of would-be Christians. Stop signs were few and far between, and Dewey would forget all about Little Melly's warnings and soar along the streets of Mennotown and out into the prairie, never mind digestion, with little Archie huddled by his side. The cow pies flew apart.

Next, Jan decided he would build a replica of Apanlee. That was what Josie wanted. What Josie wanted, Josie got. She wanted Apanlee.

Jan pleased her every way he could, for she was still the little Josie of his heart, and if she wanted Apanlee—why, Jan built Apanlee! When, at last, the stubborn snow drifts melted, and the sap of yet another spring surged to the top of every tree, Jan bought a special tract of land to build his wife a home. A separate home from Lizzy's. By then, he had white hair, and Josie had seven daughters.

"You can come visiting," said Jan, who sensed his mother's anguish. "As often as you like. It's only a short walk."

Did that help ease the devastation of rejection? "I'm old now. Old and useless," said Lizzy, sniffling bounteously. "The few years I have left, to spend with my dear family, matter not at all. To anyone." For Lizzy, this was just like giving up the throne. She had hoped to live out what remained of her life with her family under one roof.

Jan soothed Lizzy, as best as he knew how. "We'd love to have you come and visit. Come visit every Sunday, Mom. Be sure. And don't forget."

"No. No. I would be underfoot."

"Come early. And stay late," Jan pleaded earnestly.

"You mean that, Jan?"

"Of course."

"I would be underfoot."

"The very thought!"

"You're sure? I won't be underfoot?"

"Please come. As often as you like."

So that is what she did, by way of compromise, the family album wedged beneath her arm.

The couple's new home was magnificent. No edifice in all of Kansas offered more by way of quality, convenience, space and

light. It had large, two-foot window sills on which to grow geraniums, which Josie promised Lizzy that she would—as soon as
she found time. It had a foreroom, a corner room, a small room,
a back room, a summer room, and an enormous parlor. The parlor
had a huge brick fireplace—the biggest one around!—but Josie
wailed she wanted two; why had the builders not built two, as
she had specified?

Her new home had a porch up front and bright, blue shutters
all around. She decided she wanted them beige. The painter
came and changed the colors, muttering under his breath.

She took the brush out of his hand and added an elegant trim.
That idea was Hebrew as well. They were gaudy, and Josie was
gaudy. They were tawdry, and Josie was, too. That was the sentiment.

Not that Jan cared. He could have bought himself as much
of history as anyone around; by then, he had great wealth, but he
had little use for Apanlee or memories of Apanlee. Jan had no
use for history. He was a real American that way—deep into
electricity.

Jan built a U-shaped buiding, where wheat was cleaned and
dried, then carried onto moving belts which fed adjoining silos.
The windows of Jan's mill and silos—just squares of warmth
and gold!

"It's Satan who's driving the light through the wires," cried
Little Melly, never one to wear her Faith lightly. Once, when she
reached to flip a switch, a soggy dish rag in her hand, the demons
rushed right through her fingertips. For days, she couldn't stop
shaking, but in the end, prayers proved potent antidotes.

"The magic power," Jan explained, as always hugely animated
by Little Melly's terrors, "runs straight uphill. Uphill! Around
the corner. Through the walls. In fact, in any old direction."

"No! You don't say! Are you a sorcerer, or what?"

He smiled at her. "Just practical."

She cast down modest lids. "No one but you! Incredible!"

This was their weekly ritual. He would explain the modern

world to her; she listened. She'd dress in checkered skirt and
flowered blouse, put on pink socks, shake out her skirt to make it
fall in swells, then take the young fry in her charge to be weighed
in—and thus compared!—to Josie's bony son.

"Half-starved, the little fellow," said Little Melly pointedly,
as soon as she spied Josie with practiced eagle's eyes. "And is
that any wonder?"

"What do you mean by that?" jumped Josie. She always
jumped when stung.

"You know as well as I."

"My son is first in all his classes. Go ask. Just go ahead. Ask
anyone."

"Too skinny. Far too skinny. Watch out for scurvy, Josie."

"The Lord has given lavishly," said Little Melly next, while
sitting as a Sunday guest on Josie's davenport. "We must give
something back. I'm here collecting for my brother. I hope I
kept nobody waiting?"

"The very thought," said Josie, removing another damp diaper. "Go help yourself. Here. Have a cup of coffee."

"I'd rather have tea. Tea, please, if you don't mind. How old
is that jam?"

"Last year's."

"It has a touch of mildew."

Just as the swallows came in May, so Dewey's sister came
collecting for his missions in November. She came and didn't go
away; and her message was always the same.

"We must surrender ten percent. Maladies are sure to strike if
we neglect to tithe."

"Here. Have another piece of strudel, Little Melly. It won't
hurt your digestion."

"Dewey's doing wondrous things for Alabama's shut-ins."

"And for the Indians in Alaska."

"Why, Josie! You remember!"

"I wish you luck," said Josephine, who could be cruel beyond belief. "And I wish Dewey luck. But I support the causes

of my choice."

Lizzy, on stand-by, chirped brightly: "She's kidding. Stay put, Little Melly. She's joking. Sit back, Little Melly. She's merely teasing you."

"She heard me. She has ears." Josie's pulse began to race; her neck was growing mottled. "I said that I support the causes of my choice. That's what I said. That is my final word."

"And what is that supposed to mean?" asked Little Melly, already roused for battle.

"As if you didn't know. Speak up. Don't beat about the bush."

"Oh, Little Melly, hush! Don't get yourself excited. All Josie meant to say was—"

"I can speak for myself."

"The Lord has blessed you lavishly," said Little Melly, hugely entertained. "You've got to share. You've got to."

"She's got a point." Already Lizzy wrung her hands, but fact was fact: the evidence stared everybody in the face: ever since the margin child had started taking elocution lessons, Jan's offerings had fallen off alarmingly.

"Is that a fact? What point is that? I have no say in Jan's donations. All I'm saying is—"

"Now, lovey, hush. Please. Hush."

"—all I'm saying is he has his charity; I have my charity. Why can't I have a charity? What's fair is fair. If Jan can have a charity, then I can have a charity."

"What charity," asked Little Melly pointedly, "is that?"

"Look for yourself. Here is my can. Next to my labeled spices."

Little Melly shook the tin can carefully. She shook it first against her right ear, then against her left. Next, she put on her glasses.

"Go on. Read what it says."

"It says Susan B. Anthony."

"Who's she? I never heard of Susan Bee." Lizzy was edging closer.

"I'll bet you haven't. That's my point."

"Who is this Susan Bee? The head of the Salvation Army?"

And Josephine, triumphantly: "A pioneer to stop the slavery of women."

Lizzy all but swooned with shock. Little Melly sat waiting, inspecting the tips of her fingers. The silence stretched and stretched.

In the end Josie cried, choked with feelings: "You two. You listen. You two listen hard! I support the suffragette cause. Do you know what that means? Do you know what being a suffragette means?"

"Yes," whimpered Lizzy. "I looked it up. It's worse than misbelieving. It's renegading, Josephine."

"It's not. It merely means—"

"Have you become one of those daffy females who are trying to wobble the globe?"

"It's about voting!" shouted Josie.

"Voting?"

"Voting! You heard me. Voting."

"Why would you want to vote?" moaned Lizzy.

"Why would I not?"

"Jan votes for you! You know he votes with your welfare on his mind! Is there a better man than Jan, who cares more deeply for his family and votes accordingly?"

"Voting for a candidate," lectured a beet-red Josie, who'd rather read than eat, "is an illegal act for criminals. For lunatics. For idiots. And me."

"Sit down. Please. Calm yourself!"

"I have no legal rights. My daughters will grow up and have no legal rights."

"You have more rights than you could possibly use up. Does your fine husband ever tell you no? You can order anything you wish from the wish book."

"I'm not his pet. I've got a brain. I think. That is my passion. He treats me like a child."

"What's wrong with that?" asked Little Melly, nibbling on a

cheese bit.

"Some people," Josie hissed, "will see some mighty changes around here. You'll be surprised. We're reforming the political landscape. We're revising the laws of the land. Women's prospects have never looked brighter."

The spinster looked at her with small but steely eyes. "That's what you think. That's just your own opinion."

"This is America."

"You're entitled to your own opinion."

"You watch. This is America."

"But see? Here in America, our Savior calls the shots."

"Some mighty changes! Mark my word!"

"Oh, really?"

"Really! Absolutely!"

"Well. We shall see."

"That's right! That is precisely right! You listen to me, Little Melly! When women grow at last beyond the point where they cut paper doilies to spruce up some Rotary Club, that's when they'll find themselves—"

"—left hanging by their fingernails," said Little Melly pleasantly, and picked a cheese crumb from her lap. "If you don't mind, another piece of strudel."

Chapter 33

"Reform? Yet more reform?" The mild tsar shook his head.

Reform was reform, conceded the tsar, but coercion was clearly coercion. He was obliging, courteous and lenient, but when it came to blackmail, to that he would not yield.

He offered, timidly, as a concession, that he would finish what his progressive grandfather had begun. "But at my leisure," said the tsar, to which the Empress nodded.

Yet on the other hand, he said repeatedly as well, he would not slam the door on centuries. He knew, as did his ministers, the seed of Judah was fervently behind the oft-repeated sacrilege of insurrection, and for their blasphemy, such knaves went to the gallows. That was his alpha and omega as one long century behind him turned to dust. His spies, to a body, spoke German.

While deviationists stirred riots in the cities, few farmer residents at Apanlee in the first decade of the new century paid any heed to folly. The orthodox priests, swinging their incense in arches, pronounced the harvests good.

Wealth took hard work. Thrift, moderation, prudence, diligence had stood the test of time. There were no malcontents at

Apanlee. The sons did better than their fathers; their sons, in turn, would reap richer harvests in turn. The cosmic gears meshed smoothly—much like the fanciful machinery of Apanlee, the German showcase farm all strove to emulate—reaping the wheat, binding the straw into tight, even bundles.

By then, one of the finest grain estates in all of the Ukraine had been passed down to Hein, grandson of Peet and Greta Neufeld. Hein was a handsome, robust youth, not in the least inclined to curb the ways of nature with restraint.

Born on the very day the anarchists had thrown a bomb beneath the horses' hooves that tore a mild, progressive tsar apart and changed the course of Russia forever, no one knew better than did Hein how to impose his will.

Hein took his time to find the Lord, forsake the appetites of his red, fleshy heart, and settle down to business.

The elders often sat him down for coffee and small talk. While washing down their zwieback with their coffee, they would come to the point at once: "You wouldn't want to get involved romantically with anyone whose surname you could easily forget?"

It wasn't that he wasn't willing to follow custom and tradition. Everybody, in the end, was willing. But Hein's vitality ran strong, and his hot glance had fallen on a Ukrainian servant girl— a maid with callused heels and strong, efficient hands, a splendid, healthy female.

Her first name was Natasha. She didn't know her last.

Hein harvested and leveled his potatoes. Behind him stood a kinship net that numbered in the thousands. The Lord had seen them through one century. He would do likewise in the next.

The Elders kept a strict eye on trespasses.

The nearby Catholics just sprinkled; the Lutherans dunked newborns head-first in their galvanized, wide buckets; the priests tried to stifle their yawns. The Apanlee Elders, by contrast, were grim. They baptized youngfolk thoroughly, by triple and total immersion, in the waterhole behind the trees of Apanlee, assuring salvation the trustworthy, traditional way. You had your rules;

you lived by them; it was best to leave nothing to chance.

The Elders told the congregation pointedly, their eyes on Hein's red ears:

"Remain apart. Keep pure the pool of kin. For if you do, your yield will be magnificent. Your children's future will be without shadows."

These Elders preached inspiring sermons, for if you married—as you would!—why, then their blessing was essential. Unheard of was it in those days that one might marry anyone not bred to, raised by, and furthermore confirmed in the True Faith.

The Elders' thoroughness pleased everyone. Their shortest prayers lasted seven minutes. When they came calling, the children greeted them and took their hats, then shrank into the darkness. If you knew what was good for you, you harmonized with them. In their frowns, you read your doom. If they grabbed you by the arm to reinforce a rule, sooner they'd break it before they let go.

As soon as the sun started licking the puddles, the Elders started masterminding spring conversions with customary zeal. Baptisms fed the church, as young love fed the cradles—if cleverly you knew how to combine the two, the future was assured.

The deacons took swift count: "You. You. And you and you and you. Just about old enough. You need your Savior's saving grace before it is too late."

"Right after Pentecost," most eager youngfolk said.

The earth was in full bloom; their hearts were wide-open while they were in love; the Holy Ghost marched in and set up residence.

That was wonderful spiritual acreage!

In those slow, pious, bygone days, there was something to youth, love and bonding that no words and no songs could decipher—enchanting as a falling meteor, as fragile as is gossamer. Silk stockings had not yet reached Russia.

A rooster crowed. The cows were red and white.

A muzhik let sharp vodka run across his tongue and mumbled this and that.

Jew, Christian or Turk—all were the same to little Uncle Benny. Life was like pointing with a pencil in a book; he moved from word to word.

You lived from day to day. You lived in peace. With gratitude. A few remaining oldsters who still remember Apanlee will tell you to this day that's how it was—how peaceful and how lovely life was. Just flowing as a river flows amidst the downpour of warm rain. Smooth. Effortless.

You knew exactly where you stood, in which direction lineage pointed, and where you would end up—with the Lord in celestial spheres.

And who would dare to say that that was wrong? That it was wicked? Racist?

You lived by nature's ways. You could hear snatches of a love song here and there, the even, happy laughter of a girl.

Count yourself blessed—such was the sentiment.

The acacia trees bent low to the earth with their clusters of flowers; the bachelors would pick at them and suck the sweetness from the pistil's base, surveying marriage-worthy maidens with longing. The Elders knew: "It's now or never!" to warn the young of the torments of sinners in hell.

The Elders briskly went to work, saving the lambs, not just from the Fiend, but from the missionary wiles of Catholics and Lutherans.

"Listen, you. And you. And you. Your loins are hot? Your heart is churning? You are a sinner, through and through. You need the Savior's church; the Savior's church needs you. Your warranty, you ask? The splendor of His promise. Brief are your days on earth. Eternal the hereafter."

There was no question mark, no compromise. What lay in store in the hereafter could be glimpsed merely in the exaltation of good prayers—but every Elder put his reputation on the line: when it came to the clan, obedience and discipline for now, but glory upon glory at the end.

It took little effort, for instance, to baptize Marleen. Marleen was ready. Well-scrubbed. Willing. Marleen stood poised, just waiting for the nod.

Chosen carefully by several worried Elders to counteract the lures that seemed to plague the lusty heir of Apanlee, Marleen arrived one frosty winter morning, replete with darning bulb.

She was warming herself by the pot-bellied stove, her face as serious as the moon. She came of proven stock. There was some Epp blood in her veins, warranting piety, mixed in with Friesens, Harders, Unruhs. No quirks that could have shocked the elders were known among her relatives.

She wore long braids. Each day, she combed them out with pride.

Before long, she was knitting her third pair of slippers. Above all else, she liked to knit; she would make sure her daughters would do likewise.

She was in love with Hein as the earth is in love with the clouds; it was in the natural order. She was in full agreement with the Elders: restraint was correct in someone so sure of her virtue as she.

Although Hein took his time in taking her measure, that daunted not Marleen, who, with the greatest confidence, threw herself into wedding preparations.

She had already, years ago, stitched for her hope chest all the pillows she would need. When the remotest relatives arrived, as surely they would, as soon as she and Hein prepared to tie the knot officially and with the sanction of the Faith, they knew they would receive a warm reception and a warm feather bed where they could settle down to stay.

She may have had love in her eyes; she also had steel in her spine. She tutored Hein at every opportunity. "Ready for baptism yet?"

He said to her: "Your face is as familiar to me as though you were my sister."

She spoke in warning undertones: "The hoots and hisses will come thick."

He was an unconvincing liar. "I know not what you mean."

They were of equal height; her eyes met his at level glance. She told him evenly: "I won't be branded as a fool. You have a year to think it over." That was Marleen, known for her rectitude, admired for her common sense. She washed her hands before she folded them in prayer. She leafed through her Bible, page after page; what she found there, she extracted and applied.

Now and then, she consulted the Elders in pastoral fashion. They told her that her strategy was apt.

That's what it took, they counseled—an ultimatum, the Bible and a moment ripe enough to take advantage of that quickening of spirit that often coincided with the quickening of body and made a man start looking eagerly for an obedient, willing wife.

Natasha seemed to say, if only to herself: "I have not a moment to lose."

Natasha was a pretty thing with hazel eyes and ample hair who radiated invitation like a wide stove stoked with pines. A Russian hamlet brought her forth; she didn't even know her birthday; she came to Apanlee while still a teenager to help bring in the harvest.

She worked quickly, expertly, her collar undone, the stains of effort showing in the armpits of her blouse. Hein noticed with a tingle in his belly that, when he spoke to her, rich hues moved over her.

His glance slid to her bosom. Her peasant odor dizzied.

She watched his eyes, enthralled, amazed, and mystified. She started to surmise: "The river is swollen with rain."

He knew that it was wrong. She knew that it was fate. There was a dark fatality in her that didn't show while she was young but marked her later years.

What happened next was easy to divine. The meadows, rife with rumor!

Natasha laughed and ducked and flirted with her lashes. Her eyes shone with excitement. Hein watched her all day long. He noticed that she, too, would start to tremble helplessly whenever he was near.

He told her when they were alone: "I'll trade you a new hay rake for a kiss."

She noticed that his neck turned pink, then red; she was nobody's fool. At *vespa* break, she set herself apart to give the heir of Apanlee a chance to speak to her. That was, she knew, an act of shrewd diplomacy.

He leaped to the challenge at once. He came and sat, squatting, before her.

"How pretty you are." With his thumb, he was stroking the soles of her feet. "A beastly heat, right? Just look at you! You're soaking wet with sweat!"

She unwrapped the rich food that Marleen—deaf, dumb and blind, and probably dead where it mattered—had packed for them both. "Here. Have a bite." Onions and bread, cold cutlets and zwieback, a jug filled with kvas. "I'm surprised at you," she laughed. She poured the kvas, leaning back into the shade of the acacias. "Well? What's on your mind?

"You must be hot. Are you hot? How your blouse sticks—"

"I am drenched with perspiration to the skin. Look at me. Just look at me." She prompted him to treachery. "Why don't you look at me?"

He struggled to obtain firm footing. "Are you alone? Where do you live? Your eyes are glossy as satin."

She held a piece of sugar between her even teeth and let the kvas surge through. "All alone. Just a pig and a goat."

"Look what I wrote for you," he stammered, slipping her a small piece of paper. "It's a deal. I'll make you a deal. You hanker to better your future?"

"What's it to me?"

"What do you mean?"

"You know that I can barely write my name."

"I'll teach you," said Hein, heavy with meaning. "Depend

on me. I'll teach you everything."

She wasn't born a simpleton. "You will?"

She knew a man's desire. Just like a horse—no matter where it started out, it never missed the stable. "I might teach you a thing or two," she offered wantonly.

Hein knew he loved his chosen well enough. He knew Marleen would serve him faithfully; she would never belittle his mustache. She had an impeccable family name. He knew she knew as everybody knew: "This is an interlude."

"I'll wait my turn," Natasha said and fell, laughing, on Hein's shoulder.

Had she let go of pride, Marleen might well have willed a miracle, but she did not—why should she have?—since Hein regarded her with awe. The Elders were already polishing their sermons to tie the wedding knot.

Marleen said calmly, more than once: "So? And so what?" The falling leaves kept dancing at her feet in heedless, jerky gusts.

Natasha kept teasing. And teasing. And teasing.

Hein stared at her, enthralled. He kept pulling loose the strings of her apron—the antics of a young boy with a slingshot in his hands compelled to hurl that pebble one more time into the glossy leaves before surrendering his boyhood to the somber duties of the corncribs and the stables and the fields.

"What will you teach me? Say?"

"You'll see. What? Are you doubting me?"

"Anything that I don't know already?" She blew against the tufts of hair that sprouted on his knuckles. "I might teach you a thing or two."

"You will?"

She patted her belly after the meal. "You know what I mean. This is your one and only chance. There's a fellow who's waiting for me."

Fire and brimstone!

Hein knew about fire and brimstone from many a blistering sermon. He turned and tried to walk away from her with butter in his knees. In fact, he tried to run.

"I might wait to be taught," she called after him, just tumbling her long hair about; she knew him well; he never had a chance; he turned and seized her hand and pressed it with moist palms—and blast the firing squad!

"Come to the barn after dark," he whispered fervently. "I'll forget to drop the latch." The sun kept on shedding its heat on them both. She smiled at him, dazed by her luck, confirmed in her Faith, her youth and her icons.

"I'll wait for you," she said, "to find your way to me."

Chapter 34

From deferential ministers, at intervals, came word that all was well across the Russian land, in every respect. The courtiers doubled up in bows. Ambitious poets composed spicy songs. The gentry boasted about foreign travel.

A muffled roar rose from the river bank where a progressive priest plunged a fat cross into the icy waters of the Neva after having blessed it lavishly with ornate, garish words. The people in the streets watched as it sank. A raw wind drew tears to their eyes. Flags rippled. Music soared. The East began to pale. The soothsayers kept whispering.

We live and die; the tsars do what they want. God save our little tsar! God save his haughty *nyemka*! We live and die; unless the tsar throws us a bone. Is this a life worth living?

They stood there in a stony silence. Their thoughts were like poisonous smoke: "Day-in, day-out, toil and wear and stinging nettles. Day-in, day-out, cabbage soup and buckwheat gruel. Our foreheads touch mud in obedience. We trap for squirrels and sparrows; we starve to death on a pallet of straw. Our lyrics are soft, but our melodies carry our anguish."

The peasants in the countryside sank to their knees repeatedly and crossed themselves with ample gestures: "We? Humble beasts of burden. You sold us land we had no say in choosing, for debts we cannot pay. Our children are weeping with hunger. God save our little tsar. We long to see your face. We yearn to read your eyes."

The people dropped their heads like grain before the breeze: "Everything yours—my land, my life, my sons, my bones. You rule us, control us. We gratify you; the sun itself gratifies you. We bow like oats during harvest. What are we? Who are we? But leaves in the merciless wind!"

They said, and it became a chant and then a moan and finally a roar: "Be good to him, oh Lord. Shield our Little Father."

The roar rolled to the Palace of the Fifteen-hundred Windows that sparkled with the sheen of many polished candelabras. The servants threw open the curtains. The courtiers stood aside respectfully. The tsar, whose heart was blind, whose mind could not sustain a single thought for any length of time, smiled amiably and waved with a weak wrist.

The whispers picked up speed. The wind scattered the words: "The throne will fall, a house of brittle cards."

The offspring of an Emperor so strong he bent a horseshoe with his hands, a ruler who cut off the heads of dissidents with his own well-oiled saber while roaring in his mirth, whose bronze horse statue reared its hooves right at the edge of an abyss, turned his attention to his dominoes.

The night was dark as ink. The rivers waited, paralyzed.

The prison roof moaned with the storm that came in broadside gusts. The cold pierced the prisoner's marrow and gave a blue tint to his nose.

"My brother climbed the scaffold, but not before he kissed the crucifix," the prisoner wrote haltingly. "His note books—always orderly. His name—without a blemish. He had a brilliant future. Save for the fire flaming in his veins at seeing peasants lying in the ditches with frozen feet and broken hearts, he would have been a bureaucrat. Our mother hoped for that." On his eyebrows formed crystals of ice. "She walked him to the gallows. Before the hangman broke his neck, he kissed the crucifix—"

The raw air had worsened his cough. A cotton wick was flickering in a small dish filled slovenly with kerosene.

"—the pride of his teachers; the head of his class; a student with a promising horizon—"

On his lips formed a pledge by itself: "May my tongue cleave to my roof if I do not remember you as you should be remembered. And may my right arm wither if I don't right your wrong—"

That was the legacy. An unforgiving mandate settled down around his shoulders like a mantle. His inner eye saw nothing but a sea of upraised faces. A drowning man, he knew, will take an outstretched hand.

"What did the tsars decree? No building should be taller than the palace?"

Therefore, why not level the palace?

"Hack down the imperial emblems! To the dust bin of history, all!"

Thus wrote a bald-headed, tormented man, much better known to history as Lenin.

While brooding on his brother's execution, this man with slanted eyes and a maternal grandmother with rumored links to those the Lord had kept adrift upon the globe for ancient, ageless sins, wrote next with stiffened fingers:

"Bring the workers to power. Turn the world upside down. Be done with the knout and the whip. Throttle oppression with your bare hands. The sun of liberty will shine on you forever after!"

From black, sticky bread he had fashioned an inkwell into which he dipped a pen he had managed to hide from the guards. He kept it in the hollow heel of one of his torn boots. He never parted with his boots, not even when he slept; they kept his toes from freezing.

"The barns and silos of the manors? The country mansions of the rich? Their stables full of trotting horses? Those animals are given better fodder than your little children, your aging parents have to eat—" He wrote with milk saved from a meager meal. He blew on it to let it dry. "Their end is etched into the brand new century with brilliant clarity. The Revolution will undo the tsars' fool's paradise. How? You ask how? Ivan the Terrible wrote you a script."

Death to the oppressors!

Destruction to the rich!

"Be done with your needless submission. Land is as free as the air. Take to your pitchforks. Fell them by the butt of gun. String them up like Christmas ornaments. Strangle them and drown them and dismember them—they are your mortal enemies. When you have taken your revenge, your precious foreigners will cling with broken fingers to a cliff."

When Erika, in her research for *Left and Right*, delved into this part of her troubled history, she found to her amazement the Kansas folks had simply no idea. They did not want to listen when she told them, in both her fists the damning documents: "The usurers, who lived like moles within the canyons of New York, sneaked him a tattered document."

"Not true!" insisted every relative, and that was that. No further argument.

"It is true, too! It's true!"

"This is America."

"You can't destroy the truth."

"It's anti-Semite talk."

"You check that out," said Erika, but no one had the time.

If it is true, it could not have been difficult. The Russian underling who was supposed to guard the prison gate had never learned to read. Why should he have been schooled when he was born to live a brutish life in squalor and vulgarity inherited through centuries? When he would die that way—if he was lucky, numbed with vodka?

"*Da! Da!*" he said, glad for a chance to please, with not a single bread crust in his hovel to feed his hungry brood. He didn't even bother glancing at the paper. He jovially waved him on.

As leaves began to fall from trees all over Russia, a bitter man escaped across the border. The serpentines, so we are told, were there.

For quite a while, he hid himself in Switzerland. Before the year was out, his rhetoric and fame jumped borders. A helpful Jew gave him some money. With it, he purchased a small press. He started publishing *The Spark*.

Despite the Elders' pointed admonitions, Natasha kept on baiting Hein, until one Sunday afternoon he went in search of her. He rode his horse without the benefit of halter, armed only with a switch.

Natasha sunned herself out in the open air, to give him a chance to survey her. She squinted at a thundercloud that piled behind a tree. It was a hot and muggy day.

"Well. Here you are. Say what you will." She had confided to a friend: "I'll lead him away by the bridle."

In preparation of his visit, she had already scrubbed herself until she almost swooned. The friend had issued warnings: "Fire and water, Natasha. Fire and water!"

"He who stops, rusts," said Natasha. She believed that.

Her friend was not convinced, but Natasha explained herself clearly: "I want a bowl with yellow flowers. The saints are on my side."

For an entire week, she had moved her icons from corner to corner to give them additional light. "One step at a time," said Natasha. "One day at a time. One kiss at a time. That's how it will be, from now on."

"You never know whence danger lurks," she told Hein now, while he stood, smiling shakily, admiring the unbroken smoothness of her skin. He leaned toward her, whispering. "What are you doing here, alone?"

"I live here. Don't you know?"

"You do?"

"Whatever brings you here?" she asked with dancing eyes.

His ears were turning purple. "I can't imagine. You?"

"Eat salted cucumbers," laughed Natasha. "I will have none of your excuses. Keep your excuses, Hein!"

The storm broke suddenly.

"At your own risk and peril," she said, invitingly, to keep him from being pelted by raindrops. She knew that she was safe that day. The gypsy, with whom she had huddled, had promised.

He took her naked elbow, about to give up the ghost. "What do you want? A scarf?" Her frock with the convenient shoulder straps permitted him to push them down with ease. "A necklace with many unbreakable beads?"

"A dish with yellow flowers." She leaned against him cozily—a girl about to sin grossly.

All summer long, and deep into September, Natasha's dancing eyes never left the small, round beads that Hein had given her.

"A little something for the heart," Hein said to her, good-natured and in love, and she smiled back at him—two ill-matched lovers from the start, stripping leaves from swaying trees and laughing at each other throughout a long and violent summer, with many sudden thunderstorms. To the tossing of the wind and the cackling of the chickens, they fell asleep, content and sated both, while, outside, nature howled.

"I can't wait for the cold days," Natasha said to Hein when next he came to visit her, and rolled her hair in paper rollers to spruce herself a bit. She walked with lithe and happy steps, her feet in neatly plaited footwear, a present from Berdyansk where Hein would travel now and then to sell a load of grain.

"Why so?" he asked, his voice on the trigger of fire.

"More time for this and that," Natasha laughed at him.

These days, Natasha laughed. Marleen just clattered with her dishes. There was still a praiseworthy patience, but yet a hard finish, to her.

The rains dissolved the summer, and still Natasha laughed. The melancholy days arrived; and then came fog; next, snow.

Marleen was resolved to sit out the siege.

Natasha, by contrast, fell asleep with a smile on her lips.

She was in love, and so was Hein; when passion struck, the heir of Apanlee was merciless in his rapacity but filled with tenderness and rue when all was said and done. That dish with yellow flowers was a start.

So, then: Natasha laughed.

An Elder heard that laughter and reached for walking stick and Bible. Two stalwart deacons joined adroitly. They spread the facts before the scofflaw, one by one: "Her father was a bonded serf. So was her grandfather. So was her great-grandfather. She is a bonded serf in anything but name—"

The guilty sinner sulked. "So what? It matters not." By then, his heart lay in a hammerlock between Natasha and Marleen.

"So what? What are you saying, Hein?"

"She's an obliging girl. She means no harm. She wouldn't harm a beetle."

"But water keeps on dripping from her ceiling. Her soup has too much salt. Her bread is black and sticky. Her straw is full of fleas."

Hein knew all that, yet could no more have stopped himself than could have restrained a cloud from raining.

"I'll think your warning over," Hein offered, but those three men of God were not about to leave before the matter was resolved. The deacons and the Elder pointed out: "Hast thou but three small grains of sense, thou wouldst see what to do. Take thee this minute to thy prayer corner."

The thous and thees were harder to resist. They pricked Hein's conscience like salt sprinkled into a wound.

"I cannot hate her," argued Hein. "She is a kindly girl."

"We do not hate them," said the preachers. "But neither do we love them."

"I never said I loved her." Hein's mustache kept on twitching with his lie.

"And don't thou know—thou fool, thou wastrel and thou braggart—that Natasha has passed through a number of hands? Would thou not want an untouched maiden to bear thy progeny?"

At that the culprit, overwhelmed, lurched to his feet and dusted the straw from his trousers.

Marleen was faultless to a fault. He saw her merits now. He saw, by contrast, that Natasha couldn't darn and wouldn't learn; she went to church with her collar unfastened; she kept her hut too hot, her sheepskin untidy, the corners of her dwelling full of cobwebs. The Elders forced the issue at every opportunity.

But still he frowned with indecision. The Lord might come with thunderbolts and fiery darts, but he was a young man, built like that oak that grew securely by the waterhole, his tap root anchored in the earth—and every little leaf, like naked skin, lay exposed to the onslaught of seasons.

"If thou don't keep thy promise," growled the Elder, "then God will surely strike thee dead."

"I'll try to keep my promise," pledged Hein, but wouldn't be specific.

Hein knew the rules as well as anyone—to marry within clan was in close keeping with your station; it was in keeping with the bargains the creed had struck with Providence. Yet still Natasha lured. A song was always on her lips. She admired his masterful mustache.

The Elders tried their best to lure the heir of Apanlee away from his temptation: installing untried melodies into their sermons fore and aft, inviting him to prayer breakfasts well fortified with chicken legs, and making sure the girl they had approved of was at hand and seated down beside him.

"No progress yet, Marleen? Then place an extra egg for him in your own samovar."

"Not yet. There is yet time." The girl spoke evenly, her

quote book in her lap. At night, Marleen lay awake in her clean, narrow bed, struggling with the misery that rakes an untouched body.

"1902. Hein N." said the letters, cut in the bark of the old oak Peet Neufeld had grown from a seedling.

That was the year a young, squat man with webbed toes and pockmarked face was exiled to Siberia—yet one more dissident, enmeshed in one more strike, to die, the monarchs hoped, of want and overwork.

His property was one exhausted horse. His name was Joseph Stalin.

At Apanlee, none would have known.

By then, Hein stood crushed against the wall of rectitude his bloodline had thrown up, resolved to be done with temptation. Beneath his name, he tried to carve: "Marleen."

His knife slipped, and he, bleeding profusely, went to the kitchen where Marleen watched the Sunday rooster sizzling in the pan. He let her bind his wound. She kept her eyes downcast. She knew the spinsters kept on gossiping in undertones; the children craned their necks.

When Hein returned a fortnight later, a stranger's hand had carved into the tree above his name, in smaller, slanted letters: "Natasha."

He took an ax to hew out every trace. The sap oozed from the wound.

That week, Natasha broke away the gum that formed to heal the tree. She ate it for good luck.

Chapter 35

The firstborn didn't make it, sadly, past McGuffey's Reader, and that was partly Doctorjay's and partly Josie's fault. It was this elocution business, and it was just as Little Melly had predicted from the start—the Lord meant business: He'd snarled the youngster's tongue to teach a haughty soul a lesson. The boy kept his pronounced and hopeless stammer. No ointment diminished the ailment.

It would not have mattered to anyone else, for a fault was a fault, all people had faults.

But it mattered to Josie. She wanted perfection. She flinched when the margin boy stuttered. She never lived down speculation that she herself had brought on the affliction, since her premarriage days were not as pure as snow.

But Josie didn't shrink from trouble; that was not in her nature. Instead, she tried to force the heavy hand of God, Who had given the stutter and could likewise have wiped it away.

She took her son's small hand, spurning the fine basement Special School for Backward Children at the corner of Maple and Main, manned by rotating volunteers, insisting: "There is nothing the Wichita doctors can't fix."

She worked it out with Doctorjay that he, still swapping mail and politics each Wednesday afternoon, would take the youngster once a week to Wichita for his elocution lessons, and likewise bring him back. She wouldn't take no for an answer, not even from the weighty hand of God.

It was a wretched accident.

She loved to read when snow fell thick and soft; she pushed her nose through yet another book and didn't sense that night was falling; she never noticed anything; she just assumed that Doctorjay would pick the little fellow up; he always picked him up returning from his rounds on Wednesdays—but Doctorjay forgot.

His mind befogged, he thought that it was Tuesday.

The constable would later piece together the details. The little boy tried hitching rides from passersby, and when that effort failed, tried hard to make it home alone, while a tremendous snowstorm built and started blowing fiercely. The railing of the bridge was broken. There was a snowdrift, way below, atop the frozen creek. He must have leaned against the bridge to catch his breath. And slipped. And fallen in.

Barn lanterns flickering like witches' tongues, the neighbors looked for him for days—no time for drink and food. But all in vain. They never found the child. The wind erased all traces.

The winter lasted long that year. The snow lay deep and hard. The only thing a neighbor found, right before Easter Sunday, was just one little shoe. It was lying in a furrow where overflowing waters carried it when spring's thaw caused a flood.

One outcome was that Doctorjay tried hard to stop all drinking. He promised that he wouldn't touch another drop for many cheerless years.

The neighbors nodded, fortified: embedded in sorrow lay blessings. The neighbors knew: the Lord takes care to wash thine eyes with tears so thou canst see thine guilt.

The healer stood before the grieving parents, hat in hand, his heart wrung like a dishrag, as his tears disappeared in his beard. "Will you ever forgive an old donkey like me?"

As soon as Josephine could speak, she told him that she shared his burden. She was so pale she was translucent; all color had been drained from her.

"It was my fault as much as yours," said Josephine. It was as if she scattered mental petals on a non-existent coffin that held not just her child but a large part of her—that radiant Josie of Jan's heart whom he loved more than life.

"Don't say that," muttered Doctorjay, at long last sober to the marrow, and she leaned over briefly and touched his trembling hand.

For the rest of his boisterous life, he would cling to that merciful gesture.

But what was one small, accidental death to Mennotown, where life went on as always? If Josie wept, none saw her tears— not even Jan, not even Lizzy. No one.

She went into one of her many disguises. She hid herself away.

Lizzy, on the other hand, kept keening. She cried and moaned and wailed. She simply couldn't stop.

The death was hard on Jan as well, but he had friends; he had his church; he had his mother and his sisters and his daughters. He tried to comfort Josie. He delved into his duties. He forged ahead with many plans, and sought his balm in work and yet more work. His grain lay waiting in the sun; another century was here, rife with opportunities; he had no time to waste another day.

Josie, who loved privacy, sat by herself, alone, all wrapped in stony silence. The rivers roared; she grieved.

The household put the tulips in her charge, and still she grieved. She grieved.

Time passed. She grieved. She didn't cry, although her shoulders shook.

The prairie turned all emerald before it changed to sapphire, and still she grieved. It would not end; she couldn't help herself. Relatives arrived, in droves, to lend their company and offer prayers; yet Josie grieved. They left their Bibles sitting on her window sills. But nothing helped. She grieved.

The answer, she was told with ever greater stridency, was to be born again. "There's peace in surrender to Jesus," they told her. "You must cleanse yourself in His blood."

She said that made no sense at all. "That's monstrous. That's obscene."

Josie wasn't buying. The accident was etched into her memory as if with diamond on clear glass.

"You'll greatly benefit from loving company," said Lizzy, pleadingly. "Please. Here. Just blow your nose. Come join our quilting circle."

"I am a stranger and do not belong," said Josie, but put on a pair of galoshes and went.

The neighbors hovered over her with low and clucking noises:

"A tragic mishap," said one.

"A lesson somewhere," said another. "We warned you. Did you listen?"

She ducked as she had ducked that long-remembered night before she flung her songbook in the fire.

"Do not be deceived, God is not mocked, for whatsoever a man sows, that will he also reap."

All afternoon, they carved new chasms in her grief. The creek, too deep to cross? The temperature just plummeted? One darling little shoe? And that without its laces?

A horse fly has a mission.

"Hath not the potter power over clay? If thou shalt now confess with thine own mouth your Lord Christ Jesus—"

She sat there, trapped, wedged in between huge shanks. Teeth gritted. Face aflame.

The oxen were long gone, the finest surreys going out of fashion. The shiftless Donoghues still clucked their carts along.

With Doctorjay hard on his heels, Jan bought himself a flivver.

The motor car Jan ordered from St. Louis turned out to be the ultimate in betterment and class, and Little Melly was so overcome to see Jan motorized she nearly burst with pride.

Though Little Melly never altogether lost her fears that such unholy speed could do real havoc to her bowels, when it came to Jan and his beloved flivver, she was as devoted as ever. She raised her pudgy finger: "Shhh!" as soon as he revved up his engine.

Jan loved that Model T. He relished the roar and didn't mind fumes. He could recite a flivver manual from memory. When Jan spun the tires, they started to smoke. He had grease splatter inside his ears.

It was a fine contraption—flat-nosed, full-bellied, fully maneuverable on any country road. In height, it measured seven feet.

Little Melly dressed it up with fine, embroidered curtains. He stored it in an old, abandoned chicken shed where she squashed several spiders. He told her flivver jokes. She liked Jan's flivver jokes, but she herself was no vehicular fanatic. She didn't lose sight of the signal that her feet belonged on the ground.

The race for honor and prestige it was that spurred the men of Mennotown to own a motor car.

The slowest sluggard knew: a new dawn had arrived.

As candidate for chairman of the Mennotown Chamber of Commerce, Jan bought his flivver just in time to tip the balance in that race. Doctorjay, who likewise hankered for that honor— though he would never have admitted such ambitions to his wife; her hoots might never stop!—gave up his surrey, retired Annetta, and vouched to go motorized, too.

For many years, Doctorjay had done his doctoring atop his one-horse shay still pulled by his old horse, albeit now on thick, arthritic legs. He and Annetta both were fixtures—near legends, by that time. The two had been a feature in the paper. Behind them stretched a history that no one could deny.

The day that article came out, Doctorjay came near exploding with vanity and pride. He flicked the reins across Annetta's ears and shouted himself hoarse: "*Pascholl*, Annetta! Giddap, Annetta!" as he passed envious pedestrians, rolling slow and proud.

Now this? Who would have ever thought he could betray Annetta?

"What can a fellow do? Can't argue with success," boasted he, the tip of his nose getting redder and redder.

Doctorjay went off and bought himself a flivver of his own with lots of chrome and a loud horn. His new possession offered him unheard-of, undreamed freedom. Now he could disappear periodically into the haunts of Wichita, exchange as many hand-shakes as he liked, return in time, and not offend the town. He claimed he didn't drink. He merely visited.

"I'd like to see it first," said Noralee. "You promise, then forget."

She, for her part, was skeptical. He had black patches in his mind where memory should be.

She noticed that he kept forgetting things, events and places: everything. She forecast disaster and worse.

"One of these days—" she pointed an accusing finger, "you'll not remember who you are. You'll forget what to do. One day you'll lose your head."

And all the while his friends were saying to themselves: "There's nothing that can hold him back! Just look at Doctorjay!"

The speculations had it wrong. Now that he had a motor toy to fill his veins with warmth, his flask lost some allure. Not all, but some. He used to keep it hidden in the waistband of his trousers: that's where he now stored oily rags, screwdrivers of assorted sizes, a small can of expensive motor oil, and a much-thumbed-through manual. It came replete with etiquette: "Above all else, do not poke with a stick into the mechanism. That is the height of rudeness."

And, oh, how he babied that engine!

He came to know his flivver with an intimacy with which he never knew another human being; he could have taken it apart blindfolded, then put it back together, and still it would have run. He took good care of it; it needed shade, just like a horse; it shook and trembled when he paid attention, emitting soot and smoke. The joy, the wonder of it all!

"That is America for you," he said to Jan, and slapped him on the shoulder.

"Right. Right you are," said Jan, who seldom contradicted anyone, not even Josephine.

The two grown men were ape about their flivvers. There was no greater pleasure, then as now, as any woman knows, for a man in love with cars to come across another faulty gauge.

This suited Noralee. No longer did she have to ask: "Now, Doctorjay. Where were you, Doctorjay?" and watch him struggle for excuses.

Now she knew where she should look. Chances were that she could find her husband in Jan's company, or Jan in Doctorjay's, stretched out, full-length, beneath the chassis—inspecting, greasing, polishing. They hammered, and they patched. They ripped out screws and hoses, and put them in again.

"See? Once we get this baby rolling, an easy forty miles an hour," they bragged to passersby.

"I say that's modest! Modest! Take on another five!"

"These babies, built for speed!"

"As much as fifteen hundred miles out of a single tire!"

For hours, they computed fuel consumption, chalking up imaginary savings. They turned on the ignition and spun at the crank. The motor caught, then sputtered, caught again. They stroked the hood as though it were a living being—there wasn't any end to the suspense of what a motor car could do.

"Just watch the bridge! Watch out!" shrieked an excited Noralee.

Mocking laughter, that was her reward as she watched the two mainstays of the neighborhood—grown, somber fellows—become two mindless boys and roar the length of Mennotown, cascading fountains of dirt. Their voices grew lustier and lustier. Cows leaped aside for safety. Annetta was left standing in the dust.

Wherever Dewey preached, the angels played their harpsichords. Therefore, to no one's great surprise, Dewey chose to preach full-time.

"I was not meant to waste the land," he said to Jan, apologizing. "I must bow to the burden of my calling."

He up and sold the second parcel by the brook that Jan had given Daisy for her dowry. He sold it at a loss, without first giving Jan the courtesy of purchasing it back. Only after all the paperwork was signed did Mennotown discover with dismay that he had sold it to the Donoghues, a bunch of brutes by all accounts, who smothered their chickens with pepper.

"No way to get it back?" asked Lizzy, guiltily, still thinking of the missing title.

Jan read the bill of sale in silence before he passed it on. "No. It's too late. It worked to their advantage that the title wasn't clear."

Lizzy could have kicked herself. She'd turned every corner in her attic, turned every drawer inside out—she must have put it through the wash; the crucial deed was gone.

She tried to be a charitable Christian, but the full evidence was there, it couldn't be denied: the Donoghues were trouble; they were up to no good. On more than one occasion, the constable had tried to run them out of town; by nightfall, they were back.

Now the detested Donoghues had gained not just a toehold but a foothold: they now resided next door, practically—and smirking at her rooster.

Modernity was in the air: more was yet to come.

Gone were the days of flails and hand-driven fans; long gone were the ornery mules—which didn't, on the other hand, need brush and paint and linseed oil to keep the rust away.

Only yesterday, the farmers stood in sweaty shirtsleeves on the platforms, to bind the grain and drop the sheaves in piles. Now modern threshing outfits moved from farm to farm in early August, gigantic caterpillars built of steel. Jan's binders came and bound with wire, while he stood by and watched.

Josie started flirting with further modern notions. Her zeal to catch up with the world was so extreme that even Lizzy, already sensing Jan's heart breaking, bit by bit, stood tremblingly behind the door to listen.

By all accounts, the most progressive female, by that time, in all of Sedgwick County, and beyond, was Josie. She willy-nilly pulled the lead out from her hem to keep her skirt demurely at her ankles so she could climb aboard Jan's flivver, unhampered and headstrong. She even shortened it to two inches up above her ankle. Away she roared, hair flying in the wind, and gave no second thoughts to fanciful disorders of the digestive tract believed to be the outcome.

In months to come, Josie and Jan argued a lot. Their voices grew louder and louder. A shadow formed over their union.

His love was a burden, she argued, for it led to additional children—one in her arms, two more at her legs, a forth not even potty trained—where would it end? Such was her litany. She had no shame. She used peculiar words, and didn't draw the shutters. The arguments went on through the night and sometimes spoiled Jan's breakfast.

Jan tore down his outdated mill where stones had ground the wheat. His new mill was talked of as a miracle: a hundred barrel rolling mill, its wires spreading tentacles all over the expanded, airy attic; its power-driven belts kept sorting kernels from the chaff.

"This makes God weep," said Dewey. It couldn't last, said Dewey. What about tried-and-true, old-fashioned elbow grease? You freed up leisure time, and that gave Lucifer more margin.

Though many disagreed with Dewey—for it was either electricity to top success or else fall hopelessly behind—none laughed.

With progress came new problems.

Soon afterward, the Lord called Herbert home. One day he was still here and well, the next day he was gone. The Lord plucked day by day from Herbert's simple life until his time was up.

"A quiet, modest man," said Dewey with approval. He did, by then, all funerals. "The Lord be praised. No suffering."

"Death comes because God wills it so," sang the community of deep believers. Here was a man who passed away, as he had lived, with quiet, somber dignity, next to his maple syrup. While still alive, all loved him well enough.

Jan did his best to honor him in death, as he had honored him alive; he saw to it that Herb was taken to his grave in style and lowered in respectful silence. Lizzy sprinkled a handful of dust.

That week, Josie was on her best behavior. She put her best foot forward. She lent a hand without a murmur with the dishes, while Lizzy sat and wept for Herbert lavishly and watched the fading season—watched how the fog crept over the acres, watched how the first October snowstorm started powdering the roofs.

Noralee was a wide-awake sister. "You're hoping that a guest will come?"

"I want to be of use."

Pause. Heartfelt sighs. By the window sat Lizzy, unseeing. She, too, was young just yesterday. She hoped for a harmonious tomorrow.

Here was the balance sheet, enumerating Lizzy's ills: Arthritic knees. Short breath. Lapses in memory.

"Enjoy being old. You've earned it a hundred times over."

"Yes. That's what Herbert always said."

"The past is now the past," said Josephine. "He was a good, kind, honest man. He's dead now. He is gone. He lived an obscure life. Such life is not for everyone."

Lizzy pressed her lips together hard and swallowed a ready reply.

Little Melly served coffee in polka-dot cups that Josie had

recently bought from Sears-Roebuck—not going there herself to inspect and to compare, but ordering from catalogs as though Jan's money came like hay.

Feet on a heated brick, her knitting needles flying, Lizzy tried to heal herself from being snubbed by relatives because Jan's wife was still so quarrelsome, and no one liked to visit. She kept on reaching for her handkerchief, but still, no change in Josie.

Now Herbert was no more; she, Lizzy, on the sidelines. She longed to overwhelm her relatives with hospitality to show that, grief or not, she was as ever centered in her Lord. But after the initial flurry that follows every funeral—why, hardly anybody came to visit Lizzy any more.

Jan said to Lizzy, gently: "Mom, life goes on. Why don't you pack your suitcase? Go visit Winnipeg."

"Who wants a useless woman? It's just as Herbert said—"

It snowed upon Herb's grave. It rained upon Herb's grave. Her time was heavy on her hands, her eyelids still inflamed with weeping.

" You haven't seen the Dycks for years. Go. Take a small vacation."

" I guess I should. Well, next year. Maybe next year. It costs a lot."

"I can afford it, Mom."

"You've spent too much already. On Herbert's funeral."

"Don't even mention it."

"It pays to save, I always say. It's hardly worth that I should run a separate household—"

Josie unfolded her napkin, pinkie extended, as though she dined now with the Finkelsteins, downtown in Wichita, instead of having afternoon coffee with her mother-in-law, sister-in-law, husband and very close family friend.

Josie spoke as brightly as she could, after a long and swollen pause: "And, anyway, the latest word is that I'll soon have in-door plumbing, just like the Jews in Wichita—"

They had their antidote. The clan strolled down memory lane.

Remember the buffalo chips? Remember the year the potatoes froze in their buckets and all of our chickens succumbed? The year of the rampaging grippe? The lessons we learned? The hardships we endured? We learned how to eke out a sliver of soap. Let alone buy our soap cakes, perfumed.

Lost in her secret world, Josie stared out the window. Her face was blank. She was famished for knowledge and news.

"It's hard for me, these days, to climb the stairs to Bethel Church without assistance," hinted Lizzy. "But I can always count on Josie's helping hand. Right, Josie? Josephine?"

"*Ach ja,*" sighed Noralee into the yawning silence. "If so you say, it must be true. *Ach ja.*"

The young grew old. The old grew useless. Remember the corn stalks? Remember the stones, the marginal land, the locusts, the contrary Indians? Remember how Jan set the unhewn rafters? While Little Melly watched? Remember how we searched for nails to hang that Russian clock? How Herbert's oxen took us visiting on Sundays—clear across that bumpy road to Hillsboro?

Spade in hand, we took to the land. The roads—still unfinished. The bridge—yet unbuilt. And now you reap the blessings, the credit be always the Lord's. A winterized home. A babe every year, so we hope, Josephine. And money to spare for Christmas!

Chapter 36

Hein grew a patriarchal beard. The harvest kept him busy.

"Come winter, then," Natasha said. She carefully studied the palm of his hand. "Just you remember, Hein. He who stops, rusts. I believe that."

He laughed at her. "You're telling me?"

He saw her once or twice, to tie up some loose ends. The chickens still cackled; Natasha still laughed. For weeks on end, he stayed away, but he was always back.

Winter came. Gray days set in. "The river," Natasha told a loyal friend, "turns into a mere trickle."

Hein practiced scales for church songs with Marleen. He wore a belt with buckles Marleen had given him. She leaned against him happily. Natasha poked about—just like a blind, abandoned kitten.

Natasha poured her heart out to the Gypsy. "What do you see? What is in store for me?"

"I see the shadow of a crow that falls upon a coffin."

"These days, it takes a mule to haul him in!" Natasha wailed unhappily.

"Try fasting," said the Gypsy.

"I did," wept Natasha. "I fasted till my hands shook. My waistline grows thicker and thicker."

"So he must know. Tell him at once, Natasha."

"He'll beat me!" howled Natasha. "He'll beat me black and blue."

"Go home, dumb girl," the housemaid told Natasha. "There is no need to show off your misfortune."

"No. I'll wait here."

"He is so busy, nowadays," the servant said, while casting scornful looks. "He scarcely knows himself."

"You tell him. Tell him I am here. Tell him that I feel faint." Natasha sat down, exhausted, on an overturned bucket, resting her hands on her knees. She blew her nose repeatedly, and tried to take deep breaths.

"Fool girl! You'd be lucky to merit a ladle of borscht."

She struck out at her tormentor but missed, so swam her eyes in tears. Natasha could barely bridle her sorrow, so mixed it was with wrath and worry and regret.

"Why did you come here?" Hein scowled when forced to face his own dishonor. "I asked you not to come. Did I not ask you not to come here any more, Natasha?"

The tears rushed to her voice: "It's too late. I now expect the worst."

Hein gnawed at the ends of his mustache. Natasha sat there on her bucket, wrung her hands, and gave free rein to tears.

Hein couldn't help himself; he stroked across her hair. "Well. Now. Let's see. What might be done? I recommend that you start looking for a husband."

"You loved me, and you promised me. Can you deny you did?"

"All that is past."

"For me, you have no mercy?"

"Once my mind has been made up, why would I want to change it?"

"What priest will marry me?" she wept, cradling her belly with fluttering hands. "What man would want spoiled goods?"

"I'll help you search," he offered, and twirled his mustache thoughtfully.

Hein called on Ivan, the newly bonded village herdsman.

"Five rubles," Hein replied, delivering a clever speech. Though he was young, not even twenty years of age, he had a head for business.

"Too little," sniffed Ivan. "Just think. What will the neighbors say?"

"A strip of pasture—fenced! I'm willing to add to the bargain."

"Your name! Imagine the disgrace!"

"Here. Take this flint. A goat?"

Ivan took the flint and sniffed it several times before he let it glide into his pocket. "And all the spiteful tongues. A goat and six fat chickens?"

"Would you like to see me ruined?"

"A cow?"

"And a calf."

"A cart?"

"Plus a wheelbarrow, too."

"Well, come to think of it—"

"Better sign here now," said Hein quickly. He was a prudent man; he had a document in hand. "See what it says? You'll yet make a pauper of me."

Ivan, a shepherd in need of delousing, smacked the bottom of his vodka bottle with the flat of his left hand. "All right. All right. Why not? A cross is good enough?" He was a coarse and uncouth fellow but with a sullen loyalty. The cork popped out and danced into a corner. "Just one last small request. Perhaps a pair of boots?"

"The finest pair of boots," said Hein. "Brand new. The finest leather I can find. And treat her well. That is my one demand."

"Make sure they squeak," said Ivan.

"I'll spit in your face," howled Natasha, rotund.

Hein sat and cracked his knuckles, waiting out the storm. "Shout all you like. There's nothing more to say."

"You took my heart and tore it out."

"Why did you trust the Gypsy?"

"I trusted you. Did I not trust you fully?"

"Don't play such sorry tricks on me. You made a bad mistake. Ivan is not that bad. He says he'll marry you."

She refused with a hot flow of tears. "The dog bites him! The goat hates him!" shrieked Natasha.

Hein studied the tips of his fingers.

"And his lice?" wept Natasha.

"Just strip him, put his clothes in the oven and bake them for an hour."

Hein walked off, hands in his pockets, and left her sitting there. Through floods of tears, Natasha saw her future had a blueprint now that not the deftest saint could change. She wept until her anger melted.

Her belly swelled and swelled. Her tantrums subsided. Compliant shudders shook her frame.

Hein's confidence grew; his comfort increased. The four Gospels were welcome again.

In the end, Natasha gave in: "I am now at the end of my rope."

"I'll let you do some chores around the house," he offered in return. "You'll earn some extra kopecks. I'll put you in charge of the geese. I'll sneak you this and that."

"Is that the truth? You won't forget?"

"You have my word. Why would I lie to you?"

She looked at him, exhausted. "It's your child, too, you know."

"I know."

"Just so you know."

"I know. Have I ever denied that, Natasha?"

"You have. You have."

"But not to you."

"So, then? I am waiting for something to happen."

"I'll let you light the fires. I'll let you wind the clocks. I'll let your husband scrub the drinking trough and pay him handsomely. That way, you won't go wanting—"

"And meanwhile, you and I—"

There was a brief but heavy pause. Hein cleared his throat and promised: "I'll see you now and then."

"He stinks," she argued weakly, to have the last word and save face. Hein stroked her neck. "Good girl. Good girl. I'll send him to the steam bath every month."

Natasha settled for reality. A sensible woman, at last she gave in, but not without first dropping hints of trouble yet to come. She gave her hair an extra careful combing with tiny dabs of butter, slicked it down across the ears, and settled for Ivan.

She said: "I'd rather step a small rung down than stay an old maid at the top."

Hein summoned an Orthodox priest: "This is Ivan. And this, Natasha."

First, the priest scolded, then he married them to quench the buzz of gossip. Natasha kissed the crucifix. She had expected better than to have to settle for a herdsman, but she would get herself a brand new saint, and let the rest be jealous.

Marleen beamed a triumphant smile. She wore stiff lace cuffs on her dress and an embroidered collar, both virtue and victory hers. She searched her heart and found benevolence and generosity: that came with having won.

"Luck. Double luck. And triple luck," intoned the priest and swung his censor hard.

Ivan sneezed lustily. Hein guffawed while Marleen gave the new bride the triple Easter kiss, since it was close to Easter and her heart was light and free.

Natasha blinked away her tears. "This marriage will remove all doubt," she offered timidly. "Marleen, let me ask this. Will you now have a laugh against me?"

Marleen replied, an earnest Christian: "I'll never laugh at your misfortune. That much I promise you."

Her wedding date to Hein was entered firmly in the Elders' ledgers. What was one muzhik, more or less? She would bear many sons and daughters—offspring beyond comparison.

The priest wrapped up his incantations.

Natasha sniveled.

Ivan glowed.

Hein tied the couple's hands together with his red-checkered handkerchief. He told them they could keep it.

"The best of luck," said Hein, relieved. He let the newly-weds pick several of his piglets to start a modest household.

A little later, a vermin-ridden monk arrived at the imperial gardens to shed his rags and fix his eye upon the palace. His name was Grigorij Rasputin. Sandals made of bark and stolen twine hung on his unwashed feet. His nails were black with grime. Dirty strands of hair fell to his ears. He cursed, told purple jokes, and had atrocious table manners.

He claimed that he could tame the wildest horse.

He spiced his tongue with peppery profanities. He crushed a frog with his flat hand.

By meditation, he proclaimed, he had arrived at universal truths. Through prayer, he insisted, he had acquired powers to drive away bad luck.

Some said that the holy man was Lucifer, disguised, but not a few insisted that he was a saint, a prophet sent to earth. Still others said of this: "The very thought is ludicrous."

"A man of the people," cried many, gullible and credulous. "He's worthy of our trust."

Soon, swarms of girls of casual virtue sought him out. He showed them how to dance: with total and joyful abandon, arms spread wide, swinging back their skirts and kicking up their heels. He leaned into the dusk and played the balalaika while they danced. They felt at ease with him—he spoke their spicy language.

They took to him their maladies: "Will you please feel my heart? It makes a hollow sound."

He next expelled a demon that had plagued a damsel of the gentry, and thereby spread his fame. They came to him, these shallow, idle females, hands buried in their sable muffs. They looked at him beneath their lowered lashes: "A would-be ravisher, perhaps?"

"All is forgivable," the monk said with a belch, "and, therefore, nothing is forbidden."

The icon lamps kept flickering. The palace lay in slumber.

"When you are thirsty," said the monk, "you will awake from deepest sleep." He looked at them and smiled: they were but silver darts that quivered on his hook.

"Let's cover the icons," he said softly. His gestures were like water lilies growing quietly on the slime. "You. You. And you and you and you. I bid you kneel before me, before we settle down to love."

They said of him in awe: "A man of God. A real man of God."

His name began to ring in the medieval city of the tsars.

One day, he fixed a pinpoint stare upon the Winter Palace, then said in a low whisper: "When I decide, the Emperor will have an heir. But when I die, the throne will fall with me."

At first, the courtiers laughed: words spoken by a drunken babbler. It was no secret that the timid Emperor sired only useless girls. The German Empress taught them fancy needlepoint. The nannies spoke to them in German.

But then, to all's surprise, a baby boy was born, a child with thin lips and wide cornflower eyes.

"A primrose baby," said the Empress. "This child will bring nothing but joy."

It was a wondrous world, that year; blue the sky and soft the clouds; young people fell in love; oldsters died in peace; tulips stood in bloom. Apanlee was bursting at the seams with far-flung, watchful cousins. The Elders preached their Sunday sermons to open doors and windows. The countryside was bountiful. The orchards swarmed with bees. Spring drew the sap up from the earth; it surged up to the tree tops. The field hands oiled their pruning shears. The Elders, to a voice, beseeched the Holy Ghost to bless the monarchy.

A darling, this imperial child, much wanted and much-longed-for.

The cannons thundered their salute. The German Empress lay there, pale and wan, replete with a small smile and a hot water bottle. The tsar knelt by her bed and looked the baby over. It bled a little at the navel. He pulled a scented handkerchief to blot the tiny spot.

"What's this?" he asked with a proud laugh. He held the stained cloth aloft as if it were a trophy. "Already up to mischief?"

At once, the red droplet returned. He blotted, carefully, again.

The tsar drove Russia to useless war. The papers claimed the fault lay with the Japanese; the Japanese objected angrily; additional details were harder to come by. The cannons boomed. The shrapnel crackled. The country bled. Two armies moved on one another. Somewhere, a banker laughed.

Halley's Comet came and went. For a long, brittle summer, the clouds withheld their moisture.

For the peasants, this meant hardship. For the merchants, business slumped.

But for the folks at Apanlee, all this was of no consequence, for Apanlee had forged its soul, by then, by trusting in His word.

If things went well, He took the credit. If things went badly, now and then, it was a test of Faith. You put your trust in the good Lord; He never punished you without good cause—if chastising was called for, that purified your soul and cleansed you of trespasses.

You lived, if you were part of Apanlee, both for the privilege and the duty of bringing scented bread loaves to the table—and when you died, what did that mean? Not much.

You slept beneath a wooden cross until His trumpets' call would rouse you to glory—rouse you to rhapsody and splendor greater yet than anyone could comprehend.

And, meanwhile, every Elder preached—and no one disagreed!—you had your duties, one by one, and if you did them, one by one, that translated to joy. Joy sprang from harmony, which came from discipline. Joy meant good neighbors living within wave and shout of one another; it meant the shine of hoes, pitch forks and sickles being readied for the wheat.

It was so simple. Earnest. Clean. It was a potent elixir. It took a robust man to steer the plow that turned the soil that grew the grain that fed the world you knew. It took a worthy woman to stir the yeast to bake the bread that fed your children and their children's children and then their children's children, too.

And if a willing couple—between them holding values honed to gloss by centuries of ethnic strength—chose to unite in holy matrimony and to the benefit of land and kin and tsars—why, that was Hallelujah time and yet more Hallelujah time for all!

There came a ghastly pogrom. It came in the wake of a plot. There was no escaping the Cossacks. Not since the times of the Cossack uprisings more than two centuries ago had such blood purges raged as were now unleashed on the Valley of Jews.

The howling rabbis shaved their beards and hid in barns and attics, but mounted sentries of the Crown charged village after village and pried at them with bayonets, digging through the straw. The guilty and the innocent hid in cellars, under beds, in closets and in sheds, but still the sentries pulled them out and battered them, until the victims spat out broken teeth and wailed for mercy, which was rare, or death, which followed swiftly.

It was an ancient conflict—part of the country's tapestry.

Did ever someone ask: how can you tell the good Jew from the bad? If so, the question drowned in the tumult as rifles crashed against the doors. You knew a Jew. By his profile: that's how you knew. If that was not enough to tell, you checked by pulling down his trousers—if need be, by the flicker of a candle.

But take account: it wasn't just the tsars. It wasn't just the German settlers who held corrosive attitudes—and least of all the ones who lived and sowed the seed of Apanlee. In truth, it barely touched them where they lived, and where they hoped to die.

Here was the universal sentiment: a different breed; down through the centuries, so were they known, a devious breed, a plotting tribe. Not one of them paid honor to the Crown.

In the declining years of the last century and several years into the next, this was the universal puzzlement: what was it with the Jews, discounting that they made you shiver?

If you sought out a malcontent, odds were it was a Jew.

Just point a finger at a Jew, and you were pointing it to someone who had tricked someone somewhere.

You noticed, furthermore, that they were always looking left and right, as though afraid of being caught. If innocent they were, why be clandestine, pray? The tsars, though known as fair and trusting monarchs, had never trusted them. The tsars had had no choice but take the culprits to the pits of execution—where they received their due. What if they sobbed while pulling out their sidelocks? While being broken on the rack, their tangled shame emerged.

So with these latest strikes. So with this newest plot.

The mortal enemies of Christ, disguised as beggars in the cities, kept thrusting leaflets and pushing discontent into the hands of passersby.

It happened more and more. It happened everywhere.

Yet all the while, the folks of Apanlee stayed clear of the festering conflict. Their task was to speed progress by buying farm machinery to better serve the soil they loved, the Crown they honored, and the Lord they revered as the ultimate judge. Such riches as they had, acquired honestly by diligence of generations—who dared to say: the Devil's way? Who dared to say: that kind of wealth is wrong?

Behind them lay a century of sowing, harrowing and reaping, swinging their scythes in mighty half-arches, binding and stacking and loading. Their way of life had stood the test of time. That proved that it was sound.

The Elders told the congregation, as in past centuries: "Remain apart. Keep pure the pool of kin."

Thrift. Order. Hard work. Diligence.

Time wasted—wasted opportunities.

Once do we pass through life. Since journey we must, since struggle we must, nothing is sweeter than work, nothing more precious than God's golden kernels.

Wasted minutes add up to an hour. Hours soon total to days.

And squandered days are like the feathers of a carelessly ripped down comforter—once scattered to the winds, no way to bring them back.

Chapter 37

Ivan gave Natasha a moderate beating.

"If it's a boy," she shrieked, now checked but not defeated, "he'll be a ticket inspector! If a girl, a needle worker! I'll see to that! You mark my word, you smelly oaf! You hear?"

"You are the greatest simpleton on earth." A three-day stubble on his chin, Ivan fell asleep, his head upon the table, content with life and luck. Natasha moved her icons back and forth, to give them ample light.

"You two. Have you been gossiping about me?" asked Hein the following week when he came visiting. Hein came to visit often. He came with a thundering rap at the door. They sat together peacefully.

"Let her deny it if she can. This woman here? As faithful as your shadow."

Natasha hissed at him: "For heaven's sakes, be quiet." She glanced at Hein—arched eyebrows, that was all. All three broke into laughter. Ivan slammed his fist down on the table. "What's done is done. I close my eyes. What else is there to say? Perhaps a tiny favor?"

"What do you want? Speak up," asked Hein, and slapped him hard across his back so that his shoulders shook. "Stop hinting. Speak your mind."

In olden days, if any serf dared speak against the well-established order it meant the knout, and sometimes death. If land was sold, the serf was sold; and now? Here sat Natasha, implanted with the seed of Apanlee, and was there punishment? Nobody said a word.

"Once freedom comes to Russia—" Ivan said, belching softly, and let the words hang in the air. Should Revolution ever come, the handy knowledge of the bargain struck between Hein and Natasha would be a weapon in his fist. But that's where Ivan stopped.

Hein spoke complacently. "What? Not in a hundred years. What is it now? You want my boots?"

Ivan looked at him slant-wise. "Not just your boots. Your sheepskin, too—"

Yet in the deeper parts of his nature, Ivan knew his limits. So, for that matter, did Natasha. He had already called down every fiery curse he knew upon her for her unseemly ways, for she was nothing but a peasant girl, born into endless squalor. Already, he had bloodied her to gain the upper hand in his rude hut; now here she was, just beaming her approval. "I like your mustache, Hein," she told him smilingly. Her eyes were glistening with glee.

Natasha, too, had listened with attention to the endless talk that had it of the bottom rising in the future to the top, the top collapsing to the bottom, once Revolution came. Such chatter never ended; it never went away.

"You do? You really like my mustache?" Hein told her, speaking friend to friend, that he had plans to cultivate it lovingly into an upsweep masterpiece to rival an old Prussian nobleman whose portrait hung above his bed.

"A show-off, right?" said she.

The tacit understanding between Ivan, Hein and Natasha

didn't change as the time of her confinement drew nearer.

"What else?" asked Hein, accommodatingly, for labor took its time. "A hay cart? A bucket? Don't tell me that you want a horse."

"We hate to be hurried," said she while lying, panting, in the straw. "A discard mare, perhaps? A roof for the family cow?"

Her husband came in handy. Had he been less content with how things were and surely would remain, he might have kicked her, might have cuffed her, had she been on her feet. But she was not; this birth was hard on her; Natasha suffered quite a bit. He even offered her his thumb. "Here. Bite it as hard as you like." Crude and barefoot though he was, when it came to the basics, he never turned the tables. Perhaps he asked himself: "After the horse has been stolen, what is the point of burning the stable?" He might have simply been a muzhik of good will. All he grasped now was this: if he, Ivan, pulled out a bottle and settled down to joviality and shouts of "Bottoms up!" Hein felt too guilty and too mortified not to do likewise, even louder: "Bottoms up! Hey, everybody! Bottoms up!"

Meanwhile, Marleen spread Uncle Benny's shredded bulletins along the entrance of their hut to deaden the noise of a difficult birth. She stuffed the holes along the walls with Uncle Benny's chiding editorials about the haves and have-nots to keep the stray cats out.

"Hear me! Hear me! The sky's the limit!" Natasha shrieked. Hein waited nearby, pipe in his mouth. By then, he was bewhiskered like a schnauzer.

"Do you need anything, Natasha? Are you just about done with your struggle, Natasha?"

Natasha lay perspiring in the straw, although the roof was silvery with frost. "I am as eager as you for tomorrow!"

"Be glad you weren't singled out for spinsterhood," said he, a patient man. "What can I get you next, Natasha?"

"Were you a cat, I'd brandish you by your own tail. I'd smash your head against a rock!" screamed Natasha.

This was her opportunity; she made the most of it. Tomorrow was tomorrow; it would come soon enough. She would fall back again, tomorrow, on the laconic ways that marked her stock and kin, but now she shrieked with rage and pain, as loudly as she could, as often as she needed, Hein's old, discarded sheepskin pulled up hard against her chin.

"Your heart is black with discontent," said Hein, while waiting patiently. "You're making an infernal noise. You want to wake the neighbors?"

She gasped with wrath. She had momentum of her own and rode it to exhaustion. She knew that it was now or never to cast aside her inhibitions. To shriek with her betrayal, as loudly as she could, was only natural. Natasha shrieked her ire until she lost her breath.

"Now, take it easy. Tell me when. Just tell me when," Marleen demanded, long-backed, serene, her fingers stiff with cold. Her presence opened eyes. Such dignity. There are still people living to this day who will attest that she was there, to watch Natasha bear the bastard, to help and criticize.

Explanations come to mind, but none of them suffices. All who knew Marleen in her youth tell you there was no bravado. The greatness that would mark her life came later.

So we are left to guess. Could it have been mere tolerance that came with having won? Or might Marleen have been a saintly Christian who turned the other cheek? Perhaps she asked herself: what do I need but Jesus?

Could be. She must have surely suffered.

But on the other hand, she had the stoicism of her ancestry in her. She was a pious soul, that much we know—her roots deep in the Gospel. Restrained in all she did, she struck a righteous stance but did not drop a single word that would reveal her feelings. Her pinkie kept twitching and twitching; that's how her husband knew. What else was she to do? The village midwife, meanwhile, lit the stove with nimble fingers. Her bosom rose with doom.

At last, Natasha bore a son. Marleen, her lips compressed, washed the infant's pinched visage with the rich milk of Apanlee.

"Be glad it's over, Natasha," said Marleen. "A tadpole. Now, are you satisfied?"

Natasha's heart felt light with the release. She made herself as small as possible. "Can money repay me?" wheedled Natasha. "No. Nothing. Not a thing. Just a small goat, maybe, Marleen?"

"A goat? Did you say a goat?" The triumph of her challenger was gall.

"A shaggy goat, that's all."

"You swear?"

From now on, life would be like fishing in a barrel filled with carp. "I swear."

"You'll get a goat," promised Marleen. "Swear by your patron saint. Your mulishness is known."

"That's all. I swear upon my favorite icon." Natasha sank back in the straw. This was her finest hour. Since she'd survived this birth, she knew she could survive most anything. "Just hand me that soaked towel to cool my swollen eyes."

"Here. Careful now. Your husband and my husband heard you. You're sure a goat, and nothing more? That's all?"

"*Ja. Ja.* For now, that's all." Natasha was a clever student; she'd gathered here and there some snatches of High German. No longer was she pale with terror. Now she could dip into the handy fountainhead of motherhood, as often as she needed—a source as filling as hot corn. "I put my trust in God," Natasha said, reflectively, "that you will treat me fairly."

"You have my word."

"I could use a small cart, Marleen. To pick the fodder for the goat I am about to get."

Marleen turned her eyes heavenward, or else toward the ceiling. "By hook or crook, that's how."

"And why not? By and by."

A small, beguiling smile lit up Natasha's face. She had her own defenses—if all else failed, a tantrum now and then.

"Now hold your tongue; you are a glutton," Hein roared, to

cover up his pride.

It had happened. Life went on.

At the core, there might have been discord; there never was corrosion. Whatever the reason, whatever the motive, an understanding had been forged.

As years piled upon years, there was much bickering. There were sly ploys. As often as not, there was quick-flaring anger. When Hein drove either of his women in ways that pleased him more than them, the fur began to fly.

But all in all, both women bore the troika's yoke with mute tenacity. It worked; each knew her place; there was no basic conflict. Natasha always wore Marleen's discarded dresses until they fell apart—but not without a lecture from Marleen. To enter through the back door was no problem; it opened into Marleen's heated kitchen all the same. She could snoop there; her rival was snoozing; she could thaw her feet out by the pot-bellied stove.

Natasha reasoned cleverly: if she worked hard, kept to herself, avoided being quarrelsome, and did what she was told, she had no need for conflict. So what if she was shouted at? It didn't happen often—and when it happened, she grew sullen, deaf and dumb, which gave Marleen a headache.

When she was sent to run an errand, Natasha went—but at her speed, in her good time, and like as not, with the umbrella Hein had given to Marleen. To own that fine umbrella was the height of aspiration, to keep from getting wet when thunderstorms arrived—but probably asking too much.

"I have a feeling deep inside that all this has happened to somebody else," Marleen confided quietly to Dorothy, with whom she was best friends.

To the misbegotten child she said as often as she could: "You ugly creature you. A ticket inspector? Don't make me laugh. You're as good as a pickpocket already."

The baby, meanwhile, kicked and spit and howled, and every time Natasha saw a priest, she held her son up to be blessed.

Natasha called the infant Dominik, named for a favorite icon. She told the saint named Dominik that she forgave him, though he had failed her miserably.

"How could you? How could you?" she chided. "Did I not trust you fully?"

The saint smiled back at her with clear and vacant smiles. She gave him a resounding kiss. She was a practical woman; she knew she might need him again.

Her young heart swelled with pride.

Hein came around from time to time to check the hut in need of thatching, or else to scold Ivan for small trespasses. "Sit down. Sit down," Natasha cried, as ever on the lookout for bonanzas.

At first, she welcomed Hein with eagerness, for there was peat smoke in his eyes—and throw precaution to the winds! She sat him down, pulled off his boots, and heated up the samovar. The visits were no secret. Sometimes Ivan would leave both of them alone, and sometimes not: it didn't matter much to Hein, nor to Natasha, either.

For quite a while, Hein visited with fire in his loins, but in good time, he cooled from holiday to holiday; it happened of itself.

All parties were content.

Hein never lost Natasha's friendship. She never lost his genuine goodwill. She combed his hair and beard; she trimmed his fingernails; the toddler they both owned would climb up on his knees. She sat and watched and grated her potatoes in a dish, chipped all around sufficiently to have warranted thieving it from under Marleen's eyes.

"Don't spit on him, you naughty boy!" Natasha scolded Dominik.

She tried her best to teach some manners to her son, but that was easier said than done. She brushed his lips with Ivan's vodka—to quiet him.

Hein was a patient man with any child; he was so with this

youngster. When he was in a mirthful mood, he gave Dominik galloping piggyback rides.

"A rascal," Hein said proudly, and cuffed him on both ears.

"When he grows up," Natasha bragged on more than one occasion, "he'll seek the company of talented and learned people."

Hein laughed uproariously. "What? What?"

She argued on her son's behalf. "His toes do not curl inwards. That means that he is smart."

"It does? Well. We shall see." Hein smiled at her approvingly. She smiled right back, albeit through a tear. She knew that she looked pretty while smiling through a tear.

"You will make sure? When he grows up, you will make sure he'll travel in compartments filled with padded benches?"

"I will?"

"You will. I know you will make sure."

"I'll see what I can do."

"He will be a ticket inspector. To the end of his natural life."

Ivan broke into roaring laughter and slapped Hein on both knees. What next? No limits to her dreams?

"In olden days," Hein shouted gleefully, "I could have sent her to Siberia for her pains."

The olden days were gone. The future smiled on them.

"Take me," Ivan said boastingly, still sitting on a dented pail, exchanging banter with the head of Apanlee while nursing an infected foot. "This is the modern age."

Fresh oats for the horses. Fresh milk from the udder. A wish, barely uttered—fulfilled!

He had no quarrel whatsoever with the unfolding century, and neither did Natasha. She knew that Hein was satisfied; so was Ivan; come push to shove, so was Marleen. In olden, bygone days when serfs were serfs and masters masters, Hein could have flogged her, sold her, even thrown her into prison—nobody would have cried a tear.

Modernity was on the march; the olden days were gone.

Young love had fallen on Natasha's heart, with the sudden force of thunderbolts—but now she felt sedate and tranquil; she gently shut her doors. Marleen, when in a wrecking mood, might holler to her heart's content, but given the odds, and counting the choices, what else was there to do?

Hein was providing well enough, and there was room for all.

Hein liked the restive youngster. He tickled him and tossed him high into the air. By the time his second spring thaw came around, the infant, growing rapidly, made a sure dash for him.

Marleen said little, then or later, except perhaps to Dorothy. Self-discipline did not permit her hate; but neither did it nurture love; and in the interim, she trained herself to self-respect; she trained her heart with songs she learned each Wednesday afternoon at female sing-alongs where she sang harmony. She had a small but trilling voice; she practiced every week. When a friend or a relative died, nobody sang with more feeling.

"Who is Natasha, after all?" was how she summed it up. "Debased as an old kopeck." A false spring was just that—a brief inflammation of nature. From that had come a child—and what an ugly toad!

This boy with his small, beady eyes was clearly a mistake, an irritant. By contrast, she herself was firmly grounded in the seasons. By then, Marleen was having baby after baby of her own, and all of them were fat.

Uncle Benny watched these family developments attentively. He noticed: the soothsayers' eyes did not blink.

The cripple had not changed at all—still frail, still cultured, still reading to himself, all the time. He still saved envelopes from almost any nation; sometimes he slept on them. The scent of fresh-cut hay still made him slightly dizzy, but Dorothy was there, on standby, with hot tea.

Bespectacled and pale, with rheumatism bending every aching joint, he kept on worrying his brittle documents through all the years that followed. The secret of his background lay forgotten: those eager to make sure the scandal never died had died themselves, by then.

In his own way, he was a busy man. Publishing the weekly *Voice of Peace* took two days, sometimes three; on other days, he went for walks with friends—friends who arrived at Apanlee from every corner of the empire, all worldly gentlemen. They came from Orenburg and Zaparoshe, as well as from St. Petersburg. They told each other many times, as they sipped honeyed tea at Apanlee:

"The man who has two horses should willingly relinquish one."

It was a tiresome refrain: "Unless reform—then Revolution."

Nobody paid any attention—not even Natasha; not even Ivan. For these two stalwart souls, and with them Dominik, to live in peace and plenty was enough.

They wintered, and they summered, like everybody else.

If Dominik was naughty, Natasha and Marleen, both shrieking like two shrews, would chase him down the street.

Soon after Dominik was born, Marleen gave birth to freckled twins. Such was the joy of Apanlee that even Natasha was feasting on stir-fried potatoes.

This happened on a gray and melancholy day. Hein named the two infants Yuri and Sasha, beside himself with pride. "Hear, you foul-smelling muzhik!" he bragged to Ivan. "Everything double. Blue eyes. Blond hair. Strong hands. Square feet."

Natasha glared daggers at Hein. Her face turned red with rivalry. She spoke from jealousy: "Why two, I wonder? One isn't enough? Is there no limit to your greed?"

Hein laughed and cuffed Natasha playfully: "The doctors ordered bedrest for Marleen. I do not want her thin and nervous. How would you like to come and help out in the nursery? "

And what a stroke of luck!

Natasha simply could not spurn such golden opportunity. She played a little hard-to-get to savor every nuance. Inwardly, she was jumping at the chance.

"As if I haven't work enough with mine."

"Consider it an open offer," Hein told her laughingly. "You can refill your plate as often as you like."

She took the *Voice of Peace* and swatted Hein to keep a fly away. "What am I? A black market piglet?"

The truth was already well known. Hein was a man with the voracity that marked a man; Marleen had painful spasms in her back and stubborn headaches throbbing at her temples; the headaches stayed; they wouldn't go away. Trustworthy bonesetters arrived from Alexanderwohl to check her chronic malady. They counseled her repeatedly: "Perhaps you need more sleep?"

Marleen confided quietly to Dorothy, who wrung her tiny hands: "My heart is as still as the grave."

She spoke so softly, by that time, that Dorothy concluded, worriedly, that cottage cheese was all Marleen could eat, and still hold down, when the migraines struck full force. How could she match Hein's ardor?

Marleen put up as brave a front as possible. She kept her eyes downcast. She told her husband quietly: "Do what you must. I won't be in the way."

Hein felt released and gratified. Had he been more demonstrative, he might have worshipped her; he certainly adored the twins she had presented him. Hein propped her up within her feather pillows to get a better view.

Marleen sat there with pounding heart. "She will not have a laugh against me?"

He shook his head, a patient man: impossible to penetrate her feelings.

"You mean it? Tell me now." Pointedly, Natasha stared down the narrow path where she and Hein had walked.

"I'm certain," said Marleen, dusting a speck from her skirt. "I'm thinking of the ups and downs of measles. I'll need you then. You might as well start practicing."

"You won't change your mind?"

No one had said it would be easy, but things not easy still needed to be done. "No. I gave you my word. My word is my word."

Natasha gnawed her lower lip. She had a rounded bottom. Besides, she still coveted an umbrella of her own. "What are you—in a melting mood? I do not understand."

"An offer is an offer. It's offered honestly."

Natasha looked confused and flushed; in fact, her face was scarlet. Beside her, Dominik was struggling with the hiccupss that ended in a nosebleed more often than she liked.

"But why?"

Marleen chose not to answer. Instead, she merely said: "My babies are unspoiled. They will eat anything."

There was a long and heavy pause. Marleen looked up at last and held Natasha's glance: "Tell me. Does he still ask?"

"Ask? Not only has he forgotten," cried Natasha, now eager to please and placate. "I have forgotten to listen."

"Natasha, tell me everything."

"There's naught to tell. It's over."

"Here's an apron. Here's the feather duster. Here, take this slice of soap. It's settled, then. You'll start tomorrow morning. Just keep that red blouse buttoned."

Chapter 38

Natasha was elated. She was a good domestic—nobody doubted that. Indeed, so overcome was she with gratitude that, had not Marleen been her contender, she would have worshipped her. She decidedly worshipped the twins—who had, by then, between them sixteen pearly teeth with not a single gap.

She squirreled away discarded socks and mittens for Dominik, who arched his back and howled. To quiet him, she fed him the finest leftovers—on holidays, zwieback and raisin bread, sweet tea and boiled chicken. Natasha nearly purred; she was that happy and content. Marleen was ill again; propped up by several pillows, she spoke of blinding flashes. If there were barbecues at Apanlee to celebrate the grain, Natasha served the kvas.

She listened to Marleen—to every nuance of her maladies and illnesses—with an altogether sympathetic ear. "A glutton, isn't he?" she said, which made for oblique sisterhood.

That's how it was for years.

This odd arrangement pleased Ivan as well. He felt cheerful enough to relinquish Natasha part-time; she was a nag; she nagged and nagged; she whined the rain leaked down the chimney.

"Do this! Do that! Get up! Come down from that oven!"

That was Natasha, nagging him, when all he craved was sleep in the warm niche atop baked bricks when the November snows arrived.

Years piled up on years; he and Natasha continued to argue. For quarreling, there was no end at times—the door wouldn't close, the hay needed cutting, the roof needed fixing again. Inflamed by alcohol, he pounded her face with his fist. At times, he beat Natasha hard enough so that she started spitting blood. Sometimes she hit him back.

"It's all your fault!" was Ivan't shout.

"Your fault!" Natasha would shout back.

Not that she lacked her own defenses. She had them, and she used them to the hilt. Natasha's high-pitched shrieks would soon bring Marleen running with a broom to ward the drunkard off. Later, she'd press a towel soaked in vinegar against Natasha's blackest bruise.

That's how Natasha knew Marleen was on her side. "You brute!" Marleen would shriek, in fury. In gratitude, Natasha nearly swooned.

"Say what you will. It's all my fault. I make him wild, Marleen."

"He's violent. He's vile."

"Just now and then, Marleen."

That gleeful smile of hers when she came back from Apanlee! It drove Ivan to drink. When he had peered too deeply into his vodka glass, and when Natasha smiled and smiled, that's how the trouble usually began.

Meanwhile, their door had fallen from its hinges; their windowpanes were cracked; Ivan had no nails; he lost his hammer; the wind blew viciously. He often slept, his clothes on, in the straw in one of Hein's sheds where the horses were kept, while the vodka faded from his head. The only sign of life, his beard would heave and fall.

This called for unity. Natasha took him by the legs; Hein took him by the shoulders; Marleen would run to get the gate, and Dorothy just wrung her hands—high drama all around! All pushed, coaxed, heaved and shoved Ivan atop his oven where he lay comatose for days.

"You! Don't blame others for your own misfortunes," Natasha told her husband many times. His corn stood lower than his weeds; his fields were full of thistles; the grain was threadbare; the haulms were much too short. "The Cossacks ought to rip your nostrils!" She called him names that burned.

He squinted at his meager acres—too small for worthwhile harvesting "He wants you there at night to seal his glee? So go! What's it to me?"

That was precisely what she did; she benefitted handsomely; so did Marleen, and so did Hein; the pipe just never left his mouth; all benefitted mightily.

"The day will come," she said, her eyes on Dominik, "when that boy will wear jackets and trousers that match."

"Sure. When roosters start to whistle," Ivan offered angrily before he fell asleep.

Natasha didn't fret. It was quiet, warm and clean at Apanlee, where not a single door hinge squeaked, where embers always glowed. The winter relatives arrived and stayed an entire season, exchanging faded photographs. Natasha wore the apron.

Resourcefully, Natasha fit herself into the quilt of Apanlee. There, she had sweeping powers in the nursery, as well as other liberties as long as she practiced restraint. In fair exchange, she saw to it that each of Marleen's freckled youngsters, one by one, had only blissful dreams.

As often as she wished, in turn, Natasha could fill up her cart with Hein's leftover hay. Hein trusted her implicitly to have his best at heart. He knew that she was honest. While she might steal a sausage end for Dominik, she would never have taken a kopeck.

Natasha throve on other benefits as well. Marleen might well have pelted her with stones, had she not been a Christian, and of the finest kind. Instead, she kept warm borscht right on the stove the day Natasha limped in from the cold, chilled head to toe from having queued all day.

"Here. Have another bowl. I needed that special embroidery yarn to finish my last doily."

Natasha sat and slurped her borscht and did not say a word.

Marleen stood, silent, by the window. Outside, the world was gray on gray; the rain blew horizontally. Let winter come: she was well fortified; she wore her double underwear and woolen socks besides.

"I always meant to tell you—" said Marleen next, but then bit off the thought.

Natasha kept her silence likewise. Each spoonful filled her more until she had enough.

When in a tantalizing mood, she flaunted her chain of unbreakable beads. The Apanlee feast days showed in her waist; her bosom grew wider and wider.

She bit into huge chunks of cheese whenever fancy struck her—cheese chunks the size of Hein's thumb. She made sure her son took his Saturday bath—as often as not, in the family tub, in the leftover family suds.

Small concession, she knew, to gently close the doors when Marleen found herself deep in the throes of yet another migraine. Natasha even shushed the kitchen maids, and no one said a word.

That she did, to show her good will. She did it also—no one knew!—because she took the chance to steal a hard-boiled egg to deepen the color of Dominik's cheeks.

"Better than cabbage soup, borscht and black kasha. That's what I always say," she said to Dominik.

The youngster had his father's steely eyes above his mother's Slavic cheeks. When mail came from America—for Cousin Josie still shipped poetry for Uncle Benny's benefit—he ran to fetch the letters.

With chill nights came the measles, mumps and chicken pox. These were Natasha's finest hours. The babies needed her—their fevers made them weepy. She spent her nights at Apanlee, ready to rise the moment they turned weepy and rock away their ills.

She was fond of them all, but the twins stole her heart. The twins were her natural tonic when she was torn between two worlds, not knowing where to place her feet, still dressed in sandals made of bark. She loved them as her own. She knew her share of antidotes to calm the little look-alikes and make their fevers drop.

Albeit younger than her son, the twins grew fast—they outgrew shirts and socks and trousers. Natasha took the discards home, proud of both cloth and workmanship. And no one said a word.

When she took walks along the edge of Apanlee, a freckled youngster on each hand, the admiration others paid her was enough. She kicked up the dust with her sandals and bragged:

"Look what I have here. Look. As alike as two peas in a pod. And you think I can't tell the two apart?"

"Life is a party, eh, Natasha?" the jealous field hands sneered.

For Hein, now married solidly and getting thickset in the chin, this was the perfect compromise.

He was not good. He was not bad. He was a product of his times. He authorized most anything, chiefly congregation funds. Because he gave his share, and more—he gave and gave as though he sought to buy a place in heaven to match his place on earth— the Elders tipped their hats.

Had there been serious challenge to Hein's way of life, he would have given all he had to set himself aright, but by that time, the past was done; the future fixed; the Elders deemed that what was good for Hein was good for them as well: the wheels of Apanlee meshed smoothly. There was enough for all—leftovers for Natasha.

Like all his ancestors before him, Hein loved to work the

land. He was a robust farmer. For him, as for his neighbors, life was one ceaseless round of plowing, harrowing and sowing, growing harvests. He rose at dawn, worked all day long, and came back after sunset, his overflow of energy still palpable, as often as not in an amorous mood.

Marleen despised Hein's lustiness. She passed for a humorless woman. As Hein would sometimes say when in a mocking mood, it was impossible, by then, to set a fire to Marleen. Tall, bland, opaque, forbidding, Marleen had few true friends, but not a single enemy. She was a nondescript.

Had Hein had enemies—he did not know a single one who might have said so openly—he would have shrugged his ample shoulders: to him, it mattered not a whit.

While Hein and Marleen grew apart, Natasha flourished merrily. When chance arose, there was Natasha, ready. Would she have spurned a ham, if an arch-enemy—of whom she had none either—had offered it to her? Not she. She scorned no opportunities; she was alert for them. She had elected, had she not, to live right in the lap of luxury? She wintered in Marleen's warm kitchen, in comfort and in leisure, and no one said a word.

But on the other hand, while squirreling away discards at every opportunity to save up for a rainy day, she did not hurt the folks of Apanlee. To even think she might would have been alien to her nature.

In lively prattle passed her days. All babies, round and rosy! Now that Marleen had broken down and relinquished that umbrella—Natasha would no more have stolen Hein from her than she could steal an icon from a priest. A romp in the hay hardly counted.

Surprisingly, it was Marleen and not Natasha who kept producing offspring, and every child was dimpled. They swelled Natasha's heart. She swaddled them severely so that they wouldn't scare themselves with their own tiny hands.

Each year, when measles swept throughout the district, Natasha had no sleep; she nursed the little ones. She did so till she dropped. She felt beloved, useful, still reasonably pretty. At intervals, Hein whispered that to her.

She didn't contradict him, nor would she urge him on. "That's your opinion," she would say, and swat him with a handy diaper.

When winter came and snow fell in abundance and others struggled through the flakes to find a bit of firewood, Natasha sorted socks into neat piles, and if she found a sock that had a hole, she knew to whom it went.

She took good care of Dominik who was her rightful son, but soon, the borders blurred. She mothered all; she served them all; the twin boys were her favorites.

"You two—just remarkable birds," she would say tenderly. "Who cuddles you? Who spoils you? Who gives you smacking kisses?"

She taught them how to drink without slurping; she taught them how to pee without dribbling. She wouldn't let them step in puddles. She watched them day and night.

"Why two of you?" Natasha asked with pride, as though they were her own.

She would contrive small games to get the toddling twins to laugh. They fell onto her bosom, squealing, while pushing Dominik aside.

"Who swaddles you? Who pampers you? You think I can't tell you apart?"

Her own son, by contrast, a regular Tartar! She doubled up with laughter at Dominik's angry visage.

From the outset, he was different. He didn't profit from advice, much less from punishment.

As official Baba to the twins of Apanlee, Natasha earned the right to sleep at the foot of their cradle in case of an emergency. She brought a wicker basket along for Dominik and hung it by a strong rope from the ceiling. Hein helped to hammer in the nails.

He gave the swing a jaunty push. "Hey, Dominik! Smile, Dominik! You'd like to be part of the party?"

"Your conduct is hardly becoming," Natasha chided, while crinkling her eyes.

"Says who?" he winked at her.

His laughter made her bolder. "Go soak your beard," she cried, pretending to be angry, but her strong teeth just gleamed at him and caught themselves by accident on his long mustache tips—but that was as far as it went.

"No grudges, Natasha?" teased Hein.

"No grudges. See where my hand is? Right on my heart. I swear by my favorite saint."

"You used to bear grudges, Natasha."

"*Ach!* That was long ago."

She bore no grudges. She felt no misgivings. She was as sturdy and as common as a mule, and had no doubts at all.

She bit into a zwieback crust. She meant it when she said: "The jealous times are past."

"If she is blind," Natasha told herself, "that is her own misfortune. What's there to stop us now?"

So what if her own offspring still left puddles on the floor? That warm and cozy nursery would doubtlessly do wonders for his bladder.

She took a daring risk: she tucked her son right in between the twins who were, by then, as trained to their enameled potties as kittens to a sandbox.

Hein only winked and laughed. Marleen just clattered with her dishes, pretending she was deaf.

Natasha let out her breath.

At Apanlee, there was no end to elegance—and she was part of that. At Apanlee, men drank their tea from glasses and women used small cups—she crooked her pinkie likewise.

She petitioned several saints to watch out for Marleen, which was a small concession.

Natasha had her times—as did Marleen—when angry feelings overwhelmed, when jealousy flamed in her heart. Those days were rare, however. Hein and Marleen now took leisurely strolls, especially on letter day, when bundles from America arrived. Natasha stayed behind, which might be galling and unfair, but then that gave her ample time to search the bottom drawers and check for useful items. The couple walked right down the beaten goose path where she and Hein, not all that long ago, had walked. What did they say to each other? Not much. What needed to be said, had been said. Long ago. The two would walk in stolid silence, always, each holding a fat toddler by the hand.

In fourteen years of wedlock, Hein and Marleen produced ten hardy children. After the twins came four boys, then a girl, then another, and then a second set of twins—named Annelie and Erika.

Natasha scrubbed their diapers to make them white as snow.

"Why two again?" Natasha argued weakly. "Can you explain that, Hein? My eyes just popped out of my head. One pair isn't enough?"

"Ask Uncle Benny. He will know. It's in the strain, no doubt."

Natasha sometimes went to seek the hunchback's counsel. She liked to sit and look at him and watch him think his thoughts. The fragile cripple knew most anything there was to know; the things he didn't know, nobody knew; sheet music even; that was old Uncle Benny. He spoke several languages—living and dead. His writing was hard to decipher. As years piled on years, his letters grew smaller, more cramped. He published editorials to general benefit.

Natasha asked in a low voice: "Why two of them again?"

He had no answer to that one.

"Why two at once?" she pressed. "Some people have it all. The bounty never stops."

"I can't say why or how."

"It isn't fair, is it?" Her heart was aching for another youngster of her own, now that her Dominik had learned to swallow yogurt without gagging and would soon run away.

"No. Life's not fair, Natasha."

"No doubt some vengeful saint of mine—" It didn't happen often, but there were times, rare times, when her resentment showed.

"The clouds pile up," said Uncle Benny. "A menace to the grain."

Natasha squinted hard to see if he spoke allegorically. She dabbed her eyes with Marleen's discard finery. Natasha was a human being; she had her moments, too. She said again, more forcefully: "It isn't fair. Life is not fair."

The words came of themselves, though she was seized with shame. The troubling thoughts were just like weeds that kept on coming back. No matter how she tried to root them out, they kept on coming back. She wasn't getting any younger. She would have liked another child. She had but Dominik—who was, to tell the truth, a spiteful boy, a scoundrel.

"I wish I had an answer."

She patted Uncle Benny's hump, fluffed up his pillows, and took herself back to her suds.

But overriding any animosity that might have rankled deep within Natasha's sturdy peasant soul lay the comforting knowledge that now she had three meals a day, a pair of brand new wooden clogs as often as she needed, and just as many seed potatoes as she, Ivan and Dominik decided to consume.

It was the soft road for Natasha.

When gossip moved indoors—why, so did she, with nonchalance. While field hands left and right bent forward in their harnesses to haul the load of life to make the rich yet richer, the poor yet poorer, she had a privileged station: she was allowed to stay inside and scrub the freckled fry.

Natasha was a realist. She knew her source of power. Were it not for her own resources—her pretty arms and rounded rump— her Dominik would have to eat what Ivan grew, and since Ivan grew next to nothing, that could have been the end of Dominik.

No, it was up to her to supplement, and supplement she did.

Easier, by far, to rely for her old age on Hein and Marleen.

Life was not just endurable but pleasant. She jauntily waved both hands at her beloved charges whenever they sat, high atop the water wagon, and rode off to the fields.

Sometimes she rode along to pass out the buckets of coffee, the baskets of zwieback, a queen. She had her ups and downs, as did Marleen, as Ivan did and Hein—all human beings.

"*Ach ja,*" she sighed, High German style. *So ist's. Was kann man machen?*

What could she do, except to dream? Her dream was as intact as ever. Her Dominik would grow into a placid bureaucrat. She dwelled on that a lot. He would show them. He would get even yet. But then again, when she bent down across another cradle that held another child of Apanlee, a glow like heated honey filled her heart.

Chapter 39

Dominik grew up within the warmth of Apanlee. He was a misfit from the start, refusing to obey the Elders.

He took to thieving early. He soaked a puppy's tail in oil and put a match to it. He led the twins to mischief with tall tales, told purple jokes and jabbed them with his elbow so that they laughed out loud on languid Sunday afternoons. He ran around with unlaced shoes. He smacked his lips and had poor table manners. His language was the gutter language of the field hands when they returned from market after having fallen foolishly for an inferior deal.

Here was a child with knobby knees and yellow ears who would divert himself by pulling spiders from the ground with beeswax—the horror of the neighborhood. He dipped his wooden spoon into the kasha that Natasha cooked for him and brought it to his mouth:

"Hot! *Donnerwetter! Donnerwetter!*"

"Speaking German, eh?" his mother cried, delighted. "Hein, a lace handkerchief, perhaps? Just one. That's all. I swear."

Pertaining to the growing boy, who needed shoes, shirts, trousers and, above all else, consistent discipline, the two had many chats.

And then there was Ivan who raised the boy as well, for there was much forbearance for a child, be he as cross and petulant as Dominik, in Ivan's dulled emotions. But Dominik did not repay Ivan in kind.

"You oaf! You stink of alcohol and sweat."

Thus angered and provoked, Ivan had little choice. His fist smote like a stone. "A hooligan—with not a trace of honor! I stink? How do I stink? He says I stink, Natasha. Did you hear that? I stink?"

"You do," said Natasha, proud of her Apanlee baths.

"You like me just the same. Don't you? Confess the truth, Natasha."

"So what?" said she, and laughed.

Between them still was much goodwill, despite the angry flare-ups the grain spirit caused. On summer evenings, when she was in a mellow mood, Natasha still scooted over for him.

Hein was a man who earnestly believed in discipline, and long before young Dominik shed his first set of teeth, he found himself jailed in an unheated room for stealing.

"I'll climb through the window," Dominik sobbed. He fought back with spite and resentment.

"I'll blister your backside!" roared Hein. He loosened his belt and gave the recalcitrant youngster ten trustworthy lashes. The beating left welts that stayed, purple and swollen, for days.

The boy thief hurled, retaliating, a rock right through the bedroom window that smashed a night-side lamp. He was still small. He was incorrigible. Consensus was censorious.

Here was a malcontent, a counterfeit, a mongrel, unwilling to be civilized, defiant of authority. As with lava flowing down a slope, the evil from within kept pushing to the fore.

"Robust and iron-jawed," thought Hein, vexed often past his sufferance. To be harsh with the bastard child was not much to his liking, but what was he to do? Young branches needed trimming.

The hunchback in his wicker chair was silent. The hunchback watched it all.

Natasha wished for a submissive son. "A bureaucrat. A first-class cobbler. Or, at the very least, a train conductor. Is that too much to ask?" she told the cripple daily, to which he answered nothing.

She made him write her three devoutest wishes on paper which she held to a flame to please a birthday saint. She loved her son; she loved the twin boys, too. Not even she could help comparing—at cost to Dominik.

She beseeched all her favorite icons, asking them to intervene. She, with a level head upon her shoulders, with eyes that saw as clearly without glasses as Uncle Benny did with spectacles, would often scold and sometimes even slap the ruffian, but Dominik just pulled his head between his shoulders and let the punishment roll by.

"Somebody ought to make him swallow castor oil and make him stand in the town square," said Marleen spitefully. When it came to Natasha's growing boy, Marleen spoke her mind, and not in whispers either.

"The apple falls close to the tree," she said to Dorothy.

"Oh, my! Oh, my!" wailed Dorothy, as gentle now as ever.

"It's true."

"Don't say that! Please! Don't ever say that. Ever!" Her eyes still sparkled at her husband. He still kissed the top of her head and the tip of each small, dainty finger.

Marleen just dropped her lower lip, a sign that she was angered past endurance. "Why not? The truth is already well known."

"No need to dwell on it."

Marleen did not like Dominik. She hated him with a cold hatred that started somewhere in the depths of wounded pride and always ended in a heated shouting match.

"You heel! You hooligan!" shouted Marleen, a woman otherwise in full control, sucked down into some murky depths by fear and hurt and fury.

When Marleen fumed at Dominik, Natasha knew that it was unwise to collide unnecessarily, but there were times when she spoke up to take her scoundrel's side.

"Was he born fat?" Natasha pointed out.

Most of the time, when Marleen's temper flared, Natasha quietly ducked. No matter what the provocation, Natasha waited patiently for Marleen's anger to subside before she took the path to Apanlee again.

The neighborhood stood wary. The dogs became restive when Dominik entered a room. The boy was born a hooligan, was growing up a hooligan, and would most likely die a hooligan in the tsar's prisons somewhere.

One sunny Sunday in September, the ugly youngster fixed a cold, hard stare and said to Marleen softly: "Last night, I had the oddest dream."

"What dream?"

"I watched your homestead crackling in the flames."

"Come here! And turn your pockets inside out," Marleen cried, horrified. "How often did I tell you not to thieve my matches?" Her anger sent him reeling.

"He'll end up being skewered by the Cossacks like a dog," Marleen kept shouting at Natasha.

"I could bear anything but that," Natasha shouted back.

"Quick! Feed him several radishes with butter," begged Dorothy, who mended stockings to perfection.

While Uncle Benny's little love just fanned herself in agony and whispered back in undertones that she agreed—the youngster was a shame, disgrace, and constant irritant—the full-blown evidence was there: but why make bad things worse by giving them a name?

The day when Dominik tried to castrate a cat, after pushing it headfirst into his boot, Hein took him by the hand and led him to the trusted midwife who had fished the mix-blood from the straw.

"I have misgivings," said Hein, shifting foot to foot to cover his discomfort. "Here. Take a look at him, and tell me what you see."

The midwife shone a light into the youngster's angry eyes. She took a haulm and probed his wide-spaced teeth. She rolled tobacco on her thigh and blew thick smoke around his genitals. She rapped his chest and inspected the soles of his feet. In the end, she sat back and declared: "A grumbler and complainer."

"I noticed that. Afraid of work," said Hein.

"A pair of fine, blue eyes."

Hein coughed away his tension. "I noticed that as well."

"His heart in knots. A burning thirst for power."

Hein sighed. "Is there an herb? Price has no significance."

"In olden days," the midwife said, "a public flogging would have cured his malady in no time short at all."

Hein bit his lips. A public flogging might have helped. These days, the tsars were much too lenient with their subjects. They gave them this; they gave them that. Schools. Teachers. Everything. And still the malcontents cried: "More." Still peasants shouted, border to border: "If not reform, then Revolution."

The midwife said lamely, her glance avoiding Hein's: "Find him something to do."

"How often have I offered him a job? I offered many times that I would pay him handsomely for shining my new boots."

"Take him to church."

"I did. And even on an empty stomach."

The Elders wrought their miracles by prayers, but even they had no effect on Dominik. To walk in Christ's footsteps was the law for the tsar's favored children, but if he tried, if he did that, insisted Dominik—blisters! Still more blisters!

"He has more of a temper than three Cossacks put together. There's too much energy in him. He dances till he drops."

The midwife pushed them both out through her door and shouted after them: "Sit him in a bucket, then, with ice up to the rim. Or put him on an anthill."

Precisely as the neighborhood predicted, things went from bad to worse with Dominik, a genuine recalcitrant.

Natasha tried her best to remedy the situation. She hated idleness. She knew that the bedrock of merit was work.

"Look. By example. Step by step. And rung by rung," she told her son, who sneered.

"That's not for me," said Dominik. He dreamed up illnesses as though he were a spinster. You name it, he had it: headaches, sniffles, indigestion, stomach and gall bladder troubles. He came down with jaundice; he never ran out of complaints.

Natasha told her son, her own feet on the ground: "He cannot help it, Dominik. He loves his wife's sons more. Just enter and leave by the side door."

"A heart of stone and marble."

"Be fair. You know that is not true."

"It is, too. It is true."

"He promised he would send you to Odessa to be apprenticed to a cobbler. Is he to blame the cobbler moved away?"

"He promised, then forgot." Dominik sucked his breath in through his teeth. "A cobbler, huh? We'll see."

Natasha opened all her windows to let the evil spirits out, but still there was no cure. "How I despise his waxed and upturned mustache," muttered Dominik, while doubling up with cramps.

Natasha came in tears to Hein. "Not yet a grandfather, and already absent-minded," wept Natasha.

"There's nothing else for me to do." Hein was at his wits' end. "He's practically grown. Just you be glad he doesn't tumble girls."

"He's barely sixteen years of age."

"That's old enough. Don't you remember?"

She looked at him through misty eyes. "Ah, memories like fleeting kisses. Our youthful slips. Our bitter love. Just don't desert us now."

Hein blinked in consternation. "I did my best. You could have asked for nothing more. Have I not always done my best?"

"A cursed life," grieved Natasha.

"Whose fault is that? He didn't learn and wouldn't try. He'll end up on the thieves' market. That is the common talk."

"If only you—"

Tradition spoke through Hein, and with his forebears' tongues: "He needs to work his way up. Rung by rung. And step by step. Drive that into his head."

"Right. Rung by rung. And step by step. That's what I always say," Natasha sighed, assessing Hein through lowered lashes. "And looking just like you."

"For God's sake, tell me how I managed to offend you. What do you want this time?"

"Not much."

"Just tell me what you want. Don't be so cross with me. Well? Where's your tongue, Natasha?"

She just kept munching on a crust. She spoke so softly that he barely heard her words. "Two forenames, Hein. His own. His father's. So he can walk with pride."

Hein's face turned fiery red. The cold air lashed like swords. "A new, warm coat for you."

"A handsome horse," Natasha compromised.

"Your greed is bottomless."

"There is yet fire in your heart," she told him softly, still a beguiling woman. "There is nothing but ashes in mine."

Which was the fattest lie. She knew it; so did he. He waited out her sulking with a smile.

"In any forest, Dominik," explained the crippled pundit, while cutting paper chains to make a small child laugh, "no two trees are alike. And neither, in this unfair world, are we."

But Dominik gave Uncle Benny a hard stare and sucked his fingertips. "I will not wait for heaven," muttered Dominik. "That's not for me. That is their own misfortune."

"Don't talk like that."

"You do not take me seriously?"

"I take you very seriously," said Uncle Benny calmly.

"Well, then?"

"To take you seriously doesn't mean that I agree. It doesn't mean I think that you are right. You'd better think things through."

It was a Sunday evening, the cripple's pensive time. Peaceful lay the steppe. His little Dorothy, her tongue between her lips, tried to compose a birthday poem for an old, ailing cousin who needed cheering up. Natasha tickled a baby. Marleen darned a sock by a flickering kerosene lamp. A servant was laying the table. The twins sat outside, on the porch, surrounded by numerous cousins, just wiggling their toes in the breeze. They liked to sit like that, and watch the sun slide into the orchards, watch the moon climb through the clouds. In yet a few more years, all power would shift to their shoulders.

The wind bore evening scents. The meadows were sprinkled with daisies. Ivan snored in small gasps, propped against a tree.

"You are a wise and learned man, " said Hein to Uncle Benny, chin pointing at Ivan. "Now look at him. Just look at him. Is that a hood-winked peasant? How is he suffering a bitter lot?"

"He cannot read or write. That does not mean he cannot think."

"He doesn't have a kopeck in his pocket or a clear thought inside his head."

"Does he have land?" the hunchback said, and ran his slender fingers through his corkscrew hair.

"Don't make me laugh. What would he do with it?"

"Next time, you write my editorials."

"I might," said Hein, now warming to the challenge. "His father died a frozen beggar; his grandfather, a drunken fool. A tsar gave him his freedom. What did he do with it?"

"Hein, listen to my question. What is Ivan now if not another bonded serf, in fact, if not in name?"

"Did I not give him land? One of my finest parcels. It's full of weeds and thistles—"

"He needs equality. He is entitled to equality."

Hein snorted through his nostrils. That was a Josie thought. He'd had nose full of those Josie letters; that's all she talked about. Equality? That thought grew from the sewer. In faraway America, maybe, where any fool—just any fool!—could vote to change the government, equality might work. But here? Vast power thrust into the hands of unskilled peasants?

"Do we need swollen heads?"

"Perhaps—"

Hein just puffed up his stomach. He knew whereof he spoke. His arguments were made for him by history. Equality? It had been tried with all due speed, in all good will, and it had failed— failed miserably. The serfs had been given their freedom; the serfs had been given their land. And what had come of that? The fields were too poor, lamented the muzhiks; the payments too high; it was better to be like a child, cried the muzhiks who ran to Hein's father, complaining. "In olden times, nobody worried; why fix what isn't broken? Peet Neufeld did our worrying for us."

Old Uncle Benny cleared his throat. His eyes moved slowly to Natasha. "They make convenient servants, do they not?"

"She's past her prime. She will not die of want. She'll always have a place beside my embers."

"She has a son, who has a demon's eyes."

"If you are born a king," said Hein, "you live and die a king. A pauper lives and dies a pauper. Hey, Dominik. Come here. Tell us your latest slogan."

"All people, equal brothers," said Dominik, and scrambled to his feet. "And after that, the land a blaze of glory."

"He's just a loudmouth, Hein," Natasha pleaded instantly. "Pay him no mind. I'll talk to him tonight."

Natasha did not know if she should laugh or cry. She mediated constantly. She, too, looked forward to the Revolution some folks had promised her—but in the meantime, what? To see a child at peace melt in her lap—that was Natasha's happiness. To see her apron flutter on Marleen's clothesline, next to Marleen's— that was equality.

"Oh, Dominik," she sighed. "What's gotten into you?"

"If not by goodwill, then—by force."

She smiled at his pretentions and changed another diaper. A cousin read aloud some verses from the Bible. The dogs lay sprawling by the fire. Equality, a fine and heady thing, in principle—Natasha welcomed strangers kissing strangers and clicking glasses for the sake of Freedom, Liberty and Brotherhood. All that was jaunty stuff. At the drop of a hat, celebrations. And every second day a holiday. Free rides on whistling trains, up and down the Russian countryside. She, too, agreed: More land for the muzhik, and justice for all. Such hopes were comforting when winter nights were long and bedbugs moved through cracks.

"Pay no attention, Hein," she said again. She shushed her son expertly, and winked at Uncle Benny.

The hunchback's eyes missed that; they sought his treasure, Dorothy. Her waistline had not changed.

"What do you say, my love? Give me your sentiment."

"The tsars," said Dorothy, as proud as she was shy, "received their empire from the Lord. Only the Lord can take it from them."

"The tsars and the church," said Marleen, looking up from her darning as well, "are the two greatest powers on earth."

"To think like that," said Dominik, while turning on his heel, "is just like walking barefoot in the snow." He spat in a wide arc. He had lost several front teeth, but that did not hamper his smile.

Marleen grew haughtier than ever with every new pregnacy, as pale as the moon on a wintry night. Though she was getting on in years, there was no end to dimples and to diapers, to prayers and to visitors. Fine, even wrinkles framed her eyes, but the future grew under her apron.

The fogs arrived and didn't go away. A vague discomfort lingered. It had no form, no name.

It was as though a twig of poison ivy stroked Hein's shoulder blades each time he glanced at Dominik. Outside the gates of Apanlee, dissent crept out of crevices.

The rabbis pressed on as though they knew nothing whatever.

The Cossacks kept combing the haystacks for them, and when they found them, they abused them.

The peasants shook their fists and cursed.

Bread riots broke out in Berdjansk.

There was no end to innuendo and intrigue, belittling a monarch admired by all. And at the root? Equality. That was the base agenda.

A curse, the very word.

A few insurgents were exposed as being operatives in plots to do away with monarchy and sent in irons to the north. And still, no end to taunts. And still, no end to rifts. The shaggy radicals were not the friendly sort. Their doors were always locked. Their pockets overflowed with pamphlets. Their whispers brought bad luck.

They had no country, but they were everywhere.

In Rome. In Paris. In Berlin.

No matter where they settled, they fanned the flames of greed. All betting systematically on banking and on trade.

Yes, even then. That was the sentiment. From fence to fence, the sentiment was this: Just watch them strike themselves a bargain, an abacus in hand, before you blinked an eye or took another breath—such was the way of Israel. If you were well-informed, you didn't ask. You knew. Not one of them honored the Cross. Glib talkers, all of them, who talked of taking over Palestine. Once they had Palestine, enslavement of the world was next.

All that was in the Bible.

The Cossacks rushed them, robbed them, cursed them, sometimes even skewered them on their long spears—they fasted, and for no discernible reason, and took their meals at random. It was believed by not a few that this was done for wicked cause: to throw the tsar's hounds off their scent.

It was now widely understood and, furthermore, sporadically repeated by knowing people of all sorts that this antagonistic tribe was feasting on the blood of mankind universally.

From the cradle to the grave, and in between as well, each one of them a libertine!

The dogs would growl in apprehension. Suspicions permeated everything, but proof of treachery was harder to come by. You had best cut an arc.

Hein would discuss the Jewish problem now and then with Uncle Benny, who kept an open mind.

"Some Hebrews have no eyebrows," Hein said to Uncle Benny. "Why did they shave them off?"

To which Uncle Benny said nothing.

Hein glared at Uncle Benny. "When their answers turn suddenly vague, you know mischief is afoot."

"Go on."

"They keep reaching into your pocket and make you believe they have sold you a song."

"I said go on."

"So tell me. Why are all of them on cordial terms with foreigners?" Hein asked aggressively.

Hein couldn't help himself; that just slipped out; he hand't meant to wound his little relative, who kept his own pet foreigners—specifically a female fool, a so-called liberated woman, whose name was Josephine, who had become American in outlook and in words. She and the cripple kept up a lively correspondence. She kept on sending clever clippings espousing odd ideas—ideas as disastrous as a flying ink pot. The one recurring word? Equality. That's all she talked about.

"I lack the courage," said the cripple, "to find a sharp reply."

Hein hated namby-pamby. Sometimes his mild and gentle cousin, intent on being fair to every side, made Hein as thirsty for a red-hot argument as salty soup made him crave icy water to calm a sudden thirst.

"The New World Order? Nothing new!" the farm folks sneered, when Erika came visiting from California to search out the kernels of truth.

"Go on."

"All that is in the Bible. We heard about it, even then. All this was there, for many years. It hovered at the edges. No sun was strong enough to make it disappear. It didn't have a name."

It's true: it grew in intuition, instinct and accumulating evidence. But on the other hand, none gave it extra weight. It was not of their world. To claim that it was more than a perplexing feeling of discord would give undue intensity to history. It wasn't central to existence. It was just there—a clammy presence. Nobody argued it away.

The Lord and the tsars had been bred into Apanlee's genes.

Hard work, self-discipline, pride, honor, cleanliness, debt to the rich, black soil had anchored all their rights. To challenge the established order by bringing in the concept of equality was as unheard-of in those young years of our century as suckling a small, squealing infant in a church.

"Don't make me laugh," said Hein, and laughed until his shoulders shook. He reddened, but he laughed. "Democracy? The very thought!"

It might have been a notion theoretically intriguing to the progressive mind—to pundits such as Uncle Benny. It might have spurred the priests to fervent prayers for the small Tsarevich who kept on seeping his pale blood into his joints. It might inflame a malcontent like Dominik. But it was of no significance at all to Hein, Ivan, Marleen, Natasha, Dorothy. The earth spun on its axis. You guarded against heresy. You found an extra babushka to wrap around your shoulder blades. You lit another fire.

That's how it was. For years.

At Apanlee, all was still sun-drenched days and clear and windless nights. The steppe was blazing. The Lord and the harvest were one. The churches were packed, with standing room only. Natasha scrubbed another diaper and burped another baby. The Elders lifted comfort from their prayer books and warned against the vanity of thought.

The leaves were turning red. Soon, it would be October.

And little Uncle Benny—as ever excellent at analyzing pros and cons, as ever studying the drift of history to the last dab of ink!—was probably the only one at Apanlee who read the headlines, front to back, who understood precisely why Apanlee was rushing headlong towards Golgotha.

Lebensraum! - Book II - Chapters 40 - 77

Reviewed by Michael S. McMillen

The second book of Lebensraum! opens with the German pacifists in Apanlee sowing and reaping as rumors of impending war and revolution sweep across Russia.

Hein Neufeld, one of Peet Neufeld's grandsons, continues to dismiss the threats of upheaval with naive confidence. His own family is already paying for an early mistake, his fathering of an illegitimate son, Dominik. Dominik's mother is a Russian woman, a youthful infatuation named Natasha, whom Hein and his wife Marleen take into their home as a domestic.

In Mennotown, Hein's cousin, Jan Neufeld, continues to prosper, even as his wife Josephine throws thrift to the winds and spends recklessly among the moneylenders and "progressives" of Wichita. Faith is still supreme in Apanlee and Mennotown, but it begins to grow flabby and to fraternize with presumption.

Meanwhile unanchored intellectualism masquerades as discernment while seducing its victims in the Ukraine and in Kansas. The physically handicapped but bookish Uncle Benny, an illegitimate cousin to Hein, compensates for his physical deformity by addicting himself to reading. He also writes articles advocating radical reform.

Like many who choose to soar in the rarefied realm of abstract speculation detached from reality, Uncle Benny will help to unleash the forces of his own destruction. His counterpart and correspondent in America is Jan's wife Josephine, a woman also obsessed with book knowledge and scornful of the robust, rustic virtues of her husband and mother-in-law. With itching ears she lusts after every wind of doctrine, intoning the slogans of "equality," dressing in provocative new fashions, shocking her Christian neighbours by her intimacy with the money-lending Jews of Wichita and agitating on behalf of the suffragettes.

Josephine, however, is in America, and thus has the priceless opportunity to redeem herself, or at least find her senses, before it's too late.

The theme that it is already far too late runs throughout Lebensraum! - Book II like a telltale draft in Winter. If civilisation and decency are not to wilt and fade from the earth, those who uphold them must overcome manifest temptations and redeem the times.

Book II is a tragedy of errors. Some of the characters put up a valiant fight in the midst of horrendous conditions. Some, whose primary enemy lies within rather than without, succumb and yield the field to their ravenous antagonists.

We are reminded throughout this book that as men sow, they will also reap. The earthly wages of sin, however, are seldom apportioned in any logical or just form. That's because evil itself is neither logical nor just. It does, however, exact a toll. Its effects can sometimes be modified by subsequent reform and repentance, but as everyone in Apanlee and Mennotown knows, not even God can alter last year's harvest.

Much of Lebensraum! - Book II is a horror story. First, the Russian nation is knocked out of the war. Hein's illegitimate son Dominik, who has grown into a bitter, malevolent and amoral man, temporarily finds a purpose in the military defense of Russia. He ends up in prison and is eventually released upon the coming of the Red revolution. He joins with a group of desperados now feeding upon their country.

Resentful of his illegitimacy and the lack of love bestowed upon him in his childhood, Dominik leads his Red comrades to Apanlee and betrays its inhabitants. The new revolutionaries embark on a blood-soaked spree of unspeakable cruelty and terror. Among the dead is Hein himself, the grower of food murdered by hands that know only force and fury. Uncle Benny, whose own scarlet prose helped fan the fires of this onslaught, and his wife Dorothy are killed savagely.

Some do miraculously survive. Among those who live through the first wave of terror are Hein's wife Marleen, her twin

sons Yuri and Sasha and her daughter Mimi. A cousin named
Jonathan, grandson of the ill-fated Uncle Benny, manages to escape and takes up a life as an itinerant beggar. He will find his
way to Germany and return to impose some justice on the hordes
that have ransacked and bled his native Apanlee.

Much of the second book recounts the increasingly tight
noose of terror that the communists wrap around Apanlee. Wanton shootings and deportations to Siberia begin to clear the land
of the productive.

The Reds seek to grow bread by force and issue paper quotas to people forbidden to enjoy even the meager fruits that the
blasted land will still yield. The commissars take a devilish delight in exercising arbitrary authority and in arresting people who
have done nothing.

Apanlee is decimated, but Marleen, the twins and Mimi
are able to hang on, partly because the flinty Natasha acts as a
go-between with her son Dominik, now elevated to leadership of
the collective.

Having betrayed his hometown to brutal beasts, Dominik
becomes responsible for fulfilling the quotas for his Soviet masters. His "inheritance" of Apanlee is as illegitimate as he is. Terror, coercion and crude animal cleverness are his only tools.

The thugs and hooligans who rise to fill the ranks of the
new party apparatus revel in their chance to dominate their betters and destroy them. People are taught slogans, as if demoral-
ised, terrorized innocents are likely to be inspired by them. The
slogans, however, like everything else about the Soviets, are in-
tended to cow and strike fear. In what must be deliberate and
cynical irony, schoolchildren are taught to refer to the time of the
tsars as that "before the revolution made us free."

In Mennotown the old Faith holds out longer against the
new Freedom, but Josephine chafes and pouts under restrictions
on her intellectual and social whims. Throughout their marriage,
Jan has yielded to her and indulged her every wish. He wants a
son, however. Their first son died in a freak winter accident and
Josie gives birth to a succession of daughters.

Having reached the frontier of middle age, Josephine does not wish to venture another pregnancy. Jan, however, beginning to sense that his marriage is running out of control, has other ideas. Although Josephine will come to idolize her last-born, a son she nicknames Rarey, she will never forgive Jan for the importunate passion that leads to the lad's conception.

Josephine may be a thorn and a trial to Jan, but she is a comely one. She even makes efforts at halting her own slide into modernist depravity. Eventually, she admits that she fought the law of nature – and the law won.

In the meantime, a series of disasters dooms the once proud Jan Neufeld. His wife's expenditures pile on top of his own questionable credit purchases. Previous Neufelds would never have surrendered themselves to the lenders. The Donoghues have not retreated from their aims. The nascent labour movement draws them to itself and they begin to make escalating demands on their employer, Jan Neufeld.

One of Jan's mills is burnt, and suspicion hovers around the Donoghues. It turns out that Jan is not quite in step with modern times. He never bothered to take out the insurance policy on the mill.

Jan's consequent illness symbolizes the malaise and torpor of Western civilisation reeling on both sides of the Atlantic. The old verve is gone. He does seek temporary solace in the theology of the elder Dewey Epp, but to no avail. As Jan deteriorates, Josephine hitches her star to one more pipe dream, that of moving to California!

Eventually, Jan is reduced to seeking a loan – now federally subsidized and regulated. In a scene resonating with Randian overtones, Jan draws upon his last ounce of self-respect to negotiate a loan from the Donoghue now arrogantly ensconced at the bank.

The dialogue between a man who is still trying to do business in an honest, straightforward fashion and a moral degenerate who knows only how to function as a conduit of second-hand power is an eloquent summation of the rot that has eaten its way into the entrails of a once proud and independent country.

The scene with the Donoghue "bankster" is prelude to Jan's final fall. Throughout the years, he had turned his back on the firewater offered by his tippling friend Doctorjay. At this point, however, Jan has been broken by his pressing crown of woes. He gets drunk with Doctorjay and takes refuge in the hospitality of Dewey Epp's soup kitchen.

When Jan learns that even the alms he is reduced to accepting there are underwritten by Roosevelt and his raiders, the dam bursts. He shoots Dewey dead and ends up killing himself.

Lebensraum! - Book II is an unflinchingly honest portrayal of the early year's of this now hoary century. The aspirations that animated Peet Neufeld and his sons have been snuffed out in the hissing spittle of the architects of the New World Order. The price of joy is not even quoted amid this procession of market collapse, legalized looting, war, revolution and reigns of terror.

If the twentieth century's reflection makes us recoil in disgust, the fault lies not in those who have the historic facts, artistic vision, and courage to hold the glass up steadily. The thick miasma of despair that permeates Lebensrau!- Book II is scarcely dispelled by Doctorjay's drunken defiance of the "banksters" with which the book closes.

But it does show someone still has a spine.

Faith. Hope. Charity. Not even the ravages of Soviet Russia and social-welfare America can annihilate these. Faith hangs on tenaciously in the face of ridicule and persecution. Charity is widely counterfeited, nowhere more piously than in America, where the Old Time Religion gets cozier by the day with Rooseveltian radicalism and sets up tax-subsidized soup kitchens with one hand and dispenses tracts with the other. Genuine charity manages to limp along in its own venerable, unspectacular way. The unflagging hospitality of Lizzie, the bonhomie of Doctorjay—even the mule-like loyalty of Natasha to Marleen and her kin stand out as coin of this realm.

And what of hope? What hope can survive the ruthless

Russian bear allied with the crowns and republics of Europe and the languorous strength of America?

Ask a hungry urchin taken in by a stern and loving Hausfrau. Ask Marleen Neufeld, an emaciated prisoner in her own homeland. Ask the emaciated heirs and the ghosts of those who sowed and reaped, who built and nurtured Apanlee.

Their answers will be heard.

Lebensraum! - Book III - Chapters 78 - 125
Reviewed by Michael S. McMillen

Of all America's foes in all of her wars, no enemy has been more vilified for so long as the Third Reich. Every now and again, someone wonders why.

If novelty enhances a novel's appeal, Lebensraum! - Book III should be a bestseller. The sections dealing with the Second World War will strike many readers as the literary equivalent of a photographic negative. For a change, the Nazis are wearing the white hats.

While writing this review, I came across a relevant quotation from *Founding Father* by Richard Whalen: "World War II was the liberals' war and they are understandably determined to uphold their version of its origins with all the formidable political and intellectual resources at their command."

Since the early 1940s, Adolf Hitler has been the West's Villain for All Seasons. Books, plays, movies, "docudramas," and television series feature Nazis and Germans interchangeably in the stock roles of archetype of evil and scourge of mankind. The only time National Socialists aren't portrayed as goose-stepping demons is when they are cast as hyperpunctilious, heiling buffoons.

In Lebensraum! - Book III the reader will find no such caricatures of the German Volk. He will find instead an army and a people fighting fiercely to preserve their own race, a nation stung to the core by an all-destroying, internationalist foe.

It would be petty to object that Lebensraum! Book III fails to present an objective moral study of Hitler and his Reich. As a novel, the focus of Lebensraum! is not statistical analysis of the motives and actions of its characters. Lebensraum! is not a comprehensive history of World War II. The story is, however, rooted in fact.

History attests that there were people during the Second World War who welcomed the Nazis as saviors and heroes. The German pioneers of Lebensraum! who had once grown prosperous under the Romanovs are their representatives.

When one considers the nature of Stalin's gulag state, its goal of yoking all its subject under collectives directed by a central committee in Moscow, one can understand that the people crushed under its iron boot might have looked upon the armies of the Führer with grateful anticipation.

Lebensraum! - Book III gives us an exciting and heartbreaking glimpse of one people's moment of vindication against a comprehensively brutal engine of oppression. After the hellish terror unleashed by the Soviet revolution, Justice cries out for vengeance from the skies – or from the earth.

Young Jonathan, who escaped from the Soviets and found his way to Germany, grows into a loyal soldier of the Fatherland, and is among the Landsers who reclaim – albeit temporarily – Apanlee for its rightful owners.

Eventually, owing to overextension and strategic errors on the part of the Fuehrer (e.g., his refusal to permit retreat) the Wehrmacht is driven back by the Red Army, now counted among the Allies. One of the tragedies stalking the stoic German survivors is that those who could have helped defend them, side instead with the beast seeking to devour them.

The remnants of the Neufeld and Epp clans in the Ukraine are unable to understand the world's indifference to their suffering. They cannot imagine that the rest of the world is infected with the same notions of international collectivism as the Soviet state.

They are utterly baffled and mystified when America, the land of Liberty, which received their own kin not so many decades earlier, joins forces with Stalin and his Reds.

When people are faced with such an inexplicable fact, they seek desperately to satisfy themselves with some kind of an answer. Lebensraum! records accurately the answer that many fixed upon: international Jewry.

The objective reader will bear in mind that the anti-Judaism expressed by some characters in these novels is not an invention of the author. The reader would do well to note that most of the main characters bear no animosity towards the Jews or anyone else. They simply wish to be left alone. Moreover, at one point, young Jonathan starts to tell what sounds like an off-colour story about Jews and is quickly chastised by Heidi, the woman who had rescued him from the streets. She explains that some of the good people with whom she had traded are Jews. The point, I believe, is that although bigoted anti-semitism unfortunately existed in Germany and elsewhere, it has nothing to do with the desire of the Germans for freedom and living space.

For centuries, the Jews had been viewed with suspicion throughout Christian Europe. This is not fundamentally because they happened to be adept at trade and finance; these functions are vital to an economy and constitute nothing inherently dishonourable or exploitative. Marked by their refusal to embrace the cross and creed of Christ, the Jews were frozen out of the circle of production by the economically fastidious (and sometimes woefully ignorant) Christians, and they became the exchangers, lenders and middlemen. Not surprisingly, many succumbed to the temptations inherent in such preoccupations and came to regard the people whose money they managed as convenient nuisances— profitable in the collective but of little consequence individually.

Marxism views the mass of men essentially the same way – and excoriates Christianity to boot. Socialist mythology sees its chosen people – the proletariat or working class – scattered and dispersed across the world and mistreated by bourgeois, primarily Christian, society.

Many Jews became the willing spokesmen and penmen for this new global ideology. Many were archly sympathetic to its call for a strictly secular state that would tear down the crosses and churches in deference to dreams of futuristic fraternity and equality.

Marx promised a far-off Utopia to all men in exchange for a radical break with the individualistic, nationalist Christian past. The proverbial wandering Jew became in many instances an ambitious booster for both the international banker and international bolshevik. The apparent contradiction in this union of banksters and rowdies continues to mislead the unwary to this day.

Ingrid Rimland has described the concomitant growth of these two forces vividly and dramatically in Lebensraum!, particularly in Book III. Her picture of an America slouching through the Roosevelt years convinced of the gospel verity of the New York Times is not a flattering one.

Nevertheless I, as a patriotic American who believes in the founding principles of this nation, applaud the author for penning so blunt a satire of her adopted land.

America has often been described as a country with a great and eager heart. Sometimes her eagerness does her no good: the willingness to believe the glowing and deceptive dispatches from the Soviet Union; the reflexive anti-Germanism imbibed freely from the media outlets of the era; the gullible surrender to state welfarism, so long as it is buttered liberally with prattle of "compassion" and "tolerance."; the sheep-like acquiescence in the quasi-religion of received propaganda concerning the nature and extent of German mistreatment of the Jews during the war.

All this – what one might dub a pathological obsession with acting out good intentions – is symbolized by Rarey Neufeld, who goes enthusiastically off to war to kill his German brethren for Uncle Sam (and Uncle Joe). Book III ends with a touching letter to his wife from this genuinely good man, who is killed in the waning hours of the war by anti-aircraft fire from his own

German cousin, Erika.

World War II was a disaster for everyone involved. Nevertheless, the corruption and self-hatred it fomented in the USA and Germany contributed to the unthinkable rise of the clumsy but vicious and deadly Soviet Empire.

Some claim to see in the political fall of the unwieldy beast the death of Communism. Such people are sadly mistaken. Communism today reigns and runs rampant on American college campuses and in the nooks and crannies of government both here and in Western Europe.

Today "internationalism" has become "globalism" and the UN has replaced the Red Army as the socialists' army of choice. I say here in sorrow and in anger that this very trilogy that I am reviewing will probably be banned in some of the "democracies" that helped defeat Hitler and prop up Stalin.

What God's plan for this weary world may be, I do not profess to speculate upon. I do assert, however, that the political ideas and ideals that the world needs have already been formulated - and were once put into practice for nearly a century - right here in America.

It's here in America that Ingrid Rimland's trilogy is being published. If America does not speak out on behalf of the rights of man and for the unhindered pursuit of truth, who will?

Ingrid Rimland has spoken out again - eloquently and clearly. Those who do not share her vision of America are free to disagree and to criticize.

Those who care to join her in this literary quest for Lebensraum! will find a good story well told. What more can you ask of a novelist?